GW00725471

The Haymakers Survey

- Our Secret Inheritance -

Billie Shears

Blakesware Publishing

First published in Great Britain by Blakesware Publishing, under the title, 'The Haymakers Survey' by Billie Shears. Copyright @ 2008 Billie Shears.

Apart from any use permitted under UK copyright law, this publication may only be reproduced, stored, or transmitted, in any form, or by any means, with prior permission in writing, of the publishers or, in the case of reprographic production, in accordance with the terms of licences issued by the Copyright Licensing Agency.

The characters, places and events described within the novel are a combination of truth and fictitious. Any resemblance to real persons living or dead is purely co-incidental.

ISBN 978-0-9557023-0-3

Printed and bound in Britain by Quadrant Ltd, Hertford.

Blakesware Publishing's policy is to use papers that are natural, renewable, and recyclable products and made from wood grown in sustainable forests. The logging and manufacturing processes are expected to conform to the environmental regulations of the country of origin.

First Edition 2008
1 off 2,100 copies

Blakesware Publishing
Ware
Hertfordshire

www.thehaymakerssurvey.com

<u>*Earth's Answer* :</u>

"Earth raised up her head
From the darkness dread and drear
Her light fled:
Stony dread!
And her locks cover'd with grey despair."

William Blake 1794

Presented in all Innocence and Experience...

In December 2006, we discovered a journal from the 1820's by a romantic British poet called Charles Lamb. Many historians agree he wrote the journal, but all were sure he'd destroyed it. Maybe they were mistaken. Some of you may have already seen the extracts we put online. If so, you'll know a little of what we mean by describing the find as magical. It contains a message for all humanity – 'Our Secret Inheritance'.

Given the significance of the journal, we jumped at the chance to record our recollection of the strange events leading up to its discovery and show what we did in response. None of us are writers by trade, so forgive us if our choice of words, grammar or punctuation is sometimes lacking. Our task was simply to promote the journal to the world as best we could.

The circumstances in which we found the journal add to its credibility. However, making sense of something so remarkable wasn't an easy task, far from it. The human memory has a strange habit of distorting the truth, especially when emotions stand in the way. We needed cool heads to show everything accurately, right down to the last detail. So, when we talked about the things that had happened, Ben took copious notes and double-checked any areas of doubt with our friends and witnesses.

The hardest part was trying to piece the evidence together in a logical way. We already knew the events took place in an order that matched the questions in 'The Haymakers Survey', so we decided to link everything to them. We believe in our hearts this is what the Blakesware Set would have wanted - call it instinct, if you will.

It wasn't easy to write about ourselves in a way that outsiders might view us. We also had a duty to entertain – to bring what happened to life in a way that gripped people. We tried to take a

4

leaf out of Charles' journal and add that magical ingredient, imagination!

Sadly, to protect the area, we had to change some of the place names in Hertfordshire, but we believe it doesn't detract from our message. Whether you think what we say is the truth, is for you to decide. As Lucy says, "Have faith and all things are possible." She should know!

At first, we thought the most curious thing about all this was what we found after we pieced it all together. Caleb had just finished going through everything, adding some Endnotes to the journal, when we realised someone had inserted some notes of their own. They are headed with the symbol, ⊠. We didn't take them very seriously at first, but Jonas convinced us otherwise. He's certain they're messages from the future – so we left them in. We believe people have a right to know what they say and to draw their own conclusions.

Yet the most remarkable thing had yet to unfold. We only discovered it once Ben began his Whittenbury Watch. At the start of 2007, he decided to keep an eye on world events from 'The Haymakers Survey' perspective. Looking back on the first few months, it became abundantly clear to us that something beyond our understanding was taking place. We feel the spirit of the Earth is genuinely trying to reach us. To prove the point, we've added the early experiences of the Whittenbury Watch at the end of this book.

You can keep right up-to-date with the Watch by visiting our website, www.thehaymakerssurvey.com. Whilst there, why not take part in 'The Haymakers Survey' too? It's fun, easy and free. You can check your answers against others and claim a certificate for your computer or 'phone. There's also a surprise awaiting those who do the survey - go see for yourself! However, we do recommend you read this book before you do the survey, as its true value will then be much clearer and more powerful.

We've also selected some videos on *YouTube* to further show the deep magic behind the survey; and we'll be adding some videos of our own too. Again, we recommend you look at these once you've read about our adventure. You can view these on www.youtube.com/polarbearchampion.

Oh, we almost forgot to say why we chose Billie Shears as the name to represent us as the author of this story. It was Ben's suggestion; he's a huge Beatles fan and the nature of Charles Lamb's life means he could well qualify as an honourable member of the famous *Lonely Hearts Club Band*. It was Sarah who had the casting vote on the author's name; a view swung by her experiences with Lucy and her diamonds.

With all our hearts, we hope you are enthralled, entertained and empowered. If so, the good news is we imagine there'll be more to come, although in a way the ending is for you to decide!

Ben, Julia and Sarah Whittenbury, Jonas Fosbrooke and
Caleb Hitch

- On behalf of the Blakesware Set -

Part One

Art

Q1: Do you believe your life has a purpose?

This was the first question in 'The Haymakers Survey' and the top one on Ben Whittenbury's mind. He'd spent much of his 39 years on Earth seeking his purpose. A product of 1967, the so called *Summer of Love*, Ben believed there was something profound waiting to unfold in his life. Yet the evidence was against him.

- ♥ Every second, 3 babies were born.

- ♥ There were some 6.66 billion people in the world.

- ♥ Around 100 billion humans were estimated to have ever lived.

On top of that, our lives were so short. In a way, we're like grains of sand on a planet that has existed for millions of years. This was the glaring reality of Ben's life. He was just an average guy on an Earth awash with humans.

Indeed, as the years went by he became a family man – with a wife and a daughter, Julia and Sarah. So that seemed to settle things; his basic purpose being to procreate and maintain the species. Yet the feeling that there was something more continued to gnaw away at him. It began slowly, as the stories crept into the news. Scientists and politicians started to take an interest, for something was going on with the *World About Us* - a thing called global warming or climate change.

The Whittenbury's watched the stories unfold and the seriousness of the threat begin to become reality - record temperatures, flooding, loss of habitat for creatures, seasons in a muddle. New organisations emerged to campaign for action. Documentaries on the issues became more frequent and debate on what to do took place. Many people were becoming desperate, yet sadly resigned to their fate. At 39, Ben's mid-life crisis was a belief that he could be the one to make the difference. A guy to ask questions of those who mistrusted the evidence or were apathetic and cynical. So, when he was asked to volunteer his time for the cause, he jumped at the chance.

In truth, Ben secretly had some doubts about the extent that humans were influencing things, and believed that alarmist messages about climate change were counter-productive. However, to Ben the reality of the risk was clear. Why take a chance when we had so very much to lose - the polar bear, the tiger and the rainforest? So, Ben made a list of some of the likely consequences of global warming – Ben liked lists. It looked like this.

Climate Change – the ticking bomb 💣

   Rising sea levels.

   Loss of natural habitat.

   Mass extinctions.

   Food and water shortages.

   Displaced people.

   Extreme weather.

Glum huh!

What to do? Ben's instinct was to leave the city and set up home in the countryside. He simply needed to live amongst nature. Let's call it, the voice inside his head! He was drawn to somewhere magical - Keeper's Cottage in Noblin Green, Hertfordshire. The place blew Ben away when he saw it. Remote, peaceful, old and unique; boy did he get lucky!

As we say, it was magical, enchanted even. Let's start with the haystacks found close to the cottage; they as good as spoke to him, acting like a magnet to his soul. Once settled at the cottage, he regularly climbed upon them to enjoy the views and philosophise. They symbolised his mission, so he dubbed himself a Haymaker. What's that you say?

Q2: Are you an art lover?

Apart from nature Ben also loved art. When he lived and worked in London, he regularly visited the galleries. As the thing called global warming began to grip him, he developed a passion for a pastoral painting on display at Tate Britain. Hitherto, he hadn't taken much interest in George Stubbs, preferring artists like Monet and Dali. Yet one afternoon in autumn an obsession with the painting called the *Haymakers* began.

What was it about the picture? Ben couldn't keep his eyes off it. The woman at the centre of the painting intrigued him; and the man on the hay cart looked oddly familiar. When he discovered that in 1977 the British people had shown extraordinary support for it - raising the funds needed to secure the painting for the museum - he went straight out and bought a framed copy. The day the Whittenbury's moved in to Keeper's Cottage, one of the first things he did was to hang it in the lounge. From such a vantage point, the lady at the centre could ask the questions. If Ben was flagging in his mission – he would have to answer to her. She would be his motivation. There was no escape for Ben.

You can imagine then, that Ben was really rather pleased when the locals hinted that he resembled the lofty figure in the picture. Ben quite liked that. Indeed, give him a pitchfork and the right clothing and he would dream of an idyllic life, before the machines came.

Art aside, a year in at Keeper's and Ben was confident his decision to adopt a country life was the right one. Not just for his family but for the whole of humanity. Okay, he hadn't been able to secure the local conservation job he craved; the market place was crowded and they implied he was a little eccentric, impractical and a bit of a dreamer - but it wasn't the *End of the World*. Although he didn't much like it, Ben's position at the district council paid the bills and gave him enough time to ponder and plan.

Apart from the haystacks and the *Haymakers* there was something else to inspire Ben. It was a Samoyed dog! They're a breed that resembles polar bears – well smaller versions of the endangered animal. The dog's name was Malachi. He was beautiful and loving, but untamed, so prone to odd behaviour. We'll tell you how Ben met Malachi in a bit, because it's most curious. All you need know for now is that Ben and the dog became inseparable. Malachi was Ben's mascot for the challenge ahead.

Ben's quest to satisfy his inner calling really started on the equinox, autumn 2006. He had climbed upon one of the many haystacks near the cottage and persuaded his wary dog to join him. Most days he'd have his daughter, Sarah, with him for company. Not today. She was with relatives. As Ben and his dog admired the last of a beautiful sunset, he thought of her and her future. "What kind of a world will Sarah grow up in?" he asked, as the first russet and golden hues of autumn sparkled before him.

Tragically, if the scientists were to be believed, it was all under serious threat - the plants, the animals and the whole eco-system. It was the same the globe over – a world wide woe – and, it was all down to the industrial human. What to do? Ben remembered his orders. He was desperate to find the answers to the climate change chaos. It haunted him. Bedazzled by the vibrant sunset, he looked dreamily to the heavens for inspiration. Maybe it was an illusion, but directly overhead he saw a fleeting glimpse of a rose shaped cloud. A vision that vanished in the blink of an eye, as if to confirm this was real life, void of fairy tale endings.

Whatever the evidence and predictions, Ben believed our fate was in the hands of Mother Nature. She would have the casting vote on whether to evict us from the house, so to speak. If it were a popularity contest would she want to keep us or not?

- ♥ What do they call it, Big Brother? Have we the X-Factor?

- ♥ Would you vote for our eviction or for our salvation?

- ♥ Should we hold a phone vote?

We labour the point. Ben concluded that unless we showed the planet more respect, then all hope was lost for humanity. He, for one, was ready to announce his allegiance to the natural world. He had reached the tipping point - the emergence of a deeper, curious energy rose in his soul! It came from within the core of the Earth, rising through the soil and its harvest - the hay - and into the receptive body of a man. Suddenly Ben felt driven - a new resolve and determination overwhelmed him. He clenched a defiant fist to the heavens and cried,

"NOW IS THE TIME FOR ACTION!"

Malachi seemed to nod approvingly, as though he had expected the proclamation. Besides, the dog had plans of his own – Haymaker you say? The dog was scheming.

Q3: Do you have a good imagination?

You do? Great. Well, we had a real challenge on our hands. We needed to give the animals and plants a voice in this narrative for it's their planet as much as ours. So we gave that voice to Malachi. It seemed only fair, as he had a lot to say for himself. Come on, just pretend. Let him enlighten us – it's only a bit of fun. As we said, Malachi was scheming about being a Haymaker.

🐕 I need to be part of the picture! 🐕 he said.

Malachi was a handsome and vain dog. We often caught him sat looking at the *Haymakers* painting. We think it was because there were no dogs in Ben's favourite picture. Who could blame him for being upset? Apart from the disloyalty issue, a romantic idealistic vision of the countryside that lacked a dog or two seemed incomplete. Why would Mr Stubbs exclude dogs from the painting? As ancient hunter, herder and companion, we believe Malachi had a strong case to be in the picture. We digress – it's a habit we've picked up from Charles Lamb!

Back to our story. Ben was a bit put out by Malachi's muted response to his cry for action. How could he be so blasé about it? So, Ben ruffled the mass of creamy white fur around Malachi's neck. He gave it a good strong tussle, "Give me a penny or two for them…

you cuddly bear you!" The dog just smiled. It was one of the breed's most adorable and enduring qualities. Yet, beneath that veneer he was brooding.

🐕 I really need to be in the picture. I will never forgive you if you fail. I'm unique enough to deserve a place alongside the people of this world. We can still do it. We can! 🐕

This was seemingly an impossible task as the *Haymakers* was painted in 1785, whilst Samoyeds only arrived in England some 100 years after that. But Malachi was not one to give in easily.

> ✉
> *Okay, I know they've only just started to tell you what happened and the last thing I want to do is distract you, but I really MUST convince you. Please, I speak from bitter experience. If you do one thing in your life you MUST take this opportunity for action for all our sakes. Trust me – our future depends on it!*

Q4: Have you ever wanted to stop the clock?

This is where events began to get a bit strange; as though there was an unseen force influencing our behaviour and everything about us. Charles Lamb knew; we were just finding it out for ourselves. You see, disturbed that climate change was set to alter forever the world we know and cherish, Ben wanted to bring time to a standstill. He longed to hit the pause button or even rewind some two-hundred years to the start of the industrial revolution. He wanted to find a way to warn them and say, "Hey… stop the clocks," or something similar. Still, time travel wasn't possible, so he settled on another gesture. At dusk on the autumn equinox, when the hours of light and dark were in perfect harmony, Ben removed his watch – yes he still wore one - and threw it high and long into the sky. It span around like a Catherine Wheel, before tumbling into a copse beside the dry remains of the Nimley Bourne stream. The watch face glistened as it fell – like a shooting star crashing to Earth. It was a defiant denial of Ben's will and a reminder that time was its own master. Okay, it was a futile symbolic gesture, but at least Ben eased some of his frustration.

"What use is a watch now, when we're fast running out of time?" he questioned, drawing a look of approval from his dog.

🐎 Absolutely! Tardiness, well it can lead to all kinds of mayhem. 🐎

As Ben absorbed the scene a warm zephyr caressed his face. It was a wind of change. He grew increasingly euphoric and invigorated, ready to do his duty to protect and serve the planet. He stood tall on his haystack, like a beacon of hope for humanity.

"Do you know what today is?"

🐎 Yes, it's the beginning… the middle… and the end of days! 🐎

Ben had his own views. "It's more than just the equinox. This is the day the good people who love our Earth really began to fight back. Can't you feel the magic? Use your imagination – look about, what do you see?"

Malachi did as Ben suggested. In the words of the famous song, he saw a *Wonderful World*! Beyond that, he noticed the grand oaks that had grown from acorns to stand proud and tall. Scattered amongst them were leafless trees – dead, but still standing as poignant reminders of our small beginnings and our own mortality.

🐎 Ah, this is the rub – how something mighty can grow from something small, yet that something mighty shall one day fall! 🐎

Q5: Do you believe in fate?

This was a question often on Ben's mind. "Fate Malachi, has it brought us here or did we shape our own destiny from a series of random choices?"

🐐 We're all part of something immense and mysterious. 🐐

Ben's gentle grey eyes looked out from beneath a furrowed brow, squinting to shut out the red glow of a setting sun. From his vantage point, he saw a silhouetted figure of a man cross the field ahead. Ben had expected to see him. Clearly a creature of habit, his neighbour often took the route from his house to Widford. The lean man walked slowly with his head low, appearing sullen and void of hope. He carried a rucksack; he always did! His posture confirmed that life had been a struggle for the man in question, this last year or so. Ben sympathised with the family tragedy that had befallen him. Yet today his presence roused Malachi,

🐐 Listen! The mighty Being is awake. 🐐

Malachi had quoted an extract from an, *Evening on Calais Beach* – a sonnet by William Wordsworth from 1802. It was about a sunset too and quoted for good reason. It was the perfect prelude to events beginning to unfold.

It began with the innocuous appearance of a barn owl, which flew in from the north. The bird had taken to the skies before nightfall. It came towards them in effortless and eerie silence. Was it symbolic of something? Who could tell, but the orange glow of the setting sun transformed its white foliage into something unworldly. The bird sped, like an arrow fired from Cupid's bow and passed directly over the heads of the pair. Ben enjoyed the moment immensely, but Malachi knew better.

🐐 One for sorrow! 🐐

Okay, so it wasn't a magpie, but give Malachi credit, for he knew the owl was a bird synonymous in a poet's mind with death. And, this tale was all about an unfortunate poet of yesteryear.

Q6: Do you believe in fairy tales?

This is an odd question for some to contemplate. Let's help you. Excited by the sight of the owl, Ben leapt from the haystack and marched towards home, dog in tow. He strayed from the path, leaving invisible carbon footprints in the parched soil. For, despite his mission and changes in lifestyle, Ben knew the daily business of living meant he and his family still produced carbon dioxide or CO_2. For Ben, it was a damage limitation exercise. "Let's take a new direction… grasp a second chance for a new sustainable way of living. Hey - let's sow a seed and watch something beautiful grow."
🐾 Not a *Brave New World!* 🐾
Malachi was referring to a novel by Huxley, which achieved an ironic utopia by denying people access to the things that brought happiness - such as nature. Ben put him at ease, "Come, my companion, walk with me to celebrate the miracle of creation."

Malachi had anticipated Ben's next move. The target was a curious majestic evergreen tree guarding the gates of Keeper's Cottage. Locals had long ago realised the tip of the tree resembled the head of a malevolent creature. The Goblin Tree, they called it - partly because Noblin Green sounded a bit sinister and very similar to Goblin. Funnily enough, one of the branches resembled an arm that pointed away from the cottage, which was an omen if ever one was needed! Not that Ben cared. No, he just adored the tree's quirky individuality and character. Anyhow, Malachi knew the truth – what a wise old hound!
🐾 It's Yggdrasil - the mythical World Tree. 🐾
In Norse mythology, the tree has a great power which links the underworld and Heaven with the surface of the Earth.

18

> **Q7:Have you ever dreamed of being a champion?**

As a fan of football, or soccer as it's known in America, Ben did. He used to dream of lifting the World Cup to an admiring crowd. Hey, here's the thing, if Ben – no if all of us – work together and turn global warming around, or at least limit its impact we'll win that cup? Look around you – the World Cup is everywhere and it's ours for the taking!

So, at a time of year when the land over-flowed with the gifts of nature, Ben's imagination and creativity soared. He stood beneath the scary branches of the impressive Goblin Tree. Mimicking a knight from the time of King Arthur, he raised an imaginary goblet and cried, "Waes hael," which meant, 'good health,' in Anglo-Saxon times. It was an entirely spontaneous comment; words that came to Ben from the ether. Inspired, Ben lifted an invisible magical sword - his very own Excalibur and, with much theatrics, said,
"I commend my services to you, Tree of the World - symbol of life… Do you find me pure of heart and untarnished by ambition or revenge? Am I a worthy champion of nature? Do you honour me… a simple Haymaker… with the greatest challenge ever, as Mother Earth's keeper?" Ben waited patiently for an answer. Malachi offered one.

🐈 You really have no idea what you've just done! 🐈

Beyond that there was no sign of retribution or consent. No death knell rang or triumphant bugle blew. Despite an eerie silence, Ben felt empowered, like a member of the Knights Templar who had taken a monastic vow. He had confirmed his purpose in life!

"FOR THE PLANET BLUE IN A SEA OF BLACK,"

Ben called, promising to tell Julia, about his new role. But first he knelt before Malachi to honour the partnership between man and animal.

🐕 Arise brave knight... go claim your prize! 🐕

As Ben looked into the dog's eyes, he saw the trace of tears. Julia had recently speculated that Malachi was *The Messenger* as his biblical name suggested! What if she was right? What had he to tell us? Lovingly, Ben ruffled his dog's fur, "Let it be so... you lead and I'll follow." Malachi's response was simple.

🐕 My friend, our lives to date have been mere preparation for what is about to follow. 🐕

Q8: Do you dream of a better life?

We think it's only natural for people to do this. Even Ben confessed to us that one of the reasons he moved to Keeper's Cottage was to find a better quality of life. So, what was it about the place that attracted Ben and his family to adopt it as home? Let's don our estate agents hat!

Built in the 1800s, the cottage was one of three houses in an idyllic hamlet. It was once part of a working farm and home to people who kept the land. It was unlike anything Ben had experienced before. It was a house with character, presence and perhaps – some speculated – a very soul of its own. Keeper's Cottage was the kind of place most people would close their eyes and wish for. Except for one thing; it was also a little scary, rather like Grandma's Cottage in little Red Riding Hood.

For starters, sun-bleached skulls of Muntjac deer hung on surrounding outhouses like a warning – *Danger Keep Out!* It was also very remote. So much so, that at night, the darkness and silence was so intense that the slightest movement or sound unnerved its newcomers. Every creak and groan of the old house conjured images of wandering spirits. Step outside on a clear night and the moon appeared large in the night sky, dwarfing the scenery. It took some getting used to and perhaps explained why Keeper's had stood empty for months before the Whittenbury's arrived.

However, all the darkness faded away once Malachi arrived. This was how Ben recalled it:

♥ On the afternoon of Midsummer's Day, I had taken a walk alone by the banks of the Nimley Bourne stream when I noticed a dog roaming confused, as though lost. I heard voices – a man and a woman - calling, "M-A-L-A-C-H-I." I thought I saw a young child – a boy! Yet the dog ignored them and ran straight to me instead. He seemed overjoyed to find me, showing a depth of affection normally reserved for a lifelong owner.

♥ The dog dutifully followed me home and sat for hours outside Keeper's, refusing to leave. He whimpered until we took him in and fed and watered him.

♥ Malachi showered us with love, making it impossible to turn him away. We did ask around locally, but failed to identify an owner, so we kept him.

It was the turning-point - a new beginning. The Whittenbury's grew mightily fond of Keeper's, forgetting any early fears or qualms. They began to live the dream! Yet the dream was tinged with concern, for here the impact of the changing climate really hit them - the arid land in times of heat and drought, the wildness of the storms and the intensity of heavy rain. Oh, by the way, Julia had a thing going on with raindrops - but we shall come to that. It's worth the wait.

Q9: Do you feel in control of your life?

What of Ben and his pledge to be Nature's Champion? Well, first he had to learn how best to respond to Malachi's antics. As a Samoyed, Malachi was a member of one of the oldest breed of dog known to man. Headstrong and powerful, he was just one step away from wolf, which meant his behaviour was unpredictable and instinctive. For an inexperienced dog owner, he was far from the ideal choice. Yet, as we have seen, Malachi chose the Whittenbury's, not vice-versa. The Whittenbury's often struggled to control him and no amount of formal training could put the dog to right. When Malachi lost control, there was little to be done except muddle through.

Sometimes, the most innocuous thing would set him off, such as the gentle sound of bells from distant St John's Church in Widford. As soon as the soft tolls reached Malachi's ears, he stood upright on his hind legs in the fashion of a dancing bear. He lurched forward and almost toppled Ben in the process. "Malachi... what on Earth are you doing?" snapped Ben, bemused. The dog returned to all fours, but ignored all attempts to restrain him. Instead, he dragged Ben by the heels towards hedgerows that lined a bridleway that ran from Keeper's all the way to the Nimley Bourne stream.
🐕 This is all to do with the bigger picture! 🐕

Yes, Malachi's maverick behaviour was linked to his apparent obsession with the *Haymakers*!

Q10: Have you ever seen a ghost?

Without any warning or indication of her arrival, a hunched figure of a woman appeared before them. It was as though she emerged from the soil beneath her feet. Ben felt a shiver of fear crawl over him. Had he woken the dead or enticed a spirit from another place and time? Before a cascade of indigo and reds at dusk on the equinox he could almost touch fire and brimstone. Was this a vision of Hell? No! The extraordinary image was just a woman, albeit forlorn and fragile.

"Are you lost?" he asked.

"No," she mumbled softly.

Head bowed, the woman slowly paced the ground around her. She took awkward steps to deliberately disturb the surface. "But IT is... since well, seems like an age an' all." There was something curious about her words and voice, as though they were fading away before they had even been spoken. In the decreasing light, Ben was unable to see the woman's features clearly. However, he noticed she was dressed from head to toe in dreary grey, including a ragged shawl and bonnet. Malachi was bewitched by her. He sat at Ben's feet motionless and silent, watching and listening to a Lady in Grey.

🐎 Is it you? It is you! 🐎

Ben persisted. "Can I help in any way?"

No answer. The shuffling switched to bare hands, scouring the parched soil. She was very unsteady. Ben reached out a hand, "Please listen... do let me help."

At last the woman raised her head, if only to look down the bridleway and beyond the cottage. "Listen! Listen!" she said. "Didn't you hear the bells? It's time. He'll be coming for her soon." Her voice was full of emotion.

🐎 Dare I to tell, it's those strange fits of passion? 🐎

Ben was curious. "Who's coming? What is this?"

The woman's manner changed,

"I never meant any harm. It was something anyone could have done. I just wanted a better life... I didn't know it would end that way. It was just o'matter of timing, but I made a promise to put it right.

And a promise is a promise... I must keep searching, keep trying."
Only now did she look properly at Ben.
"I'm innocent!" she insisted, with a face in shadow.
Ben looked confused.
"You doubt me?" she asked.
Malachi fidgeted. The woman stared at him and said, "Why have you forsaken me?"
🐺 You ought to have listened then, not now. It's too little, too late! 🐺
"Please, I'm here for you. Whatever it is, whoever hc is that you say is coming, I can help... I want to help." It was in Ben's nature to react in this way. He was generous in spirit and charitable – how else could he act on our behalf?

Encouraged by Ben's warmth and sincerity, the woman shook from her stupor. Her eyes widened in hope.
"Is it you? Lady Plumer must know, you must tell her you have returned. She is waiting... always waiting. We've all been denied real happiness for so long. We can bear it no longer," she pleaded. She reached out. Her icy hand touched his warm flesh. Ben pulled his arm back in shock.
"Who are you?"
She replied slowly and calmly, "I'm Fanny... Fanny Ebbs. Remember? You must remember after everything that has happened. We all lost so much, all of us. Yes, that's it. Help me, come help me."

She paused as a prelude to the unmistakable sound of a horse in gallop which was heading their way. Malachi's demeanour changed. His ears flipped back. For the sight or sound of a horse, normally brought out the wolf in him.
🐺 It's the horse. I need to run. Please let me run. 🐺

"Copenhagen comes, but it's too late. It's always too late. You, Richard, are our one hope of salvation." She reached out again, but Ben was too busy, trying in vain to control his dog. The woman persisted,

"Do it for Lucy and for all our sakes, please I beg of you... make haste!"

As soon as she had finished speaking, she moved from Ben, more swiftly than he could have imagined possible. Malachi expected such behaviour.

🐎 With a quickening pace his horse draws near. 🐎

The trees around Keeper's hid the horse from view. It approached like thunder. It dominated. It had power and purpose. Ben knew that in parts of England a creature known as the Gytrash was said to haunt lonely country lanes. But before he could feel any fear, horse and rider came into view. It was a temperamental partnership of man and beast. The steed was tall, dark and powerful. It snorted as it traversed the path in an unruly canter. Youthful and focused, the rider wore a long dank coat to keep wind and rain at bay. Coat tails lifted in the rush, revealing a splash of red and gold clothing. He resembled a highwayman in flight. Ben anticipated a pistol to emerge from beneath the cloak to shoot him dead. For a few seconds he reflected on his folly – to tempt fate with his Earth Champion pledge - or should that be Nature's Champion? Maybe they're one and the same thing - interchangeable. We digress! All told, Ben struggled to believe that what he had seen were mortal beings.

Q11: Do you believe in justice?

Malachi knew all too well what had to be done.

🐈 Quick Charles, go to her. Let me help you. 🐈

He was driven. He was compulsive.

"There is no justice," cried Ben as Malachi tugged hard on his lead, almost choking on his collar.

🐎 It's not about you or me. This isn't personal. It's a life or death struggle for all of us. So, I must go, I must. 🐎

Malachi proved too strong for Ben. He gave one almighty yank forward and broke free to pursue the horse and rider. Ben watched aghast, as they fled and grew smaller and less visible in the fading light. Poor Ben, abandoned by Malachi, to the whim of the Lady in Grey. He hesitated to look for her. Where was she? In one sense he could still feel her presence – the touch of her icy hand and the desperation in her fragile voice. But she was gone, vanished from view, leaving Ben to dwell on the curious inexplicably events he'd just experienced.

Q12: Is our Earth enchanted?

We think this is a question that intrigues a lot of people. Is there more to this world than meets the eye? For sure, our ancestors believed it. Until the 19th century, people in Britain often settled close to water or beside special or sacred places. Communities invariably emerged in the shadow of notable trees that fed the human imagination and enriched the spirit. Ben's wife, Julia, wondered if this was the case with the Goblin Tree.

As the haystacks were to Ben, so the Goblin Tree was to Julia. It was the thing that struck her most when they moved in – the intimidating, foreboding presence directly visible from the smallest of their bedroom windows. On the first night, she'd drawn the curtains early – to shut out its glare, but the more she studied it, the less she was afraid. She even began to clothe it with her hopes and dreams. She imagined its branches were connected to her mind, feeding her spirit and making her world. Julia was a bit like this – in tune with things most of us cannot see or hear.

Julia could also see the Goblin Tree from the kitchen window. She was drawn to it at just the time Ben saw the Lady in Grey and the mysterious tempestuous rider - coincidence, maybe? We said earlier that we sensed there was a force influencing what was going on. It was like this when Julia looked at the foot of the tree. To her surprise, a wryly creature popped its head out from the long grass – peek-a-boo! It was a feisty grey squirrel.

The squirrel saw Julia, she was sure of it, blinking its beady brown eyes. "Look at me, I've a secret to tell!" it might have said. We later found that in Norse mythology the squirrel – Ratatosk, or 'swift teeth' was one of the inhabitants of Yggdrasil. Perhaps she'd seen him? It certainly entertained her, making an animated scamper to the summit. The squirrel's stay at the peak was short-lived, for it promptly scurried down again, in circles about the tree, as though mimicking a helter-skelter ride. The whole affair lasted about three minutes, before the squirrel returned to the long grass again. Most odd, most delightful!

Julia was drawn away from the window by a pan that boiled over, flooding the hob of her cooker. She soaked up the mess, re-ignited the vegetable pan and added some salt. "Water, water everywhere, but nor a drop to drink," she said. Strange poetic words, but then her mind was suddenly struck by the torment of those left adrift at sea - to die of thirst, yet be surrounded by water. Oh the irony!

Ben returned to the cottage just as the water levels reached another tipping point. As Ben recalls it now, his arrival was greeted with the opening bars of Ludwig Beethoven's famous *Fifth Symphony* – the distinctive four note 'short-short-short-long,' knocked like fate from the kitchen radio. It largely disguised the back door's screech. Oh, he'd promised Julia he'd oil it, but his can ran dry. At the time, it triggered a conversation between them on how much oil lies beneath the Earth's crust. History was littered with mistaken estimates. In 1919 the US Geological Society predicted America would run out of oil by 1920! Today, we use the stuff at an alarming rate, but many are confident there's much more to come. One estimate is there's about three trillion barrels left yet! That's one hell of a lot of carbon gas. We digress – Charles' habit again.

On his return, Ben had a troubled expression that Julia recognised immediately, as he requested,
"Julia… quick … help me find the torch. Do you know where it is?"
Ben was panting. He'd obviously been running.
"It's Malachi, isn't it!" said Julia. "He's run off again, hasn't he?"
Ben nodded, "Yep. That dog, he's like a white rabbit… pops up then vanishes when you least expect it."
"Ah-ha… that's Malachi for you, full of tricks," replied Julia.
"But this isn't like before. There's something weird happening… I can't really explain quite what, but it's strange."
Ben plunged his long bony fingers into dark cupboards to search for his torch. As Beethoven played on, Ben's fingers danced like a pianist's in search of the right note. A fleeting ironic smile appeared on his face,
"Why can't I ever find what I'm looking for?"
"Because you need to know where to look Ben," suggested his wife. Ben reacted by dashing manically about the kitchen. He brushed into Julia, causing her to spill some salt.
"Ben, do be careful! Look what you've made me do," she said.
"What?"
"The salt, its gone all over the floor – isn't that bad luck?"
Ben paused to ponder.
"Come on… I've no time for games!"
Julia frowned.
"Okay… you have to throw a pinch of salt over the shoulder," Ben advised.
"Which shoulder?"

Ben sighed, "Julia, I've no time for this… left… no right. Oh I don't know. It's only salt and just a stupid superstition… Julia!"

"Only salt!" replied Julia - we think she was referring to the climate change sceptics, who take the threat with a pinch of it. Yet as the Arctic ice melts, the salt content in our seas lowers, and this is likely to have a significant impact on global ocean circulation. Who knows where that might lead? Another digression!

"Well… I'm not taking any chances," added Julia.

She chose the left. The Devil was blinded. At that, Ben immediately found his torch.

> ## Q13: Have you ever been mistaken for someone else?

Julia was an artist by trade. It was partly what attracted Ben to her. In fact, they met when Ben decided to take an art class in west London. Julia was the tutor – though she gave that up when Sarah was born. Ben didn't take naturally to painting, but continued to attend because of his affection for Julia. Their first date was a visit to Tate Britain, London. Ben had flattered Julia by suggesting she resembled John Waterhouse's, *Lady of Shalott*. That Valentine's Day, Ben drew Julia a rose and, putting his love of poetry to some use, won her heart by scribbling an extract from Lord Tennyson's poem about the *Lady* on the rear his sketch. Ben's words were:

> 'Down she came and found a boat
> Beneath a willow left afloat,
> And round about the prow she wrote
> The Lady of Shalott.'

Julia loved it, caring little that the Lady was portrayed on an ill-fated journey; that was a mere haunting, romantic detail. Julia had little fear of death. In truth, the *Lady of Shalott*, was her favourite painting, reflecting her interest in myth and legend. A copy hung in their bedroom, largely because Ben likened her to the central figure. It was the hair – a typical Leo's mane. Julia had the tawniest red hair that fell to her waist in waves. She also had 'eyes like the Mediterranean Sea and beautiful bone structure' – Ben's words, not ours. Some might choose to liken her to a mythical Mermaid, had she the tail of a fish. We digress!

Before Ben ventured outside again, he rambled on about what had happened, following his wife about the kitchen like an excited child. Julia did her best to listen,
"Did you see the woman, the old Lady in Grey... and the galloping horseman? Wild he was, like the wind. And she called me Richard... Why would she do that? She acted as though she knew me, yet I've never seen her before. She was deluded... crazy. Look Julia, she's probably still out there, right now."
"In the dark, will she be okay?" Julia looked out from the window. Ben pulled her away.
"Let's talk more when I get back. I must go. I need to find Malachi... now," insisted Ben.
"Oh Ben please... listen to yourself. There's no need to panic! Hey, if you're that worried let me come with you. Two heads are better than one! The dinner can wait," suggested Julia, uneasy about being left alone.
Ben was adamant. "NO," he demanded firmly. "You should stay here... it's much better. Besides if... no when... Malachi comes back you can let him in."
Julia curled back her lower lip. She did this whenever she felt threatened. Ben held her and gently kissed her forehead.
"Look, promise me something. If she comes knocking, under no circumstances must you let her in. Do you understand?"

Julia squinted. "Ben... should we call the police? She may be in danger."

"No... I don't think so. There's no need for that. All I know is there was something very strange about her. I can't really say what.... Now, just make sure you bolt the door – damn I should have fixed it before now... some champion I am! Then draw all the curtains. I don't want her looking in at you."

"Champion? Ben, please... I'm not a child."

Julia's thoughts instantly switched to her daughter, Sarah.

"Speaking of which, I wonder what might have happened had she been there!" said Ben.

"She'd probably have run after him... which in a way is what you're about to do... Ben, can't you just wait for him for a bit. Malachi will come home in his own time... he always does – he's just a bit of a free spirit. Just think of him running free out on those fields, having a fabulous time! It'll be fine, you'll see."

Ben was a little indignant.

"How can you be so casual about things all the time? He's still on his lead. He could get tangled up or all sorts. I hate to think of him out there... alone and suffering... I've no choice, I really must go to him!"

Julia agreed.

"Okay go... but be very careful."

"Yeah!"

There was hesitation in Ben's voice, as he recalled the spectre's icy hand.

"You know, maybe you're right. Maybe... he'll come back on his own."

It was a further two hours before Ben finally left the cottage. It was a question of logic. Malachi had often ran away, yet many times he'd come back under his own steam.

Trouble was, once Ben started waiting he thought, 'I'll wait just a bit longer. Let's see what might happen.' He regretted the indecision for the night had drawn in, making the task to rescue the 'little polar bear' that much harder.

Now, the next bit unsettles Ben these days, though at the time it meant nothing to him. "I love you... my Captain," Julia cried fondly as he left. You see Captain was one of her pet names for her husband. It used to be Ben's favourite – now he's not so sure. It's an unwritten rule between them, not to mention it anymore. Shame really! That aside, Ben left with the familiar screech and thud of the heavy back door. Julia dashed to the lounge and watched her husband depart through the wrought iron gate at the front of the house and disappear into the night.

Q14: Do you believe your stars?

Astrology was considered science in man's early history, with messages written in the stars serving as the guiding force for many. Old traditions die hard, of course, so in these supposed days of reason and facts, millions in developed countries regularly consult their stars for an insight into their future. What about Ben – what did the stars predict for him?

After Ben had left the cottage, Julia had dashed to their bedroom to watch her husband's progress. To get the best view, she switched off the bulb and peered out into the darkness. Several rooms were lit in the farmhouse opposite. It was their solemn neighbour's house. She speculated whether Ben's Lady in Grey was inside.

Julia saw no sign of Ben, so she tried a second, smaller window; one which overlooked the Goblin Tree. She had no choice but to look through its silhouette to the fields where Ben ventured. A harvest moon had positioned itself right behind the tree's crown. The moonlight turned the route to the Nimley Bourne into a shimmering pathway to a surreal and magical world. It was an eerie sight, which punctured Julia's primeval senses. An outlook made more sinister as Mars, so infamous in mythology for war and destruction, was a prominent image in the night sky. Julia took its smoky red aura as a warning.

Ben saw the planet too. He knew that in Greek mythology Mars was sacred to Ares, the God of War and Violence. He imagined Ares' chariot in the night sky, roaming the battlefields of conflict, bringing death and destruction. He craved a sacred spear and shield to protect him. In such a climate, the creatures of the night tested his courage to the full – a screeching owl, the bark of a fox and the tramp of deer. As he walked, moths danced about his flashlight and he sent startled pheasants from their roost. Ben pushed on regardless. He sought just one prize – the recovery of his beloved dog.

When he was confident he'd reached the point where Malachi had vanished, he heard a whimper. It came from within the gully that led to the base of the Nimley Bourne stream. Ben shone his torch into the depths. Its rays penetrated a maze of bush and branches, creating an exquisite kaleidoscope effect. Amid the spectacle, a pair of eyes reflected back the torchlight. It was obvious that Malachi was stuck, vindicating Ben's decision to search for him. Ben descended into the gully. He went slowly and carefully, for the copse around the stream was dense and especially treacherous at night. Things cracked underfoot and brushed against his head. All manner of unwelcome images went through his mind. He clambered on, over exposed roots to rescue the ailing dog.

🐕 Paradise lost! 🐕

"What on Earth possessed you... running off like that? I've risked life and limb to rescue you."

🐕 Just draping a watch on the branch of an olive tree! 🐕

Malachi's lead was badly tangled. It would be easier to unclip him, but Ben thought better of it. In need of two hands to set him free, Ben laid down his torch. He put it opposite a severed trunk of an old tree. The unnatural light emphasised its annual growth rings, traversed by cracks from its centre, like a star. Nothing remarkable about that, but were the trunk a clock face - at about five to midnight was something quite astonishing! Clinging to the side of the trunk was a creation that resembled a person, hunched in a foetal position. Although part of the tree, it reminded Ben of a fossilised figure - it reminded him of extinction! Yet, for a fleeting moment, he believed the fossil was resurrected. He saw a young woman - alive - looking at him, with eyes aglow like the sun. He shuddered in fear, before dismissing the vision as a trick of the eye. Mother Nature never ceased to amaze him.

Ben grabbed the torch and quickly looked about himself, for reassurance. He sent shadows dancing in the woods about him. His heart raced in his chest. His breathing became more intense. Ben was afraid. He turned the torch back onto the wooden figure. It sparkled. Wholly improbable, but Ben's watch, discarded in frustration, was there, draped over the wooden head. It was a fusion of the symbolic with the irrational, inviting yet resisting explanation.

"Huh, Malachi... do you see this too? It can't be possible!"
🐕 Come out of the circle of time and into the circle of love. 🐕

Ben recovered his watch – it had been in the family for generations, a genuine Whittenbury Watch.
"I'll take this as a sign," he told the dog, as he began to set Malachi free. Yet the dog had another surprise in store for Mr Whittenbury. He pawed the ground directly in front of the trunk Ben came to know as the 'Web-Log'.
"Hold still. You can't dig your way out... huh, what's this now?"
Malachi had unearthed a piece of jewellery.
"It looks like gold... an old heart of gold... a locket I think," Ben whispered.

He went to touch it then held back, conscious that curses were often associated with the removal of ancient treasure. He pondered the moment, "Is this your doing?" he asked Malachi. "You knew this was here didn't you?" The dog looked at him and smiled.
🐕 The flame of a butterfly before it settles. 🐕
Ben checked about him again.
"Finders keepers, losers weepers," he said softly, triggering a crack in the woods behind him which set his heart racing afresh. He grabbed the locket. No sooner was it in his hand did Ben whistle the melody of 'Yankee Doodle'. It was a tune made famous on the American frontier as a rallying anthem for the War of Independence; a song that became a stirring anthem of defiance and liberty. In England, the tune was used for a nursery rhyme, 'Lucy Locket'. Ben had no affinity to the tune - but it came as no surprise to Malachi.
🐕 Ah, the Duke and his fife entertaining the Blakesware Set – happy days! 🐕

Q15: Do you sometimes fear the worst?

Ben returned home with an impudent boyish grin on his dusty face. Julia noticed it immediately he walked through the door, with a hungry and thirsty dog in hand. She rushed up to Ben and kissed him.

"You were gone an absolute age. I've been going grey with worry," she said, before focusing on Malachi.

"I was afraid we'd lost you… come here… let me hug you! And don't do that again, do you hear!"

Julia's talk of grey changed Ben's mood. What right had he to feel triumphant given the Lady in Grey's plight? Her ghostly words stirred his conscience, "Help me find it… find it for Lucy."
Eager to do Lucy justice, Ben tucked his hand into his jacket pocket to ensure his discovery was secure. Crouched beside the dog, Julia shared Malachi's view of her husband. "What is it Ben?" she asked, reading his expressions.

"It's this."

"A blue ribbon!" she murmured, watching it slip from Ben's pocket and glide gently to the floor.

"So it is! What on Earth? Where did that come from?" he said, as they watched it settle into the shape of a heart.

"Now that's beautiful," said Julia.

🐎 She braided her hair with ribbons blue and called it 'Forget-me-not'. 🐎

"Beautiful… and a nice surprise, because I actually wanted to show you this…"

Ben dug deep into his pocket, only to reveal… his watch. "It's your watch!"

Julia shook her head, bemused by her husband's eccentricity.

"It's a magic show… next up it'll be the White Rabbit," she said.

Ben looked at the watch face. The second hand had frozen; the time read five minutes to twelve!

"Well, it beats me… I don't understand it. A conjurer's at work for sure … and the trick's on me!"

Ben finally unveiled the tarnished jewellery rescued by Malachi.

"At last… third time lucky!" he announced.

Julia gave an ironic cheer.

Ben explained the find, "It's a gold heart-shaped locket… it looks very old and ornate… take a close look at the care that's gone into its creation."

Julia touched the locket with her finger tips, which really did reveal the metaphorical White Rabbit, so to speak.

Q16: Have you ever had a psychic experience?

We mentioned earlier that Julia had a thing about raindrops. Now and then she'd claim to have seen a vision or images in raindrops as they fell and settled on a window pane. For Julia, looking at raindrops on glass was akin to gazing into a crystal ball. Her Grandmother told her she had the gift, an inner third eye - an Anja - which gave her a kind of clairvoyance. It was but one of her many talents. Ben also likened her to a Sibyl, able to see and feel things others couldn't. Ben's list of her abilities looked like this:

> *Julia's Jazzy Jamboree*
>
> ♥ *Raindrops — they dance around on window panes, forming symbolic images before Julia's eyes of what's to come.*

> ♥ *Premonitions - in dreams mainly, or she'd have an overwhelming feeling that something tragic was about to occur, like an earthquake. It normally did.*
>
> ♥ *People and things - she would sometimes meet someone or something; touch it and experience a flashback. This normally happened when a traumatic event had occurred.*

Julia often felt uneasy about her ability and tended to shut it out. However, it became impossible to ignore once they moved into the cottage. She put it down to the deep and vivid history of the place. The intensity and frequency of the experiences overwhelmed her. Worried what others might think of her and anxious to protect her family, she kept the gift largely to herself. Ben did his best to support her and tried to make light of things, jesting that witch trials were a thing of the past. Another digression!

So, back to the locket: Julia's fingers barely touched its surface, but it was enough. Her eyes glazed over and ears rung, whilst the blood drained from her complexion. She slumped to the kitchen floor, with Ben just able to break her fall. She fell into a foetal position, one to mimic the wooden figure seen by Ben. Her fingers wrapped about the blue ribbon. She was motionless except for her eyes, which moved rapidly around her sockets. Ben tried in vain to wake her. He heard her whisper, "In manus tuas, Domine," which was Latin for, "Into thy hands O Lord."

🐈 O Mercy! The work was done – the race was run! 🐈

Julia began to come round.

"Julia, can you hear me? You fainted… went as white as a ghost."

38

"Oh Ben," she said, trying to sit up. "There's no time to waste… none at all."

"Time… for whom? Julia, you're not making sense."

Julia was unsettled.

"Hang on, I'll fetch you some water."

He brought her a drink.

"Here, sip this."

She quenched her sudden overwhelming thirst.

"What did you see?" Ben asked.

"I heard the bell toll… I felt helpless. I saw a purple rose – with wilting petals, they fell, slowly, one by one into the snow." She used her fingers to gesture the descent.

"Julia, you're crying."

"Am I?" She wiped a tear away with the hand that held the ribbon.

"Try not to dwell on it… let it go," Ben advised.

"Hey, I can smell the rose… can't you?"

"Mm… I can, now you mention it."

"It smells so beautiful… so sweet, like a rose garden… it's amazing."

Ben took the ribbon from her and returned it and the locket to his pocket, for safe keeping.

"C'mon… I think we've had enough excitement for today."

Q17: Can you speak another language?

Malachi had the final say.

🐕 Tacta alea est. 🐕

Ah, the dog speaks Latin too! It means, 'The Die is Cast' and was famously spoken by Julius Caesar when he made the critical decision to take his victorious army across the Rubicon river against the order of Rome. It was a point of no return and led to his eventual coming to power. So – was Malachi trying to tell us something?

Q18: Do you let your heart rule your head?

The next day, Ben took Julia to the place where the locket and watch had been rediscovered. Julia was quite astonished by the shape that clung to the Web-Log.

"It looks so life-like... as though it... no she... it looks like a she doesn't it? As though she was real once! Either that or someone carved it. But why go to all that trouble to carve something then just leave it here?" she asked.

"I guess it could be a carving... but I think it's just Mother Nature doing her thing... just one of the quirky miracles of creation," suggested Ben.

Julia wondered if the figure was waiting to reveal a secret or two. She took a deep breath and slowly put her hand on its head. She closed her eyes to wait for a message to come through, but nothing did. If Julia was honest, it didn't come as much of a surprise for her ability was unpredictable. She knew in her heart that she was at the gift's mercy. Her Grandmother had warned her of this several times; "It has to come naturally... from the outside in. It can't be forced."

When Julia re-opened her eyes, she shook her head at Ben to let him know,

"Nothing... not a hint."

"Well... it's probably for the best."

🐎 Nature teaches more than she preaches. 🐎

However, although he didn't tell Julia at the time, as they hovered about the Web-Log Ben sensed something unusual. It was to do with time. Everything seemed to happen in slow-motion or through a haze. It was as though he wasn't really there! Oh, he did what was asked of him, taking several pictures of Julia and Malachi stood beside the wooden figure. Yet it was when Julia took some pictures of him holding aloft his watch and the locket – like trophies – that he sensed it the most. It was very intriguing.

When they returned home, Ben downloaded the images onto his computer. The pictures of Julia came out fine, but those she took of him were distorted and foggy. Julia apologised for her poor photography, but Ben understood,
"Hey, never mind. We can take some more another time… perhaps once Sarah comes home," insisted Ben. Inwardly, he was disappointed, so as a consolation he scanned the internet to try to identify the locket – its age, rarity or value. Little joy! So, he took it to some local jewellers for a professional view. No luck with that either. The locket was clearly reluctant to surrender its history or secrets. So, Ben drew up one of his famous lists.

The Liberty Locket

♥ *Found by Mali in the dirt beneath a curious old log by Nimley Bourne stream.*

♥ *Cleaned up really nice – no scratches or anything.*

♥ *It's about the size of a pound coin.*

♥ *It's in a soft rounded heart shape.*

♥ *Got ornate leaf embossing running all round the edge.*

♥ *On the back are the initials LL.*

♥ *Really difficult to judge its age or quality.*

♥ *It feels really heavy for its size.*

♥ *It's always warm to the touch, never cold – as if someone's been holding it tightly.*

♥ *We can't open it, so don't know what's inside.*

Once the list was finished, Ben had an idea. He wondered if Fanny Ebbs had been searching for the locket. It didn't take a genius to conclude that, 'The L in LL could stand for Lucy!' which is what he suggested to Julia.

"I guess so!"

"And she… Fanny Ebbs asked, 'Find it for Lucy', that's what she said… so, there's only one thing for it. I'll go find Fanny Ebbs and return what belongs to her… but where should I start?"

"Oh the Lady in Grey. Is that wise? Didn't you say she was… well crazy?"

Ben thought carefully about his response.

"Desperate Julia… but not crazy! At least if I try to find her my conscience will be clear."

"No harm in it, I suppose… better dust down your walking boots, for it could be like trying to find a needle in a haystack," suggested Julia.

"Okay. That's true enough, but come on… if my mission's to save the world, then I'm darn sure I can find one woman."

"Ben please! Listen to yourself… you're not a superhero or a caped crusader. Besides one man alone can't put things right. Climate change – it's huge. It's inevitable. We have to learn to live with the consequences."

"Okay I know. I'm not suggesting I can do it alone Julia. I can't explain it that easily. Let's just say it comes from in here," he said thumping his chest. "Not up here," he added, pointing to his head. "You big softie. Why not just join up with one of the charities… and do some recycling… turn off some lights? Let's leave it to the big boys, the institutions and the celebrities. And we can just get on with our lives… you, me, Sarah and our dog!"

"Okay… fine, I don't doubt they're doing a great job in raising awareness, campaigning and educating people, but somehow it's not enough. We need something more. I don't know what the solution is yet, but I'm working on it, for Sarah's sake, and her children and their children!"

"Look, I know Ben. What do you want me to say to make you feel better?"

She crossed her arms. He sat in silence.

"By all means go look for Fanny Ebbs, but please let go of this ridiculous idea about the planet – the climate's always on the move... blowing hot and cold... and they're bound to sort it all anyway. They always do. I bet an invention's waiting around the corner!"

"You're the fortune teller – you tell me."

"And you're the super hero!"

"Okay, I thought you were with me on this one," said Ben. He slumped into the chair in his study to stare helplessly at the Liberty Locket List on his computer screen. Julia sat on his lap, like a child.

"I am Ben, really I am. I worry about the consequences too, but there's only so much we can do. Its one huge world out there... China, India, America! How much of it can any one person influence?"

"I know you're talking sense. It's all a stupid pipe-dream. It's my heart ruling my head – just thinking about those polar bears out on the ice, whilst it breaks up around them. You remember how Sarah cried when we watched the bear drown on television because he couldn't reach an ice sheet in time? That was so upsetting."

🐗 Sometimes you just have to follow your heart. 🐗

Q19: Do you like hedgehogs?

Historically, rustics who have lived in rural Hertfordshire for generations are known as hedgehogs, because of their traditional and slow moving ways. The Whittenbury's had got to know a few in the sprinkling of villages, hamlets and farms in the Ware Uplands - most were neither prickly nor sloth like. Disappointed by Julia's response to his plans for climate change salvation, Ben donned his Haymakers hat and went, dog in tow, to visit some hedgehogs in search of clues on Fanny Ebbs' whereabouts. Over the next few days, he completed a full circle of the Uplands, covering: Barwick Ford; Widford, and the wonder of its ancient church; the impressive Blakesware Manor and the intimacy of Babbs Green.

The nomadic pair became well-known, but the unlikely tale of the Lady in Grey risked Ben's credibility. He was in danger of being labelled a 'Hertfordshire Hayabout', an expression once used to describe ignorant ploughboys. In his current plight, a hay band tied to the right leg and a straw band to the left might have been appropriate - to help him distinguish between the two. Indeed were it not for the hard evidence of a locket and a ribbon, Ben would have seriously doubted his own senses; to know what was fact and what was fiction.

Q20: Have your eyes ever deceived you?

Two days into the search, Ben's hopes of finding Fanny Ebbs had faded. His early enthusiasm evaporated, replaced with a thirst and thoughts of a long cool beer to replenish him. It was too humid to sustain the pursuit. At Babbs Green, they'd reached the crossroads, literally. Ben was on the verge of hallucinating, when Malachi decided enough was enough and led Ben towards a small mound of grass close to where the roads crossed. Ugly, swollen mummified fingers greeted him, reaching to the heavens from the verge.
🐎 Beware the murderous pie man! 🐎

Ben had heard stories of Babbs Green. How an infamous villain haunted the crossroads. Our aspiring Earth Champion no longer had much appetite for ghosts. Oh, he believed in them – who wouldn't after what he'd seen, the crazed rider and the forlorn and vulnerable Fanny Ebbs. He knelt beside the oddity. Ben had a sudden sense of being watched. Goose-pimples crept over his skin as he caught a movement, out of the corner of his eye.

"Them… they be Dead Man's fingers," said an unfamiliar voice that crept up on him and his dog like death. Ben turned to look up at the person who'd approached him.

"It's fungi… fantastic stuff isn't it! Just goes to prove that things aren't always what they seem."

The man who offered the explanation was Caleb Hitch, a flamboyant character, with a deep knowledge of the area and its history. We agreed it would be best to tell you more about him later; Caleb's a proud and humble man and he thought it inappropriate at this point to distract from our account. So we've reserved a detailed description of him until later. We would say this though, as a little research suggests that Ben and Caleb may have been misled or confused in their interpretation of what they'd seen, for Clibborn's Post was elsewhere.

Q21: Have your ever hugged a tree?

Whilst Ben's fruitless search for Ms Ebbs concluded, Julia was engaged in a task of her own. She was tidying the grounds of Keeper's Cottage, ready for her daughter's return. Julia's passion for trees led her to dwell on the remains of a deceased tree, whose few languishing branches hung dangerously over the bridleway at the front of the cottage. Okay, it was another dead tree, but hey, they're being axed the world over.

Julia's psychic traits reached into the realm of the natural world. She sensed the tree's lingering spirit; it was yearning to reveal an absorbing truth. What could it be? She stroked its fragile bark; a touch which developed into a hug. Yes, Julia was a tree-hugger! She'd hugged many in her time. She found it neither embarrassing nor futile. It was her way to give thanks to nature. She told us, "Tree hugging opens the heart – you should try it some time. Hey, don't knock it... there's no shame in hugging a tree. Trees Rule OK! They grow taller and live longer than any other living organism on this planet. They give, while we take!" Who were we to argue with Julia!

Julia spread her arms about the tree as far as they would go and squeezed gently. She placed the side of her face against the bark, closed her eyes and listened to the tree's lingering pulse. Absorbing its fading energy, she whispered, "Give up your secret." She took slow, deep breaths and imagined the tree in full bloom. She visualised its roots reaching deep into the soil. She had a vision,

'Just imagine if millions of people in the world went outside to hug a tree all at the same time. That would be such a fabulous gesture - a silent, peaceful and fun protest against deforestation - a human chain of resistance stretching across the globe! Let's adopt the spirit of the Chipko's! Let's honour a group of villagers in India opposed to commercial logging who used tree-hugging to avoid their forest from being cut down!'

Julia's reverie was broken by an unexpected blast of cold air that swept in from the North – as though it had journeyed all the way from the Arctic. Caught by the chilly blast, a small piece of the tree fell to her feet. She heard the words, "Release me!"
Julia called to her husband,
"Ben we need to do something with this tree – tackle these rotten branches… before Sarah comes home."
"We?" remarked Ben with eyebrows raised.
🐐 Make hay while the sun shines? 🐐

Q22: Do you love our Earth?

We do – it's the most wonderful miraculous place we know. Given the pace of modern life, it's all too easy to forget its deep and rich splendour. Our old, fragile spinning orb, travelling at some 66,000 miles per hour through the void of space! It's a struggle to imagine such a speed.

It was a struggle, too, for Ben's saw to slice through the decaying branches of the old tree. The saw spluttered and coughed angrily - sounds that rippled about Noblin Green. Julia did her bit to help by stripping old Ivy from the trunk. As Ben began to tire, he said, "Julia, I think we're trespassing. This tree's right on the border with Noblin Green Farm," he claimed.
"What's a border between friends? Never mind that, look here... the tree's hollow."
"Really... I wonder!"
Ben readily dipped his hand into the cavity.
"Watch out... something might bite," said Julia.
"Ouch," joked Ben, before he withdrew his hand, revealing an olive-green jar made from clay.
"Release me!" mumbled Julia. "I knew we'd find something," she suggested.
"Just for a change, eh!" replied Ben, before he blew some earth off the jar. He took a look inside. It seemed the jar contained a mix of soil and some perfect round white stones.
"Marbles perhaps?" said Ben, recalling his younger days.

The find stirred Malachi from an afternoon slumber. He strolled nonchalantly over to see what all the fuss was about.
🐎 Ah, the mystical sacred stones! 🐎
Ben offered an explanation, "Could be an old county custom – to bring good luck or ward off evil. I'll ask Caleb next time I see him.

He knows everything."

Malachi offered another thought.

🐏 Blessed are the meek: for they shall inherit the Earth! 🐏

For, simply stated, meekness is the reluctance to be assertive – the fundamental virtue, humility. So, we'll lead by example. We promise from here on in not to point the finger – or push our passions. We give you our word.

Q23: Do you believe all the laws of physics?

It's not rocket science to predict what happened next. "Ben, here... pass me the jar," asked Julia.

"I'm not sure that's such a good idea."

"I need to touch it. I had such a strong feeling that we'd find something of real significance in the tree."

"Well... okay, if you're sure then that's fine... go ahead," replied Ben.

Julia's fingertips merely brushed against the jar, when a sharp crack and thunderous sound startled her. Resembling a bolt from the Greek God, Zeus, aimed directly at her feet, a large partly sawn branch, fell under its own weight, bringing Ben's saw with it. Julia shrieked as nestled birds took to flight.

Malachi reacted too. He jumped up at his surprised owner and caught the jar with his paw. It crashed to the baked, cracked ground. "Malachi... careful... look what you've done!" cried Ben.

🐏 But we have this treasure in jars of clay to show. 🐏

Ben had been unreasonably harsh on Malachi. Let's face it, we've all had an accident or two. It's part of the human experience, to break something precious and fragile from time to time! Sometimes things were beyond repair; sometimes they could be salvaged. There's a thought!

Anyway, when the jar smashed, it sent up a puff of smoke, whilst the stones scattered, rolling where fate decreed. Julia's instinct was to try to recover them. She touched one of the stones. Her journey began.

It was dark, very dark. Uneasy with confined spaces, she was overcome by a feeling of being entombed and a sense of abandonment. She heard running water, a gentle trickle. The humidity of Hertfordshire was replaced with a clammy cold atmosphere. Where was she? She held out her hands to feel her way. Gradually some light began to filter into her eyes. Three candles flickered into life to reveal a circular chamber. Directly ahead of her was a wall. She moved forward slightly to touch it, exploring the texture and contours. She traced out the palm of a hand, which appeared to have a heart shape etched into it. She found another, and another. Each hand identical to the one before!

Julia claimed to hear a breath from behind her. Instinctively, she span quickly around. She saw a familiar picture hanging on the wall of the chamber - Stubbs' *Haymakers*! Beneath it was an ornate wooden chest. She heard breathing again. She had no fear, not even when she glimpsed a shadowed figure stood beside the chest. She kept perfectly still and looked to the floor of the chamber. The white stones - they that Malachi had knocked to the ground - began to move of their own free will. They revolved in circles, as if they were dancing, as though they were alive.

The man in the shadows spoke,
"Julia, can you hear me?"
"I hear you."
"It's our one chance Julia... our one opportunity."
"I'm afraid... I don't understand!"
"All will become clear. Live the magic Julia, do you feel the magic?"
"I can, I feel it."

Daylight rushed back into Julia's world.

"Julia… Julia it just slipped through my fingers," she heard Ben say, as he grappled awkwardly with the soil and pieces of the broken jar. 🐎 Like sand passing through the eye of an hour glass! 🐎

Q24: Do you get enough time to yourself?

As was often the way with her visions, Julia was left feeling wary. To help her recover from the cavern experience, she requested some time alone. She needed to reflect on what she'd seen and heard; to re-gather her composure. Ben helped her upstairs, where she lay on her bed to try and recall everything. She chose to write down what she could remember, for fear of losing the message. She stored her scrawled notes in her bedside cabinet for safe keeping.

It's me again. I realise so much has happened in such a short space of time, I figured you may be a little confused. I know how hectic 21st century life can be so I thought I'd use this 'window of opportunity' – I think that's what you people call it - to recap the series of incredulous events:

💜 *First, we had the Lady in Grey and the manic horseman.*

💜 *Then we had the cameo squirrel that dashed up and down the Goblin Tree.*

💜 *Then the bizarre figure clinging to a log with Ben's watch dangling from it.*

♥ *We had the gold locket that won't open and the ribbon that formed a heart.*

♥ *Ben saw the Dead Man's Fingers and found the jar with the strange stones.*

♥ *We had several of Julia's visions, some odd chants and old songs.*

🐕 *The coup de grace has been a wonderful dog with the mental astuteness and acumen of a Greek philosopher.* 🐕

Surely this is utter nonsense! It's the dawn of the 21st century - the Information Age of the personal computer, MP3 player, IPod and mobile phone. Illogical stuff like this just doesn't happen, does it? LOL!

Come on, open up, it's not as though you're being asked to believe in fairies?

Q25: Do you believe in fairies?

When she was a girl, Julia's Grandmother asked her whether she believed in fairies. She'd regularly led her up the garden path to search behind Foxgloves, Lavender and the like, in an effort to see one. "The trouble with fairies," she'd say, "Is that it's up to them whether they let you see them or not. Some say that even if they do let you, they make you forget so quickly that it's as though they were never there at all."

"They seem ever so clever."

"Oh they're very bright indeed, amongst the brightest things in

God's kingdom. But there's one thing about fairies that most people don't know… they can be extremely naughty! They do like to practice their magic and play games… you know, such as moving things around. That's why your Grandad's always losing his things."

"Even his glasses?"

"Yes his glasses… and his keys… and his marbles!"

"Did you ever see a fairy Nana?" Julia had asked.

"Well that would be telling, my sweet… and if you ever did tell, then that fairy just falls down and goes to sleep forever."

"Is that true Nana, do you believe that… as I've never seen one sleeping?"

"That's because they fold themselves up into a little ball, so tight and so small… so pure, like a pearl, that you wouldn't ever notice them."

"And they can never wake up?"

"Oh they hibernate… you see never isn't a word that fairies understand!"

"Is that why they live in Neverland?" Julia asked.

"No sweetness – that's just a story."

Julia loved her Grandmother a great deal; she'd raised her from a young age, after her mother died. Older, wiser and no longer innocent, Julia guessed that her Grandmother was just helping her to cope with her mother's loss. All the same, Julia's fascination for fairies became imbedded in her psyche. It thrilled her to think that maybe they were out there – amongst the flowers, dancing like little angels. Julia still secretly searched for fairies. She believed that if she were to see one then it had to be at Keeper's Cottage.

Q26: Do you take poetry seriously?

Just before she died, Julia's Grandmother gave her a framed poem, hand written in ink, that her own Grandmother once gave to her. "Julia, I want you to have this. It's your heritage. It's your responsibility to think about what it says. Remember, whenever you read it I'll be right with you. You won't be able to see me, but I promise. I'll be there."

"Will you really Grandma?"

"When I'm gone, think of me as your guardian angel. I'll look out for you. All you need do is look for the signs. You have the gift… you'll see them… act upon them."

Julia re-read the poem.

Shadows

See the magic in the shadows

Standing next to Nature true,

Tiny seeds of hope o'sowing

Tiny wings of Aqua Blue.

Ah, be ours the task to stop it

Ours the task this Earth to keep.

With imagination blot it,

Woe decry industrial creep.

Woe decry that Icy Tear,

"Forget-me-not," the Time is Near.

See the stones, pure o'glowing
Circles in a darkened cave.
Tiny seeds of hope are growing
Tiny hands for us to save.
Ah, be this our task to find it
So the Artist shall not weep
With imagination stop it,
Woe decry complacency.
Woe decry that Icy Tear
"Forget-me-not," the Time Is Here.

With the memory of her Grandmother alive in her mind, Julia wondered if events in the poem were beginning to unfold in the world and at home. She studied the words in detail and wondered who had written them. Why had her Grandmother placed so much emphasis on the poem? Perhaps the stones could provide the answer. Julia knew Ben had placed them in an old tankard which he kept in the study. There were 12 stones altogether; all identical in size, weight and form; none showed any sign of damage from the fall.

With Ben absent walking Malachi, Julia's curiosity led her to the stones. She was confident of avoiding a further vision; for in her experience an object would only reveal a truth to her once, and no more.

"See the stones, pure o'glowing,
Circles in a darkened cave."

Julia carefully removed one of the stones and held it in the palm of her hand. She rolled the stone in small circles, this way then that;

clockwise, then anti-clockwise. Her behaviour was compulsive; like a human machine – an automaton. The stone warmed in her palm, which she found therapeutic. She completed a hundred circles, at least. Come the end, the stone sparkled when she held it to the light. It was like nothing she'd ever known. But what did it mean?

Q27: Do you like gardening?

By the time Ben and Malachi reached the cottage, Julia had made herself comfortable on a bench that looked across the rear garden. September 2006 was a real scorcher – but what did the exceptional temperatures mean for the future? It was all too easy to lay back and soak up the sunshine – hey, was it so bad if Britain became like the Mediterranean? Just think of it: the Costa Del Cornwall!

Yet climate change was more than soaring temperatures and a good sun-tan; it could bring storms and floods too. Nonchalantly, she asked,

"Good walk?"

"Yes, of a kind... well you certainly look much brighter... the colour's flooded back into you."

"I feel really fabulous... a little rest has made all the difference."

"It sure has..." said Ben, taking a seat beside his wife.

"It was a strange walk... it went by in a blur. I remember climbing up on to the haystacks... and know we went to the ford because we paddled in the low trickle – it's just a foot deep now - but the rest is... well it's gone."

"It must be the heat Ben."

"It doesn't do him any favours... poor Mali, he kept stopping every few yards to rest. It's way too hot for him. He doesn't really belong in these temperatures. We should move to Norway or someplace. Look at him, he's exhausted."

🐎 Like the Norns in Wagner's Der Ring des Nibelungen, I'm at the end of my tether. 🐎

Malachi's point was the Norns in Wagner's tale lived beneath the roots of Yggdrasil, where they weaved the tapestry of fates - the force that guides the destiny of life and death!

"Let's bring him into the shade… I'll fetch us a drink and top up his water bowl," said Julia, as she stood up from the bench.

"You really do look incredible… what did you do to yourself?" Ben asked.

"Just caught up on my beauty sleep!" replied Julia.

"You look five years younger."

Ben kissed his wife.

"Flattery will get you everywhere," she said.

Ben wiped his brow,

"Is it me or is it getting very sticky… I think they predicted storms this evening… we could certainly do with the rain."

Q28: Have you ever lived in poverty?

There's a campaign to *Make Poverty History*, well our experience was just that, literally. It began when Malachi tried to quench his thirst. He gulped the water so eagerly, he toppled his bowl. The water streamed towards a small rockery that bordered a flower bed by the side of the cottage. Malachi followed the trail into the flowers, forcing his bowl into the plants with his snout. Presumably he wanted to lap up the last drops; though he had something more on his mind.

🐎 I wonder, was the Duke a man of his word? 🐎

Julia reached into the flowers to recover the bowl. She couldn't resist a sly look into the depths of the plants, amongst the Lavender and the Dahlia, for those tiny wings that toyed with her heart and her imagination.

"Ben!"

No response.

"Ben!" she beckoned him close. "What do you make of this?"

"Make of what?"

"There in the stones. I don't remember seeing them before. Do you?"

Embedded in the stones of the rockery were several penny coins. In shades of blue and grey, some had a left-facing laureate head inscribed GEORGIUS IIII D. G. Others had a right-facing seated Britannia with shield and trident with the words BRITANNIAR REX F. D. The coins were from 1823 – nearly 200 years ago! It surprised us then. It doesn't surprise us now. We imagine Malachi recognised them!

🐎 They're from the Maundy Ceremony. 🐎

"You're right Julia, I'm certain these coins weren't here before. It doesn't make sense. This rockery can only be a few years old. How did these coins get here?" Bemused, Ben scratched his head. Julia agreed, "I'm certain of it too! I'd remember for sure, had I seen them before."

"Wait a second, when I gathered up the stones, I tipped the remaining soil from the smashed jar onto the flower bed."

"Did you?"

"Yes. I filtered through it… as you do when searching for gold – just to make sure – well better safe than sorry."

"That would begin to explain it. Do you think the coins could be valuable?" asked Julia.

"Maybe… assuming we're not just imagining all this."

For reassurance, Ben touched one of the coins. "Yeah… they're real for sure," he confirmed.

Ben looked at his wife as if to say, "Do you want to try?"

"No Ben... not now… later perhaps," she said.

"You never did tell me what you saw earlier," said Ben, drawing his Julia close.

"Whilst you were gone, I wrote it down… it was something I had to do."

"It's okay," he whispered. "You do what you have to do."

Q29: Could you live without machines?

We struggled to understand what attracted Ben to this question, given he owns a computer, a digital camera and a car! When we quizzed Ben, he told us what happened when the storm arrived.

The weary bones of the old cottage creaked and groaned under the gusty blows of nature. The house trembled, as thunder cascaded across the skies and driving rain pounded every window. It was enough to cause a power failure. The Whittenbury's were prepared – with candles and wood-burner at the ready. As the storm raged around them, Ben and Julia snuggled up on the couch under candlelight and the glow of the fire. Malachi lay in the hall, beside the heavy oak front door, under which a draft crept in to cool him. A crack of kindling wood led Ben to say,

"This is perfect… in an odd sort of way… the candles, and the wild of nature."

"It certainly feels very primitive… apart from the television in the corner… we could be back in the 19th century… about the time this place was built!"

"As I say… it feels good to me… I could just imagine living here all those years ago. To wake in the morning and spend the day keeping the land… taking my horse to Hertford market perhaps. Not a car, mobile or plane to pollute my ears… no ugly road markings or power lines. It must have been a different age, pre-industrial Britain!"

"Yes… and a real struggle for many… no washing machines, fridges or holidays abroad."

"Well, I'd really like to go back there, given the chance!"

"What do you mean, go back there?"

"Just a way with words… that's all."

"No… it's the way you said it."

"What are words worth? It wasn't meant to be taken literally!"

Julia shuddered as a huge clap of thunder rumbled overhead. As the lightening struck close by, Ben had his eyes on the *Haymakers* picture.

"Take the *Haymakers*… so idyllic. It's everything life should be… fresh air, nature, working the land… being with friends and family!"

"You're just a romantic country boy at heart," claimed Julia, cuddling up to her husband.

"Which makes you my country girl? I could easily close my eyes and imagine you and me in the picture… me on top of the hay cart… you helping to load it."

"You… just because you resemble him. Remind me, where it was painted?" she asked.

"Do you know, I can't remember for sure, I'll need to look that up." The conversation had stirred Malachi from his sleep.

🐾 Philosopher's Point, Ben, Philosopher's Point! 🐾

Julia closed her eyes and tried to imagine living some 200 years ago. Whilst she did so, Ben continued to muse about life without machines.

"I'm a touch envious of the Amish people in America. A simple life is theirs - men in straw hats, braces and boots; women in plain dresses and bonnets riding horse-drawn buggies, shunning the modern world."

Julia re-opened her eyes.

"I don't think I could live that way… I like my modern comforts too much and the things that make life easier. To do what they do, it's weird…just one step from living in a cave." As the words left her lips, she remembered her vision of the shadowed figure in the chamber.

"Mm… maybe we've just gone too far, too fast. 200 hundred years ago nobody could surely have imagined the hunger for progress would lead us to what we have now – the threat to our climate, our world at risk."

🐏 Ah, yes the climate – that's why I was asked to come. 🐏

As if to drum home the point, Mother Nature flexed her muscles; an almighty crash of thunder and crack of lightening sent a nearby tree tumbling to the ground.

"Goodness…" said Julia, jumping to her feet with fright.

"I think that just hit a tree!" she shrieked. "It could have crashed right into us!"

Malachi rushed to her side.

🐏 Fear not Julia, there's more that shields Keeper's than meets the eye! 🐏

"Come, sit back down," invited Ben.

"You must be either crazy or desperate to venture outside on a night like this," claimed Julia, unable to resist pulling back the curtains to look for the victim of nature's wrath.

> ## Q30: Did you ever watch the rain on your window?

It was one of those storms that make hairs stand up on the back of the neck. It raged, wild and furious. Trees swayed like tormented souls. The deluge was too much for the baked hard ground. Water gushed along the bridleway and headed for the Nimley Bourne. Julia saw her own faint reflection in the window, distorted by erratic raindrops on the pane that were at the mercy of the storm. The rain spoke to her – it was a language she understood. The droplets coagulated and formed a picture in her mind.

She saw the figure of a man hung by his foot with a nimbus around his head. The radiant light above the figure's head represented a life in suspension. Her breath caused the window to mist over and the image to fade. She rubbed it clear again with her hand, clockwise, then anti-clockwise. She was greeted by a flash of lightening, which lit up a drenched darkened figure fast approaching the front door. An intense feeling of dread came over her. A heavy thud on the old lion-head knocker that graced the front-door!

Q31: Are you a charitable neighbour?

Malachi woke from his stupor. Somewhat sleepy still, he slipped his snout between the curtains in the lounge and sized up the visitor. Did sin lie without?

🐕 Fosbrooke! 🐕

"Ben, there's someone at the door… Ben, Ben!" cried Julia, nervously.

"I know… I know… I know."

There was a further thud on the door. Malachi barked again.

🐕 What do you carry in that rucksack? 🐕

The front door often jammed tight, due to the movement of the clay soil. Ben did his best to open it, to no avail. Pity, as the sunken trembling figure of their closest neighbour struggled to shelter from the elements. The rain, so abstract on the window pane, was so penetrating on the nomadic Mr Fosbrooke. His dense dark Gaelic hair glistened and contrasted with his pallid worried complexion. His full eyebrows acted as a gully that steered the rain down his nose in a funnel. It dripped like a tap. What were the charitable neighbours to do?

"Go round the back – it's stuck!" urged Ben.

Q32: Are you afraid of the dark?

Jonas sat silently before the wood burner, like a child scolded for being caught in the rain and made to stay in his drenched clothes. With a head hung low, the candle and firelight exaggerated his frowning melancholic appearance. A troubled sigh!

"I think the flame's going out," he said gruffly, whilst Ben stoked the fire.

"Yes… it does that if you neglect it."

"Amazing stuff fire – like something from another world," replied Jonas, as he stared deep into the flames with his deep-set ice blue eyes.

"It reminds me of life… the spirit that burns within each of us," he mumbled poetically, before settling into another spell of silence.

"Would you like to talk about it?" asked Ben.

This was a man they had hardly spoken to in a year. Yet Ben had invited him to open his heart, in the midst of the gloom and as a storm raged outside.

"I just had to get out of the house… it was intolerable… being alone in the dark with the sound of the wind and the rain."

"You're a brave soul. I had trouble looking out of the window, let alone stepping outside," announced Julia, as she brought Jonas a warm drink made on their portable gas burner.

"You're absolutely wet through. How long were you outside?" she asked. His roughened carpenter hands took the cup, "Thanks… to be honest I don't really know. I've spent so much time alone lately… walking, always walking. It gives me a sense of purpose."

🐕 You could always get a dog! 🐕

Jonas fell silent again, which gave Ben an opportunity to ask about Fanny Ebbs. Dare he?

"You're welcome to stay until the storm eases," suggested Ben.

"Cheers. I could do with the chance to get my head together."

"Yes. I know the feeling."

"Why so?"

"It's just things have been a bit strange these last few days."

"Still with Sarah away… it must feel odd."

"No, you misunderstand… we've seen things, heard things… and found things."

"What kind of things?"

"Does the name Fanny Ebbs mean anything to you?"

Julia looked harshly at Ben for she questioned his insensitive timing. "Ebbs you say? Fanny Ebbs?" asked Jonas, as he rubbed his hands together.

Ben told Jonas some of what had happened. In response, Jonas said, "I remember… I'd been to Widford that afternoon. I saw you running, screaming at your dog." Jonas rubbed his eyes. "I'm sorry. I haven't been sleeping well lately. To be honest I'm thinking of leaving Noblin Green… I need a new beginning, a reason to live again." A brave man's eyes welled up and glistened in the light of the fire. A single tear ran down his bristled cheek. He wiped it away then stared into his open palms. His penetrating eyes scanned his lifeline. It was broken in several places.

"These hands have created so much… yet now just long to destroy!" Strong words indeed.

"If I ever learn who was responsible, well God help me," added Jonas, as he wrapped one hand around a closed fist. Malachi sprung up from his slumber and ran at Jonas, startling him a little.

🐾 It was Clibborn I tell you… Clibborn! 🐾

Q33: Do you believe in life after death?

As Sarah was due home in the morning, Julia went to bed early ahead of Ben. She was physically, but not mentally tired. She lay awake for a while listening to the muffled sound of the storm as it drifted away, to be replaced by the voices in the lounge below. She had missed her daughter, but her last thought before she fell asleep was for her Grandmother. She entered a bewildering dream. She recalled it in her notebook,

"The first I remember is that I was sitting in a small oarless boat, lit by three candles at its bow. I held the locket in one hand and the blue ribbon in another. The boat spun in circles, until a defiant voice cried out something I didn't understand. It was like a command that blew out all but one of the candles and calmed and silenced the water. The voice took the darkness away. I'd not seen water like it before, not a single ripple disturbed the surface! It was like a mirror that reflected a tranquil, blue, cloudless sky to the horizon, whichever way I turned.

I looked overhead and saw a bird of prey circling menacingly. My mouth was desperately dry. My lips cracked, as though I hadn't drunk for days. I was so thirsty. I looked within the boat for fresh water. The old pennies from the flower garden were at my feet. Britannia's face smiled at me, in jest at the value of money when adrift at sea. "Water, water everywhere, but nor a drop to drink," I heard. The voice drifted across the still sea. The words lingered, toying with my emotions. I heard it again as the boat steered itself towards the voice.

A green jar bobbed gently in the sea, within arms reach. Inside were the familiar mysterious white stones. One by one I tipped the stones into the sea. They made no sound as they hit the water. They did not sink. They began to sparkle like diamonds. The siren's voice called again,
"Your body's weak and your throat is dry, I guess it would be easier to die."

The bird continued to circle overhead. Afraid, I tried to make myself small in the boat, fearing death at any point. I crouched into a ball and closed my eyes, as tight as they would go. I heard the voice again, "Water, water, everywhere but nor a drop to drink." I could almost feel the breath of the person who had spoken.

When I re-opened my eyes I had sand between my toes. A gentle warm breeze caressed me. I looked up. The boat had gone. I was ashore on an island before a huge palm tree which swayed silently.

"Where am I?" I whispered.

"An oasis for the dead," was the reply from the foot of the tree. An angelic figure got to its feet and walked slowly towards me, leaving no footprints in her wake. Like a flower unfolding to greet the sun, the figure held out her hand and invited me to pass her the locket. The young woman looked at me with eyes aglow, resembling the setting sun.

"Fear of death is worse than death itself," she claimed.

"Am I dead?" I asked.

"What is death?" Her hand was still outstretched.

"I'm so very thirsty," I pleaded, barely able to speak.

"Then drink with me," she said and gestured towards a pool of water beside the tree.

"Are you an angel?" I asked, using my palm to cup the fresh water.

"They call me Lucy," she said. "I need to tell you – you hold the key. You must never break faith Julia. Can you promise me that?"

"I…" I hesitated. "I don't understand."

Julia looked at her cupped palms. Rotating within it was a tiny Earth - she literally had the whole world in her hands.

Lucy tilted her head and softly sang part of a nursery rhyme, "Lost her locket, only ribbon round it." She made a heart shape with her hands.

"I will try, I will, if only I knew how," I said.

"You'll know when the time comes, you'll know."

A ripple of church bells spread across the sand. That's when I woke up."

We're really confident this is an entirely accurate account, for Julia made scrawled notes when she woke, adding them to those she made after her experience in the chamber.

Q34: Have you ever restored something?

The morning after the storm, an eerie mist hung over the Ware Uplands, as if to honour it. In the storm's wake, a huge old tree lay strewn across the bridleway by the cottage, making it impassable. The uprooted tree dwarfed debris ripped from surrounding trees. Dressed in his wellington boots, Ben tip-toed amongst the twigs and fallen branches. His mission was to conduct a local survey of the damage caused. The boots weren't really needed, for the parched ground soaked up most of the night's deluge. Malachi was with Ben. 🐐 I'm so glad I wasn't called Paddington! 🐐

The pair began with a quick review of the cottage. It was largely unscathed, aside for a few dislodged tiles.

"I'll call the landlord at Blakesware Manor, so he can fetch one of his people to get it sorted. That's the joy of renting… S.E.P… Someone Else's Problem," said Ben.

🐐 Ah, Charles at Blakesware, cherished memories! 🐐

Next in line for a health check was the indomitable Goblin Tree.

Its unsettling head appeared to bow to greet him, as if to ask, "How's my champion today?"

It retained its full glory.

"Not one scratch. I guess it'd take a calamity to bring you down! I wouldn't be surprised to find you protected by your own guardian angels," he suggested. Ben placed a tender hand on the trunk, patting it lightly, before moving on to assess the rest of the Green.

He began with the ruins of former Noblin Green Farm - a place that had gone to pigs and whistles! It dampened his spirits. Ben stood glum faced before decaying sties that had long been empty. They were crumbling and plagued with discarded beer cans, plastic bottles and rotten doors that, despite the storm, clung miraculously to rusty hinges. In Ben's words to us, "Orwell's *Beasts of England* had revolted and there was no sign of Old Major, Squealer or Snowball on Animal Farm."

🐎 Beasts of England, beasts of Ireland, beasts of every land and clime, Hearken to my joyful tidings of the golden future time! 🐎

"It brings tears to my eyes," said Ben, as he surveyed the former farmyard, littered with debris. Weather-beaten barns, storage houses and decaying outbuildings stood as ancient relics to a former golden age. Ben imagined the sights and sounds of that time. Horse-drawn carts, Aylesbury ducks competing with chickens for scraps and women carrying pails heavy with milk.

"This is a graveyard, not a farmyard. Just think Mali, this farmhouse was once the heart of something. Had I the money, I'd love to restore this place to how it used to be… sadly I need those pennies from Heaven first." Ben lifted a cupped hand to the skies to simulate catching falling coins.

The farmhouse was several hundred years old. A faded tiled roof protected a cream and black weather boarded structure. It had many square windows, some of which Ben had looked into during its

vacant tenancy. Ben was about to approach the farmhouse when he was disturbed by a vehicle that pulled into the rear of the farm. "That's not possible, surely. I thought the roads were blocked? Perhaps my parents will be able to return Sarah today after all. C'mon boy, best get out of here... we're on private property."
🐈 The cat, the rat and Lovel our dog, Rule all England under a hog! 🐈
These famous lines were once affixed to the doors of St Paul's Cathedral in the city of London. It was a form of critical graffiti directed at rulers in the 14th Century, which led the culprit to endure a cruel death in the Tower of London.

Q35: Do you trust your instincts?

It was an instinctive step. Our point being that if the human race continues to have such little respect for Mother Nature, we shall feel her wrath! We digress, our role is to show not tell. Forgive us.

Malachi was notoriously curious. He was unable to resist reacting to the arrival of strangers and a dog at the house next door. Malachi's senses were as sharp as a whistle. He surveyed every movement and sound made by a chequered black and white Jack Russell Terrier. It snapped away to announce its presence. Its owner cried out, "Come, Toby."
🐈 Ah I've been expecting you! You took your time and what a surprise, you've lost the bells to frighten away the Devil. 🐈

Malachi rose up on to his hind legs – like a dancing polar bear - barking wildly at his new neighbour. The terrier reacted by dashing towards Malachi before retreating fast at his owner's command. It yapped determinedly around its owner's boots, running rings around them. A tenacious act applauded by the owner. The man had a Napoleon-like stature with an arrogant stance to match the tenacity of his dog. He had a glaring lack of hair and the morning moisture made his head shine like the moon. The clapping ended, replaced with scornful laughter aimed at Malachi's antics.

"C'mon down boy... I don't like the look of him... smells like trouble," said Ben.

Q36: Should a good life cost the Earth?

Apart from the haystacks, an alternative place for Ben to philosophise was at the very end of the rear garden at Keepers Cottage. It was amongst the natural wilderness of wild flowers, bramble and some disused dog kennels.

🐕 In wilderness is the preservation of the World. 🐕

Malachi was quoting Henry David Thoreau, a famous American Naturalist. In 1845, Henry embarked on a two year experiment in 'easy-living', when he moved to a tiny self-built house in a forest. You could think of it as a more extreme version of the Whittenbury's Keeper's experience.

Anyhow, the wilderness at Keeper's gave Ben a wonderful panoramic view of the open undulating fields. Ben often sat upon the same upturned log. Today, as if to grace one of the main traits of his Aquarian birth sign, he adopted the pose of Rodin's *The Thinker*, right hand to chin and elbow to knee. Ben again dwelt on the potential impact of climate change.

"Take a good look Malachi! This is all under threat. It's so easy to be complacent. Yet in a blink of an eye it'll be gone... lost forever. I'm helpless to stop it. What kind of champion am I?"

The reason for Ben's sadness was clear. The news shared some facts that shocked him. This was his list:

___Climate Change – the ticking bomb___ ❤

❤ _Humans are using the world's resources so fast that the planet cannot replace them quickly enough. Many of the Earth's species of animals had lost nearly one-third of their population in the last 30 years._

❤ _Do the maths? If nothing changes, by the time a new born child today reaches adulthood the world will be entering a disaster so huge it is unthinkable._

❤ _Global warming was set to tip many countries into crisis. Mass migration, terrorism, civil war, disease, want and starvation - this was the future._

Malachi wasn't one to give up easily. He pushed his snout into Ben's lap, and dropped something into it – a fife!

🐕 Hey, true champions don't give up without a fight. We've come so far… waited so long… all of us. Just try a little imagination! Visualise success! 🐕

Ben took up the instrument.

"Where did you find this?" Ben asked, amazed at Malachi. "It's a fife! What do you expect me to do with this? Do you imagine me a pied-piper to lead the people of the world into a new sustainable way of living?"

The dog, of course, was unable to answer directly, but his tail wagged furiously. So Ben put the fife to his lips.

🐕 If music be the food of love, play on, give me excess of it! 🐕

Ben played the tune 'Yankee Doodle', lightly tapping his foot as he did so. Malachi ran in excited circles to the tune, bringing joy to Ben's face.

"What kind of dog are you? It's as though you know what's going on. You could be from a fairy story… on a stage… a performer in a tale of Shakespeare!" remarked Ben, once he'd finished playing. He held the fife in his hand, as though it were a conductor's baton.

"That's it… the human race is in the midst of a tragedy. To be, or not to be, that is the question!"

Malachi's ear's pricked up in approval.

"Maybe that's my purpose, to make the people of the world see the truth, to feel the Earth's sorrow at our destructive hands… to use art to put the love of Mother Nature at the heart of all we do! Hey… let's start with a survey, 'The Haymakers Survey'. We could put questions online and invite people the world over to take part. A one-world voice to provide the inspiration and the solutions we need: and to bring new hope and urgency. We might even develop a following of Haymakers committed to serious action before it's too late. What say you Mali?"

🐕 One planet, one people, one solution! 🐕

Enthused, Ben began to draw up the questions in his mind.

"We don't want a set of serious questions that are factual or science based. It's not about clear-cut answers. The survey should go beyond our appetite for knowledge. It must be something deeper. If we want people to think creatively about the problems, we need it to be a fun list. People need only answer those questions that interest them. Malachi, imagine this, doing the survey might teach all those logical –what do they call them, left brained people – the key to unlocking their imagination!"

🐕 Come on – what did Fanny Ebbs say – 'make haste.' 🐕

As a maker of lists, Ben was seldom without a pencil and pocket-sized notebook. He licked the end of his pencil and began to write.

"Let's get to that happy ending!"

The Haymakers Survey

Q1. Do you believe your life has a purpose?

Q2. Are you an art lover?

Q3. Do you have a good imagination?

Q4. Have you ever wanted to stop the clock?

Q5. Do you believe in fate?

Q6. Do you believe in fairy tales?

Q7. Have you ever dreamed of being a champion?

Q8. Do you crave a better life?

Q9. Do you feel in control of your life?

Q10. Have you ever seen a ghost?

Q11. Do you believe in justice?

Q12. Is our Earth enchanted?

Q13. Have you ever been mistaken for someone else?

Q14. Do you believe your stars?

Q15. Do you sometimes fear the worst?

Q16. Have you ever had a psychic experience?

Q17. Can you speak another language?

Q18. Do you let your heart rule your head?

Q19. Do you love hedgehogs?

Q20. Have your eyes ever deceived you?

Q21. Have you ever hugged a tree?

Q22. Do you love our Earth?

Q23. Do you believe all the laws of physics?

Q24. Do you get enough time to yourself?

Q25. Do you believe in fairies?

Q26. Do you take poetry seriously?

Q27. Do you like gardening?

Q28. Have you ever lived in poverty?

Q29. Could you live without machines?

Q30. Did you ever watch the rain on your window?

Q31. Are you a charitable neighbour?

Q32. Are you afraid of the dark?

Q33. Do you believe in life after death?

Q34. Have you ever restored something?

Q35. Do you trust your instincts?

Ben paused for breath. Looking back, we know now he had unwittingly drawn up questions which recorded the events to unfold since his quest began to be Nature's Champion. Ben reviewed his list,

"Whatever it takes… I just hope the survey will make people realise that a good life needn't cost the Earth… let's make that Question 36!" He added it to the list.

......

Q32. *Are you afraid of the dark?*

Q33. *Do you believe in life after death?*

Q34. *Have you ever restored something?*

Q35. *Do you trust your instincts?*

Q36. *Should a good life cost the Earth?*

Ben put down his pencil. "I'll return to the list later. I'm sure Julia and Sarah will have some suggestions. I'll share it with them." He casually placed the note book and pencil into his back pocket.
🐐 Hey, you need to take more care of that – it's priceless. 🐐

Ben walked nonchalantly back to the cottage, playing another tune on Malachi's magic fife.

Well, I wasn't expecting that! It's a bit 'out-there!' Let's take a few minutes to reflect on what Ben suggested? How could a seemingly random set of questions - some profound, some trivial, some just plain odd, help with the big issues – global warming, deforestation, pollution and poaching?

♥ *It doesn't make any sense – but does life make any sense?*

♥ *Maybe it'll help if we begin with Question 1 –*
'Does your life have a purpose?' Is it collectively for us to do

whatever it takes to preserve our planet for the pleasure of future generations? Is it for each of you to see that YOU COUNT? Your planet needs you – we cannot succeed without you!

♥ *It's a really big ask I know, but so much is at stake. It's so much more than turning off a light, having TVs without stand-by buttons, or growing a few more trees. What do you people call it – ah yes – a cultural revolution!*

♥ *We need to be creative – to do that you need to open up and think laterally – maybe the survey will help to achieve that. From acorns do oak trees grow!*

♥ *Still sceptical – Come on, say no to Climate Chaos and join the Culture Change Club!*

Okay – enough preaching from me, let's have some fun. ☺

Q37: Do you know how to have fun?

Sarah Whittenbury certainly did. She was a child who lived for the moment, was nearly always active and craved adventure. Just ahead of puberty, she still had a certain innocence, naivety and freshness. In many ways her behaviour was rather like Malachi's. She was kind, loveable and playful – yet sometimes misbehaved or meddled in things that weren't really her concern. She was untroubled that her journey home from Ben's parents had been delayed. Although Sarah enjoyed her time in London, she was delighted to be home again.

"So Mum… Dad… what's been going on whilst I've been away?" she asked, playing with an excited Malachi. Ben and Julia's pensive look made Sarah suspicious.

"Well… have I missed anything fun?" she asked, breaking the silence.

🐎 The World Games have been declared well and truly open. 🐎

"A few things…" said her father.

"Mm… it's been eventful," added Julia.

The other thing about Sarah was her curiosity, hardly surprising given the genes she'd inherited.

"Oh… really… Keeper's Cottage, the house of fun! I want to know all about it… but only after I've said hello to Dixie first," she cried, fleeing to her room to search out her golden hamster; she'd initially called him Trixie because he got up to lots of tricks, but Trixie was a girl's name and the vet said he was a boy, so Sarah did the decent thing - "Well, Dixie sounds like Trixie!" she'd said.

Once she'd dashed upstairs, Ben turned to his wife and said, "Do you think she'll believe us? I'm having trouble believing it all myself. She's just a child, what shall we tell her?"

He held Malachi's magic fife in his hand.

"Oh Ben… what's to tell other than we found a locket… pure and simple?"

"I suppose not, when you put it like that."

It wasn't until the *Day After Tomorrow* that Sarah began to find out some of what had occurred during her absence, and she had plenty of fun in the process. It began with heavy rhythmic thuds that echoed across the fields at the rear of the cottage; thuds that sent wood pigeons sky-bound in wonderful chaos. Jack O'Legs, a Weston Giant and ancient Hertfordshire legend, could well have been marching across the countryside, but the answer was more mundane. Julia and Sarah were playing on a discarded single–axis wooden trailer, which they used as a novel seesaw.

"This is great... make it go faster... c'mon please Mum," implored Sarah.

"It won't... go any... faster," said Julia, puffing between the thuds. "And there's a risk... it might break."

"C'mon please. It's fun. Trust me, it won't break," cried Sarah shrilly. Malachi joined in. He jumped on to the trailer to stand in the middle, between mother and child, our ambassador from the animal kingdom. He stood on the tipping-point.

🐎 Life's full of up's and downs! The trick is to keep things in balance. 🐎

That's just what he did.

"So what happened... when I was away?" Sarah asked, between thuds.

"It was Dad... he started it... by making a pledge... to be Nature's Champion!"

"Oh... I see."

"He saw a ghost."

Sarah stopped the trailer.

"A ghost... *Freaky*... Where?"

"At the bridleway... in front of... the cottage."

"Was he scared?"

"No. It was... a woman."

"Oh... was it... a young woman?"

"No, it was a Lady in Grey."

"Oh... what did she say?"

"This is... ridiculous," said Julia, stepping from the trailer.

"Ben thinks it was an SOS, from Mother Nature."

"What's that?"

"She wanted Ben to save us... to do it for Lucy and all our sake's."

"Lucy! Ah, I knew it."

"Lucy Ebbs?" asked Julia.

"Oh, it makes me crazy… just having fun Mum. Ghosts eh… boo!" she cried, before racing indoors.

Q38: Have you built a house of cards?

We think this question is really a metaphor for the high-energy, fossil fuel consuming, carbon producing societies the world over. We are gambling with our future – one slip of a card and the house will surely tumble! Still, as Julia and Sarah experienced, building a house of cards takes patience, determination, craft and guile. It can take several attempts to build and once constructed it brings pride and satisfaction. Once made, there's a determination not to destroy it.

So it was with the house of cards they built on the dining room table.

"Yes… we did it," announced Sarah gleefully, her mind seemingly untroubled by the revelation about Lucy.

"Well… if you put your mind to it you can achieve most things. It's just a question of will power, sacrifice and perseverance."

"I suppose so," replied Sarah. "But I've still one card left. What should I do with it?"

"What is it?"

"It's the Three of Hearts, here look."

Sarah flashed the card at Julia.

"It's my favourite," said Julia, taking hold of it. "Shall I tell you why? Well three is a really special number. Let's see… we have a mind, body and a spirit."

"Is that it?"

"The world is made of earth, sea and air."

"Okay."

"There's recycle, reuse, and restore."

"And reduce!"

"And reduce! There's also faith, hope and charity… and the Earth, the sun and the moon."

"I see! Okay Mum, anything else?"

"But most important of all you were born on the third of the third."

"Oh yeah!"

"And the Hearts?"

"Oh yeah... the Hearts."

"Well that's easy really. We think they stand for Art, Love and Nature – let's face it if we didn't have a Heart we'd be well..."

"Dying... like Lucy."

"Lucy... *dying*! How do you mean?"

Malachi's ear's pricked up.

"Oh nothing. It doesn't matter really."

Sarah playfully snatched the card back from Julia.

"It's her favourite card too."

"Lucy, you say."

"Mm... can I tell you a secret Mum? You promise you won't be cross." Sarah took her mother's hand. "She told me last night."

"Last night?"

"Yes, she was in my room when I woke... oh, I wasn't scared or anything. I'm still not scared. She was holding this card... she gave it to me and said, well, actually she sung me a nursery rhyme, which annoyed me a bit because I'm not a child now, I'm almost a teenager."

"Sarah... are you sure? Maybe it was just a dream."

"Oh no... it can't have been a dream because she left the card on my bed. It was there when I woke up in the morning."

Julia was bemused.

"So I've got to look after it, because it's very special."

"Just like you Sarah," said Julia, hugging her daughter. It led Sarah to sing,

♫ Lucy Locket lost her Pocket going to the fair, Lucy Locket lost her... ♫

Malachi found her song irresistible. He stood beside her as proudly as a show dog at Crufts. He looked disappointed when Julia interrupted with,

"Shall we play a game now? How about Solitaire!"

Malachi had other ideas,

🐕 I'll take that... thank you very much. 🐕

The dog snatched the card straight from Sarah's hand. In doing so, he brought the house of cards down and a shriek of dismay from the young girl. Unperturbed, Malachi scampered out of the lounge, through the dining room, into the kitchen and out of the back door with Sarah in hot pursuit,

"Give that back... you naughty dog. It doesn't belong to me."

🐕 Sarah, battle if you may, for all's fair in love and war. 🐕

Q39: Do you believe in magic?

"Damn that door, I must have asked Ben a hundred times to fix the bolt, BEN, BEN," shouted Julia.

"BEN, WHERE ARE YOU? WE NEED YOU NOW?"

Sarah was well ahead of her, running to the door in a vain attempt to grab Malachi before he reached the garden.

"Sarah... SARAH! You can't go outside like that. You need something on your feet," cried Julia, as the youngster ran to the outhouse.

"You mad dog! It's Lucy's card... she'll be so cross," insisted Sarah, as she hurried into her trainers. "Oh come on... he's getting away."

"BEN!" shouted Julia again, "Come on, we've not a second to waste."

"What's that? What's going on?" said Ben, as he emerged from the cellar.

"It's Malachi. He's run out of the door."

"With Lucy's card!" snapped Sarah, stamping her feet in annoyance.

"Whose card? Look there he goes," said Ben, catching a glimpse of Malachi as he headed from the front garden to the bridleway.

"Oh Daddy please, hurry we have to get it back," she insisted.

"Hey what am I, a magician? He's long gone," advised Ben with a shrug of his shoulders.

"Come on Sarah, we don't give up that easily," said Julia, grabbing her jacket.

Sarah followed her mother out of the kitchen door.

"Who said anything about giving up, not me!" said Ben, but his words went unheard. He grabbed his coat and slipped into his Wellington's to join the chase.

It came as no surprise that Malachi headed for the place where he'd dug up the locket. An athletic Sarah was ahead of the chasing pack.

🐾 Run, run as fast as you can, you can't catch me, I'm the Gingerbread man! 🐾

"Malachi... Mali," called Sarah. "You have to stop... I promised to give the card back to Lucy!"

🐾 Don't let me be misunderstood, my intentions are good. 🐾

Sarah claims she saw Malachi scurry into the copse that was home to the felled tree with the wooden figure clinging to it. We'd no reason to doubt her.

"THIS WAY!" she shouted, gesturing to her parents with a wave.

"This feels so familiar... as if I've been here before," said Ben, as he caught Julia up.

She laughed, "You should see yourself, running in those things."

"If they were good enough for the Duke, they're good enough for me," Ben cried back, as he passed his wife.

"So she's seen Lucy too," replied Julia, between pants and lengthened strides.

"Eh," Ben slowed to take one look into his wife's eyes and knew instantly what she meant. "When?"

"Last night!"

"He's headed for the Nimley Bourne," said Ben, as he managed to keep the dog in view.

He cried out to his daughter," NOT TOO FAR... BE CAREFUL, IT'S A LONG WAY DOWN."

Sarah's head dipped from view as she entered the gully, where the trick unfolded, thus.

Ben and Julia reached the peak of the gully. They saw their daughter sat beside the mysterious log where the locket was unearthed. Sarah was obviously upset and startled. She put her arms to the skies and waved furiously at her parents.

"I'm down here... he's gone!" she called.

"Okay, we're coming."

She was on the verge of tears, "Mali's just vanished... I'm not lying. One second he was here then he went." She clicked her fingers, "Just like that. Whoosh... gone... vanished!"

"How do you mean gone? You must have lost him," said Julia. She hugged her child, whilst Ben continued to hunt for his dog.

"No, you don't get it! Parents really! He got to here, right where I'm sat now, and disappeared... as if by magic!"

"That's not possible," replied Julia.

Sarah folded her arms, "You told me the impossible can happen, remember – well he's gone and taken the card with him, and that's that! Lucy is going to be really mad at me... really mad!"

"Mm, I doubt Lucy's like that," insisted Julia.

"Oh she can be. She's really unhappy with us already. This will just make it worse."

"Us... what exactly have we done?"

"Not just us, all the people, all around the world. And she won't stand for it much longer."

"Oh... I see. There's obviously more to Lucy than meets the eye."

"Yes Mum... much more!"

As she spoke, Ben mumbled something about, "Destiny brought us back to this place… I just know it. I mean a dog like Malachi doesn't just disappear without good reason surely!"

"With Malachi, who knows," said Julia, which was her last word on the subject, before she and her daughter decided to head back home. Though Sarah added,

"Remember Dad… we're all counting on you! One… two… three!" which sounded most causal for someone who saw her pet dog vanish in front of her eyes, or so she claimed.

Oh Ben – the pressure of being Earth Champion. Can you show the leadership needed to bring out a sustained change in lifestyle?

Q40: Can you play a musical instrument?

When Sarah returned to the cottage she had a bright idea. She brushed away her tears and grabbed the fife her father had given her; the one Ben claimed Malachi had presented to him.

"Dad says it's Malachi's magic fife, well let's find out shall we!"

So she picked it up and began to play. Sarah was a bit of a whiz with the recorder, so the fife came naturally to her. She marched about the grounds of the cottage, heading upstairs, then down, round the back and down the bridleway. She even sat, unwittingly, upon her father's favourite log in the wilderness. She played the same tune, over and over, occasionally breaking into song,

♫ Lucy Locket lost her Pocket going to the fair, Lucy Locket lost her… ♫

Imagine her joy when she saw Ben and Malachi walking back up the bridleway towards the cottage.

"It worked… it worked!" she cried.

Her celebrations were premature, for although Malachi was back, the card was lost. In its place was a handkerchief! Yes, that's right, a handkerchief! It was just a little thing, but within the handkerchief laid the seed of Ben's destiny; he just didn't know it yet. It was the strangest thing.

Ben had spent a good hour seeking his mischievous dog, only to find Jonas Fosbrooke leading him home from one of his regular jaunts to Widford.

"I found him on the Hertfordshire Way, dodging between the cars... darn near caused an accident," Jonas explained. "He really scared me! I just managed to catch his collar in time."

"Thanks Jonas... we owe you. Heaven knows what might have happened were it not for you," replied Ben.

"That's fine... I was saying my final goodbyes... but saving him has made me think again! It's good to know I've still something to offer."

Ben gave Jonas' hand a mighty shake, and then took Malachi from him.

"Thing is, he's carrying something in his mouth. He won't let go of it, snarled like crazy when I tried to take a look," said Jonas.

"Ah, Sarah will be relieved," replied Ben.

"C'mon boy... give it up!"

"It's some kind of rag," advised Jonas.

"So it is. Guess you're in trouble now my friend, somebody's not going to be happy!"

"Is that music I hear?" Jonas asked, as they approached the cottage.

"Sounds like my fife... yes, it's 'Yankee Doodle'... that tune's haunting me, I can't escape it."

Q41: Do you like surprises?

With seemingly ceaseless energy, Sarah ran up the bridleway to greet them.

"Well... has he still got the Three of Hearts?" she asked, already fearing the worst because of the frowned look on her father's face.

"Afraid not Sarah, still at least he's okay."
"He's always okay... but I'm not... I should have taken more care of it, how silly of me."
"You're not silly," suggested Jonas.
Sarah folded her arms in disappointment.
"Hello Jonas," she mumbled.
"Sarah! Okay, I have absolutely no idea what's going on... but as your Dad says, at least Mali is safe and sound... I found him running on the road you see. Down at Widford!"
"Oh... All the way down there! Gosh, this dog is so weird. We don't know what he's up to from one minute to the next."
🐕 What you don't know, can't hurt you! 🐕
"So what's that in his mouth?" she asked, as they walked through the shadow cast by the Goblin Tree.
"It's a rag... or something similar," claimed Ben, in between saying farewell to Jonas.
"He won't let you have it," insisted Jonas, as he waved to them.

Once back inside, Malachi sat humbly in the kitchen to soak up the words of indignation. After everyone had finished bemoaning his character, he let the rag fall to the floor.
"What's this?" asked Sarah, with a look of disdain.
🐕 It's a kind of magic! 🐕
Malachi was quoting a famous song by the British rock group, Queen! A good choice, as it captured perfectly everything that seemed to be going on!

Not that Sarah thought so. She went to pick up the rag, but said, "It looks like a handkerchief. Ugh... that's disgusting!"
"Hmm, a Samoyed that thinks he's a Retriever!" quibbled Ben, aware that Malachi had a habit of finding and presenting things to them; that's three things now – the locket, the fife and a hanky!
"Don't touch it... it could be covered with germs," said Julia.

🐕 What is it with humans – this obsession with keeping things clean and tidy? 🐕

Sarah was most amused as Malachi used his nose to try to unfold the hanky. She laughed,

"Oh you silly dog, bringing me a hanky... they're for old people with runny noses. Most people don't use them... but I love you all the same. And besides, I'll just tell Lucy what happened and that's that! Mum says she'll understand."

🐕 They've been going in and out of style, but it's guaranteed to raise a smile. 🐕

It was Ben's turn to have an idea; something to turn Sarah's mind from the lost card. He encouraged his daughter to follow him upstairs.

"Don't mind that... I've some things I've been meaning to show you."

So the pair left the room, Julia and the dog behind. Julia was ready to bin the hanky. The tips of her fingers were a whisker from touching it when the stitching, 'Charles Lamb,' caught her eye.

"Oh... Lamb eh... that name's familiar. Mm. Let me see now!"

Upstairs, Ben had invited Sarah into his study and sat her down at his computer desk. He rubbed his chin.

"Now, you'll remember when you came home from Nanny and Grandad's you asked us what had been going on... and I said, 'A few things,' well one of those things was this."

On a shelf beside his desk, Ben kept a small wooden box with a picture of a horse and rider upon it. He'd picked it up at a local antique fair for under £5. It was where he put things such as stamps and pins, so Sarah wasn't expecting much when Ben took it down from the shelf and put it in front of his computer.

"Open it!" he suggested.

She smiled at her father.

"What is it?" she asked.

"Just take a look. Inside are a couple of things Malachi found. Go on, open it."

She lifted the lid. A gold locket and neatly folded blue ribbon greeted her.

"Oh… what's this, a locket?"

"Go ahead, pick it up."

"It's really pretty… it's warm and heavy – that's weird!"

She fiddled with the locket in her small hands.

"Malachi found it at just the spot you say he vanished. Did he really vanish or do you mean he ran into the woods… you know disappeared into the trees?"

"Dad really! Can I have this?"

"Why of course… you may as well. I did try to find the person who may have lost it, but…"

"Eh… oh my God – the ghost! I remember… Mum said you saw a ghost whilst I was gone! Does this belong to a ghost?"

Sarah put the locket down again.

"Did Mum say that? No, it wasn't a ghost at all, just an old woman… a very old woman in grey! Her name was Fanny Ebbs! But that's not important anymore. She said she was looking for…"

Ben was going to mention Lucy, but thought better of it.

"So I asked around if anyone knew who Fanny was, but they didn't. So that's that. We'd like you to have it. Just think of it as a way for Malachi to say sorry about the card. He's just a dog with wild ways… and you said you still love him."

"I do. Maybe I could put his picture inside it?"

She picked the locket up again.

"It won't open. The clasp is broken – jammed shut," advised Ben.

Sarah shook it gently. Not one sound.

"Oh bother! Never mind… oh look, it has the letters LL on it," said Sarah.

"Do you want to try it on?" Ben asked.

Sarah looked at her father in a way that said, "Now that's a silly question!"

Julia and Malachi came into the room.

"The hanky has a name embroidered on it!" said Julia, adding, "Oh you've shown her the locket!"

"We need a chain!" said Ben, with an apologetic look in his eye, as they had promised to present it together.

Julia headed for her bedroom to find one. Everyone followed. They settled by the dressing table as Julia found a chain and helped Sarah put the locket around her neck. Sarah twisted it gently between her fingers and thumbs.

"It suits you!" said Julia.

"LL for Lucy's Locket?" she smiled.

"She'll be so surprised to find me wearing it!" said Sarah as she made a little heart shape with her hands in front of the mirror. Her parents were speechless.

"Dad I need the ribbon!" Sarah asked.

"The ribbon?"

"Yes. The Ribbon! It goes with the rhyme:

> ♪ Lucy Locket lost her pocket,
> Kitty Fisher found it.
> Not a penny was there in it
> Only ribbon round it! ♪

Malachi barked.

🐕 Watch out, there's a Clibborn about! 🐕

"Thank you Mali… I don't care about the card now, because you found me this wonderful locket, you clever doggie!" She kissed the top of his head.

Sarah's fondness for Malachi increased further once she went to bed, for when she pulled back the duvet the missing card was waiting for her.

"Way-hey! I don't believe it! Where's that dog?" she shrieked, running downstairs with a playing card held tightly in her hand.

"Look… look what was in my bed. It's the Three of Heart's."

She held the card high above her head and jumped up and down triumphantly in silly circles.

♫ I got the Three of Heart's… I got the Three of Heart's ♫ she sang.

Ben had a huge beaming smile on his face. Julia took hold of the card.

"Hang-on, it's got something written on it. What's it say? Looks to me like… '*Thank You, Ben*'."

"What's that?" sparked Ben.

"Daddy! I bet you did this, didn't you! You can do magic after all."

"Well, it would seem that way I guess."

Ben began to laugh.

"Right, that's not funny. You are going to pay for that," announced Sarah. She jumped on to him and began a tickle fight with her father.

🐴 To assume is to make an Ass of U and Me! 🐴

Q42: Do you enjoy drawing?

Julia was keen for Sarah to develop her artistic skills in the hope that she may one day follow in her footsteps.

"An artist needs an open mind Sarah," she said, as they organised the art materials and paper.

"It's what feeds the imagination. It's about seeing the possibilities in what's around us," she said.

"Is that why you believe in fairies still, as a grown up?"

"As I say… keep it all open."

They'd packed pencils, water colours, brushes and sketch pads.

"Is that why we're doing this today? On Halloween… going out in the mist to paint?"

"Of course, c'mon let's see. Who knows what secrets we might find? Take your father. He wants to change the future – our Earth Champion!"

Sarah smiled.

"And I plan to help him to do it, which is why I'm wearing the locket. From now on my name is Sarah Battle!" she cried, doing a strong-girl impression with her arms.

"Good for you, Sarah Battle!"

So they ventured into the early morning mist - a curious layer of moisture a few feet high that hovered above the ground. When Ben saw the mist he decided to go with his wife and daughter on their field trip. In Ben's inventive mind, the combined wandering souls of deceased locals had gathered. For, according to Caleb, our ancestors believed that on Halloween, the disembodied spirits of all those who had died throughout the preceding year returned to search for living bodies to possess for the next year.

Spooks aside, the mist dampened the boom of shotguns that echoed across the open landscape. Booms that confirmed the shooting season was underway. A few startled grouse flew over our group - Ben, Julia, Sarah and Malachi – as they went in search of things to draw or paint. Except that Ben took a poetry compilation with him to read whilst the others created! As for the dog, well he had his own special brand of creativity.

"She's wearing the locket," Ben whispered to Julia.

"I know. She said it's to show her support for you as the Earth's Champion. She's even got a nickname too… it's Sarah Battle!"

"She does that alright!" replied Ben.

The group meandered along until they reached the words, 'PLEASE DO NOT FEED' on a sign bordering a field between

Baker's End and Babbs Green. It was home to Jim, an ageing chalk-white horse. He was one of only a few local horses that Malachi tolerated. In fact, whilst the Whittenbury's showered Jim with compliments and attention, Malachi sat as though in meditation.

"There you go Jim," said Sarah, offering him some long grass.

"Guess what, we've come to draw you, so you have to be really good and keep still," she insisted.

Jim's tail flicked to signal approval.

🐎 Fifteen minutes of fame! 🐎

The horse co-operated for precisely that long, until,

"Stay still Jim. Oh Mum he keeps moving. Now he's gone to the other side. Dad can't you stop him? I haven't finished drawing him yet."

Sarah put her pencil down.

"Show me," asked Ben. "I like it, I do. You have your mother's natural flair. Julia have you seen this?" he asked.

Julia was deep in concentration and scribbling furiously. Sarah carried her drawing to her.

"Mum, what are you doing?" said Sarah. Julia kept quiet.

"Two dice! Where's Jim?"

"Oh, just using my imagination. It's an impression, that's all. The cubes came into my mind whilst sitting here at this place."

"They look so real. You're so brilliant at drawing, but where's Jim?" asked Sarah.

"Oh… here," Julia flipped over the page.

Sarah shrieked, "Mum, you've drawn Lucy!"

"Have I?"

"Yes and she's wearing the locket."

"Is she, where?" asked Ben, setting his poetry book down.

"Did I draw this? I must have done," said Julia. Her family looked over her shoulder, as she flipped through the pages in the sketch book and found her picture of Jim.

"Wow! Look Jim… see how handsome you are."

🐎 What about me? I keep saying that I need to be in the picture! 🐎

"Can you go back to the other picture," asked Ben. "Hurry, I'd really like to see what this Lucy looks like!"

Julia skipped back through the pages, but the drawing had vanished.

"Eh. What's going on here? Are you two teasing me?" asked Ben. He took the sketchbook from Julia and flicked through the pages.

"It was there, honest!" said Sarah, as she chewed the end of her pencil.

"I'm as puzzled as you Ben," replied Julia.

"Is it you Dad, up to your tricks again?" asked Sarah, giggling.

"Nothing to do with me!"

"Cross your heart and hope to die," asked Sarah.

Ben grimaced. Given all that had occurred recently, he wasn't inclined to pledge to anything of the kind.

"Double-one," he said, to change the subject.

"Eh?"

"You chose double-one as the numbers on the dice… any particular reason?

"Did I? No… just coincidence, they're only numbers Ben."

"It's just they seem a bit… well… threatening," he whispered. "Just like two staring eyes… mocking us."

🐎 Snakes eyes! 🐎

"I suppose so," replied Sarah nonchalantly.

"One and one makes three, because you and you made me," announced Sarah, waving her pencil at her parents in turn to illustrate her curious logic.

"Can't argue with that!" said Ben.

Malachi had a theory of his own.

🐎 Alter ego! 🐎

It means a second self. Some people believe there is another world somewhere in the universe identical to our Earth and on it is another you reading these lines right now! Why not wave to each other? We digress, again.

"Well, all I know is the drawing of Lucy's gone!" confirmed Julia, after another sweep through her sketchpad.

"Assuming it was there to begin with," replied Ben.

"Are you calling us liars Ben?"

"No. I'm suggesting it may have been an illusion!"

"An illusion?"

"You know, smoke and mirrors!"

"Now you see me, now you don't," said Sarah, hiding her face with her hands then uncovering it again.

"Peak-a-boo!" teased Julia.

"That's Lucy for you - you just never know what she's going to do!" said Sarah.

Ben began to get unsettled by his daughter's behaviour.

"Okay. I think we've had enough talk of your invisible friend," he said.

Sarah smiled. "Oh Daddy, Lucy's not invisible. She's all about us, in this leaf… in the grass… in the trees!"

"If you say so."

"Not me. Lucy says so."

With that Sarah rolled up her drawing of Jim, tucked it under her arm and signalled for everyone to troop back home.

"Come on, let's go play hide and seek," she announced. Malachi stood up, anxious not to let Sarah out of his sight.

Ben called out after her,

"Don't expect me to go looking for Lucy…"

"You don't have to. She'll find you," replied Sarah.

Ben clearly had a very witty and feisty child as his daughter.

Q43: Do you believe in happy endings?

Just before they reached home, the Whittenbury's met the Napoleonic neighbour with Toby, the small chequered dog. Ben remembered Malachi's reaction to Toby. He was right to fear the worst from the encounter, especially as the road ahead was narrow with little room for manoeuvre. When face to face, the two dogs snarled at each other. The imbalance between them was striking. Malachi dwarfed his neighbour.

🐕 The lengths we go to, just to make a point! 🐕

"Can't you learn to control your dog?" snapped the new neighbour, chewing gum.

"I'm sorry, he has a thing against small dogs!" said Ben, apologetically.

"You need to show him who's boss. Try a firm hand and a clear command. Watch me! Get here Toby!"

The dog yelped as the man grabbed his collar.

"I don't think I've had the pleasure," said Julia.

"I'm Bill... Bill Darvill! I just bought the house next door. It sure needs a lot of work on it. Still I've got great plans for the place... got acres of space to develop," he said, still chewing furiously.

"Really...oh that's nice," she replied. "I'm Julia and this is our daughter, Sarah... she's ten."

"She's going to be a heart-breaker when she gets older," said Bill. Sarah blushed, but wasn't misled.

"It's not like a fairy tale," she said, kicking some fallen leaves.

"What's that you say? I'm afraid you've lost me," said Bill.

"What I mean is you can't just put a spell on Malachi to make him good. Dad says its part of his nature. He doesn't like most horses either - but he likes Jim."

Bill Darvill chuckled. He squatted to Sarah's eye level.

"Hey, that's a real pretty necklace," he said.

"It's not a necklace, it's a locket."

"Lucky you!"

"Oh it's not mine. I'm just borrowing it… it belongs to Lucy."

"Lucy eh!"

"Yes, look, it says LL on the back."

Bill Darvill smiled as he placed his hand on the top of Sarah's head, as if to claim ownership.

"So it does, LL for Lady Luck!" he suggested. Sarah nodded.

"Malachi found it," announced Ben, proudly.

"Good for him! Well, I can't stand here all day and idle my life away. I've a business to run," said Bill.

"How nice… we're going to play hide and seek!"

"What exactly do you do?" Julia asked.

"This and that… I do a bit of everything. I go where the money is. How about you, what exactly do you do?" asked Bill, in return.

"Julia's an artist," said Ben.

"And my Dad's a 'Haymaker!' " said Sarah innocently.

" 'Haymaker' you say, what's that exactly?"

"It means he wants to help stop global warming!" said Sarah proudly.

"Oh!"

Ben jumped in, "Okay… actually I work for the Council. Waste disposal policy! You know recycling! It's not ideal, but it pays the bills, so…"

Bill Darvill's eyebrows raised up his shiny forehead.

"Recycling eh! What a load of rubbish! Ha, ha! No, I'm sorry but I've not got the time for any of that, I'm far too busy me. Anyway global warming, it's something and nothing if you ask me! Nah, best just get on with it, that's what I say. I for one won't be losing any sleep over it. C'mon Toby, let's go… before the sky falls in!" he said, thrusting his hands together in a load clap. Then, to top it all, as he walked away, he put another piece of gum into his mouth and casually tossed the wrapper into the hedgerows.

🐏 Beware, for Nature's wrath knows no bounds. 🐏

"Strange how a man like that should choose to live in a place like this!" remarked Ben.

"Still… we'll show him, won't we Dad!" replied Sarah.

"Maybe Sarah, but, sadly, the truth is there's plenty of people out there who feel that way," Ben replied.

"And that's what you're up against Ben – still keen on the challenge?" asked Julia.

"I believe in happy endings Daddy," said Sarah, grabbing her father's hand.

"Then a happy ending it'll be," Ben replied.

> **Q44:** Is there anything worse than a fly buzzing around your room at night when you're trying to sleep?

On Halloween of all nights, Julia lay awake unable to sleep. She stared into the darkness at the ceiling, with her mind awash with all the things that had happened since the equinox. The list in her head rolled on into tomorrow and she was unable to make sense of any of it. She twisted and turned in her bed. The more she dwelt on it, the more confused it became. It didn't help that a bluebottle buzzed about the room. The sound amplified in the darkness. She followed it with her ears, from one corner of the room to another. It was attracted by her warm breath, darting towards her incessantly. She tried to sweep it away. How could Ben sleep through it? Frustrated, she sat up in bed and contemplated switching on her bedside lamp, when she heard,

"Fear of death is worse than death itself."

Goose-pimples crept over her body, like clouds that blocked out the sun. Was she dreaming? The darkness of the night teased her imagination. She heard the words again.

"Ben… Ben, did you hear that?" she whispered.
Her husband grunted, but slept on.
"It came from outside… I'm sure of it."

She rose from her bed and crept slowly to the small bedroom window that overlooked the Goblin Tree. Under the cover of darkness, her heart raced. She drew back the dank velvet curtains. Condensation was on the window. She wiped it clear to watch the Goblin's gaping mouth at the head of the tree sway. Clouds directly behind it parted to allow the moon to break the density of the night. In the eerie gloom, something moved at the foot of the tree. It was a figure. A woman seemed to bury something in the soil. Julia shuddered, whilst her breath misted the window. Was this Ben's infamous Lady in Grey, our forlorn Fanny Ebbs?

Julia re-wiped the window pane. To her horror, the haunted pallid face of the woman stared up at her. The hands of the ghostly figure clasped its cheeks, whilst the mouth opened slowly in the style of the famous work by Edvard Munch. An infinite scream seemed to pass through Nature; a silent agonised wail! Julia rushed from the window and tumbled back into bed. She clutched her husband for warmth and security. The fly had gone. At last she was able to sleep.

Q45: Are you good at marbles?

The next morning Julia awoke to erratic thuds coming from the landing outside her bedroom. She lay next to her husband for a good ten minutes listening to the sound and waiting for Ben to wake. To encourage him, Julia drew one of her fingers down from Ben's forehead, across the contours of his face and onto his chest.
"What is that noise?" Ben asked, once he stirred.
"It must be Sarah… I think she's playing. Ben…"

"Mm," he mumbled.

"I had a crazy dream last night. You know the painting, what do they call it. Oh, it's on the tip of my tongue. Oh, heavens… I can see the face as clear as day."

"It's not helping me," replied Ben. "But a cup of tea would," he asked.

Sarah had obviously heard their voices, for she momentarily put her head around the bedroom door.

"Thank you for my present," she said.

"Eh?" muttered Ben.

"I love them. So does Mali. He's playing too!"

"I thought he was quiet," said Julia, as she searched for her slippers. She was greeted in the hall by her daughter's crouched figure.

"Watch me Mum," asked Sarah.

"What are you doing?"

"I'm playing marbles, watch me."

"It's a bit too early for games."

Regardless, Sarah rolled twelve small balls along the carpet, each taking turns to tap some skirting at the end of the hall.

🐕 Tis not for gravity to play at cherry-pit with Satan. 🐕

Our learned hound was quoting from Shakespeare's *Twelfth Night*.

Julia wiped the sleep from her eyes.

"So that's what we could hear."

Sarah scuttled along the hall to begin to gather the balls together again.

"They're great Mum, can you get me some more… I need more than twelve for a proper game!"

"I'm sorry. Are they new?" asked Julia, about to step over her child.

"Oh Mum, c'mon. You left them beside my bed last night. They were wrapped up in the hanky Malachi found… the one with Charles' name on it."

Julia almost fell over herself.

"If you look at them carefully, they sparkle like the stars in the sky," Sarah said, with her curious dog beside her.

"Look!" invited Sarah, holding aloft one of the stones.

"I am looking!"

"What's the matter Mum? You look like you've just seen a ghost."

"Ben, did you leave Julia the stones to play with?"

A grumble from the bedroom!

"The stones from the tree! Did you wrap them in the hanky Malachi brought back with him?"

No response.

"I need a cup of tea!"

"Okay. I'm going to make a circle," said Sarah.

"No… I don't think that'll be a good idea."

"Why Mum?"

Julia knelt before her daughter.

"Because they're magic stones," said Julia.

"Oh… if I throw them out of the window will they grow into a beanstalk?"

"No sweetheart. Don't do that. Just keep them nice and safe. Now, I'm just off to make some tea and toast. Want some?"

"Yes please. Peanut butter today!"

Julia nodded.

"Yep! So long as you look after those stones, they're precious!"

When Julia returned with a tray carrying breakfast, she found Ben sat upon Sarah's bed talking to her about the stones.

"They were just here… all wrapped up like a parcel," Sarah said, directing her father to the exact place on her bedside table.

Sarah took a bite of her toast.

"It's a very clever hanky because it keeps the marbles nice and warm and clean!" she said.

Ben bit into some toast, then spoke with his mouthful.

"We found them inside a jar… inside an old tree."

"The Goblin Tree?" asked Sarah, excitedly.

"No. The old tree at the front of the house," said Ben.

Fed by the talk of trees, Julia's mind flashed back to last night. Had she been dreaming?

"Oh, so if they're not really marbles then what are they?"

"Hey if they look and feel like marbles then maybe that's what they are," replied Ben.

"Well, yes they do roll as good as any marble I know. The big difference is they all sparkle in the light… like diamonds."

"Do they?"

"Yes Mum, like tiny twinkling stars."

Sarah had been protecting the stones. She had kept them in her lap wrapped up in the handkerchief. She unfolded the hanky and let the stones fall on to the bed covers.

"See!" She held one in the glow of her bedside light. "It's like tiny things are moving about inside," she added.

"Like one of those ornaments at Christmas! You could almost give one a good shake, then watch the snow fall around Santa!" said Julia.

🐈 Snow – did someone say snow? 🐈

Sarah smiled as she watched her father chomp through his toast. Malachi raised a hopeful paw.

"You must have left them for me!" said Sarah.

Her father's eyes widened, as he threw some crust into his dog's mouth.

"So, who's Charles Lamb?" asked Sarah, as she put the stone back with its companions.

"Mm, I think I've heard of him," said Julia, whilst her hands hovered over the handkerchief. Dare she touch it?

"Lamb eh, I think there's a Lamb in my poetry collection," said Ben.

"I wonder if Charles is Lucy's friend?" Sarah asked.

"Could be… shall we try to find out?" asked Ben, as he flicked bits of toast from his fingers.

"Dad… the crumbs… be careful!"

Sarah immediately gathered up the stones and tucked them back into the hanky. The risk of harm to the stones caused Sarah to remember the locket. She'd worn it when asleep, and was reassured to find it around her neck.

"What can I do to keep it safe?" she asked.

🐏 Beware. It's all hanging by a thread... which is why I'm here! 🐏

Q46: Do you value a good education?

There was just enough space in Ben's compact wooden box to store the handkerchief, the dozen stones and the blue ribbon. "I think it's a good place to keep them," said Sarah as she ran her fingers across the lid.

"Me too, because the painted rider can keep an eye on them," suggested Ben.

"So can we go on the internet now?" she asked, keen to learn all about the man named Charles Lamb.

Assuming they had got the right person, they discovered:

The life and times of Charles Lamb

💛 He was born in London in 1775 and died in 1834.

💛 He was the son of John Lamb and Elizabeth Field.

💛 Lamb believed his destiny was to be a poet.

💛 This was probably due to his long-lasting friendship with Samuel Taylor Coleridge, honoured for his love of nature.

💛 He was an English essayist, best known for the *Essays of Elia* and for the children's book *Tales from Shakespeare*.

💛 He regularly stayed with the aristocratic Plumer family at Blakesware Manor, a mansion just outside of Widford.

♥ In 1795, Charles spent six weeks in a psychiatric hospital.

♥ On 23 September 1796, his sister Mary, in a temporary fit of insanity, attacked and killed his mother and stabbed his father.

♥ Charles became Mary's guardian.

♥ The shadow of her madness plagued his life.

♥ Following the tragedy, he destroyed most of the things he'd written.

🐈 Contented with little, yet wishing for more. 🐈

Sarah grew disinterested as Ben ploughed into the detail, until he mentioned that Charles' sister killed his mother.
"Oh Dad, did she? Poor Charles!"
"Yes, that's very sad, isn't it?"
"And he lived near here."
"He did."
"But that was a long time ago, so it's not the same Charles Lamb, is it?"
"Probably not, but hey, who knows?"
"Did he ever get married?"
"It doesn't appear so… it says here that he spent his life caring for his sister."
"He sounds really kind, bless him. I'd love to have been able to meet him."
🐈 Relax Sarah, all in good time. 🐈
Ben hugged his daughter.
"Can we visit Blakesware Manor?" she asked.
"I don't know if we can; it's private property."
"Oh, so we can't just take the handkerchief back?"
Ben frowned.
"I love your serious face," said Sarah.

> *Charles, if we only knew then what we know now.*
> *If anyone deserves a place amongst the exalted ranks of*
> *English poetry it's you! How true your words ring now –*
> *"All, all are gone, the old familiar faces."*

Q47: Do you know your history?

Once Sarah's enthusiasm for facts about Charles faded, Ben did further research on some of the significant things that happened during Charles Lamb's life. He surfed the internet again and cherry-picked:

1776 – Congress carries the Declaration of Independence.

1778 – Ludwig van Beethoven presented by his father as 6 year-old prodigy.

1785 – George Stubbs' *Haymakers* painted.

1785 – James Watt and Matthew Boulton install a steam engine in a cotton-spinning factory at Papplewick, Nottinghamshire.

1789 – Paris mob storms the Bastille.

1789 – First steam driven cotton factory in Manchester.

1790 – First steam powered rolling mill built in England.

1791 – Tragic premature death of Wolfgang Amadeus Mozart.

1795 – First horse-drawn railroad in England.

1796 – Napoleon married Josephine.

1797 – First copper pennies minted in England.

1798 – Malthus' first essay on the *Principle of Population*.

1799 – Rosetta Stone discovered.

1800 – Bill Richmond – a former slave, became one of the first popular boxers.

1801 – Union Jack becomes the official flag of Great Britain and Ireland.

1806 – Thorvaldsen's *Hebe* sculpture.

1807 – England prohibits slave trade.

1811 – Luddites destroy industrial machines in Northern England.

Ben chose to pause at 1811 and reflect on the many monumental events to occur during Charles' first 36 years. It was a remarkable list. Charles was obviously in the midst of things - the birth of literature; a golden age of classical music – Mozart and Beethoven; the spirit of the French revolution; independence for America; and the birth of equality for all. All this magic – unfolded under the shadow of the industrial revolution! It all served as a catalyst for globalisation, mass population growth and climate change!

Q48: Have you ever played Solitaire?

Whilst Ben took his history lesson, Sarah played cards in her room. Driven by a growing infatuation with the Three of Hearts, she chose Solitaire; a game also known in Scandinavia as Kabal, which translates to 'Secret Knowledge!' Sarah wanted Dixie to watch her play. To protect him from Malachi, she closed her bedroom door, took the hamster out of his cage and placed him into a transparent round plastic exercise ball. She lay on the floor beside him - her back arched and elbows dug into the carpet.

Sarah shuffled the pack then dealt the cards carefully. She played Solitaire the challenging way – by suit and turning only every third card from the stockpile. This was Julia's doing, for she preached, "If you succeed against the odds it's much more fun." So, Sarah refused to cheat. She believed in herself; that she would win.

Now and again she encouraged Dixie to roll across the cards in his ball. It amused and inspired her.

♪ I wish I was in Dixie. Hooray! Hooray! ♪, she sang.

Just the one line, it was all she knew. Abraham Lincoln's favourite song, it was sung in all innocence. Bizarrely, in the space of a few days she'd sung the unofficial anthems from both sides in the American Civil War. She had peeled back the veneer that our five senses experience; such was life in Sarah's 'House of Fun'. Only trouble was, try as she might she could not win.

When Ben interrupted her, Sarah's patience had worn thin.
"Oh come on… this silly game is driving me crazy. I just can't win!" she told her Dad.
"That looks like Patience!"
"No, its Solitaire because you play it on your own… Mum taught me it."
"But it's also called Patience, Sarah, because that's what you need to win. Here let me have a go!" he suggested.
"I bet you won't win!" she claimed, passing him the cards.
"Whittenbury, watch!" her father said, as he squat on the floor and shuffled the pack.
"Okay… but I bet the Three of Hearts won't let you win!" Sarah said before stooping to rescue Dixie from his plastic ball.
Whilst Ben dealt the cards, Sarah gave Dixie 'hammy snuggles', which meant kissing his head over and over again very quickly. In response Ben sang,
♪ Look away, look away, look away, Dixie boy! ♪
" Hey… I was singing that tune just now. I could get my flute and play it!" she suggested.
"It's a fife Sarah, not a flute!" said Ben.
It prompted scratching at the bedroom door. Malachi wanted to come in.
🐕 You can't blame the Captain for that one! 🐕
For the record, Ben couldn't win either.

Q49: Do you ever think about the old days?

The following weekend, Ben pondered a visit to Blakesware Manor, where Charles Lamb once stayed. Beneath the shadow of the *Haymakers*, Ben weighed things up in his mind by reflecting on how far the countryside had changed since the poet's time:

♥ The Shire horse had been replaced by tractors, and haymakers by combined harvesters.

♥ Cottages once lived in by people that worked the land, now went for premium prices, often to commuters to London who craved a bit of green and pleasant land.

♥ Open sweeping fields had replaced compact ones, once penned in by hedgerows that were home to many beloved species.

♥ The regimental sound of birds of steel often drowned out natural birdsong.

♥ Country lanes, once trails for the tranquil horse and cart, were now tarmac with fossil-fuel emitting vehicles that sped along and left casualties in their wake – rabbits, foxes, hedgehogs, birds, rodents, and sometimes people.

♥ Electricity and telephone pylons now stood alongside trees; ironically often with flocks of birds settled upon them.

♥ Light pollution from nearby towns and the ceaseless creep of London reduced the spectacle of stars by night.

So, Ben concluded it would be good to take a step back in time. He was ready to invite Sarah to put her walking boots on for a trip to Blakesware Manor. The best made plans! For just as the instructions were on the tip of his tongue, three rhythmic knocks hit the aged oak door.

A proud elderly man dressed in country greens stood outside. When Ben first saw him, the man appeared to caress one of the two wooden pillars that supported the porch; behaviour which suggested a familiarity with the old place. Ben tugged at the front door, but it was stuck fast. As he pulled, he overheard the visitor thinking aloud about the lion-head brass knocker on the front door; something about Brasenose College, Oxford!

Ben called, "Just give me a minute!"

"You can have five!" suggested the man.

Ben went to the lounge window and said, "I'm sorry but the front door's jammed!"

"Yes. I expected as much!" The old man smiled, from under his cap. "It'll do that… it's the movement in the clay soil."

"You used to live here?" asked Ben.

"This place is very special to me these days… I'm Peter Scott by the way. I dropped in to see how things are going… to congratulate you on following a little in my footsteps!"

"I see… well I'm Ben Whittenbury!"

Peter came over to the window and offered a hand of friendship. Ben accepted the offer. The handshake was friendly yet firm.

"It's really good to meet you my friend," said Peter.

Three inquisitive souls - Julia, Sarah and Malachi - joined Ben at the window. As Ben introduced his family, the dog's paws rested on the window ledge.

" ♪ How much is that doggie in the window ♪," sang Peter, which amused Sarah.

"Oh, he's not for sale!" she said.

"But he's very handsome. Isn't he an Arctic breed?"

"He's a Samoyed. His name's Malachi!" replied Sarah.

Peter stroked the dog's head.

"He like's you!" said Julia.

"He's probably just a good judge of character… that's all. Dogs are capable of so much more than you might imagine, especially this one. Trust me, I've cared for a few animals in my time."

"Well you've tamed this one, so you clearly have a way with dogs!" said Ben, as Malachi behaved like putty in the man's hands.

"Tamed him… never! He was born free… and free he'll stay."

"Some people find Malachi a bit, well… intimidating!" said Ben.

"This one… he's just a little bear. My father would have adored him."

🐾 So says the patron saint of conservation. 🐕

"Oh, come on Mum, Dad… we can't leave him waiting by the window. Invite him around the back," urged Sarah.

The adults obliged.

"Do, come take a look around," insisted Julia.

"I'd like that, thank you."

Peter made for the rear of the cottage. Every step taken was a cherished one.

"She's certainly inspirational… doesn't disappoint in the slightest. It's a great place for Art, Love and Nature… and I feel it's in such safe hands."

"Couldn't have put it better myself," said Julia.

"I've passed by a few times… but this is the first time I felt the time was right to knock and wish you every good fortune."

The curious visitor chose to stroll up the garden, hand-in-hand with his vivid imagination. Ben followed in his footsteps for a bit then stood back and let him alone with his thoughts.

"He must have lived here before us," Ben said quietly.

"That's what I was thinking… best let him wander," replied Julia before disappearing into the cottage.

Sarah was less discreet. She ran to the swing that hung from the apple tree. Malachi dashed to her side.

"Hey little girl, do you like the swing?" asked Peter.

"I do. I can reach for the stars. Its magic – like this house," replied Sarah.

"Yes. She's magic alright. No doubt about that!"

"So was it magic when you were here too?"

"What's that you say?" Peter lowered himself to Sarah's eye level. "I'm going deaf you see. It's all the noise in the modern world."

"*Noise…* I like to hear the birds sing… and nice things… but I also like the Goblin Tree!"

"The Goblin Tree?"

Sarah pointed at it. Peter smiled.

"Surely that's not a Goblin! I think it's a horse's head! You could almost take a ride on it off into the sunset!" claimed Peter.

"Oh, for a happy ending. I'll tell Mum."

"My daughter liked to swing too."

"Can you push me?"

"Why, of course."

Sarah began to head skywards.

🐎 A little something to lift your spirits! 🐎

"It still looks like a Goblin to me," she claimed, as the swing changed the tree's perspective.

"Then a Goblin Tree, it shall be!" he concurred.

Peter looked about as he pushed Sarah towards the heavens.

"I believe you've covered up the old well!" Peter said to Ben.

"What old well?"

Peter pushed Sarah again.

"There, beside the flower bed. You've concreted it over. Good job… always was far too dangerous for my liking!" he said.

"Someone must have covered it before we arrived. But that's really useful to know, thanks."

"They left the old coins though," said Sarah, her long hair catching in the wind, as she swung to and fro, resembling a pendulum on a Grandfather clock.

"What old coins?" asked Peter.

"Why… these," said Ben. He pointed them out.

Peter stopped pushing Sarah. He wandered to the rockery which bordered the site of the old well. He crouched down. His ageing knees cracked.

"Most fascinating! These coins look extremely old!"

"Its part of our adventure… my Dad likes adventures."

"Really… my Father did too!"

"We don't know what to do with them," said Ben.

"Well, as you love animals so much, why not use them to support a World Wide Fund for Nature?"

Sarah giggled, "The WWF… I'm already a member."

"Good for you," said Peter.

"Should we tell him about the jar in the old tree too?" asked Sarah, as she leapt from the swing in mid-flight, like an acrobat in training.

"Eh?"

"It's nothing really. We found a jar inside a dead tree bordering the cottage. It contained some really odd stones."

"Stones eh, what was so odd about them?"

"They're like marbles," cried Sarah.

"Marbles huh… just make sure you put them to good use… that's what I say and take care not to lose them!"

🐾 You never know what you've got 'til it's gone. 🐾

"If the well was still here, I'd make a wish."

"Make that three, Sarah!" said Julia, re-emerging from the cottage with some tea.

Peter swiftly changed the subject.

"Do you know if Jonas is at home?" he asked suddenly.

"Jonas doesn't live here," claimed Sarah, kicking her heels.

"You mean the man who lives over there," replied Ben, pointing to the house opposite.

"Jonas. It's about his wife… it's a surprise."

"Oh, we didn't know Jonas is married," said Julia.

"Was my dear, was!"

At which Peter touched Julia's arm.

110

Q50: Do you miss someone you love?

Julia was really reluctant to reveal to anyone what happened after Peter touched her. In fact, for reasons that will become clear, she kept it all to herself for weeks. It was only when she reviewed her note book, *Julia's Jazzy Jamboree* did she find the courage to speak of it again. It wasn't especially horrific but, in her words, it was an experience she'd closed the door on. She'd shut it away in the deep corridors of her mind. These were her notes:

"This was unlike anything I've ever known before, the feeling I had when I held the child in my arms and looked into its eyes. The feeling went beyond the maternal; different from the way I felt when I first held Sarah. It surpassed the smell and touch of a young child. The little boy had a mystic air about him. He was cherub like with tiny wisps of hair. I teased a few strands with my fingers; they were as soft as satin. I kissed his sweet forehead,

"You're simply adorable. What's your name?" I asked.

The infant smiled and wrapped his fingers around mine.

"If you could speak, what would you say?"

"Julia don't break faith, you hold the key!" said a voice.

I remembered that voice – I could never forget it; a voice with the warmth of the summer wind.

The baby closed its eyes to sleep. Slow, gentle and effortless breaths.

"His name is Adam! He is your future… all our futures."

I believe the voice belonged to Lucy - the woman in one of my previous visions! She walked about me and drew a circle in the sand with a long stick. She spoke or chanted. I cannot for sure remember which,

"I circle our world with this rod and trust, against the sore stitch, against the sore bite, against the grim dread, against the great horror that is hateful to us all, and all evil that enters this land."

As I looked at the infant in my arms, his laughter turned to tears. Lucy reassured me, "To survive he needs food, water, shelter and love. That is all!"

The circle complete, she passed me something. I took it.

"Wipe his tears dry Julia!"

It was a handkerchief. I did so.

"Adam must rest," she said, directing me to a basket at my feet. I laid him in his bed, only to step outside the circle of protection; an unwitting act for a Whittenbury! Alas, fate was cruel with my carelessness.

"Stay!" she cried. But what happened next is a fog in my mind. A blur! It happened so fast. I heard footsteps come up behind me. I turned… I saw… I faltered! I couldn't see his face. He was too quick for me. He took her. He had the basket. I tried to stop him. Another man ran passed me, crying out, "No… leave him be… he's so young… much too young. His time here isn't done yet!"

I think this man was Peter Scott.

That was all I can remember. I just know the boy, Adam; he was like no other child I have met. He was the face of the future. I failed him. The guilt overwhelms me. I shall never speak of it again."

When Ben shared his recollection of what happened, it was more about his frustration that he had no say on when these things took place. He knew Julia was very disturbed by her vision; not immediately because Peter made a real fuss of her after she'd fainted - almost as though he knew what she'd witnessed. It was in the days that followed. All she would say was, "It was the eyes Ben… I'll never forget his innocent little eyes – so full of love. And the feeling that we'd betrayed him. One child lost; one giant loss for human kind!"

Q51: Have you ever taken part in a protest?

As Mother Nature's Champion, Ben Whittenbury was prepared to go to any reasonable lengths to promote his cause. As a first step he decided to grow a moustache! He vowed to keep it as another reminder of his mission. The hair would stay until he'd taken a clear positive step as Earth Champion. He knew that Julia and Sarah would surely tease him but Ben's independent streak carried him through. Besides, he had a much more maverick idea to distract them; Ben bought a polar bear on the internet. Not a real one of course, but a costume complete with polar bear mask, hands and feet. He also made up a little sign to hang about his shoulders with the simple words, 'SAVE ME' written upon it.

Ben had thought about buying the costume for sometime, but he was finally driven to act because of a protest taking place in central London seeking action on climate change. Ben really felt quite excited when the costume arrived. He took it from the box with the enthusiasm of a child opening presents at Christmas. If truth be told, he found the outfit a bit scary – for the bear's mouth was agape, revealing pointed teeth, whilst the hands and feet had sharp claws; it made Ben appreciate that the polar bear was in reality a powerful and fearsome wild animal worthy of respect.

When Ben put the costume on for the first time and looked at himself in a full-length mirror, he felt rather unsettled by his reflection.
"Is that really me?" he said, adopting different poses. He gave himself the thumbs up and said, "Sarah's going to just love this!" before he descended the stairs at Keeper's to find her. He stalked

from room to room, only to find the cottage empty, until he heard voices in the garden. He meandered through the kitchen and the outhouse to find Julia and Sarah with their backs to him seeking a lost shuttlecock.

"Let's leave it Sarah – a north wind is blowing in... so it's really far too cold for badminton now," he heard Julia say.

"Oh Mum, I was winning!"

"But it's not too cold for a bear," roared Ben, already feeling the heat from his exploits in the fur suit and mask.

Julia and Sarah span around, rackets in hand. The pair shrieked, waking Malachi from his mid-afternoon slumber. Ben still can't recall who screamed the loudest! Sarah tried to hide behind her mother.

"I'm a sad polar bear," said the bear.

"Dad... is that you?" said Sarah, as she'd recovered from the surprise.

"I'm sad because global warming is melting my home... please stop playing games and help me!"

🐑 An Inconvenient Truth! 🐑

"It is you... you look really cool!" cried Sarah. She ran to her father.

"Oh Ben, what have you done?"

Ben sought out the bench beside the rear of the house.

"I don't feel cool... I'm burning up in here," he said and removed the mask. Sarah, Ben and the dog huddled about him like bees around a honey-pot.

"Are we going to a fancy dress party?" asked Sarah, "And can I go as Tinkerbell... please!"

"No Sarah. I got this outfit to help with our campaign! It... we're... going on a protest."

"We are?" said Julia and Sarah as one.

"But I've never been on a demo' in my life Ben," said Julia.

Ben put his mask back on.

"Save me!" he said glumly.

114

Well, the protest took place in ideal conditions on 4 November 2006 – the eve of fireworks night! The Whittenbury's arrived early and found a good place beneath Nelson's column. Julia took a photo of Ben dressed as a polar bear adopting the same pose as Admiral Horatio Nelson's statue.

"Thank God, I have done my duty," said Ben – as the bear - mimicking the Admiral's famous last words. The outfit certainly helped Ben to get noticed.

The Whittenbury's were joined by more than 25,000 Earth loving Earthlings. Young and old, people from all ages, races and faiths came together. A sea of faces with a common goal - to commit to action to stop climate change! There was a kind of carnival atmosphere with other people in costume to highlight the cause, including a giant panda and mermaids. "I COUNT… I COUNT… I COUNT!" chanted the Whittenbury's in the heart of London. "Remember Sarah, one day when you are older you'll be able to say, 'I was there the day it all began … I helped to start it off. I helped to change the world!'" claimed Julia.

"Just imagine the numbers next year and the year after that. The momentum is growing. We'll see events in other towns and cities across the world." Ben was certain of it.

Sarah picked out her favourite banners.

Save Our Home – It's The Only One We Have

Cheap Flights Cost The Earth

NO2 - CO2

Enough Hot Air

Our Shared Future

Act 2day 2 Save 2morrow

Fossil Fool

It's Not Easy Being Green

Ben you're our hero. We love you – those of us who are left.

Hey some more facts. Then it's on with the show, I promise. Trust me, things are really going to warm up!

Q51A How many people does it take to fill up the Earth?

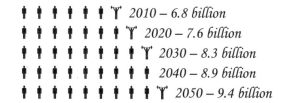

- **†** *Human population reached 1 billion in 1802.*
- **† †** *In 1927, 125 years later, it reached 2 billion.*
- **† † †** *In 1961, 34 years later, it reached 3 billion.*
- **† † † †** *In 1974, 13 years later, it got to 4 billion.*
- **† † † † †** *In 1987, again 13 years on, we hit 5 billion.*
- **† † † † † †** *In 1999, only 12 years after, we got to 6 billion.*
- **† † † † † † Ψ** *In 2006, we reached 6.66 billion – isn't that a scary number?*

So, in Ben's lifetime the world's population had doubled! As to the World beyond that, the United States Census Bureau predictions were:

- **† † † † † † Ψ** *2010 – 6.8 billion*
- **† † † † † † † Ψ** *2020 – 7.6 billion*
- **† † † † † † † † Ψ** *2030 – 8.3 billion*
- **† † † † † † † † †** *2040 – 8.9 billion*
- **† † † † † † † † † Ψ** *2050 – 9.4 billion*

Well, well! All these people in need of food, water, shelter, clothing. Assuming, of course, the potential full impact of climate change has been taken into account.

Q52: Do you believe in miracles?

The Whittenbury's returned from the protest with mixed feelings. Okay, it was encouraging to be amongst so many people eager to make a difference, but some of the facts and predictions about climate change alarmed Ben. Part of him was angry, part of him upset, another part apathetic. Weary, he folded away the polar bear outfit, took a shower then stood before his beloved *Haymakers*.

Sarah noticed his glum mood,

"It's not easy being Earth Champion, is it Dad?"

"What makes you say that?" asked Ben, under the inquisitive eye of the woman at the heart of the picture.

"Its just you were so quiet on the way home and now you've come in here to stare at this old painting."

"You are growing up, aren't you?"

"Mm. Mum says I'm an inch taller than I was last month!"

Ben smiled.

"I just wonder what I'm getting you in to, that's all. I can't work miracles, can I? Maybe I should forget all about it."

"Oh Dad, come on sit down with me."

"It's just you should be having fun at your age, not worrying about what may happen in the future with the planet, and the animals. It's not fair. It's not right."

"But Dad, I had great fun today."

Sarah smiled and kissed her father's cheek.

"Did you?"

"Yes… and I took the locket with me too. I've decided that if we ever open it, I'm going to put in it the picture of you dressed as a polar bear being Lord Nelson!"

"Ah… I thought you were going to put a picture of Malachi in it!"

"Oh yes… oh I can put them both inside. Anyway when you were dressed as the polar bear you looked so very like him."

"I suppose I did really!"

"And I like your moustache… it looks really cute!"

"That's good… I thought you'd tease me about it!"

Sarah giggled. With her head tipped to one side she quipped, "Even if it does look like a little caterpillar."

Ben pursed and wriggled his lips, as if to bring the caterpillar to life.

"Well caterpillars turn into butterflies… and moths," said Ben.

"Exactly… well, at least it's not an ostrich."

"An ostrich?"

"Yes. Mum says most people are like ostriches because they put their head in the sand."

"To try and ignore a problem, if it scares them."

"Like an ostrich."

"Yeah, like an ostrich."

"Oh."

"Did you know that they actually don't bury their head in the sand? When they sense danger and cannot run away they flop to the ground and stay very still. Because their necks and heads are lightly coloured they blend in with the soil. So from a distance it just looks like they've buried their head in the sand, when actually they haven't."

"Is that really true?"

"Yep. And they can't fly either."

🐎 I wish I could fly right up to the sky, but I can't! 🐎

Q53: Do you like to keep warm?

Still raw from their climate change protest, the Whittenbury's were less enthusiastic about bonfire night than usual. It was only Sarah's youthful interest that led to Ben agreeing to take her to a small fireworks display in the grounds of the White Horse public house in Wareside. A light drizzle was enough to dampen any interest Julia had in the display, so she used Malachi's welfare as an excuse to remain behind at Keeper's.

Ben and Sarah were greeted at the White Horse by the supernatural cracks and dance of flames from a bonfire in the centre of the pub's courtyard. An effigy of Guy Fawkes burnt at the top of the fire, whilst the whiz and pop of some rockets lit up the night sky. About the bonfire stood a host of Waresiders, young and old alike, feasting, drinking and enjoying the warmth of the flames. Their forms and faces were distorted to extremity in the glare of the ever-changing fire.

Amongst the madding crowd was our eccentric friend Caleb Hitch – his words, not ours. Now, first off, Caleb wanted us to stress how grateful he was to Prometheus for his bravery in stealing fire from the Greek Gods and giving humans the ability to tame and use it for our own ends. This was Caleb all over; a man of history, curiosity and a real passion for mythology. In fact, he'd once been a contestant on BBC's *Mastermind*, so he says; he came second in one of the qualifying rounds.

Caleb believes his interest in mythology began during the Blitz on London in World War II. As a child, whilst the bombs fell from dark skies to destroy the street where he first lived, he sensed forces unseen were governing his fate. This was partly explained because the Blitz left him orphaned, but it was probably because he had two thumbs on his right hand. When he hid in the bomb shelter he'd kept folk amused with his thumbs. Even now, all these days into his long and varied life, Caleb would sometimes be in awe of his thumbs; he saw them as a blessing. Oh, he enjoyed flaunting them – entertaining young children at village fetes, birthday parties and the like.

In recent years – since his wife sadly died – he took regular daily jaunts along the Hertfordshire Way and waved determinedly to passers-by, doing his best to make sure they caught sight of his two thumbs. On hot summer days, Caleb walked with his shirt off. In cooler times, he held his flat-cap in his hand to greet travellers with it.

So, this was Caleb Hitch – a man who'd settled in the Ware Uplands 40 years ago. He knew nearly everyone and nearly everything about the local area. He was a walking library on the social history of the Ware Uplands, dating back generations. Everyone loved him. He was a local celebrity; or should that be a calebrity?

Caleb was the first to spot Sarah. He welcomed her with the gift of a sparkler and enjoyed watching her make shapes with it in the dark.
"That looks like fun," he claimed.
Sarah noticed how the folds of his crinkled face seemed to roll up in the eerie light of the fire. She later told her father that Caleb looked like one of those odd dogs on the television that advertised insurance. Not that Caleb cared – if he did, we'd have left that bit out! We digress!

Caleb watched bemused as Sarah made heart shapes, before the spark went out.
"Do you have any more sparklers?" she asked, cheekily.
Caleb shook his head.
"Here. Take mine," offered another friendly voice.
"Jonas!" nodded Caleb. "It's good to see you my friend. I see you've lost none of your generosity."
Jonas shrugged his shoulders.
"Well, what can you do? I can't live in the past or fear the future! Besides I've got a new job too."
"That's good to hear… what'll you be doing?"
"Let's just say I'll be collecting things, mainly. I'm not sure yet if it'll be worthwhile or I'll like it but I'll give it a go and see what happens."

"Ah, well… good luck with that anyway," replied Caleb,
reluctant to probe further. He gave Jonas a firm pat on the back as,
for once, he was without his rucksack.

Sarah held out her sparkler.

"Here." Jonas lit the end.

Ben encouraged his daughter to thank Jonas.

Sarah smiled.

"She's a lovely girl… you're a very lucky man," said Caleb.

"Show me your thumbs again," Sarah requested, before forming
fresh heart shapes with the tip of her pretend wand.

"Wragghhh!" he cried, wriggling them in unison, causing Sarah to
giggle.

"This one's called Tom and this one's called, Tom too!"

"At least they're not Dead Man's Fingers!" said Ben, ahead of the
last crash of fireworks and a spectacular show in the heavens above.
It was the signal for most people to head for the warmth and comfort
of the old inn.

Q54: Do you enjoy a bit of a mystery?

The White Horse was built in the early 19th century. It was a
compact low-ceilinged patchwork of an inn with the main bar held
up by four large beer casks. Ben and Sarah found their way to an
inglenook fire, and wrestled a seat next to Caleb and Jonas. It was
the first time Sarah had been inside the pub. She felt quite grown
up.

"Did you enjoy that then?" Caleb asked Sarah.

"Yes, but we missed most of it… we should have got here
earlier."

"Still young lady, you've got me for entertainment now!" Caleb
replied, exhibiting his three thumbs once more.

"Have you ever painted them?" Sarah asked, in between
requesting lemonade and crisps.

"How do you mean?"

"You know, drawn little faces on them… eyes… a nose and a mouth!"

"Yes… I've done that; makes for quite a little family!"

"Could I draw something on them?" she asked.

"Faces?"

"Here's a pen," said Jonas, passing her one.

Caleb threw a sly discerning glance.

"It's a red pen!" replied Sarah. "That's just perfect."

Reluctantly, Caleb held out his hands.

"Close your eyes!" asked Sarah.

"I don't like the sound of this."

Sarah drew three red hearts – one on each of Caleb's thumbs.

"Okay – open them!"

"What the blazes… hearts?" Caleb wriggled them close to her face.

"Do you like them?"

"Eh, not really sure… I was expecting three faces."

Sarah scratched her head and pulled her hair into a ponytail, tying it with a hair band.

"It was Lucy's idea!" she said. "This one stands for Art… this one stands for Love… and this one's for Nature!"

"That's very interesting. Who's Lucy, do I know her?" Caleb asked.

"Oh yes… everybody knows Lucy! It's just sometimes they forget she's their best friend."

Ben intervened.

"She's got an invisible friend!" he whispered in Caleb's ear.

"I see."

Caleb changed the subject. He took hold of his drink from Jonas.

"Speaking of invisible people, did you ever see that ghostly woman again … the Lady in Grey?" asked Caleb.

Ben took a mouthful of beer and licked the froth from his lips.

"Dare say, I'd almost forgotten all about her," he replied.

"How come then… when we went to London yesterday… you

couldn't stop talking about her," said Sarah.

Ben frowned.

"Hardly!"

"You did… in fact when you were dressed as the bear you said it too."

"Sarah! You promised not to talk about the bear."

"Did we?"

"Yes… we did!"

"Is this a private conversation, or can anyone join in," asked another local – he by the name of Bill Darvill.

"So it was you in that outfit!" he claimed, "Running about the garden. Mr Polar Bear!"

"Very funny," said Ben, folding his arms.

"Great outfit though… did you buy it to hide the moustache!" joked Bill, with a wink. "Can I join you? Don't think I've met your mates," he said.

"If you like," said Caleb.

After the introductions and some further light ribbing about the bear costume, Caleb steered the conversation to the possible whereabouts of the Lady in Grey and the mysterious horseman. "The whole thing is so intriguing. I just had to try to find out who the ghostly horseman on the equinox sunset might have been," he said.

"A ghost you say," said Darvill.

"One, possibly two… It was something and nothing really. Hey I could have imagined it all… a trick of the eye against a setting sun," replied Ben, keen to play things down.

Sarah slurped her lemonade from a straw, before blowing bubbles into it.

"Sarah please," said her father.

"What? If you want to play games, then so shall I," she said.

"Mm, okay."

124

"Is your house haunted then, you know, goblins and stuff?" asked Bill Darvill, as he leaned forward from his bar stool.

"Look… all I know is that I saw a frail elderly lady in grey and a mad horseman who dashed along the bridleway at the front of the cottage, that's all. A horseman dressed in clothing from a couple of centuries ago, by looks of…"

"We think it may have something to do with the locket," said Sarah.

"Ah…the locket! I remember."

Sarah wrapped her hand about it and held it there for minutes on end, until her arm tired just to stop Bill Darvill from looking at it.

Caleb finally got the chance to present his research.

"So, the identity of the horseman, the 'sunset kid'. First off, there's Sir Geoffrey de Mandeville, a powerful baron in Hertfordshire from the 12th century… doomed to everlasting torment because of a terrible curse he made when founding the Priory of Walden. However, I've ruled him out as he wore a red cloak and was normally accompanied by wailing howls and a headless hound."

"Nope… Noblin Green's not Sleepy Hollow!" said Ben with confidence.

"Next up was the Wicked Lady of Markyate?" said Caleb. He introduced her with a ditty,

> ♪ Near the Cell there is a Well,
> Near the Well, there is a Tree,
> and under the Tree the Treasure be. ♪

Sarah wished she'd brought the fife with her, to play along.

"Fascinating! A woman eh," responded Darvill.

"No! This was a man, I'm sure of it," said Ben.

Caleb persisted, "Please, there's more… Lady Katharine was a lonely and impressionable figure with an appetite for danger. She met a highwayman and regularly took part in night forays in Hertfordshire. Legend has it that her highwayman's treasure still lies buried under a tree near a well close to her cell or hideout, where she died after being fatally wounded in a robbery. Thus the song…"

"Unbelievable," said Darvill.

Sarah reached the bottom of her glass. Her straw made an annoying noise as she sucked up air.

"She was buried in the church of St Mary at Ware, but her grave is said to be unquiet. Her phantom is sometimes seen galloping along country lanes."

Ben shook his head.

"No… I'm confident I saw a man."

"But the best I save for last. He's the murderous pie-man of Ware."

"Who?" everyone as good as asked.

Sarah stopped sucking her straw.

"He was the leader of a vicious gang who used to rob and sometimes murder traders on their way home from the fairs at Hertford. He was called the murderous pie man because he sold pies as a rouse to help identify suitable targets to his gang members for ambush.

"Clever," said Ben.

"Anyhow, one Christmas the leader was overpowered by one of his victims! It was considered a justifiable murder and the felon – the murderous pie man of Ware – was denied a Christian burial in consecrated ground. They buried the bugger by the side of the road where he'd been shot."

"What's to stop his ghost from walking?" asked Jonas, in all seriousness.

"It seems they drove a post through his body to keep it down."

"Like they do with vampires," said Sarah, folding her straw to make pretend fangs.

"You ask as though you've seen a ghost too," suggested Bill Darvill.

"No, no… no. Just curious about the spirit world, that's all."

"Where did they bury him?" asked Darvill.

"He used to live at Babbs Green, near Wareside."

"Dead Man's Fingers?" said Ben.

"Yes Ben… Dead Man's Fingers."

"What's this man's name?" asked Jonas.

"He went by the name of Clibborn… Walter Clibborn."

Everyone took a mouthful of their drinks, except Sarah of course. She had the make-do fangs in her mouth, and feigned to bite Caleb.

"It doesn't really explain the ghostly rider though," added Caleb, keen as ever to have the final word on matters of folklore. "But I'll tell you something Ben Whittenbury… you'll never guess the name of the individual that shot him! Not in a million years!"

"Go on," he said.

"A certain B. Whittenbury Esq."

"What?"

"Go look it up for yourself, if you don't believe me."

"That's too weird," replied Ben.

Sarah got to her feet and tried to speak with the straw fangs in her mouth.

"Could I please have another lemonade?"

"Do you want ice in it?" asked Jonas.

"No ice, thank you… I want to save that for the polar bears."

Q55: Do you believe in truth?

As the debate continued, with Bill Darvill in particular, rubbishing the arguments, Sarah began to grow restless. Even Caleb's attempt to cheer her with the three hearts drawn on his three thumbs failed.

"Action not words," she whispered, "That's what Lucy wanted. She'll be cross… very cross indeed."

Sarah had a plan.

"I've got something to show everybody," she said as Bill ranted on about the folly of returning to the Stone Age.

"It's a stone of my own," she said. "Now… first I need a clean and dry space," she added, shuffling some glasses to one side. She dipped into her bag and drew out the handkerchief that Malachi found. She spread it out on the table – taking care to flatten the corners and exhibit the embroidered name of Charles Lamb. All the while, she made sure the pure white stone remained at the centre of the hanky.

"Here… this is the stone."

She placed her index finger upon the stone and guided it in a full circle about the cloth.

"The magic stone circle!" she added.

"It's a Rolling Stone!" suggested Bill dismissively. "Probably Mick Jagger!" He mimicked an air guitar.

Wry smiles on the adults who watched, including Sarah's father – who, if truth be told, was surprised that she'd brought it with her.

"No… it *is* a magic stone… I'm telling the truth!"

"I believe you Sarah!" said Caleb, giving her the thumbs up – three in fact.

"What's so magic about it?" asked Jonas.

"Well, my Dad found it… twelve of them inside an old tree next to Keeper's Cottage!"

"It's true… I did!"

She picked it up and placed the stone in her palm.

"Look it glows… and inside there are things that move around and sparkle … like snowflakes… and the stone is always really warm, even when it gets very cold."

"What's it made of?" asked Jonas.

"Stardust!" replied Caleb. "Everything's made of stardust!"

"We're not sure… but definitely not glass or plastic."

"I hate to disappoint you Sarah but it looks just like a plain old stone to me!" said Bill Darvill, as he gathered his grey leather jacket and gloves together.

"C'mon, where's your imagination?" asked Jonas.

"I don't have one. I deal with facts, pure and simple!" he replied.

"I play marbles with it!" said Sarah.

"There you go… it's nothing but a plaything – a child's toy… well I bid you folks a good night. Keep up the ghost hunting! Woooo!" said Darvill, mimicking a spectre. In response, Sarah grabbed her folded straw again and put it back into her mouth, vampire style. Bill Darvill laughed aloud, and made a fake cross sign on his chest to ward Sarah away. Then he left the pub under the brass sign, 'Duck or Grouse.'

Once Bill had gone, Jonas Fosbrooke picked up the ghost theme again.

"What did Fanny Ebbs look like again?" he asked.

Ben scratched his head, "Do you know, Jonas; I can't really be sure… I can see her in my mind's eye, her image – how could I ever forget – but it… she's just a blur of grey. In fact my memory of her is all monochrome… everything in shades of black and white."

"No colour?"

"No colour at all!"

"How odd."

"Have you given up looking for her?" he asked.

"Not yet, not entirely… I ask about, where I can."

"I see."

"Why do you ask?"

"Just curious!"

Caleb changed the subject, as Sarah reached out to gather up the handkerchief.

"This Charles Lamb eh… he was a local poet, wasn't he?" asked Caleb, running his thumbs over the embroidered letters, whilst he had the chance.

"That's right… he," began Ben, before he was rudely interrupted.

129

Q56: Do you believe rules are there to be broken?

Bill Darvill dashed back into the White Horse, with the sound of crisis in his voice,

"Hey – Whittenbury – get up. Your dog's running amok out here in the car park. He's out of control... I think he's trying to kill someone!"

Angry words indeed.

"Malachi! My dog? Are you sure?" asked Ben, as he shuffled from his seat.

"I'm dammed sure," replied Bill.

"But he's at home with Mum," insisted Sarah.

"Exactly!"

"Well... do you know of any other mad Samoyeds?" asked Bill.

"Malachi's not mad," snapped Sarah, as she quickly tucked the 'Magic Stone' into the handkerchief and put it back into her bag.

Ben, Sarah, Jonas and Caleb followed Bill out of the White Horse. The dying embers of the bonfire greeted them. Beyond it an overturned beer barrel rolled noisily across the pub's car park, and crashed into a fence. The barrel's contents gurgled out across the tarmac.

"Over there. He's over there," called a voice in the dark.

"See... there... is that your dog, or is that your dog!" said Bill smugly as flashes of creamy white dashed about in the night in the fields close to the inn.

"Could be!"

Ben ran into a children's playground at the rear of the pub. Caleb and Jonas followed him.

"Is it him?" cried Sarah, trying to catch them up.

A familiar bark echoed in the open country. Ben's calls to his dog were punctured by the sound of a rocket which lit up the sky.

He ran to the top of the slide and called again.

"There, there he is, chasing someone across the fields."

🐕 Clibborn… give back that painting! 🐕

"I think it is him!" cried Ben. "How did he get out? What's he doing so far from home?"

"Where's Mummy? Is she with him?" asked Sarah.

"I don't understand. He hates fireworks – they scare him," insisted Ben, as he slid down the other side.

"If we split up we'll have more chance of grabbing a hold on him," suggested Caleb.

"Where'd he go… can anyone see him?" asked Jonas.

Sarah had an idea. She fumbled in her bag for Charles Lamb's handkerchief, taking real care to ensure the 'Magic Stone ' was safe in a little zipper pocket. She jumped up and down and shook the handkerchief wildly in the hope of attracting Malachi to it.

Out of the darkness emerged a shadowed figure pursued by the Samoyed. They both ignored Sarah and ran directly at Jonas instead. Malachi's target breathed heavily and looked disorientated. He held a long rolled-up reel of paper – like a canvas - and seemed oblivious to those around him. Jonas met the gaze of the stranger. Puzzled at what to do for the best, he stepped aside to let the man pass and tried to grab a hold of the dog's collar.

🐕 Why won't you people have more confidence in me… trust me, please! 🐕

Jonas crouched down to try to smother the dog, but only succeeded in grabbing his fur. It was sticky, pungent and smelt of beer.

"MALACHI!" cried Sarah. "OVER HERE!" She waved the handkerchief furiously. It worked. The dog ran towards her. She reached out hopefully.

"SARAH… BE CAREFUL!" called Ben.

"IT'S OKAY… MY PLAN'S WORKING," she shouted back; that was until Malachi snatched the handkerchief from her hand and fled with it.

"Oh no…" she cried, and stamped her feet in rage.

"Give that back to me!"

Yet Malachi disappeared into the shadows.

🐕 I know my behaviour seems crazy, but I'm putting a wrong to right. It'll make sense soon enough. Just trust me! 🐕

Ben's instinctive reaction was to think about his wife's welfare.

"Sarah, c'mon… we'll have to head home. I'll need to check on Mum… make sure she's okay."

Sarah nodded and they dashed to their car – Yes our Earth Champion has a car!

"I'm sorry Ben… I nearly had him there," said Jonas.

"Why don't you call her?" asked Caleb.

"We can't. I don't have a mobile phone yet!" bemoaned Sarah.

"Does anyone have a phone?" asked Caleb, as people poured out from the pub to find out what was going on.

"Here… you can use mine," offered Bill Darvill.

"Why… em… thanks."

In Ben's mind was the thought, "If needs must…"

He got through, but it just rang and rang.

"No answer!"

"Dad, can we go… please?" asked Sarah.

"You go… we'll sort things out at this end. If the dog reappears well…"

"Yeah… yeah! He breaks every rule in the book that one!" agreed Ben, as he hopped into his car.

"Don't worry… I'll settle up!" claimed Caleb. As they drove off, his painted hearts flashed at the window of the passenger seat.

When Ben and Sarah reached home they ran through the dark to the rear door. "MUM!" cried Sarah. She thumped the door, as Ben fumbled for his keys.

"Hurry Dad… it's cold."

132

"The lights are still on!" said Ben, hopefully.

"MUM!" she called again.

The commotion awoke a sleepy dog inside.

🐕 Let sleeping dog's lie! 🐕

"Malachi!" said Ben and Sarah together.

"He's indoors… what? That's not possible!" claimed Ben.

He turned his key and pushed the door.

"Damn… it's bolted."

Ben need not have worried, for Sarah had looked through the outhouse into the kitchen and saw Julia in her dressing gown headed for the door. Her mother brushed Malachi aside to let them in.

"Thank God!" said Ben.

"I've been so worried," said Sarah.

"You've been worried! We've got no water… not a drop in the house!"

"What? Oh… no… you see, we were in the pub after the fireworks…." began Sarah.

Well, it turns out that Malachi was safely tucked up in the cottage all evening and the reason why Julia didn't answer the 'phone was because she'd ran a bath and was in the middle of washing her hair! "Almost the second after you rang, the water stopped… go on try for yourself. I wouldn't mind but I had to rinse my hair in bath water!"

Ben tried every tap in the house. He assumed a local water main had burst, so rang the authorities. It was news to them, but they'd check and ring him back; they didn't bother! He rang Caleb and Jonas to reassure them that everything was fine with Julia and the dog and to see if they had a similar problem with their water, but they hadn't. Ben shared the news with his family, interrupting Sarah's story of how Malachi – or a dog that looked just like him – had grabbed Charles' hanky again and fled with it.

"Well, I can't begin to explain any of it," said Julia, as she headed for bed.

So, with lights out, and Sarah lying awake with her fake fangs in her mouth as midnight approached, it happened. At *The 11th Hour*, well five minutes to twelve to be exact, all the taps that Ben had played with gushed out water! In the still and quiet of the night the water roared, as though a mighty flood had entered the cottage. Startled, the Whittenbury's sat up in their beds.

🐈 Ideo dimissum est reliquum terrae cum factum est diluvium. 🐈
Which translates from Latin to,

"Therefore was there a remnant left to the Earth, when the flood came."

Now, before we go any further with all of this – we're very conscious it may have crossed your mind to ask why Bill Darvill wasn't represented in our little group. Well, it's a fair question and we don't blame you for asking. When everything came to light, Bill wanted nothing to do with our idea to share our account of events to the world. Put bluntly, he was cynical and distrustful; claiming much of what we had said was a pack of lies. In fact, he threatened us with defamation of character if we said anything against him or misrepresent him in any way. It's not our choice – we're just doing our duty! So Bill, if you're reading this remember: the door's always open for you to join us. We digress!

Q57: Have you ever spied on anyone?

A week or so after the fireworks on bonfire night, another of those haunting mists settled on the Ware Uplands. It was an ideal stage for Hertfordshire's famous old ghosts to roam unchallenged. Not that this prevented Julia from taking Malachi on one of his regular hikes. Julia claimed that what she did during the walk was totally spontaneous. It began as a curiosity:

'Where does Jonas go and what does he carry in that rucksack?' Julia hadn't set out to follow him. It just happened that way, one step after another. She started the pursuit at the Nimley Bourne, where Jonas took a public footpath that led towards Blakesware Manor. Even Malachi acted out of character, with his head down and focused on the road ahead, as he guided Julia to the Manor. Fortunately, Julia wrote everything down in her notebook, the *Jazzy Jamboree*.

The day of the long lingering fog

The experience was like watching a movie on a high-definition widescreen television set! The mist and leaves that lined much of the route acted as a sponge that absorbed sound and light. Everything, especially my footsteps, sounded weak – as though they had no strength or presence at all. To be honest, Jonas walked so fast that we struggled to keep up with him. In fact, when we reached the grounds of the private estate he was almost out of sight. As the fog thickened, I said to Malachi, "Oh this was a ridiculous idea. What have I got myself in to?"

🐾 "Come into my parlour," said the spider to the fly. 🐾

Ahead, I heard a hunting horn and hounds. Behind me came the rumble of wheels turning on gravel. I heard horses too. The figures and forms ahead of me emerged slowly. A trespasser on private land, I left the path to hide behind an abandoned cart which, now I think of it, could have been right out of the *Haymakers* painting. I hid behind one of the large wheels, with Malachi at my side. His creamy coat helped to camouflage him in the fog. He looked at me and smiled. I just put my index finger to my lips to encourage the dog to be silent. I peered through the spokes of the wheel to spy upon the travellers.

To my right emerged two women. To my left rolled in two horse drawn carriages. Their silhouetted outlines stopped directly ahead of me. The heads of the impatient horses nodded in the gloom. Vapour spread from their nostrils and steam rose from their flanks. There was a conversation.

"Excuse me good ladies, I am right in assuming this to be the road to Blakesware Manor, residence of Lady Plumer and the Captain? Only the cursed fog has clouded our view... and may have affected our judgement."

I'd say the accent was Scandinavian.

One of the women answered. By her stance, I judged it the elder of the two.

"Right you are, sir."

The other woman spoke.

"You are on the estate. The Manor will come into view shortly. Just follow the road ahead... and take the first turning to your left at the hounds."

"Hounds eh! That would be right... it really is a mighty relief to be close to our journey's end at last."

"Have you travelled far... Sir," asked the eldest woman.

"Madam, it's been one long arduous journey," he replied. "But at least my creativity has been fuelled by the cruel hand of fate... and that's taught me to know beauty when I see it."

The horses began to tread the ground whilst they waited. One snorted. I expected Malachi to react, but he sat in silence. We observed. We listened.

"Good Afternoon!" I heard another man say.

"Americans?" asked the eldest woman, with a slight bow.

Another man broke into verse,

♪ Yankee Doodle went to town riding on a pony. ♪

It was that anthem of American Independence again!

I heard foot-tapping, laughter and cheers from within the carriage. It moved off with the sound of barking within.

🐈 I spy with my little eye, something beginning with M! 🐈

"Hope to see you fine people again," called the Scandinavian.

I imagined the women smiled, as we watched the carriage begin to fade in the mist.

"Independence has gone to their heads," I heard the eldest say.

The other replied, "Do you see… they've brought the tree with them."

I could just make out a small potted tree, which bumped along at the rear of the carriage.

"Charles says they're bringing a magical tree from the Nordic mountains… Lady Plumer plans to adorn it for the festive period."

Either side of the tree were a couple of cages. Within them were small creatures – I took them to be squirrels, but I may be wrong. Yet the most enduring sight of the whole day – in the long lingering fog – was the face of a creamy white puppy that seemed to look across in our direction.

🐈 I spy with my little eye, something beginning with M! 🐈

"Look… a baby bear."

"Prey for the highwayman! Well, such is the way of their kind… heads full of foolishness. Lucy, remember your place… you're young with so much still to offer."

I now assumed the women to be mother and daughter. The younger one fell silent as they walked away without a further word. I led Malachi from our hiding place. Only then did it occur to me – was this our elusive Lucy?

- ♥ Sarah's invisible friend?
- ♥ The angelic woman from my dream?
- ♥ The woman I sketched that day the fog last settled in the Uplands?

Sadly, the poor visibility meant I couldn't distinguish her features. Yet as I dwell upon it now I find the conversation most strange – talk of the American War of Independence, as though it happened but yesterday!

Despite the unexpected intrusion, I was determined to learn of Jonas' destination, so I continued the pursuit. As we passed the Manor, I saw the ghostly shapes of the horse-drawn carriages creep towards it. They were greeted by fervent barking from a pack of hounds. Despite the mist, I saw the shadows of many tails kept high and proud amongst the pack. I assumed they were kennelled at Blakesware, but their presence surprised me as I'm sure Ben once said that hounds hadn't been kept at the Manor for well over 100 years!

🐕 It's the Puckeridge Hunt! 🐕

Q58: Do things happen for a reason?

Before we return to *Julia's Jamboree*, Ben wanted to say that one of Julia's more curious talents was an instinct on when to follow an action through. At such times, she often felt as though she was being pulled by an invisible thread that affixed to her heart and stretched out ahead of her. It was like this when the couple first found Keeper's Cottage. Julia had chosen Hertfordshire over more obvious places for an artist – such as Cornwall or the Cotswolds. She'd driven at random, East of Ware, and was taken in by the undulating countryside, which led to the discovery of Keeper's. Why are we sharing this now, you may ask, all these pages in? Well, it's because in the later part of her pursuit of Jonas, she had nothing to lead her but pure instinct. It was this that steered Julia in the direction of the steeple at St John's Church, Widford.

According to Caleb, the good people of Widford claim that over the centuries the church's tired grey prosaic stone structure had absorbed the spirits of generations of locals buried within its grounds. Built at the head of one of the Upland peaks, the church had fabulous views, including across sleepy Blakesware Manor. The church had three burial yards; the oldest dated back two hundred years or more, with the names of those at rest eroded by wind and rain. Locals claim that not everyone in the cemetery was at peace. At symbolic dates and times in the year, when the bells of St John's tolled, the spirits remembered past torment and returned to the world of the living to let loose their woes. So says Caleb – always the showman! What say thee Julia?

"I first saw Jonas through the wooden arch that led to the burial ground farthest from the church. The foot of the arch was decorated with wreathes from recent Armistice Day celebrations – it felt like an invitation for the living to share the world of the deceased. It came as no surprise to find him here, hunched over a gravestone – to be honest, it confirmed my suspicions. I stood dithering on what to do next – whether to turn back for home or approach Jonas, when he solved my dilemma. "JULIA, IS THAT YOU? IT IS YOU!" he called.

"Eh yes… hi Jonas," I said, reluctant to shout for fear of disrespect. So I waved back.

He beckoned me over.

"What took you so long… I thought you'd never get here," he said, when we reached him.

"Oh! Were you expecting us?"

"Well – as the pair of you followed me this last hour or so… I was actually a bit worried because of this creepy fog… and was going to look for you, but thought well… you have that beastie to defend you so…"

I was dreadfully embarrassed.

"Oh Jonas… I'm so sorry, honest I am. It just started out as…"

139

He stopped me with a shake of his head.

"Julia, there's no need to explain. In fact, it's reassuring to know you care… and it's good to have some company. It can be lonely out here with a head full of memories!"

His eyes switched from my gaze to look to the headstone that read,

Anne Jane Fosbrooke
beloved wife and mother – died aged 29

Adam Fosbrooke
beloved son – aged 3 weeks

Oh heavens – mother and child. Poor Jonas! I felt so helpless and pitiful. I reached out and touched his arm. He looked up at me.

"Two and half years ago now… yet it doesn't really get any easier. It's why I walk you see… I think of the things we've done together. Our happiness when we were younger."

I breathed deeply – more of a sigh really.

"Still, she has a fabulous view."

"Jonas… I…"

"I've tried to work it out in my mind. It had to happen for a reason, surely?"

"I can't begin to imagine how you feel."

"Seldom does a day go by without my wishing they were here with me… but the misery goes on."

"Jonas… you know you can talk about it whenever you like."

"I… thanks… it's just I know what people think, they think 'come on Jonas Fosbrooke it's been over two years now, it's time for you to move on and start anew, whilst your still young.' It's what her parents think – I see it in their eyes. But it's not easy, not easy at all."

He placed a hand on the top of the headstone.

"Of course. You just need time Jonas."

"Aye… that and closure. I don't have any closure – that's the real problem."

"I see."

Jonas removed the rucksack from his shoulder. He dug into one of the side pockets and took out a framed photograph.

"Here – this is us together when Adam was born. Anne never really recovered from the loss."

Jonas' voice choked.

"I lost my mother when I was young… my Nana raised me. She used to say that everything happens for a reason… but I'm not sure I believe her… hey, she told me fairies were real?"

Jonas nodded. "If only real life was like the fairy tales – you know the bad guy gets it and they all lived happily ever after! Still… I believe my luck's changing for I have a new purpose now."

"You do?"

"Yes… I've a new job… I'm no longer doing carpentry."

"Oh!"

"I'm a collector of things."

"I see… we've been doing a bit of that too. What do you collect?" I asked.

"Now, what was it he said? 'Things to support the message for the benefit of future generations.' Yes that was it!"

"Ah!" I said.

"I'm not crazy you know… It's a real job. 'One of the most important duties ever asked of a man'… those were his words and I believe him."

"Do you think the fog will eventually clear?" I asked, discreetly changing the subject.

"Do you believe me?" he asked.

"Hey Jonas… look… you do whatever you feel you need to do to get through this."

"He said he chose me because he had faith in me… he said I had the right contacts. That I was the only one he could trust! It's given me a new lease of life. I came today to tell Annie. She would be real proud."

I tried not to patronise him.

"I'm sure that's right Jonas."

"What time is it? Is it noon yet? We can expect to see Caleb any second now. He's regular as clockwork that one… normally gets here at the stroke of midday."

"He does?"

"Absolutely! His wife's at rest in this cemetery too."

"Oh, okay."

"Look… here he comes now, right on cue," said Jonas.

I looked up. Sure enough Hitch waved furiously in our direction.

Yet it was the figure beyond Caleb that most intrigued me. The owner's scarlet jacket stood out like a beacon in the gloom! He leant against a large Celtic cross on a tomb within the oldest part of the cemetery. My lips barely parted. "Ben. Is that you?" I whispered. You see, a sunbeam had cut through the fog to reveal a man who looked just like my Ben. He was dressed in full military finery – the dashing scarlet and blue of the British Life Guards! Although it was just a glimpse, I saw a short scarlet jacket girdled with a gold sash, bleached buckskin breeches and knee high black boots. A gilded Grecian helmet with a plumed white tuft was tucked under his arm. Malachi appeared to recognise him.

🐴 I say. It's Captain Richard Lewin KB. 🐴

He escaped my grasp and ran excitedly to him – my Ben – straight for the busy Hertfordshire Way without checking for traffic.

I screamed, "CATCH HIM… MALI'S MAKING FOR THE ROAD!"

"I'll stop him," replied Caleb.

Fearing the worst, I shielded my eyes.

"It's okay… he's made it across," I heard Jonas say, which was a bizarre consolation to Jonas, given what happened on bonfire night. Next, I saw the military figure give Malachi a warm welcome.

I ran towards the road. I dodged the traffic on the Hertfordshire Way, with Caleb and Jonas in close pursuit. "Over here... this way," I said, and led them to the Celtic cross. The tips of Malachi's ears stuck out from behind the base of the tomb.

"There he is... Ben! Benjamin."

I found Malachi totally alone beside an impressive grave.

"Malachi! What were you thinking? You could have caused an accident! Ben should know better. Where is he?" I asked. I circled the tomb and looked all about it, into the shadows, amid and under bushes.

"Come on Ben...this isn't funny. Now's not the time for games!"

Caleb and Jonas stood side by side at the foot of the tomb, arms folded.

"I saw him, I'm sure of it. You saw him too right... Ben... dressed in a scarlet uniform?"

The men looked at each other bemused. Caleb spoke first,

"Julia, let me tell you about the military figure buried within this tomb."

"Military figure!" I replied.

"Yes... he was quite a dandy! It's said he fought alongside the Duke of Wellington against Napoleon Bonaparte. The memorial was constructed in his honour."

"Wellington... really! Is that so?" My patience for local legend was wearing thin.

"Quite so... facts is facts my girl! It's also said that the tomb's benefactor once owned Blakesware Manor. Do you know, on a clear day this huge cross was once visible from the top of the Manor. Until those cottages were built and blocked the view?"

"The Manor!" I asked. "Don't talk about it... that creepy place... with its people living like Amish folk."

Another bemused look from the men! Despite my cynicism, Caleb persisted in telling me of the local myth,

"Where you're standing now… well the site's revered by Widford folk of old, as sacred ground, as he who rests beneath it took a secret to his grave about a person of blue blood who once lived in the area. They say the time will come when the lost royal will reclaim her place… as Queen."

"Oh, come on… this isn't a Hollywood movie. This is Widford Caleb… Widford. We're dealing with fact not fiction!"

"How then do you explain the soldier?" he asked.

"Well. I don't know… but what I do know is my Ben was here in flesh and blood. Hey… come on this is down to you, isn't it? You put him up to it didn't you?" I insisted.

"Ah, I wish it were so," I heard Caleb utter under his breath.

Q59: Do you like surprises?

So, how would Ben Whittenbury wriggle free of this one? In his words:

"I'd finished work early that day and had stopped off in Ware to pick up a few things to repair the bolt on the rear door. These items ticked-off my list; I had a little wander in the charity shops on the High Street to scrounge around amongst the unwanted things. Well, lo and behold I found an amazing military jacket, unlabelled and un-sized. When I tried it on, I felt like *Mr Benn* from the 1970's children's TV series; 'what adventures might I have today?' The woman behind the counter remarked on its uniqueness – "Oh, I don't remember putting this out! Peggy."

"Yes!" came a cry from the rear of the shop.

"A gentleman here wants to buy a jacket, but it's not priced up."

"Jackets are normally ten pounds!" she said, coming to the counter.

"Will you take five for it? It's all I have on me."

They accepted five pounds for it. Five pounds for what seemed like an authentic military jacket potentially over 100 years old. It had to be a replica, but who cares! Just wait until Julia and Sarah see this, boy will they be in for a surprise.

As soon as I reached home, I brushed the jacket down and polished its buttons. I put it on a wooden hanger in my study and switched on my computer to do a little research. Cursed technology! I was unable to log on due to a local exchange problem. Frustrated, I chose instead to model the jacket again. It could have been tailor made for me, as it was a perfect fit. Once on, it inspired me.
"Captain Benjamin Michael Whittenbury… Defender of the Earth… Duty awaits!" I said, as I admired my reflection.
"Prepare to fight and die for our planet blue in a sea of black!"
My mind flashed back to the equinox when I stood aloft on the haystack at Philosopher's Point – and my cry,

"Now is the Time for Action!"

Yet what had I done since? I remembered my list – 'The Haymakers Survey'!

So, I lifted the lid on my wooden rider's box – and found my old list folded neatly beneath the stones. I removed the list and made my way downstairs to stand before the *Haymakers* painting. Mother Nature's studious and critical eye looked right back at me, hay rake in hand.
"You reap what you sow!" said a voice in my head; her voice?
So, sporting my new jacket, I made for the old log in the wilderness. I reviewed the questions on my list:

'Q1. Do you believe your life has a purpose?'

"Yes," I said in my head. I licked the end of my pencil and added to the list.

Q36. Should a good life cost the Earth?

Q37. Do you know how to have fun?

Q38. Have you built a house of cards?

Q39. Do you believe in magic?

Q40. Can you play a musical instrument?

Q41. Do you like surprises?

Q42. Do you enjoy drawing?

Q43. Do you believe in happy endings?

Q44. Is there anything worse than a fly buzzing around your room at night when you're trying to sleep?

Q45. Are you good at marbles?

Q46. Do you value a good education?

Q47. Do you know your history?

Q48. Have you ever played Solitaire?

Q49. Do you ever think about the old days?

Q50. Do you miss someone you love?

Q51. Have you ever taken part in a protest?

Q52. Do you believe in miracles?

Q53. Do you like to keep warm?

Q54. Do you enjoy a bit of a mystery?

Q55. Do you believe in truth?

Q56. Do you believe rules are there to be broken?

Q57. Have you ever spied on anyone?

Q58. Do things happen for a reason?

Q59. Do you like surprises?

I based the list on our recent life experiences. A quick review reassured me it had developed into an unusual mix. It lacked obvious ones for an Earth Champion, like:

- ❤ *Do you believe in a Divine Creator?*
- ❤ *Do you recycle?*
- ❤ *Do you worry about climate change?*

But it was a list I was generally happy with; a people's survey – diverse, interesting and fun! I'd just added,

Q59. 'Do you like surprises?'

when everything went dark. Someone had crept up behind me and covered my eyes with their hands. The shock caused me to let go of my pencil and ruffle my list, but the perfume gave her away.

♪ Solider, soldier… won't you marry me with your musket, fife and drum ♪ she sang.

"Julia!" I said.

"Benjamin Whittenbury!"

I knew that tone of voice.

"The jacket… do you like it?" I peeled her fingers away from my eyes and kissed the tips. The bristles of my moustache tickled her.

"I knew it was you all along… just tell me how you did it?" She came around to face me.

"Did what?" I asked.

She smiled wryly. "Okay… mister super hero, have it your way!"

"I'm sorry Julia, but I really haven't a clue what your talking about!" I insisted.

"Oh come on Ben… lunchtime at the cemetery… I bet this was Caleb's doing. I bet he told you about the grave of the local war hero."

"Have you been drinking?" I asked.

"What kind of a question is that, of course not?"

"Well it sounds like it."

I straightened out my list.

"So, where were you?" Julia asked.

"Eh! I stopped off at Ware to drop off my watch at the jewellers, pick up the things to repair the door and popped into one of the charity shops... where I found this little gem. Isn't she a beauty?"

"You bought that today?"

"Yeah... must have been about midday-ish!"

"And you came straight back here?"

"I did... to polish the buttons... then I came out here to continue with my survey!"

"So you didn't go anywhere near St John's Church."

"Which church?"

"The church at Widford!"

"Why would I want to go to Widford?"

Malachi came running over.

🐎 There's a little magic in every place name, for someone thinks of that as home. Me, my home's planet Earth! 🐎

"Because I saw you there today at lunchtime... so did Mali. He ran straight across the Hertfordshire Way to reach you. Damn near caused an accident too. He frightened me half to death!"

"You must have imagined it... I've not been anywhere but home... honest!"

"But you were wearing this jacket!"

"Wasn't me. Hang-on... I'll prove it. I've still got the receipt."

I dug into my back pocket, and drew out a little slip of paper. It had the date and time upon it... 11:55.

"So it couldn't have been you!"

"Finally, I keep telling you... it wasn't me, cross my heart, hope to die."

148

Q60: Have you ever experienced déjà vu?

"So, if it wasn't you, then who was it?"

"He looked just like me you say?"

"Identical… right down to the moustache!"

"And he was wearing this jacket."

"Well one very similar, if not the same."

Julia closed her eyes to trigger her visual memory.

"I can see him now… yes he definitely looked like you. He was holding a helmet. Did you buy a helmet?"

She re-opened her eyes.

"No Julia… no helmet."

"It's strange… maybe I did imagine it because neither Jonas nor Caleb saw him."

"Jonas… Caleb. What were they doing at the church?"

"It's a long story."

"Come to the point, what were you doing there… you don't normally walk Mali that far, do you? And on a miserable misty old day like this…"

Julia began to explain what happened, but paused midway through, "Oh Ben, I'm cold and worn out. I need to go inside, sit down and warm up."

"I'm not surprised."

So we went inside for a late lunch, during which I shared my list with Julia. We sat in the lounge beneath a copy of the *Haymakers* and she skipped through the questions.

"So, what do you think?" I asked.

"It's obviously one of those days Ben."

"You don't like it do you?"

"No Ben… it's not that!"

"Let me explain the idea. You see most people on this planet have an idea what's going on… that the way we produce energy – the cars we drive, the planes we fly and the factories where things are made... all mean CO_2... mountains of the stuff."

Julia had her head back in the chair with her eyes closed.

"I am listening Ben," she said, when I paused.

"Okay... most people know that the forests are being cut down to provide food or space for us to live."

"Ah-ha."

"And that all this is bad news for nature... and us because the sea ice is melting and the weather's getting unpredictable. You know, droughts and so on. Are you listening still?"

"Yep... but what's your point Ben?"

"We have an idea what can be done to help change things... stop it from being so bad... and there's loads of stuff out there telling us all the time how bad things might get and what needs to happen and what the average person can do to make a difference."

"And?"

"The thing is... well... I think it runs deeper than this. Did you know the Earth has an annual CO_2 cycle – it actually breathes in and out with the seasons? It breathes in during the summer and breathes out at winter. This, and our experiences since the equinox, has convinced me of something.... that our Earth is enchanted, a living being in its own right and unless we... the human race... show it more respect... well!"

🐃 The Earth is the one thing we all have in common. 🐃

"Okay Ben... I'm tired and confused!"

"And I think this survey... which follows our recent experiences... might somehow be the answer. A way to get people to look at the issues in a new way and explore creative solutions to balance things out! We're part of nature, not separate from it."

"Ben! It doesn't make sense..."

"You're not convinced, are you? You're right. It's a stupid idea... a survey to save the world, what was I thinking!"

I took off my hero's jacket.

"No Ben. The reason it doesn't make sense is because I'm sure I've seen this list before."

"Really! No... it's my list. I made it up."

"It's just a feeling – call it déjà vu, if you like?"

"See... that goes to show you. Maybe I was right... let's make that Question 60, shall we?"

Ben, you should have had more confidence. To succeed, champions need enthusiasm, determination, drive, resilience, patience, courage, flair and self-belief. But your star quality – humility is also your Achilles' Heel. To be heard, amongst the bewildering media noise of the early 21st century you need to shout louder!

If I may leave you a tip – it's this! Keep an eye on events in the world about you - see what you make of them. Find the links Ben... find the links that demonstrate the survey's deep rooted magic!

Q61: Have you ever worn fancy dress?

The town of Ware has the distinction of being one of the oldest continuously occupied places in Western Europe. A former thoroughfare of medieval and Tudor England, the wagon ways and facades of the buildings at the centre of the town reflected its history. It was an ideal location for a Dickensian night - in honour of the great author. The locals loved it. In aid of charity, people dressed in period costume, drank mulled wine and feasted on mince pies and roasted chestnuts. Folk music and side-shows, helped to recreate a lost age.

The Whittenbury's entered into the full spirit of the evening. Ben chose to wear his new military colours.

"Goodness me Dad, you look so smart. My friends from school will be so jealous," said Sarah, as they arrived at the festival.

"Thank you Sarah, I'm glad about that because I thought you wanted me to wear the polar bear outfit again."

"Oh did I... well it is cold... but you're allowed a night off from being Nature's Champion sometimes."

"Am I?"

"Of course... but only if you promise to play the flute."

"The flute?"

"Yes... here. The one you gave me."

"Oh, the fife!"

Julia joined in with a song designed to tease her husband again,

♫ Soldier, soldier won't you marry me, with your musket, fife and drum. ♫

Yet this time Ben completed the verse,

♫ Oh no, sweet maid, I cannot marry you, for I have no hat to put on. ♫

"Then let's go find you a helmet Daddy!" said Sarah excitedly. She jumped up and down – just a once or twice, for she didn't want people to think her childish.

"Got my fingers crossed!"

"Me too," replied Sarah.

"And me," said Ben.

"That makes three of us!" said Sarah.

"It's certainly a great night for it... a starlit sky," replied Julia.

"Pity Malachi's at home. Still, it won't be for long and I've fixed the rear door now, so there's absolutely no way he'll get out!"

"I wouldn't put it passed him," said Julia.

"Still, Jonas promised to keep an eye on the house for us."

Julia and Ben looked deep into each others eyes. They knew of the horrid ordeal Jonas had been through. It drew out the protective instinct in them.

"Sarah… just make sure you keep close by, eh… it's very crowded!" Julia was prompted to say.

"Mum. I'm nearly a teenager now," she said, which may have explained her sudden interest in mobile phones.

In fact, the absence of a mobile phone trader at the event left Sarah a little downhearted, so whilst on their way to the drill hall for the evening's finale, Ben lifted Sarah's mood with a promise to buy the latest flip-top model. In response, Sarah gleefully announced,

"Oh, look it's a magician!"

The magician's stage name was, 'The Emperor.' The light of the full moon shone brightly on his masked face; perhaps, as legend suggests, as a reminder that the moon was the keeper of misspent time and wealth, unanswered prayers and unrequited love? It added glamour to his tricks of chance with cards and dice; a performance which left the audience in awe. As the applause faded from a successful trick, he sought another volunteer. Sarah had squeezed her way to the front of the crowd, just within view of her parents. The sparkle of her locket attracted the conjurer's eye.

"What's your name, my child?"

"Sarah."

"Are you cold Sarah?"

"Yes, but that's okay."

"Sarah, do you believe in *magic*?"

"Oh yes… it's because of the Captain. He likes to play tricks on people."

The audience cheered.

"He does? The Captain you say! Where is this hearty fellow?"
"There! He's the soldier, just there." Sarah pointed to her father.
Ben's scarlet jacket was a magnet for searching eyes. Although embarrassed at the attention, he waved to the crowd.
"Three cheers for our hero, the magnificent Captain. Hip-hip…"
"Hooray!" cried the crowd, ahead of more cheering.
With impeccable timing, the Emperor marched in front of his audience and declared,
"Allow me to give you an education. Dice have a history as rich and old as man. They were very popular with the Greeks and Romans. They say too that departed spirits in the underworld play at dice! Oh, and these dice I have in my hand are no ordinary dice. No… they were found in mysterious Royston Cave, when it was excavated… some say the Knights Templar brought them to the cave from the Holy Land."

The magician paused beside his volunteer. He held the dice in a closed fist next to an ear, implying the need for us to listen.
"They talk to me and me to they… so cast the dice and I will control their will." He whispered some instructions to Sarah, then knelt before her and passed her an eye mask.
"Blindfold me?" he requested.
Sarah did as he asked.
"Tacta alea est - the die is cast and I am seeing double."
Sarah threw the dice across the cobbled streets.
"Snakes eyes!" he cried.
The magician had correctly predicted a double one. Triumphant, he removed the eye-mask to generous applause, whistles and cheers.
"Can you see into the future?" Sarah asked, as the magician led her away.
"Time Is… Time Was… Time's Passed!" he advised.
"I don't understand."
"Trust me my child… one day it will all make sense."

The Emperor's voice quivered with emotion as he drifted back to his audience.

"Do you have any questions for me?" asked a man from the shadows, presumably acting as the Emperor's assistant.

Ben had weaved through the crowd to meet his daughter. He heard the request.

"May I ask Sarah a few questions to include in our survey Captain? It's essential we include the views of the children."

"What survey's this?" asked Ben.

"It's a survey to guide the future."

"Is it? In that case, yes go right ahead… of course," nodded Ben.

"I need just three questions… no more… any order will do. There's an incredible prize on offer… think of it as a competition."

"Yes, a competition," said Ben. "Please go right ahead."

"And you'll add them to the list?" she asked.

"Ah, so you know about the list?" asked the assistant.

"The Captain's preparing a list for a survey too," she said.

"Is he?"

"Yes. The Captain like's lists… he says they're a life-saver."

"Good for him."

Ben shrugged his shoulders, "Just helps me to prioritise."

Sarah was ready to offer her questions, "Okay then, three questions. Oh, that's easy my favourites are:

- ♥ Have you ever helped the poor?
- ♥ Do you have a favourite flower?
- ♥ Have you ever searched for buried treasure?

That's it. Those are my questions."

"Thank you Sarah. They're wonderful, beautiful questions."

"Come on – the Drill Hall, they'll be starting in five minutes," said Ben.

"Quick Sarah, do as the Captain says… hurry along. There's no time to waste," said the assistant.

"How will I know if I've won the prize?" she asked.

"Don't worry Sarah…you'll know, everyone will know. I promise." The unassuming man waved Ben and his daughter farewell. As they left, the assistant was joined by an inquisitive creamy-white puppy.

"There you are Malachi… good boy… a job well done!"

🐕 Every dog has its day. 🐕

Q62: Have you ever helped the poor?

Sarah was so excited at her participation in the Magic Show.

"I did that, in front of all those people!"

"Oh Sarah, we were so proud," said Julia.

"You were really brave!" replied Ben, as they made their way to the Drill Hall.

"My heart was thumping in my chest…oh my! And he guessed right. How did he do that?"

"Probably able to see through the mask!"

"No way Mum, I checked it."

"Maybe he had a wire to his ear and someone told him the numbers."

"But Dad… he guessed the numbers before the dice stopped rolling."

"And it was double-one… like in my drawing!"

"Oh my God, so it was. That's so weird," said Sarah.

"I know… okay, I don't have all the answers," insisted Ben.

"No, but you have lots of questions."

"I do!"

"It's funny that they're doing a survey too, don't you think!"

"What's that about a survey?" asked Julia.

"They're doing a survey for the future!"

"Another one… I gave the magician's assistant three questions to add to his survey."

"Well… if they're good enough for the assistant then they're good enough for me… I'll put them on my list."

"Our list Ben!" claimed Julia.

"Yes, our list!"

They reached the Ware Drill Hall. A crowd had gathered about the entrance. The venue was full! The Whittenbury's stood nearby and pondered what to do. The famous carol, 'Silent Night' echoed in the street.

"I love this one… it's my favourite!"

♫ Silent flight, owl of white ♫ sung Ben, much to Sarah's amusement.

"Where did that come from?" asked Julia.

"Out of the blue!"

A person dressed as Frosty the Snowman approached them seeking donations for a leading charity for disadvantaged children.

"If you look at your reflection in that window, you look a bit like a polar bear!" said Sarah.

The person did so and nodded.

"My Dad… the Captain… he has a polar bear outfit!"

The person nodded again.

"You can't talk can you?"

The person shook his head from side to side.

"Look Mum, Dad… in the window, doesn't he look like a polar bear?"

Julia looked into a vacant shop window of the old building opposite the Drill Hall, whilst Ben dropped a few coins into the collection box. Frosty nodded again, waved then walked away.

Caleb later confirmed that a Ware workhouse – for orphans, maddens and debtors - once occupied the spot opposite the Drill Hall. There, the poor had laboured for their survival, whilst the parish kept any profits. To survive the desperate occupants span hemp, weaved and made sacks. The premises now stood vacant, as previous owners have claimed their businesses were cursed and haunted. Lately, nobody was prepared to let it.

Julia had watched Frosty's reflection walk away. In its place stood the faint outline of a person – a Lady in Grey. The ghostly form raised a hand to her ear to imply she was listening to the carol – Silent Night! The spectre approached the window and put her palm onto the glass, leaving a print behind – that of a hand shape with a heart in its palm. The heart shape was pierced by three swords. The woman's image faded away behind it.

"Ben... did you just see that?"

"See what?"

"There, inside the shop... look, here at the reflection!"

Ben looked at the misted window pane, "What am I looking for?" he asked.

"The Lady in Grey!" replied Sarah.

"What was that?" said Julia.

"The Lady in Grey... she was inside the shop. She put her hand on the window and left the heart shape behind."

"You saw her too! Why didn't you say anything?"

"Because she looked afraid... I didn't want to scare her," claimed Sarah.

It had been an eventful Dickensian evening, for sure.

Q62a: Is life logical?

If life on Earth started from scratch a million times over, chances are it would never again produce mammals, let alone people, so why expect the questions in this tale to flow logically?

Think of it as casting a million dice at the same time to find they all landed on the number one!

🐏 *The most widely improbable feature of the universe is a lump of matter that can fret over its improbability.* 🐏

Q63: Do you like the way you look?

In the days following the Dickensian evening, Julia developed a disturbing affliction. Whenever she closed her eyes, she saw the face of the woman from her island dream from the night of the storm - when Jonas had come to the cottage to take shelter from the rain! It drove her to distraction, such that she struggled to sleep or think. Eventually, she let Ben know what was troubling her. As she spoke, they paced the cottage – from room to room - trying to fathom it out.
"The thing is that I see her face whenever I close my eyes."
"That's not good."
To prove the point, she closed them.

"It's like it now… she just won't go away."

"I don't know what to suggest. When did this start?"

"After the Dickensian evening!"

"Has it got any worse?"

"Well… yes in a way… I'm starting to see her face in the mirror instead of mine."

"You are?" The tone of Ben's voice reflected his concern.

"Yes… if I look into my eyes, she's there… blurred with my reflection."

"That must feel strange."

"It does. It feels like she's taking me over."

"Are you trying to say that you're possessed?"

"It sounds real scary, I know… but it's not that. It's just I feel she's trying to tell us something."

"You're confusing me."

"She's trying to get a message to me. It's been this way all the while… except it's becoming stronger, more powerful."

"Julia… I…"

"It scares me that each day she looks weaker… more fragile… more vulnerable."

"Maybe it's that simple … she just wants you to help her."

"Help her to do what?"

"I don't know… think laterally."

"All along she's been telling me to have faith, that I hold the key!"

"Well… you're the one with the gift. What does she want you to do?"

"That's just it… I feel she wants me to paint her portrait, but why?"

"So paint her Julia! It might keep her from haunting your every move."

"She doesn't haunt me Ben. She's just here, with me."

So, Julia took to her brushes and painted with a fervour and brilliance that surpassed her usual ability. She created a perfect resurrection of the angelic woman from her island dream.

When she arrived home from school, Sarah was surprised and overawed,

"Mum, you've painted Lucy… and it's brilliant, really brilliant," she enthused.

"It's so realistic… so life-like. You could almost imagine her emerging from the canvas. What do you propose to do with it?" asked Ben.

"I really have absolutely no idea," said Julia.

Beyond that, Lucy's face no longer haunted the mind of Julia Whittenbury.

Q64: Do you know whether or not you are sometimes indecisive?

The Whittenbury's were a little uncomfortable at the prospect that ghosts from a former age - the military hero, a fragile elderly lady, and an angelic young woman – had crept into and were shaping their lives. Trouble was, they couldn't decide what to make of everything and how best to respond to the seemingly endless flow of strange supernatural experiences and odd discoveries.

"I feel responsible for all this as everything goes back to the day I pledged to be Nature's Champion… maybe I should shave off the moustache," said Ben.

"Don't Ben. It's fine, honest!" replied Julia.

Sarah had other ideas, "Oh do stop fussing… I think it's really exciting… all the magic tricks… friendly ghosts… free gifts, like my marbles, this beautiful locket and best of all… I'm going to get a mobile phone!"

She clapped her hands. Malachi ran to greet her.

"And Malachi!"

🐏 The wonderful optimistic energetic voice of youth! 🐏

"So … I just love it."

Her parents looked at each other in tacit approval. "I think it shows that something amazing is happening… and it's all thanks to my Mum and Dad, how cool is that?"

The parents smiled.

"We hadn't thought of it like that," said Ben, speaking for the two of them.

"Yet I can't decide if the signs are good or bad," said Julia.

"So… that makes us Earth Detectives!"

"Earth Detectives?"

"Yes… I'll go grab my magnifying glass… then let's go looking for more clues!"

So, the Whittenbury's began to go over all the evidence. They went back to the start – well, to the place where Malachi unearthed the locket. Sarah went equipped with a torch and spy glass. Julia took the camera and Ben took Malachi. They were a little surprised by what they found. Fallen leaves lined much of the route, which made their venture a touch hazardous. Sarah grabbed a long stick and used it to help retain her balance as they descended into the gully. Yet, when they reached the Web-Log they noticed three things:

♥ A flawless circle etched into the soft moist ground directly in front of the fallen tree. It was just big enough for a person or two to stand within. None of the surrounding autumn debris spread onto its edges.

♥ At the very centre of the circle stood a white feather with its shaft pushed firmly into the ground.

♥ The wooden humanoid figure that clung to the log was breaking up.

"This deserves a closer look," said Sarah. She put her stick to one side and peeped through her magnifying glass at the feather in the circle. Her parents were more cautious.

"Keep out of the circle Sarah... just until we decide what's going on here."

"It's just a harmless feather... that's all!"

"But it's sticking out of the ground in the middle of a circle... right where I found the locket, which is a bit odd, don't you think!" insisted Ben.

"A magic circle?" speculated Sarah.

The adults were perplexed. Julia took a photo of the circle.

"What does a white feather mean?" asked Julia.

"Cowardice... Peace!" suggested Ben.

"So it won't hurt us then... the feather."

Sarah knelt in front of the circle and looked through her glass – like a young female version of Sherlock Holmes.

"Oh... it's all blurry!"

"That's because you're too far away!"

"Oh!"

Not one to be bound by fear, Sarah reached into the circle and pulled the feather out of the ground.

"See... no harm done, was there!"

Her parents looked at each other and nodded. Sarah studied it closely through the looking glass.

"See anything?"

"It's still blurry... it doesn't work."

"You try."

Sarah passed the feather and the glass to her father.

"You're right... it's like looking through a kaleidoscope!"

"Isn't there a feather in that song you keep singing... how does it go?"

"Why... yes ... so there is."

♪ Yankee Doodle went to town riding on a pony, stuck a feather in his hat and called it macaroni. ♪ he sang.

Julia took another photo.

"How silly naming his hat after some pasta," said Sarah. "Grown-ups, huh they really have no idea."

🐎 Try telling that to Samuel Langhorne Clemens. The ditty's a profound expression of the creative spirit. 🐎

For those that wish to know, Samuel was better known by his pen name, Mark Twain. We digress!

Ben passed the magnifying glass back to Sarah. She used it to examine the rings in the fallen log.

"It really does look like a spider's web, doesn't it!" said Ben, "You know... the way the rays spread out from the tree's centre!"

Sarah agreed and began to count the rings - from the outside in, "One... two... three..."

As Sarah counted, Ben and Julia observed the wooden figure clinging to the log. It had changed considerably from their last visit. The features were eroding.

"Sixty-one... sixty-two... sixty-three."

It now barely resembled a person.

"Ninety-eight... ninety-nine... one-hundred!"

"Which makes it one-hundred years old... fancy that, a whole century," claimed Ben.

"Oh my, hang on... what's this? There's something sparkling... here inside the star at the middle of the tree," announced Sarah.

"Not another... not again?" said Ben, contemplating the unlikely discovery of yet another gem. Sarah coaxed the object out of the heart of the tree. It fell into the palm of her hand.

"It's cold... I think it's frozen!"

"Let's see!" asked Julia. "It looks like a frozen raindrop," she said.

"Or a tear!" claimed Sarah.

"Woe, decry that Icy Tear," said Julia, quoting from the *Shadows* poem.

Malachi finished the verse.

🐾 Forget-me-not, the time is Near! 🐾

Julia took another photo.

"Well… I can't say I'm surprised!" said Ben.

"What should I do with it?" asked Sarah.

Malachi offered a view.

🐾 It's a frozen polar bear tear! 🐾

"You're the Earth Detective Sarah… you decide!"

"That's typical. The grown up's leave it to the kids to sort it all out… I'll just have to be a Secret Earth Detective?"

"Well… I guess so," suggested Ben.

"Yes! So cover your eyes… you're not allowed to look."

They did as she asked. Do you think Sarah kept the frozen teardrop or did she put it back? Her parents were undecided, but one thing was clear – the decision to return to the place where it all began had been eventful and worthwhile.

Q65: Have you ever wished you could fly?

When they returned home, Ben tucked the feather into a vent at the top of his computer screen.

"There… think of it as a symbol of peace!" he declared, "Peace between humans and nature. No more rape of the land, or pillaging of the soil and the air. We shall give the animals back their kingdom!"

🐾 Paradise regained! 🐾

"What kind of bird do you think it's from?" asked Julia, setting a warming cup of tea beside her husband.

"Probably from the wing of a barn owl, by looks of," he said, gently stroking the feather's barbs to make them uniform and glossy.

"I remember now how a barn owl flew right over me that night I found the locket!"

🐾 Ich Dien! 🐾

According to Caleb, the Prince of Wales' heraldic badge consisted of three white feathers behind a gold coronet and a ribbon beneath the coronet bears the motto 'Ich Dien', which was German for, 'I Serve'. We digress!

Sarah dashed into the study,
"Have you uploaded the pictures on to the computer yet?" she asked impatiently.
"Earth Detective… you're right on cue!" Ben replied.
The evidence appeared on screen, including images of the magic circle and the frozen tear. Ben had to tinker a little with the images as some were a bit dark, whilst others were out of focus.
Malachi wasn't troubled,
🐾 I'm a fabulous mascot, quite the Handsome Dan! 🐾
To Ben, the most striking thing about the pictures was the obvious difference with the Web-Log when compared to their previous visit. He flipped up the original images to allow a clear assessment of the changes.
"It's disappearing… day by day," he said.
"It was so amazing before. Once it's gone, we'll never get it back again," claimed Julia.
"Maybe that's what the frozen tear was… maybe Nature's sad!" said Sarah. "Can't we do anything to stop it?" she asked.
"What can you do? Erosion and decay it's just a part of nature," said Julia.
"Is it because we took what didn't belong to us?" asked Sarah, barely parting her lips.
"How do you mean?" replied her mother.
"Well… I've got the locket… and the ribbon!" said Sarah quite slowly. It was clear from the tone of her voice that she had no wish to surrender them. Julia sensed this and changed the subject,
"No… I'm sure that's not it. Hey, pity some of the better pictures are spoilt with these annoying glares!"

Ben enlarged the image of the magic circle.

🐎 Curiosity is the key that opens the door to learning! 🐎

Tiny balls of light appeared to be orbiting the circle.

"Hey… what do you make of these?" asked Ben.

"They're balls of light… they're spinning around the circle!" said Julia.

"See… I told you it was a magic circle!" claimed Sarah.

"Goodness… they look just like Christmas lights… this is so exciting, don't you think?"

"But this is impossible!"

"I think there are twelve of them," said Sarah.

"Yeah… I make it twelve too."

"They're growing bigger!" said Ben.

In defiance of all known laws of physics, the lights left the circle. Sarah shrieked in surprise.

"They're flying!" claimed Julia. "Oh, my, what are those things?"

"It's like a computer video game… but this is for real!" said Ben.

"They remind me of the stones… our marbles," claimed Sarah.

Ben slid back from the screen a trifle. His finger reached for the Escape Key.

Sarah opened the little wooden box.

"The marbles are gone… where are the stones?"

It was true - the stones were out of the box.

The balls of light whizzed about like a Catherine wheel mesmerising the viewers. Ben pressed the Escape Key; an act that seemed to catapult the balls of light from the computer screen into the Whittenbury's study. The lights hovered over the family's disbelieving heads, sparkling like stars. Although no music played, their presence inspired Julia and Ben to waltz, hand in hand, about the small study. In the surreal setting, a voice called to Sarah. She answered quite slowly,

"*Yes.*"

"Don't let me down!"

🐏 Lucy's in the sky with diamonds. 🐏

The lights clustered together into the shape of a rose.

"Close the box!"

Sarah did so. Everything ground to an abrupt halt: her parents immediately stopped dancing, the lights disappeared and the computer crashed. When Sarah re-opened the rider's box she found the marbles restored to their temporary home. The Whittenbury's were astounded. It was some while before the silence was broken.

Q66: Do you have a favourite flower?

The following day, Sarah continued with her detective work.

"I still can't believe what happened yesterday... in the study. Did we just imagine it?" she asked her father.

"No Sarah. It was real, I'm sure of it. I can still picture the balls of light swirling about us. Why I even dreamt about them last night."

"Did you? That's so strange... so did I!"

Sarah hugged her father.

"Can I look at the stones again... with the magnifying glass."

"Sure Sarah... go right ahead."

She opened the box and peered at the stones. She touched one or two. "They're still warm," she said, as she tried to bring them into focus.

"Say what you see... that's what the best detectives do," advised Julia as she entered the room.

"I think I can see little flowers inside them..."

"Little flowers... are your sure?" asked Julia.

"Yes Mum... here you have a look."

Julia took the glass.

"Oh... I think it's the reflection of the blue ribbon underneath... and yes, they do look like tiny flowers, don't they?"

"What kind of flowers, Julia?" asked Ben.

He turned off his computer and rose from his desk, with Malachi's walk in mind.

"My favourite… Forget-me-nots, I think. You know, tiny sky blue flowers with five petals… a yellow centre like the sun, with a small white star beneath it… radiating light into the blue petals."

"Wow… that's a lot of detail."

"Why… of course… 'Woe decry that Icy Tear, Forget-me-not the time is near,' I should have guessed."

"Don't tell me… it's the *Shadows* again!" said Ben.

Unperturbed, Julia dashed to the lounge and returned with the framed copy of her poem. Malachi was in pursuit. His tail wagged feverishly in anticipation of his daily exercise.

"It's all coming true… every word," insisted Julia.

Ben looked afresh at the poem.

Shadows

See the magic in the shadows
Standing next to Nature true,
Tiny seeds of hope o' sowing
Tiny wings of Aqua Blue.
Ah, be ours the task to stop it
Ours the task this Earth to keep.
With imagination blot it,
Woe decry industrial creep.
Woe decry that Icy Tear
"Forget-me-not," the Time is Near.

See the stones, pure o' glowing
Circles in a darkened cave,
Tiny seeds of hope are growing
Tiny hands for us to save.
Ah, be this our task to find it
So the Artist shall not weep.
With imagination stop it,
Woe decry complacency.
Woe decry that Icy Tear
"Forget-me-not," the Time Is Here.

Sarah had another thought,
"What about the survey, what does that say?"
"Excuse me!"
"The survey… question number twelve. What is it?"
"It's worth a look, I suppose."
Ben passed the poem back to Julia.
"Oh that's it…go ahead. Just ignore the poem."
"Mum!"
Ben unearthed the list of questions.

Q10. Have you ever seen a ghost?

Q11. Do you believe in justice?

Q12. Is our Earth enchanted?

Q13. Have you ever been mistaken for someone else?

Q14. Do you believe your stars?

"Look… there. Question 12 'Is our Earth enchanted?' said Sarah.
"I'd say!" claimed Ben.
🐾 There are more magical things on Earth than can ever be imagined – the fantastic is all around us but invisible to the naked eye. 🐾

170

Everything was starting to come together.

Have you heard of something called the 'Boiling Frog Syndrome'?

Please don't try this at home, but if you put a frog into a pot of boiling water it will naturally jump right out again.

But what happens if you place a frog into a pot of cold or lukewarm water and turn the heat up? At first the frog will swim about happily and may even grow to like the warmer water. Trouble is, if you don't throw him a life-line, he'll slowly boil to death!

Q67: Have you ever decorated a tree?

When we agreed to describe our collective experience, Sarah was really keen to set out part of the story herself. Her inspiration for the idea was Anne Frank, a remarkable teenage girl whose diary remains the most poignant story to emerge from World War II. As Sarah had a particular love for hanging decorations at Christmas, we happily agreed with her wish to write the answer to Question 67. This is what she had to say,

"I really love Christmas. It's not just because of the presents. I love it because of the decorations. I know that seems a bit strange. I like to decorate the tree most of all. Every year we buy some new ornaments for it. This year we bought one that looked like a polar bear. We also got a squirrel. Mum wanted a grey one, but the shop only had red!

Remember how much my Mum loves trees. Well, this year we bought a real tree. One that had been cut down! Now let me tell you we had some big arguments in the cottage about that. Last year, we bought a real tree in a pot, but it died. I know we've got our very own Goblin Tree right outside our front door, but it would be silly to decorate that, wouldn't it!

The thing is, a real tree smells great and looks fabulous. Anyway, Caleb told me that in northern Europe the fir tree is called the Paradise Tree. They think they have special powers that keep away witches, ghosts and evil spirits. Now that's cool!

Dad says that for every real tree they cut down in a managed tree farm they grow another and they provide a home to wildlife. You can recycle a real tree and mulch them. And, they reduce the amount of CO_2 in the air while they are growing. Dad thinks they are better than the plastic trees, as they just end up buried in the ground and don't rot and pollute the Earth. Caleb even told me that the man who set up *GreenPeace* once wrote, 'Whether you choose a cut or growing tree to enjoy this season, I believe the sensible environmentalist would opt for renewable over non-renewable every time.'

So we got a fresh cut Norway Spruce from an organic crop farm. Some of my friends at school think organic is a waste of time. I can't believe them! Dad says it's because they don't really understand what organic means. It means growing things naturally without putting lots of chemicals on things to make them look better or grow bigger or taste nasty to bugs.

When we brought the tree home my Mum said, "I feel so guilty. I really do."
I said, "Don't be Mum. If you want a tree at Christmas this is the best way. I think we should just say, 'thank you' to the tree."
So we put our lights on the tree and I hung up my polar bear too. We put him near the top of the tree, just under the angel.
"Maybe the angel will look out for him. What do you think?" Mum asked.
"Yeah… save, save, save the polar bear!" I screamed, as I jumped up and down with excitement at the sight of the decorated tree.

When I think about it now, I'm a bit too grown up to do things like that. I was going to take it out of the story, but Mum said to leave it in because it makes a point. I was also going to miss out the stuff about the lights because I like to switch things off to save energy. Yet my Mum said we only have the lights on for a few hours each evening and we do so much in other ways. I think she's right. As she says, we can't go back to living in a cave, can we?"

Q68: Does the Earth have a spirit?

The lines from the *Shadows* poem that appealed most to Ben were, "Ah, be ours the task to stop it. Ours the task this Earth to keep."
If Julia was right about the poem – that every word was becoming reality – then these two sentences captured the essence of his mission. So, early on a clear winter's morning, whilst frost lay on the ground, he chose to walk with Malachi to Philosopher's Point on the Ware Uplands. His head was awash with questions.

♥ How was it that a poem written many years ago could foretell events today?

♥ What did all the events and discoveries mean?

♥ Was a force unhidden writing the script?

When Ben reached the Point, he was surprised to find a few damp reels of hay remained from the autumn harvest. He placed a reassuring gloved hand upon one of the reels, as if to welcome an old friend. It felt secure enough to support him, so he climbed up and sat cushioned, with his legs dangling idly above the hard ground below.

"Don't let me down," he said, pondering the words heard by Sarah the day before last - when the balls of light emerged from the computer screen.

Ben closed his eyes to meditate a while, dog behaviour permitting. He dwelt on the Frozen Tear that Sarah had discovered. The timing was symbolic, for in the news was a report on how the Arctic ice was melting more rapidly than previously predicted. The polar bear's future was bleak. Something, somewhere had to give – but what and where?

When Ben opened his eyes, someone was sitting right beside him. Ben nearly leapt out of his skin!

"Caleb Hitch!" he stumbled, when he caught his breath.

"Ah… got you there, didn't I…"

"You can say that again… you came right out of the blue!"

"I saw you both asleep on the hay. Crept up I did… quiet as a mouse."

"Was I asleep?"

"I'd say! I heard you snoring from way back there."

"Ah… its just so nice to come out here and breathe the fresh air… watch the flock of wood pigeons circling overhead, and enjoy the sounds of nature – that is until the planes soar in overhead.

You know sometimes I envy those of yesteryear who may have come to this place... able to enjoy the tranquillity... without that," said Ben, as another plane flew overhead.

"Indeed... they're every few minutes now... though I love it here still, all the same. Shall I tell you why?"

Ben nodded.

"We're at the tip of the iceberg... the top of the triangle."

Caleb flagged his three thumbs.

"Now you've got me!"

"It's true... the Uplands Triangle runs all the way from here to Widford. From Widford to Wareside... and from Wareside to here again. It's exactly three miles from point to point... an equilateral triangle."

"I didn't know that."

"Have you heard of ley lines Ben?"

"What? Do you mean Earth lines?"

"Yes, some folk call them that. The last time I came here I realised that along each of the routes there's a curious mix of old buildings, places of worship and ancient trading routes."

"Really?"

"Ever since your series of curious events with time and space began, I started to wonder... maybe the triangle runs along ley lines!"

Ben nodded.

"The lines could run underground, with energy currents that ebb and flow with the tides and the lunar cycle... and are at their height at significant celestial events, such as when the hours of light and day match up, and at Halloween or the Feast of St Thomas."

"The Feast of who?" Ben asked.

"How's it go...'Thomas Day, Thomas Gray, the longest night, and the shortest day!' Yes that's it."

"What's the supposed effect of these lines?"

Caleb lifted his cap to scratch his head.

"Well, some say it allows for the appearance of spirits… manifestations… time travel."

"Come on… time travel!"

"Well portals in time… where axis cross."

"Is there any evidence for this?"

"Evidence… no of course not. Nothing of the kind… just speculation."

Malachi grumbled in his sleep,

🐕 Nothing ever becomes real until it is experienced. 🐕

Ben rubbed his hands.

"Gosh it's really cold this morning… I can't believe I fell asleep out here."

"Well you are at the apex… and all the activity has been focused around you… and your dog. Maybe you're recharging your batteries for the challenge ahead!"

"Really?"

"Apparently, if you sit or lie on a ley line for an extended period it can make you hyper-active or melodramatic… especially if you're sensitive to such things!"

"Like Julia! That would explain a great deal."

"But ley lines can be destructive too… just depends on the person."

"Okay!"

Ben jumped down from the hay. He tried to wake his dog. He was twitching and yelping in his sleep.

"He's in another world!"

Ben ruffled his dog's fur. Finally he stirred.

"C'mon Mali… home."

He stretched and got to his feet to walk with the men back in the direction of Keeper's Cottage.

"But the cottage isn't on an axis, is it?"

"No, but if you do the maths, it and the tree… what do you call it, the Goblin Tree? Well it's at a point directly beneath the apex that captures most of the deflected energy… so all kinds of everything

176

could happen there!"

"Anything goes?"

"Put it this way. If there's a secret hidden force with a conductor controlling everything… call it the Earth spirit… then Keeper's is at the heart of the action."

"Really?"

🐎 They stretched out strings of Gold and fastened them under the hall of the moon. 🐎

Which Caleb says is a line from a collection of old Norse poems preserved in the Icelandic medieval manuscript, Codex Regius. We digress!

The pair fell silent for a while, obviously thinking things through. Ben broke it,

"So… assuming the Earth was alive… had its own spirit as you say… and it was, for argument's sake, afraid, upset… even angry with humans for the disrespect we show it, and it wanted to get a message across, a warning even, then where better to do it than at Keeper's."

"Absolutely! And yet… there's something else I neglected to tell you."

The trio stopped in their tracks. Caleb looked about himself,

"If you follow the general direction of the ley lines outwards… one runs towards the famous ancient stone circles of Avebury and Stonehenge in Wiltshire, right the way through to mystic Cornwall. Another joins an old roman road to Cambridge which passes a place in Royston… called Royston Cave… then heads up towards Scandinavia."

"I've heard of that place… the Royston Cave! Someone else mentioned it recently and I vaguely remember going there before."

"It's amazing. I went there with Jonas not long after he lost his wife. It's a dome shaped cave with mysterious medieval carvings and symbols. It was only discovered by chance about 200 years ago."

🐎 No sign of the mythical treasure of Lady Roisia de Vere, wife of

Eudo Dapifer, steward to William the Conqueror. 🐎
"And the third?"
"Well that's a bit of an enigma… it stretches out for many a long mile! All the way down to the place most people think of as the Holy Land."
"Israel?"
Caleb nodded.
"But that's far too far to count," said Caleb.

Malachi grew restless in the shadow of the Goblin Tree and tugged at his lead. Ben resisted and continued his conversation,
"Do you know what's really strange?" asked Ben.
"What?"
"I've not seen sight or sound lately of Jonas on his jaunts to Widford Church."
"Ah … he's given up now because of his new job. He's off to London today… to visit some art galleries to pick up a few things for his boss!"
"Really… that sounds great. Good for him!"
"He said he could put it off no longer… that he was under strict instructions." Which leads us nicely into the next question!

Q69: Do you ever put off until tomorrow what you can do today?

Ben was really intrigued by Caleb's suggestion that the presence of the Ware Uplands Triangle might provide a gateway through time. At first, his head ruled out the idea all together, but a part of him wished it were so. In fact, his search for rational solutions to some of the things he had seen and heard, stirred his curiosity. The suggestion also prompted him into completing the list he started of the key events in the life of Charles Lamb. He'd reached 1810!

1811 – George III of England judged to be insane.

1812 – Elgin Marbles brought to England from Greece.

1814 – Napoleon abdicates and is banished to the Island of Elba.

1815 – Corn law passed in Britain, leading to poverty for many.

1819 – 'Peterloo' massacre in Manchester of demonstrators against Corn Law.

1820 – Albert Thorvaldsen's, 'The Lion of Lucerne,' sculpture.

1820 – Walter Scott's 'Ivanhoe' novel published.

1821 – Napoleon died.

1821 – Coronation of George IV and death of Queen Caroline of Brunswick.

1822 – First iron rail-road bridge built.

1823 – Death penalty for over 100 crimes abolished in Britain.

1825 – Beethoven's Symphony No 9, 'Ode to Joy' first performed in England. It's since been adopted as the theme music of the European Union.

1828 – The Duke of Wellington becomes Prime Minister.

1832 – New England Anti-Slavery Society founded.

1833 – Abolition of slavery in the British Empire.

1834 – William Morris born, craftsman and designer – he predicted the unsustainability of industrialisation.

The list completed, Ben shared it with his daughter.
"You do love your lists, don't you Dad," claimed Sarah.
"Well… as I keep saying, they may be a life saver one day!" smirked Ben.

"Let me see… I am the detective remember," insisted Sarah.

She reviewed the list and paused at 1821.

"Who was Queen Caroline?"

As Ben flipped up information about her on the internet, Malachi wandered into the room.

"Well you enjoy a fairy tale, don't you?"

"Dad, I'm eleven now!"

"Well, on her grave it says, 'Here lies Caroline, the injured Queen of England'."

"Why was she injured?"

🐎 Ah the spectre of the unfortunate 'Delicate Investigation'. 🐎

"I think it means the people of that time feel she was harshly treated. When her marriage to the King fell apart, she was banished from England. When she came back to England after her banishment there were riots. She fell ill on the day the King remarried and died three weeks after."

"Oh… my!"

"It also says her only child died shortly after birth."

"Oh, how sad. Is there a picture of her?" Sarah asked.

She studied the image for a while, then said,

"Dad… don't you think she looks a lot like Lucy!"

"Well, I guess so… remember, I've not actually seen this mysterious woman!"

Sarah sympathised with her father,

"Still, at least you both have white feathers. She's got a lovely one in her cap too."

"So she has… now that's what I call detective work!"

Q70: Do you like to look at the stars?

On the shortest day of the year, Ben joined Jonas and Caleb for a few drinks at the White Horse. It was a spontaneous thing; Ben met Jonas on the train returning from another journey into London, and they chose to stop off at the pub for a spontaneous pre-Christmas drink. Caleb – a regular patron – was already inside. They caught him performing one of his party tricks; he stood at the bar with a clear glass of water and dipped one of his thumbs into it. As the glass distorted its shape, Caleb quipped,

"Does my thumb look big in this?"

The barman laughed.

"Great isn't it. Just a trick of the eye… a distortion of light!"

Trouble was that a few drops of alcohol distorted Ben's mind too. It also freed up his inhibitions, such that he soon found himself sharing 'The Haymakers Survey' idea with his friends. The first impression was one of stunned silence, interrupted by the mechanical crunch of dry-roasted peanuts by a man at the table next to them who sat with his head buried in a broadsheet newspaper.

"Look, Ben, you know I like the idea of doing what we can to help, but this seems well… a bit out of the box! A survey to save the world?" said Caleb.

"I know… it sounds crazy. All I can say is that it came from inside, not up here," he said, pointing to his temple.

Jonas was more supportive, "It fits perfectly with what my boss wants!"

"Who is your boss, Jonas?" asked Caleb.

"To be honest, I don't know. I get my instructions by a third party."

"What's the name of the company?"

"Doesn't have a name."

"You're kidding, right!" said Ben.

"I know it's strange, but when I asked I was told, 'Why does everything have to have a name'; all that matters to me is that I'm doing something really worthwhile and I'm being paid for it."

"In what way's it worthwhile Jonas?"

"In the same way that the survey's worthwhile!" he replied cryptically.

It was a prompt for the man at the table next to them to put down his paper. Ben and his compatriots hadn't anticipated such a hostile reaction. It began thus,

"Listen to you guys! Personally, I don't know what all the fuss is about. The world's always changing temperature – warming up and cooling down. And I'm not convinced about the evidence of the so called scientists... it's misleading and biased, and not all scientists agree either. In fact, it might easily be a conspiracy – you know to help keep down the number of cars on the road. Nuts anyone..."

"Bill Darvill! How about that?" replied Ben, declining the offer. Caleb took one.

"But what if they're right?" asked Jonas.

"Okay...okay. So what if they are right. It's only a matter of time before something else wipes us out... remember the dinosaurs for goodness sake! Be it a nuclear war or a meteor from outer space, one way or another, we're doomed!"

"That's what we like to see, a go-getting, positive attitude," suggested Ben.

Bill smirked.

"That could be thousands of years off, millions even... yet human induced climate change, well its here today...now... and the worst of it is just a step away. We can smell it... almost touch it," said Ben.

Our Earth Champion hadn't imagined having to fight for his cause. He swirled the ice in his empty glass. It was melting. He took a tiny drop in his mouth.

"Fair enough, but what's the point in us bothering as other countries like China just go on making it a whole lot worse... I say if you can't beat 'em, join 'em! Let's face it anyway I'll be long dead before the shite really hits the fan... so I'm going to live it up!"

Caleb crossed his arms.

"Pity you're too young to remember the war!" he said.

"Which war's that then?" replied Bill, rubbing some grit from his eye.

"Why the big one, World War II! Rations, bombs on our door step. Do you know we had something then… it was called the war spirit! We'd have gone down without it. We need that spirit again today… turn off the lights, recycle…"

Darvill laughed.

"I don't see much point in it really. Too much trouble… takes too much time, with too little impact. Anyway scientists will sort it out before it gets much worse. Technology will be our salvation!"

He took out his mobile phone. He had no new messages.

"Do you think so?" asked Caleb.

"The same technology that's caused the problems in the first place… cars, planes… on we go."

"Well gentleman. Forgive me, but I must leave this most enjoyable conversation. Got to make hay whilst the sun shines!"

It was like a bolt sent direct to Ben's heart.

"Remember the spirit of unity across the world after the terrible tsunami that boxing day, well for me that proved the power to do public good and solve common problems is greater now than at any time in history. It's just a matter of harnessing that power. I for one am not going to sit back and let it all happen. I love this beautiful planet and its animals and I'm bloody sure I'll do all I can to preserve what's left!" he snapped.

"Oh, by publishing a survey and sitting in a pub drinking scotch! Right!"

Ben could feel a rage within him.

"And isn't that your car out there? Don't you burn oil to heat the cottage? You have your head in the clouds Ben Whittenbury."

Ben was furious. He got to his feet. His face flushed.

"Tiger, tiger, burning bright!" joked Darvill.

"How dare you!" replied Ben.

"Ah! Does the truth hurt, Earth Champion? That's what I've heard people call you round here. Huh, Earth Comedian more like!"

Ben wasn't a violent man by any means, but he found he'd clenched his fists.

Caleb intervened, "Just ignore him… he's not worth it!"

Bill Darvill tipped out the last of his nuts and held them in the palm of his hand.

"As I say… nuts!"

He tossed them into his mouth.

"Well, God forbid if you ever have children, for I hope your conscience is clear when you're old and grey and they turn to you and say. 'Grandad, why didn't you do more to stop it?' "

Bill Darvill munched on his nuts.

"Stop what? It's not going to be as bad as you make out. It never is… all the predictions of death and destruction. And whilst we're on the subject, is it me or has anyone else noticed the small fact that when it's sunny it's called global warming, and when it's not its called climate change?"

"Well… that may be so… and I can see the confusion but the truth is *Life on Earth* is at a crucial crossroads. The choices we make today are critical for the forests, oceans, rivers, wildlife and other things that we and future generations depend upon. When the last wild polar bear lies dying… I hope you'll be satisfied."

"I don't get all this fuss about the polar bear! If the ice is melting in the Arctic, why not ship them south to Antarctica instead!"

Jonas spoke, "Or to a greatly expanded Museum of Natural History… alongside the Dodo... and the countless others on the endangered list."

"So what if a few species die out… it's happened before and will happen again. Evolution will see to it that in a few million years we'll have new versions of the tiger or the polar bear running about."

Our Earth compatriots were astonished at Bill's casual comments. "It's like trying to convert a condemned man," said Caleb, as Ben watched Bill tip the last remnants of the nuts into his palm. They reminded Ben of grains of sand. Bill Darvill licked up every last granule.

"Maybe your survey will persuade me otherwise Ben... and if by some miracle the bizarre idea catches on, just think of all that energy people will use up answering the silly questions!" He raised a critical eyebrow at Ben. "Tell you what, just email me @turnuptheheat.com."

With that the cynical, apathetic man departed the White Horse, leaving the empty nuts wrapper behind. Jonas Fosbrooke grabbed it off the table and screwed it up in his fist, tight as it would go. He held on for so long it made his fist turn red.

"I'll add this to my collection," he announced, studying the words, *'Warning: This Product Contains Nuts.'*

Aware that Ben was ruffled, Caleb leant forward in his seat and placed a peanut on the table; the one Bill Darvill had given him. Caleb gestured to Ben to pick up his empty tumbler and use it to crush the nut. Ben did as he suggested and enjoyed the crunch as the nut broke into tiny pieces.

"Feel better?" Caleb asked.

Ben nodded.

"There... what did I tell you about the ley lines here? They can do all sorts to a man, good and bad!"

"That they do!"

"C'mon let me buy you another whisky... it's not known in Gaelic as the *Water of Life* for nothing!"

Ben and Jonas both accepted Caleb's offer, even though it meant a long cold walk home. They spoke of many things, including news from Caleb of Darvill's plans to redevelop the farm – they were far from Ben's liking. It encouraged him to drink more than he had planned.

When Ben finally left the White Horse he was greeted by a dusting of snow and a star-spangled sky. Acting irrationally because of the drink in his bloodstream, he chose to walk all the way home, rather than order a taxi. Caleb thought him crazy for suggesting it, and reminded him of the significance of the evening.

"Caleb, thanks but ghosts really don't trouble me… I've plenty of experience of them already, remember!"

"Here… take the empty peanuts packet, as a secret weapon!" said Jonas; for he was spending the night in one of the rooms above the pub. So, Ben left his car and wandered off into the night, empty peanut wrapper in hand, singing, ♫ Blue Moon. ♫

The moon followed Ben most of the way back to the cottage. It was behind him and cast a long unsteady shadow across the snowy white landscape, presenting the illusion of a giant of a man. Ben loved the sound of his footsteps, as they crunched the freshly fallen snow. Such solitary tranquillity was beautiful and rare in the modern world. Yet the cold began to bite, so he pulled the collar of his long wax cotton jacket up around his ears. He shivered as he passed the enclosure of the living white horse, Jim. A check of his repaired watch – 5 minutes to 12! Ben had hoped to reach home before midnight! From here on in, Ben wanted to describe what happened. Bear in mind that he had drunk a fair bit, so whether the alcohol had an effect on his memory – who knows. But this was his account:

"At first, when I heard the snort of a horse and the hard sound of hooves on frozen ground I assumed that Jim was unboxed and was coming across his field to greet me. Yet, as the horse drew near in a quickening pace, I knew otherwise. I spun on my feet – right next to the sign, 'PLEASE DO NOT FEED' to see the frightening image of a tormented dark horse bearing down on me. I was right in its path. I raised my arms in a desperate attempt to warn the rider and shield my eyes from death - yes I was convinced I would die. I felt a whoosh of icy air! I saw a flash of silver stars before my eyes; reflections of two horse-shoes that looked down on me as the horse rose-up and threw its rider to the ground. I was frozen still with fear and surprise. The horse regained its footing and paced about nervously, snorting and nodding its head, as if in discomfort. I tried to grab its reigns but the horse eluded me.

The fallen rider laid strewn face-up and motionless in the snow. Adrenalin stirred me into action. I ran over, fearing the worst. Yet he lived, or so I assumed. He uttered,

"Is it to end thus... me alone with the stars?"

I knelt beside him. Blood trickled from the back of his head. It turned the surrounding snow a shade of crimson.

"You, okay... you're bleeding!" I said.

The man slowly turned his head to look directly at me. It was a face I'm sure I'd seen somewhere before, but where? His eyes widened as if in disbelief,

"Captain Lewin! Ah, so it is all over!"

"Try not to move. Be still," I advised.

"Is Lucy with you? Pray, do say it is so! Let her come to me!" asked the wounded man.

"Lucy!"

"Aye, Richard. Lucy Ebbs... Do say it's so. Is she waiting?"

"Hay... hang on. You... no matter. Look you've had a bad fall. Though Heaven alone knows why you were out here at this hour, riding an' all."

"Please..."

The man could hardly speak. He was painfully pale and weak.

"Try not to move or talk. I'll get help."

I reached out to touch him, just a hand of reassurance.

"Woe decry the icy tear," he mumbled.

"Forget-me-not, the time is near!" I replied instinctively, as my hand passed directly through his image. A shiver of fear crept over me. What kind of devilment was this?

I got to my feet, wishing I'd heeded Caleb's advice not to venture home alone on such a night.

"This isn't real. I'm dreaming... it must be the drink."

"Drink Richard, Satan's best friend!"

I shook my head to try to awaken my senses. I cast a Hades like shadow over the man.

"Woe… all reason has deserted me in the name of love… and now my mind deserts me for I see and hear the dead! Pray, tell, was this Fanny's doing?"

I was speechless.

"I was too late… now I see no happy future at all."

I felt powerless to intervene.

Yet the mystery had hardly begun to unfold, for out from the deep of the night emerged another figure. She came from the direction of an ancient house on the hill, known fondly by Baker's End folk as the White House – which I have never really understood, given its actually painted a shade of green. I imagined temporarily that it might well be the return of the Lady in Grey, but that idea was quickly brushed aside. I can best describe the figure as a luminous impression. I think of her now as a kind of First Lady. The woman's features were blurred, like looking at someone through a frosted window. I doubt she saw me. She spoke as she walked, or might I say glided, across the light fall of snow,

"Charles Lamb, we have all failed you. Such a fate doesn't befit you…. a cruel blow for one who sacrificed so much."

Charles Lamb! I wondered could this be the man I had researched so thoroughly. If so, I felt as though I knew him better than my own brother! He was like a celebrity to me. I was in awe of his presence. Yet my actions had led to his downfall.

The woman knelt beside him.

"It was for Lucy," I heard him tell her, as the woman picked a rose up from the frozen ground; an iconic emblem of love.

"You romantic fool," she told him, "What good did it do you?"

"Yggdrasil, I implore… help us now!"

I guess some people might have fled this ghostly scene – for I'm certain these were apparitions – but I held no fear. I tried to intervene.

"It was my fault," I explained. "Please… I am so sorry. It happened so fast. There was nothing I could have done."

But, the First Lady ignored me. She stood and turned to face me with a questioning stare.

"Shall I go for help?" I asked; which, now I think of it, was a mighty odd thing to suggest to a spectre.

Oblivious to my presence, she cupped the head of the bloody rose in her hands and walked as if in a procession. The thorns of the rose's stem snagged on her clothing. She left a trail of drips of blood in her wake. She came directly at me. I held out my hand to stop her.

"Let me pass, I am your Queen," she whispered.

I recollect it so; she passed straight through me with a force, like pushing through water. I still find it had to accept, even in the cold sober light of day, but the sensation was real. It shall never escape me. I watched her disappear into the darkness.

I knew not which way to turn. All I remember now is that when I looked back at the fallen rider - Reader I shall be brave and call him Charles Lamb, for I believe it was him – there was but an impression in the snow. The man and his bloodstains had vanished before my very eyes, and there was no sign of the horse. In Charles' place was the scrunched dry-roasted peanuts wrapper, the letters WARNING looking up at me. The packaging slowly unfolded, before being caught on a breeze, to flutter into the night. I was alone with the elements – a silent white glistening landscape and a sudden appreciation that it was mightily cold. With all my strength I ran to the sanctuary of Keeper's Cottage, such that my chest hurt from inhaling the freezing air deep into my lungs. As I closed the door of the cottage behind me, I promised a vow of abstinence – never to drink again."

Q71: Is there something missing in your life?

When Ben woke the following morning he was laying on his back spread out like a starfish with his hands hung over either side of the bed. He sensed the spin of the room and thought of the Earth revolving at some 66,000 miles per hour as it orbited the sun, which was a strange thing to do in his condition. To think it was simply the force of gravity that tied him to the planet and the planet to the sun! It was as though the Earth hung by an invisible thread. For Ben, there had to be something more – part of the puzzle was missing. He heard a rustling noise beside him. Malachi was digging about the empty peanuts wrapper. Ben turned his head and saw the tips of his dog's ears. His head thumped.

"Malachi please… now's not a good time."

🐾 But it's five minutes to twelve and I'm still not in the picture! 🐾

Julia came into the room.

"Ah, finally. Do you have any idea what time it is?"

🐾 Time Is… Time Was… Time's Passed! 🐾

"Time… no, sorry… oh my, I feel ill… my head!"

Ben sat up slowly, supporting his brow.

Julia opened the curtains.

"I'm not surprised! What possessed you? It's so unlike you to drink."

Ben squinted to greet the day, "Just some things someone said, that's all."

"Oh…well Jonas just rang. He said you left the car at the White Horse. Good job too. But Ben, really I can't believe you managed to walk all the way back home in that condition… and it had been snowing," she passed her husband a warm drink.

"Snow!"

"Yes Ben snow... don't you remember? Why anything could have happened to you last night. Why didn't you just catch a cab or hitch a lift?"

"Julia, please not now."

Sarah put her head around the door,

"But at least he brought back the rose!" she said.

"The rose?" Ben took a sip of tea.

"Yes, the rose. It was on my dressing table this morning. You should have put it in some water though as it'll probably die now," replied Julia.

"It's so beautiful Daddy, you are very romantic sometimes! It's a rose fit for a Queen."

"But... it's..." Ben was about to offer an explanation, but it was easier to say, "Yes... I guess it is."

"We put it in my favourite vase," said Julia, recovering the nuts wrapper. She scrunched it tightly in her hands,

"Warning, this product contains nuts!" said Ben; puzzled as he was sure the wrapper had been taken by the wind.

"Sorry!" replied Julia.

"Just stating the blatantly obvious!" he replied.

Ben got out of bed and stumbled, puppet-like, into the bathroom. He felt as though someone was pulling his strings.

"So you touched it... the rose?" asked Ben.

"Well, no... Sarah did it, I think!"

"Just wondered!"

Q72: Are you a good time keeper?

🐈 Serius est quam credes. 🐈 That's Latin for, "It's later than you think."

Q73:Do you like nursery rhymes?

Ben spent an hour or so sat musing in the lounge. He drifted between piecing together the facts from last night and absorbing Bill Darvill's cutting remarks. It made for an odd cocktail. For guidance, he looked afresh at Stubbs' *Haymakers*. Besotted, he was unaware that Sarah crept in and sat beside him.

"Dad I have to tell you, you were talking to yourself," she said.

"Was I? I hope I didn't say anything I shouldn't have."

"What about my Christmas presents you mean?"

"Christmas!"

"Yes… it's only a few days away now."

"Well… we made a list didn't we? Anyway, your Mum sees to that mostly."

"But will a mobile phone work out here?"

"Maybe… still they got by without phones… and they look pretty happy to me," claimed Ben with his mind on the painting.

Sarah wanted to take over from here. This is how she remembered it,

"My Dad was acting really seriously. Mum says it's always the same when he's had a drink or two. I can't believe he almost forgot that Christmas was just a few days away and how could he have left the car at the pub? When I'm old enough to drive, I won't do things like that.

Well, the thing is Mum told me that Dad told her that he thinks he saw Charles Lamb on the way home last night. He also said the rose belonged to Lucy and that he wanted her to have it. The weird thing is that Mum believes Dad. She hasn't said so exactly, but I can tell it in her voice. I think it was the rose that did it. My Dad doesn't lie, so I believe him too. I so wish Lucy would come to me again. I've not seen her in such a long time. Maybe I'm too old now! I'm not really a child anymore. That's why when Dad was feeling a bit confused about everything and staring at that silly painting again, I decided to behave a bit like a child.

"Daddy... I think we should call her Little Bo Peep, don't you?"
He looked very surprised.

"You know, the woman from the nursery rhyme," I said.

"Why? Do you think she looks like her?"

"She does Daddy, she really does. Look she's wearing sky blue and white and she's got a stick like hers too."

"I guess she does, doesn't she. It's just well... you thinking about nursery rhymes at your age!"

"Well, Mum says not to grow up too fast, so I'm slowing down a bit... w.a.t.c.h... m.e... s.l.o.w... d.o.w.n!" I said, as I spoke in a deep voice, like a robot.

"Good for you Sarah!"

"Only thing is, she's not wearing a blue ribbon," I said.

"Should she be?"

"Well, she is the best, isn't she," I claimed.

Now this is where I got really childish. I remembered Lucy liked nursery rhymes. So, I wrapped my hands about her locket and began to sing,

> ♫ Little Bo Peep has lost her sheep,
> and doesn't know where to find them.
> Leave them alone and they'll come home,
> wagging their tails behind them. ♫

I think it worked for a while – well in cheering up my grumpy old Dad. And I do so want that mobile phone! All my friends at school have one and I do feel like I'm missing out."

As Sarah suggested, her show of childish enthusiasm cheered Ben for a short while, but he soon fell into a sombre mood again. A sense of helplessness and humility had unsettled his ambitious and scheming head. There seemed no escape for the human race from the climate chaos. How could his lone voice be heard?

🐏 Benjamin Whittenbury the term, 'haymaker' has two meanings you know – you have to find your sucker punch! Stand up and be counted Ben – this world needs you. 🐏

Q74: Do you like puzzles?

Ben Whittenbury was totally puzzled by everything that had taken place these last few months. Last night's events were the proverbial icing and cherry on a multi-layered cake of bewilderment. What was Ben supposed to do in response to all the signs and experiences? He figured that retracing his steps would be a good start – the new day might provide some answers. So, confident he'd sobered up, he strolled back to the White Horse to collect his car, pausing beside the 'PLEASE DO NOT FEED' sign to help refresh his memory.

"It's always five to twelve!" said a voice inside his head. But that was the extent of his new understanding. At least he was confident that he hadn't imagined the whole affair; how he wished someone else had been with him to witness it.

Still, having collected his car, Ben's mind refocused when he heard news on the radio about the living Earth that seriously troubled him. Re-settled in the lounge at Keeper's he drew up another list.

> *Climate Change – the ticking bomb* 💣
>
> ❤ *It's official – 2006 was the hottest year for the UK on record, and by some distance too! An extraordinary year with several records broken.*

> *There's likely to be worse to follow, with extreme 'phenomenal' weather on the cards, including flooding, drought and blistering heat!*
>
> ♥ *The extent of sea-level rises due to global warming may be worse than first thought, but this was difficult to predict. All that melting ice in a warming world had to go somewhere? More rain and flooding perhaps?*
>
> ♥ *By the time Sarah was 40 years old all-year round sea ice in the Arctic may be lost forever. That's a nightmare for the polar bear!*

Ben rubbed the head of his attentive dog.

"I don't know what to do for the best any more, my friend... any ideas?"

🐈 The trouble, Ben, is that all you do is talk. What were your first words to our audience, 'Now is the time for action.' How many more times do I have to remind you about that picture? 🐈

"I need a sign Malachi - something to guide me!"

At which point his daughter came into the room with the playing card that Malachi had toyed with. It was the Three of Hearts, with the words, '*Thank You, Ben*'.

"What about this? If you did that, you can do anything. So, can we play cards again... we have a full set!"

Ben accepted the offer. They chose Blackjack. Sarah shuffled the pack as best she could and dealt Ben's hand. His cards were the Jack of Clubs and the Eight of Spades.

"Stick or Twist?" asked Sarah.

"Twist!" replied Ben expecting to 'Bust.'

Lo and behold, he drew the Three of Hearts, which took him to twenty-one.

🐈 Vingt - et - un. 🐈

"Stick!" he announced, believing the card was haunting him.
Sarah took her turn,
"Twist!"
She drew the Joker.
"Hey… that's not right!"
They removed the Jokers from the pack and resumed the game. So, Ben - our Earth Champion - played cards with his daughter – the Earth Detective - whilst humans all over the industrialised world carried on regardless, with millions of carbon footprints fossilising the globe for future generations to weep over - a frozen tear for each step taken. Something had to give. A mere mortal, Ben could use a little help.

Q75: Have you ever put on a show?

The Whittenbury's were clearly a family of game players for no sooner were they through with cards, did they turn to Scrabble. It was Julia's idea. She was attracted to it because the word's definition included, 'write down quickly without much attention.' It also meant, 'grope about frantically.' Ben was doing plenty of both lately, so Julia thought it a natural progression. However, nobody was prepared for what she was about to uncover. If she was a performer on the stage, her introduction by a man in a top-hat would have been,

"Ladies and gentleman, children of the world, allow us to introduce the mysterious… the curious… the beautiful, Mrs Julia Whittenbury… our very own Lady of Shalott and Earth Artiste!"

Okay you already know all about her, but that's the kind of announcement she deserved for the trick she was about to perform. Here goes. Pay attention now. Hold on to your hats, for this will astound you.

"Fancy a game of Scrabble?" she asked.

"But I never win, unless you let me," said Sarah, trumping her father.

"Everybody's got to learn sometime," he replied.

Julia set the board out.

"C'mon, I'll make it fun… promise. It's a game of chance and skill… a craze the world over."

Sarah agreed.

"Okay then… but only if Dixie can watch!"

At which point, she dashed upstairs to find her hamster and returned with him in his exercise ball.

"I bet I get the Q without a U," said Ben as they picked their starter tiles.

They played. Ben was wrong about the tiles for Sarah got the Q and U and spelt the word QUEEN on a triple letter score, which made her happy.

"See… and you said you couldn't play," said Julia.

"It's not so hard – you just have to look at the letters and see what they say – it's funny isn't it how the same letters can spell different words, like EARTH and HEART, they're the same letters aren't they."

"Ah the pupil has become the teacher," said Ben proudly.

"It's called an anagram, isn't it?"

🐎 Ars Magna. 🐎 which is Latin for 'Great Art'.

"No Malachi… you're scaring Dixie. Keep away!" said Sarah as she swept all the letters from the board and hunted down, A,A,E,E,E,H,H,K,R,R,M,S,S,T,U,V,Y and Y. She lined them up in the middle of the board, and put the last three letters in the centre a couple of rows beneath.

"What are you doing?" asked Ben.

"Come on Dad, you're looking… but you can't see?"

Ben studied the letters, adopting Rodin's *The Thinker* pose once more.

"You are so slow. Do hurry up," she teased.

"Hey, the letter scores add up to 39, which is my age!" said Ben.

"Oh there's so much more to this than meets the eye," replied Julia, obviously preoccupied.

"No, no, no!" said Sarah cheekily, peeping up at Ben's beloved picture; he saw her do it.

"The Haymakers... eh hang on... The Haymakers Survey!" he cried excitedly. Julia interrupted his enthusiasm,

"Clever, but do you want to see something truly amazing?" she asked.

Husband and daughter nodded. Dixie stopped spinning in his ball. Malachi sat attentive with ears pricked up.

Julia lifted the K from the centre square to reveal the star underneath. She placed the K above the other letters and added E and Y from the line = KEY.

"Julia what's this?" Ben asked.

Fixed in her mind were the words of the woman in her dream - Lucy. The woman she'd painted and the one whose image looked down at them as Little Bo Peep from Stubbs' *Haymakers*.

'Remember Julia you are the key, do not break faith,' she'd been advised in her dream. At the time she knew not what to do. She did now.

♥ She lifted the U from the end of the line and replaced it with an H.

♥ She took a T,E,A and R from the line to form the word EARTH.

♥ She put an M and a Y together = MY, and set them next to the EARTH.

♥ She took an E,V,A and S to make the word SAVE.

♥ She took the last four letters, U, H, S and R and made RUSH.

The message was as clear as the light of day. An anagram of 'The Haymakers Survey' was:

KEY
'RUSH SAVE MY EARTH'

Are you clapping yet? I can't hear you! Louder! See it's incredible what a little creativity can achieve isn't it. So, are you ready to play? Do you want to be part of the dream, involved in the magic? To take part in this one chance to help preserve what should be? What are you waiting for, GO DO IT NOW?

> **Q76: Are you going to take action now to save our world?**

The discovery stirred the Whitttenbury's into action; they were through with hesitation. Ben was at his computer quicker than you could say 'Haymaker', furiously developing the material for the website hosting the survey. Beneath the owl's feather tucked into a vent on his computer screen, his fingers scrabbled the keyboard. The opening bars of Beethoven's Fifth played in his mind as the website www.thehaymakerssurvey.com was at last becoming a reality. Picking up where he left off, he added many more questions based on his journey of discovery. He also tried to be clever by adding a couple as after thoughts - Q51a and Q62a.

🐱 ♪ He's 'Walking in the Air' ♪ 🐱

As in the magical song written by Howard Blake and used in the delightful animation, *The Snowman,* which involved a visionary trip to the Arctic.

So, excited and triumphant, he sat back in his chair to review his list.

The Haymakers Survey

Q1. *Do you believe your life has a purpose?*

Q2. *Are you an art lover?*

Q3. *Do you have a good imagination?*

Q4. *Have you ever wanted to stop the clock?*

Q5. *Do you believe in fate?*

Q6. *Do you believe in fairy tales?*

Q7. *Have you ever dreamed of being a champion?*

Q8. *Do you crave a better life?*

Q9. *Do you feel in control of your life?*

Q10. *Have you ever seen a ghost?*

Q11. *Do you believe in justice?*

Q12. *Is our Earth enchanted?*

Q13. *Have you ever been mistaken for someone else?*

Q14. *Do you believe your stars?*

Q15. *Do you sometimes fear the worst?*

Q16. *Have you ever had a psychic experience?*

Q17. *Can you speak another language?*

Q18. *Do you let your heart rule your head?*

Q19. Do you love hedgehogs?

Q20. Have your eyes ever deceived you?

Q21. Have you ever hugged a tree?

Q22. Do you love our Earth?

Q23. Do you believe all the laws of physics?

Q24. Do you get enough time to yourself?

Q25. Do you believe in fairies?

Q26. Do you take poetry seriously?

Q27. Do you like gardening?

Q28. Have you ever lived in poverty?

Q29. Could you live without machines?

Q30. Did you ever watch the rain on your window?

Q31. Are you a charitable neighbour?

Q32. Are you afraid of the dark?

Q33. Do you believe in life after death?

Q34. Have you ever restored something?

Q35. Do you trust your instincts?

Q36. Should a good life cost the Earth?

Q37. Do you know how to have fun?

Q38. Have you built a house of cards?

Q39. Do you believe in magic?

Q40. Can you play a musical instrument?

Q41. Do you like surprises?

Q42. Do you enjoy drawing?

Q43. Do you believe in happy endings?

Q44. Is there anything worse than a fly buzzing around your room at night when you're trying to sleep?

Q45. Are you good at marbles?

Q46. Do you value a good education?

Q47. Do you know your history?

Q48. Have you ever played Solitaire?

Q49. Do you ever think about the old days?

Q50. Do you miss someone you love?

Q51. Have you ever taken part in a protest?

Q51a. How many people does it take to fill up the Earth?

Q52. Do you believe in miracles?

Q53. Do you like to keep warm?

Q54. Do you enjoy a bit of a mystery?

Q55. Do you believe in truth?

Q56. Do you believe rules are there to be broken?

Q57. Have you ever spied on anyone?

Q58. Do things happen for a reason?

Q59. Do you like surprises?

Q60. Have you ever experienced déjà vu?

Q61. Have you ever worn fancy dress?

Q62. Have you ever helped the poor?

Q62a. Is life logical?

Q63. Do you like the way you look?

Q64. Do you know whether or not you are sometimes indecisive?

Q65. Have you ever wished you could fly?

Q66. Do you have a favourite flower?

Q67. Have you ever decorated a tree?

Q68. Does the Earth have a spirit?

Q69. Do you ever procrastinate?

Q70. Do you like to look at the stars?

Q71. Is there something missing in your life?

Q72. Are you a good time keeper?

Q73. Do you like nursery rhymes?

Q74. Do you like puzzles?

Q75. Have you ever put on a show?

Q76. Are you going to take action now to save our world?

Whilst Ben finalised the list of questions, Sarah dashed about Keeper's gathering together all the little gifts they'd picked up during their mini-adventure. You could call them clues, signs, or just coincidences. Anyhow, to help her father focus, Sarah set out the discoveries on the computer desk. It was quite a bounty. In time, we came to call it:

Julia's Set

❤ One heart-shaped golden locket.

❤ 12 magic stones.

❤ A rose.

❤ The Three of Hearts, with the words '*Thank You, Ben.*'

♥ Ben's watch, stuck again at 'five minutes to twelve.'

♥ An old penny, to represent the coins they found in the garden.

♥ An old handkerchief, not the one that belonged to Charles Lamb as Malachi had taken off with that!

♥ Julia's drawings of Jim and the dice.

♥ A frozen tear.

♥ Ben's fife.

♥ Ben's military jacket.

♥ An empty packet of dry-roasted peanuts.

Sarah also put Ben's polar bear costume, complete with the 'SAVE ME' sign, next to the desk – but as it wasn't really a discovery it didn't merit inclusion in Julia's Set.

"There… what do you think Sarah?" Ben asked, as he hit the Enter key after typing 'Save our World?'

"I can't find the ribbon, that's what I think," she replied.

"Oh that'll be the Aqua Fairy I guess," said Julia, as she joined them in the study, "Which tells me you should add my Grandmother's poem, *Shadows* to the list."

"Oh not the fairy again… come on, the ribbon's got to be somewhere!" she urged.

"Never mind any of that, you still haven't said what you think of the list," said Ben.

"Oh, very well, let me see," said Sarah. She ran her eyes down the list.

"Why have you got two questions the same? Look 'Do you like surprises?' It's there twice."

"Well spotted!" Ben went to hit the Delete key.

"No!" said Julia sharply. "It works really well as it is… look, the question after the second 'Do you like surprises?' is 'Have you ever experienced déjà vu?' When I read it I thought, hang on I'm sure we've had that question before and ran my eyes over the list again, just to make sure, so it works really well as it is. Let's leave it in as a bit of fun," she suggested.

"I think that's great," said Sarah.

She rested her elbows on the desk and held her chin in her hands.

"So you've got Q51a and Q62a, what's that about?"

"Ah, that's me being clever, you see. Most people are led by logic – things must always add up, which if you think about it doesn't really make sense. So I added one in earlier as Q51a, which is a really important question anyway, and then put Q62a in to make people understand why I did it. Look at the question – 'Is life logical?' well," said her father.

"Illogical Captain," joked Julia.

"I don't understand what number 69 means!" said Sarah, missing the humour completely.

Ben raised an eyebrow.

"Procrastinate – that means put off until tomorrow what you can do today."

"So why don't we just say that then?"

Ben pondered for a minute.

"Okay… I think that's right, let's change it," he suggested.

"Sounds good to me!" said Julia.

"Okay – Hey Dad, you've only got two of my questions. Weren't you listening to me?" asked Sarah.

"Which questions? When?"

"At the show in Ware - the Emperor invited me to let him have three questions to include in his survey. I said,

- ❤ Have you ever helped the poor?

- ❤ Do you have a favourite flower?

- ❤ Have you ever searched for buried treasure?

That's it. Those were my questions. Question 62 is about the poor, Question 66 is about the flower, but there's nothing about searching for buried treasure!" she said.

"Okay, alright. I'll make that Question 77," said Ben and he added it to the list.

"And what about Mum, doesn't she get to choose some questions?" Ben raised an enquiring eyebrow at his wife.

"I already did," she replied.

"Oh… which ones?" asked Sarah.

"All of them!" she insisted, with a knowing smile.

Q77: Do you get bored easily?

"It's a bit of an odd number though, 77 questions," Julia said.

"Let's add, 'What's happened to the blue ribbon?'" suggested Sarah.

"No, we can't put that in. It has to be a closed question… one with a Yes or No answer," said Ben.

"Like, 'How many people does it take to fill up the Earth'? " claimed Sarah, drawing attention to the error.

"Ah… no that's a trick question!" he replied.

"But Dad the big thing is this is a bit… well, a bit boring!"

"A bit boring?"

"Yes… just a list of questions. Can't we make it more fun?"

Julia agreed, "Boredom makes people do all kinds of things, like going to the shops and buying stuff they don't really need or driving their car just to get out of the house."

🐂 Sometimes he sits and thinks, and sometimes he just sits. 🐂

So they discussed how to liven up the site and came up with ideas about the things they'd found:

❤   Linking images from modern culture and famous works of art to each of the questions.

❤   An area on a video site devoted to the survey, with a suitable video for every question –
www.youtube.com/polarbearchampion.

❤   Links to fun and games.

❤   A directory of organisations relevant to 'The Haymakers Survey'.

❤   Personalised certificates for people to download.

❤   Keeping a 'Watch' on world events; and so on.

It was abundantly clear to Ben that,
"We've a lot to do… and we still have an odd number of questions!"
"We can add in 'Do you get bored easily?' " said Julia.
"So that's 78 questions."
"Oh Dad can my question by the last one?"
"Of course Sarah."
"Because of the poem, I'd like one about shadows, 'Have you ever looked into the shadows?' " pleaded Julia.
"Okay that can be question 78."
"No 79!"
"No 78… because Sarah's question's now 79!"
"Now I'm getting confused!"

Q78: Do you want to be part of the picture?

Malachi prodded Ben with his nose.
🐾 Pick me! I have a voice too. 🐾
"I think he wants us to choose a question for him. He doesn't want to be left out, do you baby bear?" suggested Julia.
"Of course… how can we do a survey about issues like climate change, deforestation and poaching without a question on behalf of the animal kingdom? What say you Malachi?" asked Ben.

"Here let me help," said Julia. She crouched down to Malachi's eye level and looked deep into his chocolate brown eyes.

"What say you Malachi?"

🐎 At last the people are listening. 🐎

"I've got it, 'Do you want to be part of the picture?' that's what he wants us to ask."

"Eh! What does that mean, 'part of the picture' I'm confused," said Sarah.

"It means - being involved... and doing your bit to help.

"I count!" replied Sarah, nodding.

"Okay that's Question 79 sorted. Which means we have 80 closed questions. Does that sound good to you?"

"Sounds great to me."

"Me too."

🐎 Let's ask the world in 80 ways! 🐎

So the final questions were...

The Haymakers Survey (continued)

.....

Q74. Do you like puzzles?

Q75. Have you ever put on a show?

Q76. Is now the time for action to save our world?

Q77. Do you get bored easily?

Q78. Do you want to be part of the picture?

Q79. Have you ever looked into the shadows?

Q80. Have you ever searched for buried treasure?

Star Question: What happened to the Blue Ribbon?

The questions completed, Ben was finally ready to shave off his moustache. When he looked at himself afresh in the mirror, Mr Whittenbury of Keeper's Cottage, Wareside, Hertfordshire believed he was born again. Recollecting the ordeal in the snow, Ben asked his reflection,

"What would Charles Lamb make of me now? Would I still be mistaken for... what was his name... oh yes, Captain Lewin?"

Q79: Have you ever looked into the shadows?

The Whittenbury's soon realised that setting up a website to run a survey was a complicated business and they would need professional help. All the same, there was a real sense of excitement that the idea was beginning to take shape. Certainly, Sarah's idea of gathering up the little things that stirred their imagination had led to some suggestions on how to make the site more interesting and fun. However, once the euphoria about it faded, Julia became anxious about the consequences. She didn't want people flooding the area to see for themselves where everything had taken place. She wanted to protect her family too – Sarah was still young and impressionable, but there was a story to tell and the world needed to listen. So, she needed some kind of reassurance that everything would be fine.

For guidance, she turned to her Grandmother's poem, *Shadows*! In the lounge, beneath Stubbs' *Haymakers*, she began to re-read it:
"See the magic in the shadows, standing next to Nature true…"
"There's something more," she sensed.
"Tiny hands for us to save. Ah, be this our task to find it!"
Maybe the solution lay in a child's mind.
"SARAH!" she called.
Her daughter and Malachi rushed down the stairs. They found Julia stood ahead of the picture, poem in hand.
"Not that painting again… you and Dad are mad for it!"

A digression - Caleb believed she had a point – let's see! What was it with that painting? Let's be honest it's hardly a masterpiece of the class of Leonardo De Vinci or Claude Monet, is it? We have a humble work, often criticised because it's like a rhythmic ballet, rather than real life. It shows labours as graceful and without real effort. Okay, the figures are carefully organised in pyramid form, but that's common in most works. So what was it that so intrigued the Whittenbury's? Digression over!

"I just think there's something in this picture that we haven't seen yet."

🐕 Yes… I'm not in it. 🐕

"I think we need to look at it through the eyes of a child."

"But I'm nearly grown up now!"

Sarah folded her arms.

"Oh course you are… but you're the youngest all the same."

Sarah swung her elbows from side to side, and remembered her plan to be more childlike again in the hope of seeing Lucy once more,

🐕 In the eye of imagination, the child is father of the man and mother of the woman. 🐕

"Okay, I'll do it… I'll take a look."

"Just think of it as a game, honey."

"Okay then… let's link hands and sing 'Ring a Ring O' Roses first'."

We think that's nursery rhyme number three!

"What?"

"I just think it will help us to see... what we can't see!"

"Right, child's play it is then, but I haven't done this in many a year."

Round in circles they went,

♫ Ring a ring o'roses,
A pocket full of poses,
Ah-tisoo, Ah-tisoo,
We all fall down. ♫

Again, but this time they danced in the other direction.

"Now… let's take a look Mummy."

"How cute, you called me Mummy again! Now, where shall we look?"

"Why in the shadows of course?"

We suggest you try this at home too if you like? Go back to the picture of the *Haymakers* again for yet another look. You're going to love this. Shall we get some candles – three probably we think – to place on our proverbial cake so you can blow them out in your mind when you see what the Whittenbury's finally saw?

"Look Mum, next to Lucy… under the man on top of the hay - the one who looks like Dad… and next to the man with his back to us."

"I can't see anything?"

Sarah giggled. Come on Julia, a little more creativity please; just one last drop?

"No Mum. Open your eyes… the man *is* the shadow. He's been playing hide and seek, and I saw him first!"

Sarah jumped up and down with her old childish enthusiasm.

"Oh my… I see it… I see it too!"

Reader, can you see him yet - the top-hat man in silhouette at the heart of the painting? Funny that, as we began our account of events with Ben looking at a silhouette of a man on the equinox!

♥ *Abracadabra! So you've finally seen me – the lengths I have to go to just to make you sit up and take notice.*

♥ *A Magician always saves his best tricks until last - well until the interval in this case, which is coming up straight after we've had the next question.*

Q80: Have you ever searched for buried treasure?

Whilst all this was going on, Ben Whittenbury was in his study looking out at Bill Darvill scanning the barren fields of Noblin Green. Metal detector in hand and dog running amok at his feet, his neighbour was clearly seeking ancient treasure. Every now and then he'd pause to dig the soil in the hope of finding gold, only to be sadly disappointed. The frustrated man had just tossed his spade aside when Ben heard, "I see it... I see it too!" shrieked by his wife.

"What does she see?" he asked aloud as he got to his feet.

Rather clumsily, he hurried downstairs into the lounge to find his daughter triumphant.

"What does she see?" he asked again.

Ben was most humbled when he realised that all along a top-hat man in silhouette had been right before his very eyes.

"Shadows!" he remarked and rubbed his chin.

Julia winked at her husband, before being led by the hand by Sarah into the garden, muttering, "What now?"

Ben was left alone with his thoughts.

"A magician... that's what you are, pulling a stunt like that on us." A whisper, like the wind, crept up on him.

"We've all been waiting... so very long. How we suffer," he heard.

"I'm sorry... forgive us, we know not what we do!" replied Ben sub-consciously. Unclear on his purpose, he added,

"Yet, in the bleak mid-winter we have set free hope for a new beginning. It's not the Holy Grail, but the people have the facts... they've seen the magic, now it's up to them. It's not for us to tell people what to do."

Malachi, rushed into the room,

🐎 You can lead a horse to water, but you can't make it drink. 🐎

"And it's all down to you my friend. Clever boy... c'mon, let's see what they're up to outside."

Ben took a deep breath, then followed his dog out of the back door. Emerging from the shadow of the Goblin Tree, his daughter ran towards him.

"We've found the ribbon... come see, it's tied to a branch near the bottom of the Goblin Tree!"

"Really!"

"Yes... come see," said Sarah. She led Ben to the tree. "But the thing is... it's not blue anymore... it's purple."

"Purple?"

"Yes... when you were looking at the *Haymakers*, I saw the ribbon... flapping like a bird's wing in the tree!"

"Right!"

"Yes, I saw it through the small window," she said brightly.

"A window of opportunity!"

"And when Mum and I came out to get it, we saw the squirrel. That's why Jonas is digging."

Benjamin Michael Whittenbury, Earth Champion, was lost for words. He just stood and watched the activity that took place about him. Sarah explained,

"The squirrel disappeared into a burrow, right here under the ribbon. But it's stuck... under the ground. It was crying... we heard it crying."

"A squirrel, *crying*?"

"I heard it too... like a human voice," said Jonas.

"It said, 'We've all been waiting... so very long. How we suffer,' " claimed Julia.

"Which is silly as squirrels can't speak," added Sarah.

"So we're digging!" said Jonas.

"Well… well… well!" uttered Ben, as they dug.

🐀 Exactly, the Well of Wyrd lies at the base of Yggdrasil. 🐀

For, in Norse legend, every deed we do is fed into the well. The water from the well is brought up and poured upon Yggdrasil by the sisters of Wyrd, so the deeds of the past, represent the present and influence the future.

Bill Darvill was walking on by. His frustrated footsteps crunched on stones nestled on the bridleway. He paused, to listen in on the activity taking place on the other side of the natural fence. Legs astride, the metal detector swung too and fro in his hands like a hypnotic pendulum. His dog, Toby, poked his snout under the hedgerow that bordered the cottage. The pair witnessed the heavy clunk as Jonas' spade struck something buried within the soil. They also heard Sarah's excited shriek,

"Yes! We've found the treasure!"

"This could be good," said Ben, as the daring squirrel suddenly emerged from hiding to dash to the top of the Goblin Tree and survey those on the ground.

Bill Darvill stopped swinging his pendulum, whilst Toby saw Sarah jump up and down. Excited by the squirrel's escape and their own discovery, she waved the purple ribbon she'd freed from the branches of the Goblin Tree. Toby's eyes followed the ribbon's path. His envious owner, urged him back.

"Hey you," he said, as Malachi came bounding over. Toby wriggled his way back to his owner's feet. He looked up at Darvill's face. For a second or two, he saw the famous face of Edvard Munch's 'Scream'.

🐀 Open your heart, you've got to change. There's still a chance for us. 🐀

Not that any of this concerned the archaeologists beneath the Goblin Tree.

"Keep it together," insisted Ben, as though he was orchestrating things. Whilst Jonas cleared the soil from the top of the find, Ben looked up at the branches in honour. He was in awe of its diversity – in this moment of glory its flamboyance seemed to capture the whole spectrum of life, for dew on the leaves caught in the sun to reveal every colour of the rainbow in its branches.

Malachi ran back to the others,

🐏 One day this will make sense. 🐏

He watched as Ben, Julia, Jonas and Sarah each helped to raise the find from the ground.

🐏 Multorum minibus magnum levatur onus. 🐏 which means, 'By the hands of many a great load is lightened.'

This, as a simple wooden box about a foot square revealed itself to the people of the 21st Century. It was laid ceremoniously on the ground. Last touches of soil were brushed aside, to allow rays of light to penetrate its surface once more. Etched into the top of the box were three wooden hearts.

"The Three of Hearts!" cried Sarah.

"Thank you," said a voice on the wind. We all heard it!

Q80a Do you keep a diary?

Before resuming 'business as usual', Bill Darvill watched from afar as Sarah led the amateur archaeologists back inside Keeper's Cottage. She encouraged Ben, Julia and Jonas to place the box on the kitchen table, then climbed onto one of its chairs to ensure she had a bird's-eye view. The adults gathered around her – a circle of old, familiar faces.

"What are you waiting for? Go on… open it," suggested Ben. Sarah's fingertips wrapped around the lip of the lid and revealed the contents. It was one of those seminal moments – a find with the potential to change our common destiny. However, Sarah didn't see much cause to celebrate, "Oh no, it's just a dusty old book! Where are the sparkling diamonds?"

She folded her arms in disappointment and was about to climb down from the chair, when Jonas said,

"Hey you… maybe it's a magic book… maybe it contains a secret so powerful and special that someone chose to hide it away?"

"Maybe it was our destiny to find it?" added Ben.

Julia ran her fingers across the book's leather surface, almost in anticipation of one of her visions. Nothing came to her.

Sarah toyed with the purple ribbon. She wound it around her index finger, as if to point the way.

"I like magic and secrets. Can I be the first… to turn the page… please may I?"

Before the adults could agree, she lifted the front cover to glance at the beautifully written words inside.

*'Little Journal of my Foolish Passions, by Charles Lamb,
Artist, Poet and Romantic!'*

She looked at her father. The chemistry between them was electric.

"It's Charles' diary," said Ben.

"Why would he want to bury his diary?" asked Jonas.

🐎 We cannot teach people anything, we can only help them discover it within themselves! 🐎

"It's so we can discover its secrets – his secrets," claimed Julia.

"Like a time capsule!" explained Ben.

"You know what this means? We need another question in our survey," claimed Sarah.

"Yes that's true. Question 80a should be, 'Do you keep a diary?' " replied Ben.

🐎 The game is done. I've won, I've won! 🐎

So the absolute final questions were…

The Haymakers Survey (continued)

Q76. Is now the time for action to save our world?

Q77. Do you get bored easily?

Q78. Do you want to be part of the picture?

Q79. Have you ever looked into the shadows?

Q80. Have you ever searched for buried treasure?

Q80a. Do you keep a diary?

Star Question: What happened to the Blue Ribbon?

So that's it. Our account of how we found Charles Lamb's journal, assuming it to be genuine, of course. Maybe we just have overactive imaginations! Whatever the truth, there's a deep magic running through the whole experience for sure. So, let's introduce the journal itself! We trust you enjoy it as much as we did and that you come away with the same sense of awe and astonishment.

Oh, we ought to say that Caleb has added a few footnotes to the journal – to translate the Latin and clarify a few historical points. Reader, we apologise if any of you find his comments patronising or annoying. We just felt it would be helpful to some.

Read on…

Part Two

Love

'Little Journal
of
My Foolish Passions'

By
Charles Lamb.

Artist, Poet
and
Romantic.

1 May 1822

Let the world know I am writing it. Vanity I accept, but then what value art if produced for its own sake? Has not William Blake denounced the dark Satanic Mills of materialism? I join him and call for the building of Jerusalem, the city of Art, in our green and pleasant land! I take up arms to meet the challenge.

Such is the depth of the romantic in me that I am compelled to put my words to paper. In time, let these pages provide indisputable evidence of my enduring passion for the three things dearest to my heart – Art, Love and Nature!

♥ Art, let it express all that we feel, experience and believe in, and capture the very essence of life.

♥ Love, that most splendid and cherished of gifts! May it outweigh any false idols – move aside wealth, ambition, status and power!

♥ Nature, may mankind respect and live in harmony with all creation. To see, value and embrace its wonder for all eternity.

What better education than to embrace the fundamental reasons for life. Let me hold true to my word. May generation after generation rejoice in my words! Let time judge me, as I hope to capture the herald of a New Age.

3 May 1822

Heaven alone must know what possessed me on the day before last – perhaps there is something in the water at Nimley Bourne stream; such a pretty and lively brook. Still, what use is a journal if it cannot be a canvas for my thoughts and feelings, one and all? I shall reveal everything to you – my fears, my hopes, my ambitions, my dreams. I shall do my utmost to write regularly and be true and disciplined in my approach.

I feel this is my duty – my purpose in life, beyond my Essays - to record for future generations how the times are changing. For I fear it so – more than the madness. Oh horrors, the madness. Let me not be pompous - I shall write plainly and with fun and joy wherever I can, for the teller of a mirthful tale has latitude allowed him. Man is not a creature of pure reason; he must have his senses delightfully appealed to. I can be content with less than absolute truth - oh whimsical soul am I. But I make a solemn promise – no deed of mine shall shame thee.

4 May 1822

What use is a play with no stage or performers? Allow me to enlighten you. Let me begin with my heart's desire. It is only good manners. Her name is Lucy Ebbs - my Celia – the most divine girl I'll ever meet. To put her name to paper is such joy. There is nothing half as sweet in life as love's young dream. She is most delightful. Oh, I have shared the company of others who equally attract a man's eye and know of those of a noble station with the benefits of a classical education, but she rises above them. Her simplicity, innocence and gentle purity are the great attractions. In this she is unsurpassed. Oh, she is prone to light fancy, but that is a blessing – without it she would lack colour and vitality. For me, she is nature personified. Ageless and timeless, she breathes new life into all things. I sigh at her countenance divine, for the world would be a desolate and barren place without her.

Her presence uplifted my spirit at Philosopher's Point, as we rejoiced in the arrival of spring. We looked upon a landscape rich in fresh shades of green - a scene still tingling from the recent Maypole celebrations. I longed to gather up the garlands and posies hung from the pole at Wareside village green, and lay a path of flowers for my maiden's safe passage to Noblin Green.

"Lucy, the language of flowers is my gift to you. I bring Canterbury bells for our awakening and snowdrops for hope."

Her reply teased me,

"Oh Charles, flowers are as youth - they wither, fade and die."

"Not for you my sweet," I called. "I give you a rose of eternal love."

She danced away from me towards the Uplands peak. I imagined the Maypole petals cascading around her to map her way.

"And what of forget-me-not?" she asked, knowing the flower represents true love and constancy.

"Speak not of it for you imply separation and farewell." I cried, before expressing a ditty Captain Lewin taught me,

> ♪ And the lady fair of the knight so true,
> Aye remembered his hapless lot:
> And she cherished the flower of brilliant hue,
> And braided her hair with the blossoms blue.
> And she called it, 'Forget-me-not'. ♪

"Why Charles, you entertainer! You enchant and flatter me so," she said, settling on the lush grass to tuck her knees up and rest her chin upon them.

"Richly deserved, oh heart's desire! Have you no comprehension of how you inspire the artist?" I asked, as I sat beside her and began to unpack and organise my materials. She watched with growing impatience.

"Then be inspired Charles - create. Hurry now, for time is against us. Produce the picture before the moment is lost."

At her bequest, I sketched the landscape before us, to capture some part of old Hertfordshire before the creep of industrialisation – those dark Satanic Mills – stole it away forever. Before me, was the perfect setting for Lucy - serene, peaceful and idyllic! So, I sketched her. Such majesty was she. My aching heart's distraction. I lowered my drawings and sighed.

"Charles, what is it?" she asked.

I offered no reply, as I looked into her eyes - the windows to her soul.

"Tell me, do," she whispered.

I sensed a wonder beyond my imagination and asked,

"Is there something about you that you choose not to share? For I see it in your eyes Lucy. What magic lies within? How you enrich me. Lucy, I love you beyond common."

"So strange are the ways of man... for you know our love cannot be," she replied, before lying back on the grass to look skyward.

Allow me to explain. Lucy is a farmer's daughter, whilst I am of nobility in the keeping of Lady Katharine at Blakesware Manor. The division is an issue for some, but it matters not one jot to me.

"Say it not. I must give voice to my feelings. It is beyond the will of man to choose to whom we surrender our hearts," I told her.

I moved to lie beside her. She was silent.

"I want no other. Can love no other."

I turned my head towards her.

"But you are learned with great things expected, whilst I am a simple woman of the Earth," she replied.

"No Lucy, I won't have it. Of all the things you are, simple is not one of them. Let me speak plainly, you have shown me love beyond my expectation, and deepened my appreciation of art and nature. What better lessons are there in life?"

"Charles – the poet in you speaks. The truth is, you know me to be whimsical, seemingly heartless, " she said coldly, closing her eyes to the sun.

"Let me in Lucy, please. I implore you," I requested.

"I am already part of you – part of everything - I can be no more," she insisted. This was Lucy – enigmatic, mysterious… and speaker of riddles.

To convince her of my devotion, I searched the heavens for inspiration. Clouds drifted serenely from west to east, from whence it came; an ambassador of love.

"Lucy, open your eyes," I enthused.

"Look directly above us – in the zenith. There, the cloud, do you see it?" I asked.

In the heavens was an ancient symbol of beauty and love - a rose in the shape of a cloud, as though sent to us as a gift from the Greek goddess, Aphrodite herself.

"Mother Nature speaks," she said.

"Why... it's the rose I vowed to thee, to honour our eternal love," I claimed.

Lucy smiled. I kissed her.

"Hark, they call in celebration," I cried, as a peel of bells rang out from the distant St John's church, Widford.

"May this rose endure?" I called, with my arms outstretched.

"Do you wish it so, Charles?" she said, as we watched the rose travel across the sky.

"I do."

Two little words and three little letters which sang in my heart.

"Then it shall be," she claimed, but the shape of the cloud was soon lost.

Sadly, in our exuberance, we neglected to heed a gathering storm. Dark shadows spread across the land. The wind developed pace, causing trees to sway as a prelude to fury. The thunder came in ahead of the rain, with drum rolls that rippled across the undulating fields. Songbirds reacted to its approach with warning calls, shifting from vocal vantage points to seek shelter. The rain fell large and heavy. We were unprepared for the deluge. I was furious with myself for this part of Hertfordshire was infamous for its storms and electrical activity, as though Thor himself had claimed the region as his own.

The suddenness of the storm led to the elements tarnishing some of my paintings, leaving impressions of what had gone before. Lucy said it was a style that might one day be popular, which amused me. She had that way about her – an art of saying something to make light of misgivings.

"In like a lion, out like a lamb," she cried, despite the tempest.

"Come, let us get to cover before the Gods strike us down," I insisted.

7 May 1822

It's approaching the witching-hour, and I'm writing covertly in my room by candlelight. Why I should feel the need for such clandestine action at my age and status bemuses me, but it is so. My anxiety began after the storm the other evening. I had done the gentlemanly thing and escorted Lucy to Keeper's Cottage. Twas dishonourable of me I accept, but, on her return, I hid from view. Now, all I see is the fury on Fanny Ebbs' face at the bedraggled Lucy and the monologue,

"Look at you, soaked to the skin. What kind of man allows his beloved to be caught so? One with his artistic head in the clouds! A man in danger of losing his mind, that's who. You know his history… of his family's history. Be warned, he'll be the death of you. Now, Lucy, Lucy… hold back those tears. Don't waste your time on him – a painter, a poet, I ask thee? Open your eyes Lucy Ebbs to the world today - one of labour and industry. Go find someone with more purpose who can defend you. Seek a man of uniform - yes a soldier - one who will put your life and needs above his own! They abound now Napoleon's defeated."

Cruel words, for I would gladly surrender my life for hers.

I digress from why I need to write in secret. The military were firmly in my mind as I journeyed home to Blakesware. I travelled on foot as dusk approached, a mode of transport that's becoming increasingly perilous, as we seem on the verge of a lawless society. The end of the Napoleonic wars has brought peace to our shores, but our green and pleasant land is awash with many thousands of discharged sailors and soldiers with idle hands for the Devil's entertainment.

The madness and sad demise of our beloved King George and the extravagance of his opulent successor has added to the instability. Rumours are rife that the Government is on the verge of losing control. None of this explains why I was followed. I'm no radical, so what would the King's men want from me?

10 May 1822

In the wake of the French Revolution and the death of Napoleon, local speculation has intensified that spies serving on behalf of King George IV are in the vicinity. Unlikely in my opinion, but I shall take no undue risks with my writing, to guard against any accusations of treason.

15 May 1882

My aunt, Lady Katharine Plumer is, undoubtedly, a remarkable woman with a strong-will and imperious manner, embodied in the redness of her hair. She is also a gracious lady of charity and kindness, characteristics that she inherited as a member of one of Hertfordshire's most influential families. Over dinner, she plainly reminded me of the virtues of her late husband, John Plumer. I warn thee of the tedium,

"Charles, I often wish you more ambitious. John was extremely eager for you to aspire to achieve… and to do his work!" She rehearsed his title; one I knew so well,

"John Plumer, Deputy Lieutenant of the County, Colonel of the County Militia and Justice of the Quorum."

Which means he was judged able to sit on committee or senior board!

"But Aunt Katharine, I have no desire for status or power," I told her.

"So you say, persisting, despite all that has befallen you, with indulging in youthful fantasy. Will your days of learning at Christ's Hospital come to nothing? Your indifference will lead you to ruin Charles – causing you to enter the 'work-a-day' world. A mere clerk! Come Charles; is that the fate that befits you – a man of your learning? No, I refuse to endorse it. Call me stubborn or callous, if you will, but a man such as you should look to the future. There is so much at stake, and so much to lose. We need to keep the mind clear and the Devil at bay. You have the potential to become a great man, as your Uncle before you, and should so behave."

She looked at me with a sternness that afflicted her whenever she was serious or intense. My response was audacious,

"My position! I need little reminder of my circumstance. I am mere flesh and blood! Contented with little, yet wishing for more. Besides I sense you speak on John's behalf, to help implement his dying wish, so you say, that I should adopt his approach to life… to see his work through to completion. I sense, my dear beloved aunt, that you may have a different perspective, as would my mother, were she with us today. Ah, the plague of insanity - how it lingers!"

Lady Katharine leaned towards me across the dining table, "Charles, enough of such talk. May I be blunt! The spirit of revolution has been exorcised. The wheel turns. I fear it cannot be stopped."

17 May 1822

Today, Lucy asked me about the history of Blakesware Manor. I'll rehearse my answer. I wish I were able to say that the Manor owed its name to the great William Blake - an illuminating and visionary poet and artist of our time - or that he had a close association to it. Alas, the Manor and estate were conceived in the 13th Century by Nicholas le Blake - a man who infamously incurred the wrath of Ware's manorial lord, Richard de Clobbenhale, after failing to arrive at Calais, as promised, to help defend it from the French. It has since passed through a number of owners, but we are in gratitude to Thomas Leventhorp in the 1660s for much of the fine old mansion we have today, set in extensive formal gardens.

So, Blakesware has stood for 500 years in one form or another, immune to fire, tempest, war and riot. Its seclusion is one reason for its longevity. Another is the claim that it initially housed members of the Knights Templar. And, pray, they claim I indulge in fantasy and idealism!

Lucy was curious about my affections for Blakesware. I find it a place that seems to inspire in one form or another. It lives and breathes romance and nostalgia, albeit in a shadow of some tragedy. I spent the happiest days of my childhood at the Manor, under the care and guidance of Lady Katharine and the tireless dignified housekeeper, Mrs Field.

Modest by comparison with other country houses in Hertfordshire, such as Hatfield or Knebworth, it has a sense of intimacy. No more so than in the courtyard, secluded and protected; and the scene, over the centuries, of much arrival and departure. The courtyard is the heart of the Manor and often resounds to cries of greeting, commands or shouted conversation between the upper windows and the cobbled floor, or to the noise of hounds returning from a hunt.

The courtyard is reached through the arched entrance tower and leads to the Great Hall. The hall is a spacious room, with a roof that invites the eye skyward and, remarkably, has survived from the earliest days of the house. It is here that the soul of the Manor resides. When used for entertaining, tables are placed crossways at the far end for family, as few as we are today, and lengthways down the hall for lesser guests of which there are often many.

The Great Hall leads, on the right, to the noble Marble Hall, with its mosaic pavements and twelve Caesars - stately busts in marble. It also serves as a concert hall, hosting a grand piano. The Hall has an enchanting staircase which leads to the upper floor. The newel post of the staircase is carved with a lion's head, the crest of the Clobbenhale family. It is said to commemorate the banishment of Nicholas de Blake. Folklore, I would wager.

To the left is the Justice Hall, with its large chair of authority - the Justice Chair! It's the pride of Captain Richard Lewin KB. He claims it's made from the hollowed-out trunk of a sacred tree from Scandinavia. It has runic[1] carvings around its base. Richard, and others, claim the Chair induces sound judgement when sat upon. I have my reservations and for good reason. Richard has sought its wisdom often, so why does he persist with military service at this rare time of peace? I have tried the Chair for myself on many occasions in the Captain's absence, without any discernable effect on my conscience or behaviour. It's said, too, that the Chair has a darker side to its nature and is thus feared as the terror of luckless poacher or self-forgotten maiden. A mere myth perhaps to help extol the virtues of good! I digress.

Aside from the sleeping chambers, mine included, the upper floor is host to the Drawing Room, Library and Gallery. In their own way, each has served to feed my imagination and character. The Drawing Room is fondly known as the print room as it captures an emerging vogue with a remarkable selection of borders set on an Indian background. It has an air of exoticism. It is here where guests often retire after dining to gather about the hearth and philosophise, politicise or make idle gossip, to share their worldly experiences, or converse about London, Bath or life at dreary Temple Bar.

The Library is a further extension of the mind, with a rich collection of books and artefacts, many collected by my late Uncle John, and others by Captain Lewin.

I save my favourite until last - the Gallery. This has been my inspiration and is home to some major paintings. It is a classical world that has grown from sophisticated imports – but currently hosts works by acclaimed British artists, including George Stubbs, Richard Westall and Joseph Mallord William Turner - God bless their creative souls!

Lucy is more familiar with the grounds of Blakesware Manor, with its bustling stables - home to impressive stallions and mares - boisterous kennels, bristling with hounds and the often used coach house. Beyond these, we've shared many a happy hour in the gentile pleasure gardens, rising backwards from the Manor in triple terraces, leading to the 'wilderness' and Uncle John's lion head statue, partly buried beneath the ceaseless creep of Ivy.

Despite my relatively comfortable existence, I keep a sense of perspective, for the Manor is within the shadow of St John's church at Widford. The church steeple is a focal point from several of the Manor's tapestried bedrooms, including the haunted room of the celebrated family friend, Sarah Battle (now with God). I can see the steeple from my room, as I scribe. Although not a hardened religious man, I am reminded of my mortality and feel fortunate to be blest by the good Lord.

25 May 1822

It's only fair that I should tell you more about Lucy's abode. Keeper's Cottage and the surrounding farms are so very different to Blakesware Manor. The relationship of the country house to the countryside is more complex than that of farmhouses or cottages.

We who live in the country house own the land rather than farm it. The Nimley Bourne and Noblin Green farms are Blakesware Manor's home farms, and provide a supply of fresh food to the house rather than seek to make a profit. So, in a way, Lucy is at the heart of all that maintains us.

I wish more shared my love for the country. I know that nothing is labelled or displayed, but I see danger in prolonged exile from the countryside. I fear for those who are increasingly leaving the land for a new life, as they risk becoming detached from what exists outside the city. Curse the ugly creep of industrialisation - the growth of towns and cities, driven by the power of steam and the factories and railways that have emerged. Where will it end? Once all the unspoilt landscape is devoured or disfigured in grey and smog. And where does all that heat go? Aren't we at risk of warming our world! Hail the Luddites![2] I digress, as ever.

Today – the hottest of the year so far – Lucy led me on a tour of the farm. Most wonderful are the sights and sounds of spring. Leghorns and Aylesburys busy about our feet, with chicks and ducklings in tow. Majestic pigs pacing slowly about their sty, with amusing noisy piglets for company. One of the wise benevolent creatures held my eye for a few seconds, as though to plead for charity. A powerful Shire stood laden with a cart of churns. It was idyllic. I was a little envious of their simplicity and the direct access to nature. I said so.

"Don't be misled Charles, life on the land is often hard and rigorous. Just look at the weather-beaten faces of the workfolk. They tell their own story."

I looked; some were bleary eyed, due to heavy drinking from the night before.

"Pray, I suggest they ought to address you as Mistress, for do they not assume you and I be courting and will shortly marry?"

"You let your imagination rule you Charles."

"Why thank you. I'll take that as a compliment! Lucy, I wonder, ought I to apologise to Fanny for my misjudgement?" I asked, recalling the soaking Lucy received at my expense.

"Charles you should not be drawn by temptation, by false hope."

"I should talk to her."

"Charles, please show restraint. I have many who seek to claim me."

How could she be so cruel?

"No... I will hear no more of this."

"She insists it's her duty."

"Her duty?"

"She claims she has a duty of care."

Such a private discourse in a public place was inappropriate, but the grunt of pigs and the clamour within the farmyard disguised our words.

"I must talk with her. Give me the chance to explain how I feel,"
I clasped her hands.

"Marry me," I asked, with all sincerity.

"Why Charles, do you know who made thee?" she replied, releasing her hands from mine to dance, fleetingly from me.

"Is that a yes?" I asked.

"Oh Charles... my Earth needs me," she cried, as she skipped away towards the cottage, as if to honour a maternal call.

"I'll forget-the-not!" I called, as I pursued her regardless.

26 May 1822

What does Lucy mean by saying, "I have many who seek to claim me?" Is this why I cannot sleep? Do her words make me fearful and encourage the nightmares? I thought they were at an end. Maybe the Manor induces them? How I endure! Mrs Battle, deal me another hand!

28 May 1822

I have turned my thoughts to another matter - a name for my journal. I'm inclined to call you 'Gaia', after the goddess of the Earth. The Greek poet Hesiod[3] related that Gaia arose from the primeval Chaos, and so it is with my journal. My hypothesis is that the Earth is alive and I am its defender! Another wild fantasy – but I am prone to them. I have my head in the clouds.

1 June 1822

They say marriage in June is lucky. Good to the man and happy to the maid. Foolish Roman superstition!

6 June 1822

Knave of Hearts, Queen of Hearts, King of Hearts, which made me victorious in yet another game of Patience. What charm and solace cards bring to one sentenced to solitude. It serves to fill idle hours now that Sarah Battle is no longer with me. She taught me a variety of versions of the game. In many ways I sympathise with the royal prisoners of France. Patience is, of course, the literal translation of Solitaire. They say Napoleon Bonaparte often played Solitaire during his banishment on St Helena. It was said to have sharpened his wits, developed his judgement and helped with his powers of concentration. Mrs Battle told me the game would help ward off unsociable mental flaccidity. Alas, she and I can no longer play Whist together, so I resort to Patience.

When I play, I am determined to win. Cards are war, in disguise of sport. The odds of winning depend on chance and serious thought. It requires the self-discipline of being honest with oneself – I never mislead or disrespect the cards. I play with the hand I am dealt. When I play alone, I sense that she is with me still, guiding my hand with her tender presence. Why is it that the women I love are often denied me? Maybe I am cursed? Perhaps I should encourage the Captain to bring the mystic Mlle Lenormand[4] to his vision of a gathering of minds. Her divination system is said to have predicted the rise and fall of the French leader. Perhaps she could tell me my fate?

18 June 1822

The Battle of Waterloo lasted one day. It was the only time Wellington and Napoleon met in battle and both are certain to be remembered for it. Captain Lewin was awarded 'The Most Honourable Order of the Bath,' for his part in the battle, and often recalled it with vivid detail. Tens of thousands on both sides met their final hour in that legendary battle, and Richard feared he would be amongst them - to give his life whilst honouring his country. He has said many times that a soldier's real enemy is the fear of death.

Seven years have passed since the Treaty of Vienna closed the era of Anglo-French wars. In the shadow of the salutary fear of revolution, let us hope that the Vienna settlement provides a lasting framework to resolve disputes without the need for war. After a century of rivalry, the gentle sound of peace rings warmly on this anniversary. Napoleon was supposed to be a liberator but the bloodshed and upheaval he brought to every corner of Europe will remain in infamy. Let us hope we have seen the last of such megalomania and personal vanity.

The fervour to celebrate Waterloo has diminished this year, given the former Emperor's death, perhaps because people once claimed he was immortal. Even today I overheard people speculating in the White Horse at Wareside that Napoleon's power was supernatural. It is claimed he has the elixir of life and under the false shroud of death and masterly disguise has made his way to England to enact revenge on those that caused his downfall. Some Uplanders even claim to have seen him labouring on a local farm or that he is colluding with the highwayman Sixteen-String Jack.[5] Incredulous nonsense or enchanting fantasy?

When Captain Lewin returns from duty he will immediately quell the ridiculous rumours that may stem from an ulterior motive. It may be a clandestine move to stir potential uprising. We do not want a Peterloo[6] in Hertfordshire. Sedition or treason must be swiftly dealt with. Captain Lewin, do not tarry. His presence here commands total respect and authority. He is a giant among men.

21 June 1822

I was up before day break to greet the rising sun of a mid-summer dawn. It appeared, in the mist, as a swollen crimson ball suspended on the horizon. As with the ancients before me, I was overawed by the mystical significance of the event - the longest day. Sadly, it seems, there's no equivalent to Stonehenge in the Uplands at which to congregate. However, there has recently developed a fashion amongst some locals to frequent the Nimley Bourne stream on the solstice dawn, in anticipation of more than celestial pleasure. Conventional folklore has it that fairies appear on mid-summer night, but Lucy claims Shakespeare is mistaken. Mid-summer's night? Such sweet tales my friend. No, dear Bard, mid-summer's dawn, and the Nimley Bourne is rumoured to be the place to see the little angels.

I went alone to the Bourne and was the first to arrive. I found a comfortable and secluded place from which to observe. I was close to the bank and able to rest against the base of a sturdy tree. About me was a carpet of buttercups, beginning to open their buds to the morning sun. The Bourne can sometimes fall dry at this time of year, but sufficient rainfall in the spring ensured a gentle flow. Swathes of light broke through the trees, to sparkle and dance on the meandering stream. As if to celebrate, birdsong was all about me. It was tranquil and hypnotic. I was dreamy, having risen much earlier than usual. I removed my hat and placed it behind my head, to cushion the harshness of the tree. I closed my eyes to listen to the wondrous sounds of nature.

I awoke with a start; to voices descending to the stream. From where I sat, I could observe the arrivals in secret. Oh heart's joy! Triumphant dawn - at the rear of the procession was Lucy. Adorable Lucy. I let the others pass, then called to her.
"Lucy, it's me... Charles."
"Charles! Where are you?" she replied.
"I'm hiding."
"Why are you hiding?" she asked, trying her best to find me.
"So I might, bechance, see the fairies!"
"You believe... you came... I hoped you would."
"Of course, Forget-me-not," I claimed, emerging from my hiding place.

We chose to let the others move away, before we set about searching amid the shadows for fairies – our childhood revisited!
"How now, spirit, wither wander you?" I asked, mimicking Robin Goodfellow[7].
"Sh! Charles!" she placed her finger across her lips.
"Oberon, Titania[8]," I teased.
"Charles, please, fairies take offence if a mortal tries to speak to them," she whispered.
So we explored in silence, about the edge of the stream, close to where I'd slept. Until Lucy said, "Try looking for circles."
"Circles! What kind of circles?" I asked.
"Why, fairy rings Charles... where fairies love to dance."
"They love to dance!" I thought about the flickering lights I'd seen about the stream. I looked back to where I had slept. Nearby, a

curious arc was etched into the Earth.

"Try not to look with your eyes," she advised.

"But... how else can I look?"

"With your heart... kind of dreamy and unfocused."

"Unfocused?"

"And listen. Fairies so love to sing, but it sounds all muffled to mortals, and is often mistaken for birdsong."

"Birdsong?"

"Yes Charles, birdsong. But, be warned, the birdsong and the dancing can send you to sleep! Do you feel dreamy?"

"Possibly."

"Try not to fall asleep; you see fairies can be so mischievous when you're asleep."

"Fear not, I'm ready for the little people!" I promised, stretching and punching the air comically, as if a jester.

"Charles, you do amuse me."

"I'm just enthusiastic," I responded.

"Well, it matters little if we see them, for they'll wipe the memory from our mind within seconds," she insisted.

Gaia, I must confess, I am now most curious. What began as a frivolity has led me to question my senses. Once the dawn had passed, I remembered my hat. I'd left it by the stream, where I'd slept, yet it was nowhere to be seen. In its place was a playing card - the Three of Hearts - in an identical design to Sarah Battle's pack. Once I returned to the Manor, my suspicions were confirmed; the card was hers. As for my hat, it was under my pillow – as though the tooth fairy had put it there. What sorcery took place whilst I slept?

28 June 1822

We have ideal weather for haymaking. The grass has been cut and will be carried on the fourth day. The routine produces perfect hay that will scent the London streets – all the way to Temple - if borne on the wind from Hertfordshire's fields. I have experienced it myself when required in London at this time of year. The scent of haying in Hertfordshire was often a calling for me to return to my pastoral heritage. Today I witnessed it for myself. It was thirsty work just watching. When one of the labourers told me, "Bless me, you could sweat a pint out of ye every hour, leastways every etch hour a mowing of grass," I had to agree. I watched him respond to the lead mower, a ploughman known as the lord, who led an orchestra of scythes as they swept through heavy swathes of grass, which was then raked into rows.

There was some anxiety amongst the workers, for rumours were rife that the threshing had uncovered a corpse in a field in a neighbouring farm. Gossip has it that he met his death suspiciously, at the hands of a highwayman. Others speculate that he simply became intoxicated during the summer solstice celebrations and stumbled awkwardly to his death. Regardless, I shiver when I recollect that evening last month, when I was followed. Did I evade a similar fate by sheer good fortune?

I recognised many of those engaged in the work, but amongst the old familiar faces were a few new ones, probably recruits from the April fair in Ware. They have a way in Hertfordshire of sizing up folk and putting them in their proper class. I feel I am no different. People say that as a rule Herts. people are level-headed folk without much imagination or sense of beauty. They say they are unemotional, quiet and contented, seldom wanting to roam from home. Generalisations - and I am an obvious exception. However, we know the way to be happy is to enjoy the little things in life, and in the Uplands they are ever close to hand. This is infectious and furiners, as the locals describe them, soon see the sense in our ways.

Mrs Field, the plump benevolent housekeeper at Blakesware Manor, suggested to me that some of the unknown faces mowing in the fields may be inmates from the Parish workhouse hired out as labourers.

"Outdoor relief, is what they call it," she told me, as we settled before the unlit fire in the Great Hall at Blakesware. Mrs Field's cherub rounded features looked quite comical under harsh candlelight. She had an endearing smile, but it served to highlight the creep of age on her pale skin. She was seldom seen - as now - without a cream scarf, in which she wrapped her dark almost black hair.

"The inmates do very little work, for scarce any go there who are capable, besides the children. Heavens, do you know, I heard they brought a babe to the workhouse a week or so back. Bless its heart."

"How dreadful. And they say it's an easy life."

"Some do say it is," she said shaking her head.

"What will become of the child?" I asked.

"I dare to wonder."

"The place itself must strike terror into the hearts of those poor souls who enter it," I suggested.

"Some say its home to lunatics also." She paused appreciating the sensitivity of her remarks.

"Well, it's hard to comprehend why, in these modern times, the needs of the mentally ill and the poor are so inadequately met. I know Captain Lewin could justify the expense in meeting their needs."

"We already do enough, well beyond our common duty," she said.

"I owe it to mother," I insisted, recalling her fate. At this, an enthused Lady Katharine joined us.

"Charles, Betsy, marvellous news, Richard is returning from duty. We can expect him here within days." Her cheeks flushed at the prospect. So much for her loyalty to the late John Plumer!

2 July 1822

There is a myth that the Empress Josephine created the world's first rose garden. Its supposed charm was such that during the war between England and France, roses destined for Josephine's garden at Malmaison[9] were, allegedly, allowed safe passage across the Channel, carefully protected by both sides. I keep an open mind about the validity of this fanciful claim. If it is so, I puzzle at the strange ways of conflict and rejoice at nature's ability to soothe man's fury. I contemplated such as I strolled in the gardens at Blakesware and enjoyed the perfume of our roses; which I wager were established well before Josephine's.

How inspired am I at the glory of nature in mid-summer. The array of colours, scent and sounds of life, enrich me. I struggle to picture a better time to herald the return of Captain Lewin to his cherished domain. Uplifted, I delved into the wilderness that is the natural, uncultivated part of the garden and towards the ostentatious large lion head that Uncle John commissioned. Despite recent neglect, it remains an impressive sculpture.

When he was alive, any greenery about the statue was managed to ensure it was clearly visible from his chambers. As I stood beside it, I could almost sense Uncle John's eyes upon me. I was compelled to look in the direction of his former room, now denied to visitors, and caught a glimpse of a silhouetted figure at the window. In deference to my deceased uncle, I began to strip away the ivy that covered the base of the lion statue. I revealed the words, 'Time Is, Time Was, Time's Passed,' engraved, in a gothic style, about the plinth. Once done, a voice called to me from the shadows,
"Charles, it's me Lucy."
"Lucy! Where are you?" I replied, looking about me.
"I'm hiding."
"So I see! Why are you hiding?"

"To see if I can see the fairies," she teased.

"Oh, the fairies, such tantalising, naughty little creatures," I said, with the 'Three of Hearts' still very much in mind.

"Do you think it improper of me, Charles, to appear unexpectedly before you?"

"My dear Lucy, heavens no! It presents me with the chance to ask your forgiveness for my abruptness on the solstice. It was unintended. I became preoccupied with something… unexpected."

"Charles, its fine. I know… it's why I appeared. I sense you are troubled. Are you troubled Charles?"

"I confess. Yes, in some ways you are my tormentor - my heart's joy and my heart's sorrow."

"Charles please," she whispered. "Don't dwell so. History is littered with unrequited love. It makes for the stuff of legend."

"I seek neither fame nor fortune, just peace of mind. Lucy, I can no longer distinguish between truth and fiction. I'm imagining things, strange things."

"Talk to me. Tell me what happened."

"I cannot."

"You can trust me, Charles," she said.

"It's not a matter of trust - I just want to keep you from harm."

"Many wish it, but seldom succeed."

"Why torment me so? You know I fear I might wake one morn' to find you gone forever. It overwhelms me."

There was but one thing for it. An artist must do his duty. The solution was obvious. I asked,

"Let me paint you as never before. I'll capture you as perfection. Every last detail will grace my canvas. It will live and breathe for all eternity, as Lucy Ebbs my darling, lives and breathes before me now."

Gaia, she agreed! We celebrated by circling the lion statue, this way then that, faster then slower, as though we played with the very hands of time itself!

4 July 1822
(Morning)

"Oh God! It's all over," were the alleged agonised tones of Lord North when he received news of the British surrender at Yorktown, Virginia. Forty years on, and Captain Lewin has adopted Lord North's despairing words as an ironic cry of hope and glory. How poignant that on the anniversary of the official conclusion of the American War of Independence, we can expect to hear it recited once again, when the Captain arrives home. The mood of anger that swept across Britain at that time has gone, although some still claim, unfairly, that defeat against the new United States of America triggered the madness of King George III.

May they take comfort in knowing that the child of Europe is beginning to flower? Yes, the Romantic Movement[10] is blossoming in America. This is a timely revolt against the bloodless logic of the Age of Reason. In his letters from America, Captain Lewin told me resistance is building - people want to retain their strong links to nature. My kind of people! What's more, Captain Lewin has invited its pioneers to the gathering of kindred minds planned for Christmas. Emerson, I believe one of them is called. Bring him. Let them join with Wordsworth, my dear friend Samuel, Stubbs and Blake. Yes – Richard told me he could make it happen. He said, "Dear kind Charles, for you anything is possible." Oh, pray to Heaven. Let us unite against the mechanical powers and philosophy of this time, before the flood of materialism arrives.

4 July 1822
(Late afternoon)

Restless, in anticipation of the Captain's return, I took a walk from Blakesware to the White Horse Inn at Wareside. Twas stiflingly hot, arid and still. Although only a relatively short distance, I regretted venturing out in the midday sun. To catch the shade, I went across country taking in woodland and cover whenever I could. The ground was as hard as iron and dusty, as though it hadn't rained for weeks! Oh for a glass of ale to quench my thirst – but I shall keep to my decree.

Maybe it was the heat, I can't be sure, but the words, 'Time Is, Time Was, Time's Passed' - the gothic inscription on the lion plinth in the wilderness – were at the fore of my mind. I repeated them - to try to make sense of them. I sat to ponder them awhile, before removing my boots to cool my feet. I wriggled my toes – which was an unwitting invitation for some ants to crawl upon them. I find ants such remarkable creatures; so small, yet when they work together they are so powerful - an irresistible force. I think the human race has much to learn from them. I digress, sorry Gaia.

I removed my hat to wipe my brow with my handkerchief, but refused to put it down for fear of further mischief making. So, I put the hanky in my lap and twirled the hat in my hands, feeding the brim through my fingers. An idle philosopher, I thought again about the words at the bottom of the lion plinth. "Time Is, Time Was, Time's Passed - What do they mean?" I asked aloud, watching the ants to aid my thinking.

I first saw it out of the corner of my eye - flashes of brilliant white that flickered between the foliage ahead of me, setting birds to flight. Puzzled, I stopped revolving my hat, to keep as still and quiet as possible, with my eyes fixed ahead on the creature that roamed alone. Was it a white wolf? Was it a bear? Bootless, I was ready to flee on my toes. We made eye contact. I feared for my life as it raced towards me, ignoring the muffled cries of a man in the distance. I froze where I sat. Nimble and fast, it reached me in seconds. "Hey, hey, hey – please don't bite me. Don't eat me." I cried shamefully, struggling to slip back on one of my boots. The creature pushed its snout into my body, causing me to tumble backwards.

I threw my hat over my eyes to shield me from the beast. It pushed the hat aside. I closed my eyes and was ready to die, bootless and alone. Until, that was, the beast... licked my face.

The ignominy. This was no *Grimm* fairy tale. Why Gaia, the dog smiled as it stood over me.

"No, no, stop that please, whatever you, whoever you are," I asked. The dog sat back, its huge tangled tail of white flashing to and fro behind him. A saw a small metal disc hanging from the animal's collar. It was a disc with numbers and a name... 01920... I forget the rest, and the name – Malachi, as I recall. I sat up.

"What are you? You nearly frightened me to death. Why run so in this baking heat, with all this fur?" I asked.

The dog barked again, prompting a call from afar.

"M-A-L-A-C-H-I," was the distinguishable cry of a much loved and familiar voice.

I heard him again,

"MALACHI, COME!"

"Go, your master calls," I said, clinging determinedly to my hat.

The dog looked at my bare feet and barked once more - a deafening cry, as if representing all the wild things on God's Earth! I covered my ears. The dog fled, taking my handkerchief with him! It ran to the man who called him. A familiar silhouette – a familiar voice – and it transpired a familiar face once I was closer and out of the glare of the sun. I'd stumbled to my feet, stubbing my toe on a stone. I hopped in pain. It was far from the welcome I had envisaged for Captain Richard Lewin KB!

"Richard is that you? It is I, Captain! It is I, Charles!" I called, stumbling aimlessly as I tried to comfort my aching toe. Fate, I loathe thee! I struggled to beckon Richard forward. The dog barked excitedly, yet Richard shook his head and replied,

"Oh God! It's all over."

"Captain, it is you!"

"No Charles. I'm not the man you think I am. I'm so sorry Charles, truly I am. I know we have failed you, Fanny and Lucy - dear sweet Lucy. Please forgive us all for our folly. We should have listened and acted sooner, much sooner."

"But, I don't understand," I cried as he and the dog disappeared rapidly into the woods with my handkerchief.

I pushed my feet into my boots, ants and all, and limped after them! However, try as I might, I could not find Richard. I speculated that he was practising some kind of practical joke picked up from the United States. I emptied the ants from my boots and hobbled back to the Manor. It took me an age, but I had the vista that leads to Blakesware in sight, when I encountered three unfamiliar faces and a small chequered dog. The group were deep in conversation and seemed not to notice me. I assumed they were labourers, but confess they were most oddly dressed!

I was cautious, given the corpse found by the reapers recently and stumbled for cover. I was right to do so, for in Heaven's name the spectre of Napoleon Bonaparte stood amongst them. Clearly, I had not seen the man in the flesh before, but the Captain has described him often enough. Any wonder that Uplands folk say he haunts us! I have seen him with my own eyes, and, from what I was able to gleam from my vantage spot, the impostor goes by the name of William Darvill.

I caught just a glimpse of the other men, but assumed one to be the infamous highwayman, Sixteen String Jack. He had a prominent scowling brow, a sure sign of villainy in my view. As for the third, he was much older, probably an informant or spy judging by his shifty cajoled manner. I heard little dialogue betwixt them, but discerned mention of the ugly burden of two thumbs![11] These figures were more apparitions than genuine people, but, as I said to Lucy, ' I find it hard to distinguish between truth and fiction'.

4 July 1822
(Evening)

Word has arrived about Captain Lewin. He is in London on business and pleasure and will travel to Hertfordshire later this week! How can this be? I now appear to all who reside at Blakesware as a hobbling, bumbling fool. Lady Plumer was gleeful when I announced I'd seen Richard nearby, and Mrs Field hurried to finalise the last details for a suitable homecoming. But the excitement faded as the hours passed without the Captain's appearance. Questions began to be asked:

"So, he had no carriage?"

"He had no luggage?"

"There were no companions?"

"He had a white dog with him, which resembled a wolf or a small bear?"

"You believe you saw Napoleon?"

"Have you be'n drinking?"

"I can't smell any alcohol on his breath!"

"Maybe he has a fever."

"Sit him on the Justice Chair - that will ensure he tells the truth."

I have no logical explanation for what I saw, but let me put fact subordinate to instinct. I know I did not imagine any of this. Either I am again unwell or the Gods are tinkering with the natural order. Curse the theft of my handkerchief! It's so very personal to me, as my dear mother embroidered my name upon it. I am distraught at the prospect of its loss. I shall search for it with all tenacity and determination. I shall retrace my steps and urge neighbours and friends to say if they should learn of its whereabouts.

Malachi! What's in a name? In this instance, possibly a great deal! The Hebrew Scriptures suggest he is the messenger of the Lord. Well, I can't pretend to make any sense of it. My religious feelings are isolated to some fleeting moments of occasional solitary devotion. I feel a game of Patience, with Mrs Battle as my aide, will provide me with the comfort and advocacy I need and sharpen my wits for the challenges ahead. Play on!

7 July 1822

Captain Richard Lewin KB has come home. He arrived at Blakesware this afternoon in full military finery, dressed in the dashing uniform of the British Life Guards. Oh, the panache - an outlandish moustache that capped his short scarlet jacket, girdled with a gold sash, his bleached buckskin breeches, and knee-high black boots that clicked as he walked across the stone floor. Tucked under his arm was a gilded Grecian helmet, with the plumed white tuft wagging in celebration. This British officer was glad to be alive and delighted to be back at Blakesware Manor.

"Oh God! It's all over," were his anticipated first words. I said little in return, choosing instead to embrace the man who was as a brother to me.
"A man may travel far on this extraordinary globe, but nothing compares to the sweet comfort of home, the companionship of loyal and trusted friends and the allure of loved ones," he said, turning his grey eyes discreetly in Lady Plumer's direction and causing her to blush.

The Captain had been in New England for the whole of the spring and the early summer, as the King's Ambassador. He retained his lean physique but, to be blunt, looked a little sallow and drained, probably due to the arduous journey across the Atlantic Ocean. His paleness contrasted starkly with the dark skin of his companion. He was a man that had travelled with the Captain from London and now stood awkwardly beneath the arched doorway to the Great Hall. Richard encouraged him forward,
"Katharine, Charles, may I introduce Bill Richmond... a blade of the

finest magnitude."

There was stunned silence amongst the welcome party, which included Mrs Field, our servants, Reverend North, the wrinkled elderly and tremulous rector at Widford Church - dependant on his walking stick for mobility - and Thomas Wake, our collector of Tithes.[12]

In recent years, a black servant had become a fashion accessory amongst the English nobility, but Captain Lewin strongly resisted out of principle and was not one to follow vogue. Richard promptly curtailed any speculation by continuing,

"Some amongst us will know that Bill's a former bare knuckle boxing fighter. Please welcome this fine fellow of a man!"

The silence persisted; probably because Richmond's compact physique did not immediately appear to befit a prized fighter.

"Is this a wake or a welcome?" asked Richard, which prompted Thomas Wake to speak,

"Are you really Bill Richmond, the boxer who took the great Lester Crib to forty rounds?"

"Yes Sir and I would have been victorious, but for the mob – they weren't ready for a black champion," insisted Richmond. He spoke with an unexpected eloquence for one who practised the pugilist[13] art.

"Remarkable," replied Wake, with a face alight in awe. "The moustache… it's remarkable!" he added, to clarify his thinking.

"Quite a magnificent specimen," announced Lady Plumer.

"A promise is a promise," said the Captain.

It was improbable that Captain Lewin and his moustache could be upstaged on his return home, but Bill Richmond almost succeeded. I learnt later from Captain Lewin that Bill Richmond, son of a former slave, was raised in an educated household in New York, which honed his social skills. He came to England aged only 14 to enter service with the Duke of Northumberland, providing access to a gentile and cultural environment. Apprenticed as a cabinet-maker in York, Richmond taught himself to spar and was renowned for defeating men much heavier than him. Defeat to Crib had cost him the first ever world championship. Now retired from boxing, he runs an academy, where he teaches young men to fight.

"But why did you bring him?" I asked the Captain, once the opportunity arose.

"You will see. For now Charles, be clear. Know this, Richmond was honoured last year at the coronation of George IV."

"Extraordinary!"

"But the coup de grace is that John Plumer was his Patron."

I was astounded that my uncle put finance into such a primitive, brutal, bloodthirsty business. I wondered how Aunt Katharine would feel if she were to learn of her late husband's antics.

8 July 1822
(Morning)

I had difficulty sleeping last night. It was due to my excitement at Richard's return and a frightening electric storm that erupted furiously around midnight. The Manor trembled under the force of the thunder and a deluge that accompanied the heart of the storm. Rain of a furiosity I'd seldom seen or heard pounded the grounds.

Amid the tempest and my drowsy slumber, I am convinced that lightening illuminated a figure stood beside the door to my chamber. In response, I sat up sharply, ready to defend myself against the intruder. It was an age before the room was lit again, only this time the figure was gone. I rose sharply from my bed to lock the door. Thereafter, I feared to close my eyes. I slept through utter exhaustion.

8 July 1822
(Evening)

Captain Lewin has shaved off his moustache! At first, its ceremonial removal distracted from his tradition of unveiling memorabilia of his travels. But the born again Captain was quickly accepted as we gathered, as though children at Christmas, around a charming wooden chest that he deployed for this purpose – a chest with three hearts carved into its top! I helped him roll back the lid and retreated to join Katharine, Bill and Mrs Field to watch the theatre unfold.

Some people have a knack of putting upon you gifts of no particular value, but not our Richard. The smallest items appeared first. The gifts were not quite what we expected. Richard revealed artefacts belonging to the American Indian population, including a peace pipe, bow and arrowheads carved from bone, some painted buffalo hide and a spectacular tomahawk that drew gasps of admiration. Comically, he donned a fur hat made from Beaver, which he assured us was highly fashionable in America's North East cities, and fixed a white feather to it. He then entertained us with the ditty:

> ♫ Yankee Doodle went to town
> A-riding on a pony.
> Stuck a feather in his hat
> And called it macaroni.
>
> Yankee Doodle, keep it up,
> Yankee Doodle dandy.
> Mind the music and the step
> And with the girls be handy. ♫

As he sung, the Captain clapped his hands and stamped his right foot, encouraging us to do the same. We then proceeded to examine and handle the additions to the Manor's cultural library, before listening eagerly to tales of Richard's exploits in the New England.

Richard was much amused today. He had news that a vast statue of Achilles has been unveiled in the Duke of Wellington's honour in Hyde Park London. Apparently, the naked form has shocked the Ladies of England, the organisation which suggested a statue in the first place. What do they propose to do? Add a fig-leaf to cover his modesty?

Today, Richard Lewin told me how much he missed having a dog at Blakesware, this despite the hounds kept in the kennels. He was especially aware of the absence when he returned home, missing the boisterous, playful greeting of his previous canines.

"My duty for King and country fulfilled, I have every opportunity to take another, but long for something extraordinary, dramatic, imposing, strong and intelligent," he said. I could not help but recall the white wolf I'd seen, I presume, with him or his double on the Independence Day.

"Do you have a particular breed in mind?" I asked.

"I do indeed - one with Siberian Arctic roots. A dog that's one of the oldest and purest known to man"

"What colour might such a dog be?"

"As white as the snow that falls in its natural habitat."

"Have you seen one before?"

"Really Charles, not at all. I've been to America not the Arctic tundra of northern Europe."

"So it's an aspiration rather than a probability."

He wrapped his arm around my shoulder and invited me to sit in the Justice Chair.

"Where there's a will, there's a way," he advised. "Please do sit," he suggested.

"If I can bring mystic timber from northern Europe, then why not a dog too? And let us suppose this dog to be magical - worthy and capable of great things!"

The Captain winked at me, as I nestled within the carved structure.

"Charles, would you like Bill Richmond to teach you how to box?"

I was flabbergasted at the preposterous idea.

"Richard, why do you say such things? I am man of literature and art."

"But prose and painting, really Charles. Given all that has happened in the past, is not the time right for you to toughen up?"

"This is unfair; you clearly have an ulterior motive in bringing a pugilist into our home."

"Nothing could be further from the truth. Allow me to speak candidly Charles. Lady Katharine Plumer is deeply concerned for your welfare. It's essential to help you to prepare for the future. You must be able to defend yourself."

"No, no, NO. I refuse as a matter of principle."

11 July 1822

Another unproductive search in the woods for the handkerchief embroidered by my mother's fair hand.

15 July 1822

How can I contemplate bare fist fighting? I run the risk of tarnishing these hands, which must be kept in pristine condition, at least until I have painted Lucy, as promised.

Learn to fight, the ignominy – ever since mother died I have fought in one way or another! Against all that I believe in, I have agreed to allow Bill Richmond to teach me to spar. They claim it will make a man of me and ease my idealist and sentimental approach to life and love. I wager otherwise – let the art commence. The location and light for the portrait were fundamental. The location needed to complement Lucy's natural soft honey features and symbolise her personality. The light had to be sufficient to illustrate her bone structure, yet not too harsh as to make her appear gaunt or insipid.

I set up my easel in the Great Hall at Blakesware Manor. The colours were neutral and the light gentle. Lucy sat upon the Captain's Chair, wearing a striking gentle blue dress that emphasised the colour of her eyes and the honey in her long wavy hair. I was true to my word, striving to capture her to perfection, allowing every last fine detail to grace the canvas.

As I worked, the very essence of her spirit was alive in the painting. It began to live and breathe as Lucy Ebbs lives and breathes before me now. It took more than one sitting but it was my best work yet, far beyond any other piece I had attempted. History may remember me as an artist yet!

Lucy was strangely churlish about the painting. "You've removed the imperfections and blemishes. I'm not all charm Charles. Where is my rage, my unpredictability, my dark unforgiving side? You should paint all that I am."
"That's just it, I do paint as I see, to me you are perfection."
"Then your love is blind," she told me.

To my surprise, Lady Katharine was one of those full of praise for my painting. The smell of the oil was still rich and potent as I oversaw the gilded framing and hanging of the portrait in the Gallery. I wanted to display it in the Great Hall, but alas my request was refused. Oh joy is mine! Lucy can remain with me always – whenever I come to Blakesware, there shall she be, whatever our fate.

So, she was hung in the Gallery – and do you know, I had the most curious experience. Bedazzled was I, for by some quirk of fate she was displayed close to the *Haymakers*, which demonstrated how much the woman at the heart of the painting resembled Lucy. If Stubbs could see the resemblance for himself, he would chuckle so. What was it George once told me? Ah yes, I remember now. The woman in the painting represents Mother Nature herself – fertility, growth, renewal. Thus it is so – Lucy is the image of our Keeper. She is Mother Nature personified. The source and guiding force of all creation! I warned you about my romantic idealism, did I not?

What is more, sweet Lucy also looked directly upon '*Nelson and the Bear*[14]' by Richard Westall; an imaginary reconstruction of Horatio Nelson's famous encounter with a polar bear when only 14 on a Polar expedition in 1773. Portrayed as an unequal struggle – the pair make eye contact and confront each other. In the background is the ship, the 'Carcass', which sailed under Captain Constantine Phipps, Grandfather to our Reverend Phipps.

24 July 1822

Seldom, if ever, have I engaged in an activity so alien to my character. I am just relieved that I was spared the ignominy of the women in the household watching me train and spar. I am physically exhausted. Despite his age, Bill Richmond is a powerhouse of a man, agile, and remarkably fit. I watched in awe as he pulverised a punch-bag that hung in a corner of the courtyard, shaming my feeble efforts. He exercised tirelessly and effortlessly. I did what I could to match him, but it was a futile response. He left me in his wake as he did circuits of the Manor. Every sinew in my body aches. My spirit flags too at the persistent drone of Richmond's voice urging me to succeed.

"Do you know where anger comes from?" he asked me, with a toned chest exposed to the world.

"It comes from here," he pointed to the pit of his stomach. "And here," he pointed to his heart, "And here," singling out his head.

"Are you angry Lamb? Come on! Use your anger to inspire you. Let's spar... do it now!" he baited.

I was tempted.

"Uncle John spoke highly of you... do you propose to let him down? Do you know all that is at stake? Where is your faith?"

"Okay... I'll do it... for Uncle John's sake!" I replied with fervour.

Gaia, forgive me. I hit Bill square on the jaw as hard as I could. The adrenalin rushed through my veins. I hit him again.

"Enough," he shouted.

I hit him again, and know now to heed his instructions carefully in future. Some of us are better at some things than others. I now possess a badly swollen eye to prove the point. All the same, Bill Richmond was proud of my efforts.

I vowed not to interrupt Charles' mastery – but feel I must. Here is the postcard I treasure from the Maritime Museum, which shows the now prophetic painting. Take a look...

And please read the message too...

Reader,

"Today, the United States Government's Department of the Interior announced plans to list the polar bear as an endangered species. The majestic and graceful animal currently numbers 25,000. But there is growing concern the bears' ice cap habitat is melting away due to human induced climate change."

Yours hopefully,

The Curator's Assistant
28 December 2006

Nelson and the bear by Richard Westall, circa. 1806©
National Maritime Museum, London, Greenwich Hospital collection.

I have been a virtual recluse since the blow to my eye, as I wait for the swelling and bruising to subside. At birth, my beloved mother described me as, 'Weakly, but very pretty.' Not today. Ashamed by my swelling and bruising, I have played countless games of Solitaire such that the suits and numbers are embedded on my mind when I close my eyes. As for Bill Richmond, he had the good humour to check on my health. We have reached an understanding. I respect him greatly.

28 July 1822

Today, I heard the end of a discussion between Aunt Katharine and Mrs Field about the child taken into the Ware Parish Workhouse. It seems the child's welfare was the reason behind the visit from Reverend North and Thomas Wake earlier this month. I'm deeply curious about my Aunt's interest in the orphaned infant and a comment she made about guarding against making matters more complicated. She said that Fanny Ebbs' curiosity, which emerged when she visited earlier this week, should be snubbed out for fear of a misunderstanding or reprisal. I wish women were less secretive.

Perhaps the infant's arrival has something to do with the persistent rumours of spies present in the region. The spectre of revolution and civil unrest lingers. Parliament has outlawed gatherings of more than 50 people at one time, for fear of riot. The fear of an uprising of Radicals is giving new momentum to the Temperance Society on the grounds that alcohol will serve to stimulate desire for action and lead to violence. So much for the tranquillity of peace!

30 July 1822

Bill Richmond, Richard Lewin and I took an early morning run around Widford, Wareside and Noblin Green, before returning to Blakesware. I saw us as torchbearers for liberty, fraternity and equality. Although when we set out, I thought it feeble to wish to be able to keep up with the pace, but I was surprised by my level of fitness. The more we ran, the stronger I became. I felt like an Olympiad in training. I was empowered, enjoying the sun and all that nature had to offer.

When we reached the bridleway that ran adjacent to Keeper's Cottage, I was delighted to see Lucy. Balanced precariously on the wrought iron gate, she waved excitedly as we emerged into the lane. I slowed as we approached her and encouraged my associates to do likewise, but they ran ahead of me. "Can't keep up with the pace Charles... let's say we'll see you back at the Manor," cried Richard.

Lucy looked radiant. "Charles, I am most surprised and glad to see you making preparations," she said, clearly impressed by my efforts.
"Preparations?"
"Yes Charles, for the challenges ahead!"
"The challenges?" I asked, regaining my breath.
"Charles please... don't quiz me so. It's all in the nature of things."
Lucy wasn't alone in being impressed by my efforts, for Fanny Ebbs emerged from the cottage to invite me inside and, much to Lucy's joy, complimented me for my endeavour. However, an ulterior motive soon emerged,
"Charles. Please, do say you have news of the baby at the workhouse?" she asked, when we were alone in the parlour.
"The baby? I only know what Mrs Field told me."
"Folk say they named him Adam."
Fanny Ebbs was restless, unsettled even. I tried to reassure her,
"Adam? Mrs Ebbs, I do pity the infant, truly I do, but I believe he will be well cared for. Reverend North is a good man... he will see to it."

"Charles, hear me, do. The workhouse is no place for a young 'en, such as he. I'll make it worthwhile for you to find out what you can."
"Why not ask Reverend North yourself?"
"It's not my place to do so... they at the workhouse wish to have no doings with me. Please Charles... will you help? The boy needs you."
"As you fret so, yes I can ask, if it pleases you, comforts you."
"Yes Charles Lamb, it would be wise to please me – and a certain gentleman - a great deal."

5 August 1822

Today, I asked Katharine Plumer whether our local hero, the Captain, might have an identical twin. I asked in all seriousness, yet she dismissed the idea immediately.
"Charles, how utterly ludicrous! What makes you say such a thing?" she asked, as we sat in the formal gardens at Blakesware.
"It might explain the sightings, for surely a man cannot be in two places at the same time. Can he?"
"Sightings? Don't listen to the sun drenched foolish talk of ignorant farm hands. It's the season for it. The drink and the heat's turned them to simpletons Charles."
"But it's not due to the o' doubling eye?" I insisted.
"Rumours of his antics will spread like fire on the wind, Charles. People will say such things because they can, just to be popular, for gossip and rumour add spice to their lives."
"What would Richard say if he knew of the rumours?" I speculated.
"Richard knows full well that popularity lends itself to curiosity Charles, so I wouldn't trouble him if I were you."

Lady Katharine can be patronising at times. I know what I saw on the fourth of July. My eyes did not deceive me. Nor, for that matter, did Thomas Watson's. I judge Tom as a man of stoic character. I would vouch for his every word. Gaia, this morning he told me that last Sunday, after church, he saw Richard walking the

263

Hertfordshire Way towards Widford. He claims Richard walked with his head lowered and his eyes fixed upon on a wilted rose, cupped in his hands. Tom was astounded to see Richard, for only minutes earlier he had bid him farewell after the service at Widford church.

"His eyes were closed to everything but the rose," he told me.

"Charles, really, that's nonsense. You forget... I was amongst the congregation. Richard was with me all the while," my Aunt insisted.

"Ah... well I'd asked Tom, 'Are you sure it was him?' and he replied, 'If it wasn't, then he must have a double,' and I trust Tom. Why should he deceive me?"

"Did Tom not speak to him... this man you seek?"

"I asked him. He said, 'No. Well not at first as I was surprised to see him. I just let him go right pass me. I called to him as he walked away, I called more than once. He just ignored me. I was concerned so I went after him. It was easy to catch him up. I put my hand on his shoulder. He dropped the rose and shouted at me. He looked at me like he did not know me, so I left him alone,' those were his words."

"Did this man say anything else?"

"The bloody rose is dying!"

"Was he alone?"

"No. Tom said the man had a dog with him - a huge white wolf!"

Aunt Katherine shrugged her shoulders, whilst I needed no further convincing.

7 August 1822

The Ware Parish workhouse disturbed me. I accept it is a refuge from destitution born from charity, but it provoked memories of a harsh and squalid world. Paupers are sent to the workhouse for a variety of reasons, usually because they are too poor, old or ill to support themselves. However, my time in a workhouse was of my choosing and for the benefit of others. My temporary poverty was with my mind not my possessions.

As I entered the workhouse under the arch that led to the Board of Guardians' quarters, I imagined the workhouse bell ringing in my head, signalling a meal break where, 'silence, order and decorum shall be maintained.' The relative luxury of the Master's rooms juxtaposed with the stark reality of the inmates accommodation. By prior arrangement, I met the Master of the workhouse, Thomas Phipps, his wife Margaret and the school master Charles Buck. Although of proud heritage, the Phipps' were parodies of real people, with bulbous features and reddened complexions which implied indulgence in food and drink. It was difficult to accept that Phipps' Grandfather took Viscount Nelson on a voyage.

All assumed Lady Plumer had sent me. Phipps' welcome mood altered once he realised I had come under my own volition, "Mr Lamb, time is my enemy. I must insist we speak plainly."
"I beg your confidence," I implored.
"Look at my face – it is a picture of discretion!" replied Phipps, learning towards me.
"House rules," added his wife with a smirk.
So much for plain speaking. I was bemused and knew not what to say. I sought guidance from a clock on the wall behind Master Phipps. It had a slow heavy motion, but its hands seemed set on five minutes to twelve. What an uncultured thing a mechanical clock is! I wished for the altar-like structure and silent beat of a sundial.

Phipps grew impatient. He fidgeted in his seat, perspiring profusely in the oppressive sticky air of the closed room. He battled with a couple of flies that sought solace in a salty drink from his scalp to quench their thirst. He fumbled in a pocket and drew out a handkerchief. He broke our silence,
"Mr Lamb, it seems we misunderstood each other. I must bid you…"
I stopped him from continuing.
"What are you doing with that?" I asked.
"This? Why I'm wiping my brow!" he replied.

"If I may, I believe it belongs to me," I insisted.

A frown spread across Phipps' face.

"The letters were embroidered by my mother's hand."

"Is that so Mr Lamb?" He began to get to his feet.

"I speak truthfully. Please, look my name is stitched in the corner. It was taken from me last month against my will."

"Last month you say. I'm afraid you are sadly mistaken. Now Mr Lamb if you would be so kind, I insist you leave. We have a busy schedule... mouths to feed... tiny hungry mouths."

"No, please, first return to me what is rightfully mine. Then I shall leave."

"You are incorrigible Mr Lamb."

"The handkerchief... it has a sentimental value."

"There's no room for sentiment in business, Mr Lamb!"

Phipps shook out my handkerchief, as if to taunt me.

The workhouse bell rang to signal a meal break to the inmates. I clenched my fist. The Phipps' drew back in their seats, but my rage was directed at the table. I hit it hard, such that the tableware leapt in the air. I came close to toppling a single rose from its vase. Mrs Phipps shrieked, as she grabbed the glass,

"Heavens me... this is so fragile and very, very precious." The vase stabilised, she looked at me harshly and said,

"I'm sure Lady Plumer would be deeply interested in the reason for your visit, deeply interested."

I lay my hands flat on the table, "I came with good intention and this is how I am repaid. Taunted and humiliated by people who are meant to work for the greater good! I ask for very little, just for news of the child... and..."

"Do you believe in miracles?" interupted Master Phipps.

"The beggar wears all colours fearing none," I replied, cryptically.

Mr Phipps wiped his brow with 'my' handkerchief, before nervously gulping some water.

"The child Adam," he began, "Is cloaked in mystery."

Phipps explained the strange circumstances surrounding the child's discovery. Reverend North found him in early May, sheltered beneath the doors to St John's, after a tremendous storm. Although the ground around him was sodden the infant and his basket were completely dry. Aside from a light cover, within the basket with the infant were a single rose and a handkerchief. My handkerchief with my name embroidered in the corner!

"So you see Mr Lamb, if the handkerchief is yours then perhaps you can explain how it got there?" asked Master Phipps.

"Does it spell out my name?" I asked, in response.

Phipps unfolded the material. "We have the letters C and L – for Charles Lamb?"

"I see. Ah... perhaps I've misled you – the letters should spell out my name in full!"

The Phipps' looked at each other, whilst I looked, again, at the clock. Twas still five minutes to twelve!

"I believe the clock's stopped! It ticks... but the hands of time stand still," I said, digressing as ever.

Mr Phipps glanced nervously at the clock behind him, in a manner which implied it held some ominous hold over him. He scrunched up the handkerchief and wiped his brow once more. Mrs Phipps spoke on his behalf,

"So, we are no nearer giving the child a certain future. We had hoped Lady Plumer would do what was morally right, and claim the child." Although she implied disappointment, her tone suggested she was relieved.

"If you should be obliged then please do tell Lady Plumer that we shall continue to care for the beautiful Adam, to raise him - and love him - as our own until he's ready to apprentice."

As she spoke, she took hold of the rose, which I had almost toppled in my rage.

"It won't die," she said, "This flower found with Adam; it's been in bud for weeks... months even."

I left empty handed, but, on my departure, did some simple reasoning, 'rose in the sky – storm - handkerchief stolen - Adam found with rose and handkerchief!' Bewildering events were unfolding in the world about Ware, Hertfordshire. I shall ponder these further before scrawling again. I need time, Gaia, to think, to make sense of everything and to plan.

8 August 1822

Let me confess - I have seen the child. The sight and feel of his tiny angelic fingers, dwarfed around mine - how it lingers. Woe his fate. What will become of him? Cruel world!

Gaia, another confession. The thought has come to me - the letters CL could also apply to Captain Lewin. An improbable proposition, I wager. Why would the Captain possess a handkerchief[15] embroidered in my mother's hand? Surely, the letters RL would have been her choice. What ought I to tell Fanny Ebbs?

11 August 1822

Desperate news! Captain Lewin has learnt that Percy Bysshe Shelley has drowned in a storm at sea on the eighth of July off the coast of Italy. Perhaps Katharine Plumer was right after all – the spirit of revolution is dead! The injustice! Rumours abound on how it happened. I cannot contemplate such evil. Oh Skylark, bow your head in sorrow at the passing. 'Teach us, sprite or bird, what sweet thoughts are thine!'[16] All God's creatures bid thee well, young friend. Find peace through that golden key to the chamber of eternal rest. Woe, this sad terrible loss – and his poor wife Mary. How fate has forsaken her - such cruelty on her, that genius with the quill. I can scribe no more - to my bed I go.

12 August 1822

I had another of those uncomfortable nights, for the tragic news of Percy's demise has overwhelmed me. It was also dreadfully humid and a number of games of Solitaire brought little respite. Insomnia can play havoc with the mind, and bring out the darkest of thoughts. For as I laid awake staring into the darkness, I heard shuffled footsteps pace the corridor outside my room. Yet, when I eventually found the courage to take my candlestick into the hall, there was nothing but shadows to taunt my wild imagination.

Despite my lack of sleep, Bill Richmond persuaded me to take another training session. I am grateful to him. My physique has developed. I have a tautness about me that was improbable only weeks ago. There's now more to Charles Lamb than artistry, poetry and romance. Uncle John Plumer, if you could see me as I stand before you. I am stronger in body and mind. I feel equipped to defend myself and Lucy against all assailants.

14 August 1822

Gaia - let me remind you of my vow of abstinence from alcohol. It has been more than two years since ale, beer or wine passed these lips. The same could not be said for the nomadic labourers I encountered loitering, in good spirits, within the grounds of the White Horse Inn. It was just late afternoon, but the heat of the day and glasses of ale had brought on hearty cheering, laughter and boisterous antics. Amongst them was Thomas Watson - he who claimed to have seen Richard's double. He caught my eye and gestured eagerly for me to join the revelry. At first, I declined, but he was determined. He grabbed my arm and led me, uttering, 'Mr Lamb, I urge your attention. This here's a magic man... come see. He can perform miracles."

We jostled passed a wagon, with partial unloaded kegs, destined for the White Horse. A powerful chestnut Suffolk Punch stood guard over the wares, impatiently flicking his nose in temper at flies that congregated about him. The horse's actions reminded me of the workhouse governor, Mr Phipps. Restless, and with ears pulled back, the horse kicked its hooves firmly on the hard ground and snorted. The drayman had deserted him; seemingly distracted by the rowdy events.

The excited crowd circled a man squat on the ground with a masked face lowered and in shadow. Next to his feet were a pack of cards and an untidy pile of coins, which I assumed were the result of wagers. The man held something in the palm of his left hand. Blindfolded, he raised his head to the audience. He spoke with authority,

"Gentlemen, allow me to give you an education! Dice have a history as rich and old as man, very popular with the Greeks and the Romans. They say, too, that departed spirits in the underworld play at dice. Let me be clear, these dice I hold in my hand are no ordinary dice for they are made from bone and are said to come from an ancient tomb."

He had his audience captivated. They cheered excitedly. Fed by their enthusiasm, the man said,

"So cast the die and I shall read them. For I know what the die will say. They talk to me... and me to they. Ah, I hear you say! 'The dice will choose their own destiny. They have free will – like you and I'. My good fellow, I say... let me put the dice to the test!"

The group fell silent. I was sceptical as I heard him say, "You and I have work to do."

His words encouraged a figure to step forward and take the dice.

"They call him the Emperor," advised Watson, amid the hush.

The unknown accomplice, as I perceived him, tossed the dice.

"Tacta alea est - the die is cast and I am seeing double," announced the theatrical showman. "I see it. Yes it is clear now. Oh such a mystic number is three! A double three - magnifique!"

The magician removed his blindfold to much applause. Mighty fine trickery.

As the clink of coins subsided, the Emperor sought another volunteer, which led to a cry of, "I'll do it, so long as you can make me live forever?" It was Tom Watson, articulating the thoughts of the locals. I was compelled to add,

"Only one thing worse than immortality, and that's eternal damnation!"

Had I gambled with my future? I'd like to grow old as slowly as possible, so immediately regretted my words, but the conjurer just smiled and said,

"Things are not always as they seem."

Strange words indeed for a magician. I was contemplating my response, when pandemonium broke out near the fly infested guardian of the undelivered ale. I caught a glimpse of a large dog darting uncontrollably about the startled horse, barking furiously and seemingly threatening an attack. The Suffolk, contradicted the docile disposition normally associated with the breed. It rose up and kicked out, de-stabilising the dray in the process. Several barrels of ale crashed to the ground, in a tumultuous crescendo of sound. One split on impact, sending ale sprawling everywhere. The liquid behaved as a sentient being, wriggling its way downhill. Other barrels fell and rolled down the road, starting a desperate and chaotic pursuit.

The culprit, seemingly satisfied that he had made his point, fled from the scene. The returning drayman cried out in despair and rage, furiously waving his arms in a futile attempt to restrain the Suffolk. The horse pulled sharply away with an empty wagon, followed by a few good men, myself included.

"Look, there he goes... the white wolf!" cried the drayman, before the dog disappeared from view into a copse.

"A king's shilling for the man who catches him," shouted the publican, William Page as he cried over his ale. So it was that the legend of the 'White Wolf of Wareside' was born.

16 August 1822

After recent events, I craved some tranquillity and culture. Hooray for Captain Lewin! His love of classical music was one of his most endearing qualities and something I shared. On several counts, we had experienced works from Ludwig van Beethoven, Wolfgang Amadeus Mozart and others, when in London and Bath.

Heaven sings in my ears, thanks to Lewin's ability as an able pianist. This afternoon he played a number of pieces on the grand piano, including a favourite of my mother's, Piano Sonata No.16 in C Major by Mozart. I could picture mother in my mind's eye sitting on the chaise lounge in her usual dreamy manner, my sister, Mary beside her. I longed for the happy memory to stay with me for all eternity. Thank God for music. I find it an aide to memory. I hear the Sonata and my family comes swiftly to me. Mozart your sweet notes provide a special link between the present and the past. Sometimes I am close to tears of joy at the sheer beauty of the prodigies work. I wish the great man were still alive!

I wish I could be so spectacularly creative, but what are words compared with the harmony and splendour of music. It is the universal language – representative of a unity our species craves, yet cannot achieve. I am disposed to harmony, but alas, I am incapable of a tune. My only consolation is that words provide an avenue to a kind of immortality. Which makes me wonder, is this why I write?

My motivation aside, Lady Plumer, Mrs Field, Bill Richmond and I gathered today to enjoy Richard's virtuoso performance. My recent frustrations were soothed by the melodies. I felt oddly reborn.

I mentioned my sense of renewal to Captain Lewin this evening, after dinner. I told him how hearing Für Elise served as a vivid reminder to me of my dear sweet mother.

"I shall cease to play it... if it disturbs you Charles," he offered.

"No Richard, the memory is a good one. I know I can't change the past, but be assured, your music brings her to me... happy as she deserved to be."

"Then I shall play more often. I feel her loss too and am so sorry... I do wonder if I could have changed her fate."

"Who can say... but Richard, I accept it. It is the way of things. Now, I must look to the future."

"The future! Time Charles, it's one of the greatest enigmas of all! Imagine if we could conquer it, you and I. How magnificent would that be?"

"Nothing puzzles me more than time and space, and yet nothing troubles me less, as I never think about them." I replied.

"Whereas for me. I ponder it all the while. Many hours spent at sea have seen to that," he said, strolling into the Great Hall.

18 August 1822

Gaia, today I experienced something so remarkable and mysterious that I struggle to know how to scribe it. My imagination has been stirred and my soul filled with agreeable surprise. In truth, the experience has left me quite bemused. Allow me to explain.

The injury sustained to my foot several weeks ago had laid me low these last few days; I fear I pushed it too hard, too soon. Yet when I awoke this morning, I was compelled to take some light exercise. Against Mrs Field's better judgment, I ventured out into glorious summer sunshine and hobbled, with the support of a stick, beyond the boundaries of Blakesware.

I was drawn to a field near Noblin Green Farm; one rich in healthy crop. Despite the absence of wind, the tall stems suddenly swayed to and fro – before parting, as if to invite me inside! At first glance, I thought little of it; the sight of a strong crop lying ahead of me, folded in perfect unison. Yet, when I reached the flattened crop, I was astounded. I entered a circle a good ninety feet across. The wheat lay in perfect alignment, spreading from the centre as though spokes on a wheel. I stumbled about the circle in disbelief. A force had been at work that I did not comprehend. I knew of the phenomenon, but such sights hadn't been seen in Hertfordshire in my life time.

Do you know Gaia, for a while my vision blurred and I felt disorientated and dizzy. I heard a tingling in my ear. I blamed the heat – the sun was directly above me - until, that was, I had the strangest sensation in my feet. Unsettled, I sat down, placing my stick beside me. I closed my eyes, but my head still spun – as though I'd broken my vow of abstinence from alcohol. Part of me wanted to leave the circle; the other compelled me to stay. I seemed to lose all sense of time.

"Charles, isn't it simply beautiful," I heard a woman say.

I opened my eyes to find Lucy stood before me. From whence she came, I do not know.

"Goodness Lucy… you startled me so," I replied.

"Fear not the powerful creative instinct," she said.

Her presence seemed to comfort my soul. She beckoned me to stand.

"Oh… my foot, the pain has gone."

"Why yes, of course! Come, Charles…" she took my hand and helped me to my feet. I was quite healed.

"Come… this way… follow!" she said, leading me on to a path no more than the width of the spread of my arms, which went for 100 paces or so, until we reached another perfect circle, identical to that we'd just left.

"Here, there's another," she cried, leading me along a further path of 100 paces to a third circle, just the same as those that had gone before. Finally, she led me back to the circle where I'd left my stick.

"It's a perfect triangle," I suggested, conscious of a strange shrill ring in my ears. That aside, I felt an overwhelming sense of awe, peace and tranquillity.

What, I speculated, if a powerful force was behind the circle's creation? A force seeking to guide and empower us and change the direction we - the human race - were headed.

"Come dreamer... rush, save me," cried Lucy, as she ran into one of the pathways to head for another circle. 'Was she in danger?' I did as she suggested, but try as I might I could not catch her. In fact, she quickly came up behind me, and caused me to run in the opposite direction. Capricious Lucy ebbs and flows like the tides of the oceans. I felt invigorated, alive and enriched.

"Where did the circles come from?" I shouted, finally tiring.

"The living force of nature," she called back.

"What's their purpose?"

"To provide a message," she claimed, dancing about a circle.

"To tell us what?"

"To tell us who we are... to show the way," she claimed.

"It's incredible," I cried.

"Life's incredible Charles!" she said, as I caught her up.

Oh playful, enigmatic Lucy, pretending to have all the answers.

"Close your eyes and count to ten," she asked, lifting my hands to cover my sockets.

"What are you doing?"

"You need to learn your place in the natural world! Close your eyes and count to ten," she whispered.

Gaia, when I opened my eyes, Lucy had vanished, though I'm sure I could hear her crying. I called her name - many times over, until something led me from the circle. The White Wolf of Wareside had returned. He ran into and about the circle in which I stood, barking frantically.

"Malachi? Is that you? There's a price on your head my friend!"
He ignored the warning and continued to run in circles,
"Have you seen Lucy, I believe she's hiding from me?" I asked, having lost all sense of reality. The dog ran towards me, then away again, as if to encourage me to leave the circle. I followed him, back to the bridleway. I saw Lucy at the road's peak, as it headed towards Noblin Green. She waved at me; an act which encouraged the dog to run towards her.

Gaia – did I dream this? For I lost all track of time and reason. Dare I ask if anyone else has seen the circles? No, I shall wait and if it arises in conversation, I shall comment.

18 August 1823
(Evening)

Gaia, I didn't imagine the circles – they are real! Captain Lewin shared the discovery with the household this evening. Apparently news of the circles has spread like wildfire, encouraging people from far and wide to travel to see them. I guess they'll be trampled to the ground in no time. Richard told us most doubt they are genuine, as evidence of trampled ground was apparent throughout. Alas, a stick was discovered, around which it was assumed a rope was tied to make the circles. It was my stick which I'd unwittingly left behind... well, well, well!

"Some would accuse the idle travelling haymakers with little better to do on hot sultry nights then spoil a good crop with a circle or two," claimed Lady Plumer.

I kept silent, though Elizabeth Field gave me a knowing glance.
"The circles were most amusing, but the lights were the real curiosity," said the Captain.

"The lights! What lights?" I asked.

"There were sightings of strange dancing balls of light seen in the field last night."

"Who says?" asked Lady Plumer.

"Reverend North for one, and he's a man I trust," said Captain Lewin.

"Are you suggesting the lights had something to do with the circles?" I asked.

"Charles my friend, your guess is as good as mine, but the whole matter is deeply intriguing, deeply," replied the Captain.

"A curiosity indeed," I said.

Gaia what magic was afoot in this place? Is Mother Earth trying to tell us something? Are the circles a response to the emerging threat of industrialisation?

20 August 1822

Last night was warm and balmy. Captain Lewin, Bill Richmond and I played at cards until the early hours, speculating on life's curiosities – circles in crops. As the clock progressed so did the tempo of our wagers and our conversation. Bill spoke of his duels and on his time in New York, whilst Richard recounted some of his battlefield exploits. Tragedy aside, my life seemed so ordinary and uneventful by comparison.

Richard and Bill were men who clearly thrived on challenges and danger. What was the attraction of Blakesware Manor to these mighty men of the world? In one way or another they had brushed shoulders with royalty, politicians and senior military figures. I anticipated that one, or both, would depart from the Uplands once Richard's great gathering of minds at Christmas was over. Whatever they decide, at least Mrs Battle will be my abiding and loyal companion, and one that seldom boasts when she wins at cards.

24 August 1822

Fanny Ebbs came to the Manor on the pretext of clarifying arrangements for the impending Hockey - the harvest home supper. On this occasion, she came alone and it was a while before she managed to shake off the attention of Mrs Field and speak to me in private about the child. I told her everything I knew, except for the detail about the handkerchief. She was disappointed that I had failed to find out more. I asked why she was so curious but she would just say,

"I'll know him if I see him again – believe me. He came to my door. He offered money. I'll never forget his face and the way the rain dripped from the end of his nose as he stood in the doorway of Keeper's Cottage."

"The Maundy Ceremony?" I asked.

"No. No. It wasn't one of the King's men."

"One of his spies?" I asked.

She shrugged her frail shoulders.

"I don't know where to begin to find him."

"Do you recall his name, the man that waited at the door?"

She shook her head.

"I just remember his eyes. Ice blue haunting eyes – like a ghost. I don't know what to make of it."

"A ghost you say, how alarming."

"Have you ever seen a ghost Charles?" she asked.

"Why no… not that I'm aware… can't say I'd much like to either," I replied.

Once she left, I puzzled over why Fanny was so coy about the whole experience. Now I think of it, I'm also confused as to why Mrs Plumer was so interested in the boy, Adam. I think we have a mystery on our hands.

In the course of our regular run around the Uplands Triangle - involving Wareside, Widford and Noblin Green, I was disappointed to find that Lucy wasn't waiting for me at the wrought iron gate. The signs were that the novelty of my physical training had passed. I shall desist.

The much anticipated event of the year, the Hockey, has arrived. The harvest home supper represents the culmination of the rhythms of country life, where there is a time for everything – from ploughing to sowing, to harvest. For generations, a life lived in harmony with the seasons has been the natural order. I shall record the detail for fear that the practice will soon be lost in the ugly shadow of progress. The harvest-horn was blown before sunrise.

From dawn till dusk men and women laboured beneath a baking sun in the arid harvest-fields. Lucy was eager to join me, to watch the reapers conclude their work in a field near Noblin Green. Enthused by the moment, I took her hand as a noisy and triumphant performance of, 'Crying the Mare' emerged from the reapers. They sung:

"I have her."

"What have ye?"

"A mare."

"Who's be she?"

"Farmer Ebbs'" I voiced to Lucy, drowning out the name of the actual nominated farmer.

"Where'll us send her?"

"To Farmer Fosbrooke," sang the participants, but I replaced this with, "To the King of Hearts," as Mrs Battle dubbed me once she knew of my feelings for Lucy.

The culmination of the song led the reapers to focus on the last patch of grain left standing, tied or pleated to form a sheaf. The reapers threw their stickles at it in competition for the honour of the last cut. Due to the throng, it was hard to tell who won but the victor was praised with hearty cheers by the rejuvenated reapers. The last sheaf, trimmed with flowers, was lifted to the last load. The decorated wagon and horses set off and men and boys ran alongside, carrying boughs of ash and singing,

> ♫ Master he's got in his corn,
> Well mawn, well shorn,
> Ne'er heeled over, ne'er stuck fast.
> The harvest has come home at last. ♫

The verse seemed symbolic of my relationship with Lucy. Now was the time for my personal harvest - she will be mine and I will be hers. How uplifted we were, as we followed the reapers to Nimley Bourne farm. They sang,

> ♫ Hip hip, hurrah, harvest home.
> Three plum puddings are better than none,
> So hip hip, hurrah, harvest home. ♫

Once back on the farm, Lucy left my side to join those who ran out and poured water over the men, amid shouts and merriment. It was a ceremony designed to secure a good crop for next year.

The Hockey was a vibrant gathering of farm workers and an opportunity for merriment, more harvest songs and old country dancing in the decorated barn at Noblin Green. At first, I was anxious about my presence at the Hockey, given my heritage, but I need not have worried. I was made to feel most welcome, especially by Fanny Ebbs who was clearly eager to keep me in good favour because of the boy Adam.

Besides, I had Bill Richmond for company and protection, which was useful given the persistent sense that spies and villains were amongst the Hayabouts. The former boxer was the focus of much attention, and I was fearful that we might see some drink induced wagering and spontaneous offers to spar. There were a number of potential opponents, including Thomas Watson. Although I didn't dwell on the matter for long - something else surfaced that astonished me. Fanny Ebbs told me that Lady Katharine Plumer had accepted an offer of marriage from Captain Richard Lewin!

29 August 1822

I was astonished by yesterday's news, for I felt betrayed by Richard and Katharine. How was it that Fanny, and Lucy for that matter, knew of the proposal ahead of me? Thank Heaven for Sarah Battle's memory and our deck of cards.

30 August 1822

I sought an explanation from Lady Plumer on why news of the engagement had been kept from me. Apparently, it was due to a misunderstanding involving Reverend North. Captain Lewin also vouched for this. Oh, what of all the talk of loyalty for the late John Plumer, and for King and country!

1 September 1822

September – how I loathe thee! Betrayed by those I love, I made for Uncle John's statuesque lion. I was last here with Lucy, just ahead of Captain Lewin's return. We had chased each other about the lion in gay abandon. The echoes of our laughter were with me still, as I admired the stone beast. The sturdy lion had a stately demeanour that reminded me of the 'White Wolf of Wareside'. I feigned to stroke the beast, half expecting a heartbeat or a roar. Instead the tune 'Yankee Doodle' whistled in my ear. I spun about to find Captain Lewin facing me, holding the tomahawk collected from his American expedition. People creeping up on me unawares was becoming a habit. Instinctively, I backed away from Richard, catching my hand on one of the stone paws. It bled, unnoticed at first.

"It was either a lion or a unicorn for the crown, but the lion beat the unicorn all around the town," he said, realising my fascination with the statue. The Captain stood beside me - shoulder to shoulder, though he was several inches taller.

"That's how Johnnie decided between the two or so he says. Remarkable things nursery rhymes! A curious blend of fantasy and reality – a mix of the gentile with the gruesome! Isn't it strange how we impose such nonsense on our children?"

"It's all very innocent," I suggested, clutching my hand. "Opening our mind to imagination and bringing a certain magic to childhood. I'm bleeding!"

Richard searched unsuccessfully for his handkerchief,

"You are... the point I am trying to make, dear Charles, is there's a fine line between fact and fiction, they blur into each other as night and day. Do you have a handkerchief, I seem to have lost mine," he claimed.

"As do truth and lies," I said with some hesitance, consciously aware of Richard's weapon.

"Hold the hand high... it'll help stem the bleeding! Charles, I know how it must seem, but Katharine and I acted in your best interest. You are... were... vulnerable. We see it as our duty to protect you."

"Is that why you came armed?" I asked, noticing my blood on Uncle John's statue.

"This," he lifted the axe; "Really Charles I would never hurt you... not intentionally at least. Has it stopped?"

"I believe so!"

"I brought it with me from my travels as it seems so symbolic of mankind's capacity for destruction. I cannot but wonder how many scalps it has claimed in its time."

I shirked at the very thought of it.

"Sometimes Charles, I think you forget that I am a man of war. I have sent many men to their deaths... too many men, and taken life too."

"So you have."

"But I've too much blood on my hands. I plan to put my talents to better use, by tendering nature, thus the axe... to help clear away dead wood from about the statue."

We shook on the deal. My blood was on his hands!

2 September 1822

I waited until this morning to offer you, Gaia, my loyal friend, any further account of yesterday's events. The Captain suspects me of keeping a journal and conversing with the deceased or people direct from my own imagination. In the evening he said,

"I urge you caution Charles. You do remember the last time you kept a journal it led to tragedy and insanity. We can't let it happen again. Take care with your words. Be wary for your health. You've been burning the midnight candle too long," he insisted.

"You are a man of war. I am a man of art."

"Charles - think twice, lay down your pen, rest!"

Silence!

23 September 1822

I have honoured the Captain's advice for more than twenty days. Fear has kept me from writing, but I must confide in you, Gaia, about the terror of all those years ago. I can no longer keep the details within me. Pain is life – the sharper, the more evidence of life. A tear shed in secret, though silent it falls, shall stay long in the heart. Oh, I must express myself – the silence is torture. But it is so difficult to put the words to paper. I'm so afraid. No, I am terrified of the consequences. It gnaws away at me. My stomach churns as though

I am dying of hunger. I cannot settle. I pace the room. What if Richard is right? Yet all I need do is write the words. It cannot be that hard, surely. What possible harm can come from a mere journal? How can I possibly influence the future – that is pure fantasy?

All I want is a voice. I just want to be heard. Sometimes children paint or draw to express how they feel, why not me through my artistry? Besides, the pain of my loss is so immense; maybe recounting the experience will help ease it. Lucy is right, I should express all I feel. My theory is to enjoy life, but the reality is against it. What use is an artist if he cannot create? Except this is no fiction – this is fact.

Alas, something profound is restraining me. Today marked the autumn equinox, when the hours of light and day share parity. For me, there is something fateful about the celestial event. I dare not tempt further sorrow by revealing to you, Gaia, the reality of my worst nightmare.

25 September 1822

Conscious of my emotional trauma, Richard Lewin spoke to me about a philosophy he has adopted following his visit to the New World. He sat in the Justice Chair as he told me about his new belief that our Earth is a living planet. It has a spirit. We don't own it. It's not the property or estate of humans to do with it as we wish. We turn our back on Nature at our peril. I am much encouraged – there is much more to Richard than I imagined. I shall write to my dear friend Samuel Coleridge to share the news.

28 September 1822

Gaia, on one of his missionary visits, as I like to call them, Reverend North retold to me stories shared with him by his congregation. Stories embellished with fear brought about by news of another unwelcome discovery – the body of a trader robbed of his takings following the market fair in Hertford. Questions are being asked and accusations are flying. People are uneasy and suspicious. Fingers are being pointed at some of the nomadic labourers and other newcomers. One man in particular seems to be attracting attention. That man is the resident of Crooked Chimneys. I'm told he goes by the name of Walter Clibborn.

1 October 1822

September is over at last and without any sorrow. Dare I tempt fate by saying, "I am beginning to lose my fear of September?" Welcome October – despite the coming of shorter days, longer nights and All Hallows Eve. I feel alive again – as though I have emerged from mourning once more.

I feel ready to give again and leave the cards behind me. The only true time which a man can properly call his own, is that which he has all to himself. The rest, though in some sense he may be said to live it, is other peoples time not his own. However, any time spent with my beloved Lucy is everything to me. My sweet darling, I have neglected you so these last few weeks. I beg thy forgiveness and understanding. How preoccupied I have been with my own preoccupations! A head full of worry and regret whilst the woman most precious in this world carries on without me. Oh, whimsical me living in a fantasy world of war heroes, manic dogs, white wolves, art and Solitaire. The line betwixt sanity or otherwise is fine indeed.

3 October 1822

How could I have ever doubted Lucy? Her love is constant and true - unfailing despite the barriers between us. She ran into my arms, stronger now thanks to the persistence of Bill Richmond. I raised her from the ground and span her around. She laughed freely. I let her loose and chased her across the fields at Philosopher's Point. Twas a mild autumn day – the kind of day when the Earth plays tricks with you – a little reminder of the summer just gone. She wore her blue ribbon once again. I untied it from her hair.

"Sing me another ditty Charles," she requested, once I caught her and we tumbled in the grass.

> ♫ My young love said to me, "My mother won't mind,
> And my father won't slight me for your lack of kind."
> And she stepped away from me and this she did say. ♫

I paused to wait for her response. Oh it flowed like wine,

> ♫ "It will not be long, love, till our wedding day."[17] ♫

Sweet joy - Heaven's blessings! Katharine and Richard may marry soon but we will follow in their footsteps – whatever it takes. In all our interests, Lucy, sweet nature, I vow to love thee, be faithful to thee, unconditionally and for as long as we all shall be.

10 October 1822

I must not procrastinate. I long to present Lucy with a token of my esteem - to show the world how much I adore her. If I am to make a formal proposal of marriage then tradition requires that I present her with a ring as a symbol of our love and commitment, but that is so fraught with difficulties. If she were to wear one on her vein of love[18] then questions would be asked. Oh this foolish nonsense. Why should our happiness depend on the permission or approval of others? I believe I am now emotionally stable again and able to make my own decisions. I shall put an end to it. We shall commit to each other in secret for now – I will find a way.

19 October 1822

A new newspaper – the Sunday Times – has appeared. Lady Plumer has pledged to obtain a copy. Pity in some ways that a heavy stamp duty imposed on newspapers means the Radicals[19] won't be able to afford to print their own.

Lady Katharine Plumer and Captain Richard Lewin KB have gone to London on business for a few days. They went by carriage this morning. Richard wore his full military finery. A trip to the rebuilt royal New Haymarket Theatre is planned. I understand they will see Sheridan's *The Rivals*.

The play was a favourite of George Washington[20] and has received much acclaim. It is adored by the royal family. Oh the irony - the main characters are Lydia Languish and Captain Jack Absolute. Lydia is obsessed with the romantic ideals of love. She is drawn into a relationship with Jack, who pretends to be a poor soldier. Lydia's aunt wants her to marry for financial reasons, so seeks to prevent their romance. Lydia finds the idea of eloping with the soldier romantic. It turns out Captain Jack is a rich gentleman, but Lydia refuses to marry him when she learns the truth. Most curious! Maybe the play will prick their conscious – let us see!

23 October 1822

Mrs Field and the engaging Bill Richmond consented to Lucy visiting Blakesware Manor in Lady Plumer's absence. In truth, she was rather overwhelmed; especially by the Art. I just had to show her the Gallery – to give her one chance to admire and study some of the great artists of our time,
"Charles, I never imagined a collection like this – it's extraordinary."
"Seeing is not the same as looking, as hearing is not the same as listening," I advised, as she slowly paced up and down.
"Seeing involves opening your eyes – to look you must open your mind and test your intellect. Think of it as a journey, allow me to educate you."
"What about opening your heart too," she suggested. "You know - to live, breathe and feel the painting."
Such insight!

"Let's begin with this one, '*Nelson and the Bear*.' Look at the bear – can't you feel his fear. The threat to his life – such a beautiful and wonderful animal at the mercy of cruel and heartless men driven by glory and pride," she said.

"But that's Viscount Horatio Nelson. Bold, unafraid and willing to disregard orders from his seniors."

"Every man must do his duty[21] – well let's begin by looking after the bear shall we."

"It's called a polar bear," I clarified.

"Look at the ice. It's breaking up. Did the man make that happen?" she asked.

"That's not just a man. It's Admiral Nelson. Look, I'm not a man of science, but I suspect not. I do know that Captain Lewin tells me the ice caps in the Arctic are huge – the size of all of America at least."

"Imagine Charles what would happen if all that ice were to melt," she suggested.

"You do amuse me Lucy. So refreshing – able to see beyond the picture – to see the bigger picture."

"Well you've displayed me opposite the bear, so I can be its guardian angel."

"Oh, sweet nature. This is why I adore you."

"And this one?" she asked.

"That's the *Haymakers* by George Stubbs. This one is very special to me."

Lucy stood before it and tilted her head to one side.

"Is that Captain Lewin on top of the hay cart?" she asked.

"No. I asked him that before. He fully accepts the likeness. But no he says it isn't he."

"And the ladies on the left – one looks like Mrs Field - younger and leaner - and the person moulding the hay at the top – he looks like Mr Phipps."

"Really, are you sure?" I looked closely.

"Oh yes, it's him for certain."

She was absolutely right.

"What of the woman in the middle?" I asked.

Lucy placed her right hand on her hip and took a good look.

"I have a hat just like that. Mother bought it for me."

She fell silent.

"Come Charles. Show me the others."

"Don't be afraid Lucy."

I held her hand.

"I'm not afraid. It's just a painting Charles. It's not real life."

She continued, "And, what of the man next to me?"

"The one with his back to us?" I asked.

"No Charles – see before you the man in the shadows. A silhouette! Can it be that an unseen face without light can be a guiding star?"

"We see things not as they are, but as we are," I replied. "I've looked at this painting many times and many times my senses have failed me."

"Well Charles, everyone's got to learn sometime - even the most educated of people."

"How very true."

She moved to face another picture,

"And this?"

"That's by William Turner. It's called, '*Snow Storm: Hannibal and His Army Crossing the Alps*'."

"It's huge and so very sombre, yet has an amazing lightness too."

"It has so much detail down here. Look at the despair of this man with his arms raised to the heavens."

"Oh woe is me," she said.

"They're victims of Nature's wrath. You see the might of Nature is the real subject of the painting. The message is that Napoleon should have turned back whilst he had the chance, but he drove on and used up his resources. It was the cruel Russian winter that turned the tide."

Lucy clearly had a deep appreciation of art. She was overjoyed,

"A lesson for us all... they are all wonderful, most wonderful. But why are they here?" she asked.

"Because the hunger for magic and mystery will never die. Whatever the machines bring and science delivers, they will never provide the answers to the deeper questions that the human imagination craves." I said proudly.

"Quite, but no Charles, I mean, why they are here – at Blakesware?"

"Oh, we are just borrowing them until after Christmas, until the National Gallery[22] in London is complete. Call it a favour from the Duke to the Captain for his services in war."

"The Duke?"

"Wellington himself."

"Goodness me Charles. I ought not to be here amongst these treasures - me a mere peasant woman, a commoner."

"Nonsense Lucy – Art is for all the people. Take Bill Richmond, Richard brought him here to guard the paintings until they are returned, yet he finds much joy in them too. I do wish all the people in the world could discover the inner secrets of these paintings!"

"Then let it be so, Charles. A time will come when the people will witness their true glory and mystic. May they be inspired, one and all," she requested, wistfully. But I cautioned her,

"Marvellous indeed, but remember this Lucy; thieves are close at hand, ready to steal the works away!"

This is the second of my postcards. Snow storm - Hannibal and his Army Crossing the Alps, 1812.

Take heart Ben Whittenbury – you are the New Romantic. Hold a mirror in your hands and see three candles of hope for the dawning of a new age that shines bright in the reflection.

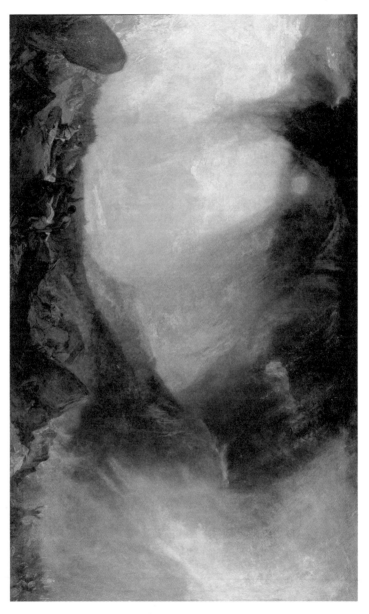

291

Dear Reader,

"This masterpiece reminds me the Romanticism period was overflowing with creativity in all the arts. Turner's era was shared by Mozart, Beethoven, Victor Hugo, Byron and Keats. In politics there were figures like Napoleon, Wellington, Nelson and Washington too. It was a time when many new ideas and hopes were born. A golden age when people believed passionately in the freedom of the individual, enjoying new experiences and taking risks. Better to be a heroic success or a total failure, than something in between."

Yours hopefully,

The Curator's Assistant
7 January 2007

Snow Storm: Hannibal and his Army Crossing the Alps by William Turner, Circa. 1806©
Tate Britain, London.

25 October 1822

Captain Lewin and Lady Plumer returned at noon through a sea of torrential rain. They arrived sodden and cold and sought solace and warmth by the hearth in the Great Hall. We were all surprised to find they were not alone. A young woman had joined them. Her name was Emma Isola[23].

"She's an orphan," Katharine Plumer advised, once she'd changed into warmer clothes.

"Call it a favour," added Richard, when Emma was out of earshot.

"She's just turned 15. Her father died when she was very young. She'll be staying with us for a while – to conclude her education."

I was bemused.

"How long is a while?"

"As long as it takes, dear Charles. We all need somewhere to call home."

Emma was certainly an attractive and educated young woman, of that I had no doubts. Slender and elegant, she had a welcoming smile that befitted her warm Mediterranean complexion, chestnut hair and soft hazel eyes. It was hard not to take to her.

"It's such a delight to meet you Charles – Richard and Katharine spoke so highly of you," she claimed. I'm honoured.

28 October 1822

I have been unable to settle since Emma's arrival. I wander the Manor like a lost sheep, asking questions of my conscience. I have seldom spoken to the young woman. She has told me a little of her past, about her schooling and her interests, but that's it. I find I am curious and resentful at the same time. I sense the feelings are replicated. My curiosity is her learned background – she has a hunger for knowledge and is studying Latin. So my resentment is purely selfish.

Lady Plumer and Captain Lewin seem besotted with her. She, a stranger in our midst, with her every word and deed admired and praised. Yet who is she to us? Have they no pride? What about the infant Adam – what of his future? How hypocritical when compared to their attitude to Lucy – cruel, heartless, discrimination based on upbringing alone. A commoner by birth, but not by nature! They are blind to it. We will neither be the best of friends nor the best of enemies. I must bear her to make her time here more tolerable, until she returns to Dulwich. I must not dwell upon the contrast in fortunes, else I shall become miserable.

31 October 1822

Seldom do I dream, but this night, of all nights, I dreamt such a vivid and horrid vision:

In blistering heat, I walked alone in a desert. Ahead was an oasis, but with every step the oasis seemed to shrink. My feet sunk deep into burning sand, leaving a clear indelible trail in my wake. From whence it came, I know not, but a thunderous roar swept overhead, worse than any howling wind I have ever known. I looked to the skies. An enormous metal bird flew over my head, with fearsome power. I shuddered to the bone, crouching low for cover.

Had I seen a star that had fallen to Earth? Was the sky falling in? To my despair, the comet, for that is how I might best describe it, plummeted into the oasis. A crash of a magnitude beyond all imagination. Flames soared to the heavens, with dark acrid smoke above them. The oasis was ablaze. From within, the surviving creatures emerged. I witnessed elephants, lions and bears – all kinds of animals, great and small, fleeing in a terrified stampede – but to where – a land of sand devoid of food, water and shelter.

Behold, another almighty roar. The sand beneath me shook - Earthquake? I slumped to my knees only to witness the sight of a mountain of water appear on the horizon, approaching moment by moment. Somehow, I sensed I was dreaming. "Wake up," I urged. "Wake up, before it's too late." I struggled to my feet and ran. The animals were about me – some in flight, others fleeing on foot, as homeless exiles – their paradise lost, never to be regained. Their future was in my hands.

Ahead of me was Lucy, dressed in grey – not her usual blue. She stood as a statue, with her right arm raised in defiance. She held aloft an Olympic torch. About the beacon, fluttered a blue ribbon. I watched it fall from grace to nestle in the sand in the shape of a heart. I feared for Lucy's future,
"Run Lucy, run," I cried.
"Why? They see no danger?" she replied.
"But Lucy, the rising seas... the heat. Extinction beckons!"
She remained frozen, as rigid as the ice on the frozen Arctic. "Lucy, do not forsake us," I cried, as the edges of the ribbon began to fray and turn to grey. I heard the tune,'Yankee Doodle' whistled on the wind.

I awoke from the nightmare in a state of shock and awe. Pray, I beg, may I never experience such horrors again. What witchcraft was at play on this night of raging spirits?

1 November 1822

Why do people have so little trust in each other? Is it because we've been let down before – misled by those in authority? Quote me the Flat Earth Society[24], with their eccentric claims that the Earth is a flat disc centred at the North Pole bounded along its edge with a wall of ice! Stuff n' nonsense and all because we can't yet see a round Earth from the heavens! I digress.

You will have gathered from this journal that I am prone to moods – isn't everyone. Call me capricious and sensitive, if you must, but these traits are fundamental and essential for an artist. Lucy Ebbs knows me and loves me for it. She says I spin like a top. Well she changes like the seasons, but shirks if I dare to say she is a Spinning Jenny.[25]

Gaia, I have a thing about circles. Remember the lion's head plinth in the gardens of Blakesware – that symbolic honour to the Clobbenhale's - when Lucy and I danced around it in the hot summer sun? We did so again, despite the slippery fallen leaves. I chased her, this way then the other. How she laughed; an infectious laughter – one to brighten the darkest, greyest day! As we circled the statue she sang the nursery rhyme, "Ring a ring o' roses, we all fall down." Are we not all children at heart?

Strange, for as we danced around the plinth we felt immortal. That was until Lucy stopped in her tracks and cried, "The sky is falling in[26]. The sky is falling in!"

"Then rush to tell the King," I said in jest.

An acorn had fallen from a nearby oak and hit her on top of her head. "Oh woe is me,[27]" she mumbled, feigning serious injury – duping me into taking her into my arms.

"Lucy Ebbs… what ails thee?"

The acorn was beneath her feet. She picked it up.

"We fear the curse of the dark Satanic Mills," she replied.

Recalling the horrors of my recent nightmare, I said,

"Then let me ease your torment. Let me protect you forever. For how dark and lost would this world be without you - flowers would refuse to bloom, rivers would run dry and crops would falter. An icy tear would settle upon the Earth."

"You flatter me Charles."

"All the riches in the world could not claim you."

"Here… Charles, take this acorn as my gift to you… think of it as a part of my heart able to grow mighty and strong."

"Rejoice in this seed of creation! Curse the fools that threaten all we cherish and adore."

Yes Gaia, I kissed her.

8 November 1822

In September, I vowed to write to my dear friend Samuel Coleridge as a presage to the most marvellous event Captain Lewin is arranging. I entrust a copy of my letter to you Gaia.

"Coleridge!

My fellow Bluecoater from Christ's.[28] I had to write. It is many weeks now since we last conversed and there is much for me to say. Hold your breath, dear poet for magic abounds. Captain Richard Lewin KB seeks the pleasure of your company this Christmas! I never was more serious. Pray, in the new United States he learnt of a new philosophy and wants to share this with patriots and artistic kinsmen. We propose the theme of our Salon[29] as, 'man's relations with Nature as the machines grow and the Jenny's spin!' It's in Percy's honour.

He embraced my suggestion that you and William should take part. We hope that Blake will join us too - how apt given the name of the Manor! I wanted to give you early notice. I feel we poets will have a collective superiority over Stubbs[30], Turner, Constable and Westall and the Danish sculptor Thorvaldsen. They have made commitments to honour Richard and the Duke himself may make an appearance. Yes, the Duke! The remarkable politician William Wilberforce has indicated his willingness to attend. Come dear Samuel, join us and let the

General honour you in person. Let our imaginations flourish beneath the inspirational Great Hall here at Blakesware. At last you will be able to take a turn on the Justice Chair. I am a dissenter!

I promise thee my countryman, my kindred spirit, that my beloved will be present too. I know some still doubt me but I shall honour my words. Oh, the riddle of destiny. She will not disappoint, my Celia. She is Nature personified – treat her kindly – until the bells of St John's Church ring to celebrate our marriage. Sweet music to my ears – a welcome blessing from my years of sadness awaits. I have had many, many, many hours of happiness in her company and have left the cards be. My long hours of solitary are at an end.

We have, too, the arrival of the beautiful young Emma Isola. At first, I cared not a farthing candle. Yet I begin to find her agreeable and she is mastering Latin. Ex silentio[31], I believe she and I have a mutual understanding, pending her return to Colebrooke[32], Dulwich.

Do write hastily Samuel, for we are so keen to learn of your decision.

Your dearest friend,

Charles.

PS: I am on the march my friend - the greatest pleasure I know is to do a good deed by stealth, and to have if found out by accident. I shall share my plans on this should you honour us with your company – I await in great expectation!

24 November 1822

Lucy can be so enigmatic. When I paid her a discreet visit at Keeper's Cottage on a cool and breezy late autumn day, she encouraged me to take a gentle walk by the banks of the Nimley Bourne stream. She is a woman for all seasons, believing each brings their own wonders. "The beauty lies in the diversity," she told me. "Of all living things, and of the sun, the moon and in the rain, the wind, the hail, the frost and the ice."
"Why do you speak so?" I asked.
"It's just all part of me, and me of it," she replied.
She ran ahead of me along the bank,
"Careful, you might fall," I told her doing my best to follow her nimble feet. I left clumsy prints in the sodden ground. She left hardly an impression.
"There, yonder, do you see him?" she cried, her voice almost lost in the rustle of the swaying branches overhead.
"Lucy. What's your game?" I cried.
"There... at the peak. He is waiting. Come Charles, don't tarry so," she urged, dancing across stones in the stream.
"Jack, be nimble, Jack be quick," I called.
"Here... follow me. It's not much further."
I kept my eyes firmly on the ground beneath my feet, to avoid falling.

Lucy had grabbed a long slender stick to help her climb – it resembled a staff. She paused part way up the ascent from the stream. "I'm neither half way up nor down," she cried. Right hand on hip and staff in hand – just the way she looked in the *Haymakers*. "Watch out for the ten thousand men!" I replied, but the grin on my face was wiped clean by the sight of the creature that looked down on her from the top of the gully.
"Seeing is believing," she reminded me.
"The wolf," I said. "The white wolf is behind you!"
The dog scurried down the slope.

"Lucy! Lucy! Lucy!" I cried in panic, trying to recover my ground. The wolf sat beside her, panting and smiling.

"Malachi," she said, nodding in approval.

What incredulity was this?

"You know its name?" I asked, looking up at the pair.

"I do."

Two little words and three little letters that spun my heart, again.

"Come closer... look... Malachi won't bite."

"I've seen him before. He took my handkerchief," I said, taking tentative steps towards them. The animal's creamy fur ruffled and danced in a wind, which began to howl.

"Who can tell what's on his mind?" she said.

"I thought I imagined it. Richard was with him... oh and the beer!"

"The old doubling eye!"

"At the White Horse."

The dog fidgeted. Lucy lowered her hand to stroke the back of his neck.

"He's just trying to protect me, nothing more."

"Whose dog is he?" I asked.

Lucy smiled.

"Home is where the heart is Charles," she replied.

"Lucy, please speak plainly, not in riddles," I requested.

She appeared to ignore me, lifting the dog's left ear and whispering something to him. He licked her hand then sprang away at pace, rushing passed me before splashing joyfully through the stream. He looked back at us and barked three times, before fleeing into the depths of the copse. Lucy offered an explanation, "He's a free spirit," she said, taking my hand.

"What did you mean when you said he's trying to protect you?" I asked.

"Look... here Charles," she replied.

Lucy gestured to the stump of the remains of a once mighty oak.

"Study the rings of this tree, and the star at its centre. Each ring is a single year and each line that cuts the rings links them."

"Lucy!"

"It's the web of life. The system on which all species depend."

"What are you suggesting?"

"Humanity is the only species capable of influencing its destiny... I need you to bear witness to my deeds."

My lips parted.

"Charles, sh!" She put a finger to her pursed mouth. Bemused, I watched her use the long straight stick she'd found to draw a clear circle around her, dragging it in the uneven wet soil. She invited me into the circle. I hesitated.

"I circle our world[33] with this rod and trust, against the sore stitch, against the sore bite, against the grim dread, against the great horror that is hateful to us all, and all evil that enters this land."

I covered my eyes with my hands, once she was through.

"Don't be afraid, Charles, you are the key. Whatever you do, do not break faith. Do you understand?"

"Who are you?" I asked, bemused by her actions.

"Lucy Ebbs... a mere woman of the Earth."

There the incredulity came to an end.

26 November 1822
(3 o'clock in the morning)

Sleep eludes me! I write by my window under the haunting glare of a full moon. Ignore the moon at our peril. Its presence on a night such as this stirs me. It pulls, it tugs. I must shy away – oh Lunar orb be gone, ease your torment on my tired mind.

What is Malachi to Lucy? How is it that the dog is entrusted to her, to protect her? Am I incapable of doing so? Am I not stronger in body and mind than ever before? I am in command of my senses. Know this Gaia; it is my solemn duty to protect Lucy, at all costs. I swear so unto thee.

Restless slumber – be gone! Perhaps Captain Lewin knows best – that I should abandon my journal, to leave you Gaia to the mercy of the wanton ways of man. I have failed to heed Richard's advice, offered in all earnest. Lest I not forget - the nightmare, the hound called Malachi, Lucy my beloved performing spells. Yet Lucy asked me to bear witness. A man cannot have two masters. Should I lay down my pen? One day, one day! Until then, oh trusted companion, window to my soul through fair or foul, I shall be loyal to the end. What will be, will be! Let me bear any heavy burden.

27 November 1822
(Morning)

I know not where to turn. Can I confide in Emma, I wonder? She knows nothing of my past, at least the benevolent Mrs Field says so. What of Mrs Field, I hear you ask? Alas, she is bed ridden, poor soul. I cannot vex her further. No, it is Emma I must ask.

27 November 1822
(Dusk)

Unrepentant, I confided in Emma. She has a wise head on such young and pretty shoulders. "Carpe Diem[34]" she advised, having heard my tale. I warm to her. I shall return to Lucy this evening – now.

28 November 1822

That night I took a horse, Copenhagen[35], from the stables at Blakesware Manor. I rode beneath a sunken evening moon towards Lucy's cottage, along paths so dear to me. I knew every twist, every inch. As my horse progressed, hoof-by-hoof, my heart thumped so - for I feared my life if Lucy were lost.

I knew the route well by day, but by darkness, on horseback, it was like entering into another world. Dream or otherwise, my horse moved on; the vapour from its breath rising before me. The eerie moonlight taunted my imagination, casting shadows that seemed to pursue me. How I feared the legendary Gytrash. I looked about me, anticipating the horror. The red and gold lining of my riding coat whipped in my wake. Its colours changed to silver in the moon's glare. I pushed my fears aside, "She shall be mine," I vowed.

At the cottage, Copenhagen pulled up beneath a silent starlit sky. Despite the late hour, I was relieved to find a light in the house; the glow of a snug fire in a small hearth to keep the cold at bay! Inside was my beloved. I dismounted and hastily tied the horse. Out of the corner of an eye, I saw a small chequered dog; lit by the moon. It sat and looked at me and the horse in pensive silence, as if to plead, before taking to its heels and fleeing when I took a step closer.

Unperturbed, I knocked. I waited. In time, a face peered out – Fanny Ebbs. Her mien was confused, "Oh cold heart, have pity on me," I urged.
Dressed from head to toe in dreary grey, she spoke plainly,
"Quickly, I'll lose the fire... Mr Lamb, what brings you here at this hour?"
"Why to see Lucy. Please I implore you. Let me speak with her."
"Were you followed?" she asked.
"Followed, no madam not that I am aware... although I saw a dog... just now under the light of the moon."
"Come round the back. Folk may see you here."
I did as she suggested, and led the horse to the rear, on my guard for the furtive dog. As if to judge my business at the cottage, a snowy owl sped over me; I wished it all good fortune.
"You say you need to speak to Lucy," said Fanny, as she urged me inside.
"Yes. Forgive the late intrusion, but it's a serious matter of the heart."

"I had hoped you had news of the boy," she said, returning to the fire.

"The boy?"

"Adam. I hear Thomas Phipps keeps him still."

"No madam. No news of the boy… if I must, I have come to ask if I may have the honour, the pleasure."

Her manner hardened. She spoke with a melancholy tone,

"Lucy is indisposed Charles. It's not the time for you to see her. Indeed you should not come. There is too much to lose. They seek her out. It has begun. I must do what I can to protect her."

"You suffer the same affliction. Protect her, why; you a vulnerable ageing woman… me a man of sound mind and body!"

She raised her hand and gestured for me to sit. I did so. She spoke slowly and quietly, as though to avoid waking the dead,

"Charles Lamb. Listen to me, please. I know you mean well and your heart is true but I have an agreement to honour – a pact. Think of it as a partnership."

"A pact! With whom?"

She stood silent with arms folded.

"Where is this written?" I asked. "Where is she? Does she sleep? Is she resting?" I called out her name. Fanny urged me quiet. Silence except for the crack of the fading fire in the hearth. I put my head in my hands.

"I just want to care for her, to love her."

"We all do Charles, we all do."

She let me by the fire, returning with a drink. At that, I slept.

I awoke to find Captain Richard Lewin KB glaring in disapproval. "We've come to take you home Charles. We were all terribly concerned to keep you well."

Riddled by thirst and a stiff neck from sleeping upright, I said little in response. He and Lady Plumer had come to fetch me. But how did they know of my presence here? Emma Isola for sure. Betrayal!

As we departed in the fly, I peered back at the cottage. I saw Lucy's face at one of the top windows. She waved gently. Our secret alone. I smiled for the first and only time this day.

1 December 1822

Oh trusted quill – your nib is misshapen and the ink well is low. I have plucked clean Lucy's supply of goose feathers – so have to make do. Compromise – such is my life. I resort to a mere owl's feather to scribe! It is such a tedious task to select, clean and trim each quill.

5 December 1822

Joy of joys! Weather and good health permitting, Coleridge has written to confirm his presence for the festive gathering – our literary and philosophical Salon.

Behold, Gaia, the widow, Mary Shelley will join him – she of such ill fortune, hand in hand with such fame. With Captain Lewin as the inspired host, we of like-minded people propose to amuse each other. We shall refine our taste and increase our knowledge with conversation, music, readings and appreciation of nature through art. We will be known as the Blakesware Set!

Samuel picked me up on one or two inaccuracies in my letter, which he put down to my enthusiasm. In no fashioned order, the distinguished list, to please and educate, now reads:

<u>The Blakesware Set: December 1822</u>
Captain Richard Lewin KB (Host)
Lady Katharine Plumer (Hostess)
Field Marshall Arthur Wellesley (1st Duke of Wellington)
Charles Lamb (Romantic poet and essayist)
William Wordsworth (Romantic poet)
Samuel Coleridge (Romantic poet)
Mary Wollstonecraft Shelley (Writer and widow of Percy Shelley)
William Wilberforce (Pioneering politician)
William Blake (Poet and Artist)
Richard Westall (Artist)
William Turner (Artist)
Albert Thorvaldsen (Nordic Sculptor)
Ralph Waldo Emerson (Son of Reverend Emerson)
Thomas Malthus (Professor in Political Economy and Anglican Parson)
John Rickman (English Statistician)
Emma Isola (Latin Scholar)

<u>Notes</u>

William Blake, he of such fantastic visions of rural England, was deeply honoured to be invited. He was most amused to find the event will be held at a venue seemingly named in his honour! Sadly, though, he believes there's a perception that he is a lesser known outsider; a mystical marginal, labelled as an eccentric, who fears his presence may distract us with dangerous philosophies. Charles plans to try to persuade him to come. I remain hopeful, which is why he features on the list. William claims, 'I wish you well in your quest to prove what people can only, thus far, imagine. May they see the Wonder in a grain of sand, and Heaven in a wild flower!'

I very much doubt that the Duke will attend – let us see. Sir Walter Scott and John Constable have sent apologies. A young man – Hans Anderson, I think from Denmark – will accompany the sculptor. I'm told the boy of 17 is fanatical about literature and knows Shakespeare by heart. There are great expectations of him. Another, Ralph Emerson is merely 19 years of age, and a very recent Harvard graduate. Richard met him in Boston and was most impressed by his thinking, "We need the voice of the New World's youth," said Richard. Apparently a four year old boy is with them, by the name of David Thoreau. Sadly, as Samuel discreetly reminded me, George Stubbs is unable to attend.

If she has recovered sufficiently, Mrs Fields shall look after hospitality. Bill Richmond will be on hand, if required. Some will bring wives or aides. It remains my deep and sincere wish that Lucy will be permitted to join us, if only as a spectator.

Oh, Gaia, how remiss of me. The Reverend North is eager to attend too. Apparently he claims he has something most interesting to share with us.

12 December 1822
(Morning)

On one of the foggiest days I can ever recall, the first of the distinguished guests arrived to stay at Blakesware. What an eclectic bunch and full of surprises too. What's more, Lucy had the privilege of helping to direct them to the Manor – highly appropriate in my view. Lucy, often so cryptic, spared me no detail.

In her guardian's company and heading in the direction of St John's Church, they met two horse drawn carriages making slow progress. The travellers pulled up to seek directions and asked,
"Excuse me good ladies, I am right in assuming this to be the road to Blakesware Manor, residence of Lady Plumer and the Captain? Only the cursed fog has clouded our view and may have affected our judgement." It was a man with a Scandinavian accent – it had to be Albert Thorvaldsen!
"Right you are Sir," Fanny had replied.

"You are on the estate. The Manor will come into view shortly, just follow the road ahead, and take the first turning to your left at the hounds," Lucy had added.

"Hounds eh! That would be right. Maybe we're not too late after all. It really is such a genuine relief to be so close to our journey's end at last."

"Have you travelled far, Sir," Fanny asked.

"Life of late for me madam has been one long arduous journey," he replied. "But at least my creativity has been fuelled by the cruel hand of fate and taught me to value above all the angelic beauty of a young woman."

At this, a couple of other men looked out from one side of the carriage, and a young boy from the other.

"Good afternoon," they said.

They were Americans. It must have been Emerson and partners.

"Yankee Doodle went to town riding on a pony," sang one. They all laughed and cheered.

"Hope to see you fine people again," called the Scandinavian, whilst they waved. Fanny believed that independence had gone to the Americans heads.

However, what excited Lucy – and me - the most were three things. First, the sight of a large potted evergreen conifer clinging to the rear of the carriage. Twas the magical tree from the Nordic mountains! Lady Plumer plans to adorn it for the festive period. Second, either side of the tree were a couple of caged tame grey squirrels, yes grey not red. I long to see them! Lo and behold, third, the most amazing thing of all – to save the best until last! Lucy saw the curious face of an adorable creamy puppy peeping out at them, with its paws nestled beneath his jaw.

"Look, it's a baby bear."

Fanny though, was less enthusiastic, claming it was, "Prey for the Highwayman!"

12 December 1822
(Evening)

Following my secret rendezvous with Lucy, I returned to Blakesware with great expectations. These were fulfilled, as the white-bear cub was adorable. I first saw him sat upon the Justice Chair in the Great Hall. Sunlight shone through the arched window overhead. It fell directly on him, turning the Samoyed's creamy fur a spectacular shade of orange. We all gathered about him; Richard, Katharine, Emma and our various visitors. The dog's arrival even encouraged Mrs Field to rise from her sick bed. Hail the miracle maker! That smile! Happy puppy, happy puppy! Those ears fit for nibbling. The face so artful, mischievous and sweet! However, if the behaviour of the infamous White Wolf of Wareside were a guide, these characteristics disguised a host of secrets.

Captain Lewin, that heroic man of war, was besotted by the creature. I had seldom seen him grin so widely.
"He's perfect, just perfect. Everything I anticipated. I can't thank you enough Albert, really I can't," he announced, shaking enthusiastically the hand of the distinguished sculptor.
"Richard, think of him as a wedding present my friend. See him as an ambassador for the cause. Does he not resemble a little lion in many ways? He'll keep you amused, of that I'm certain," advised the Scandinavian.

I spoke, "Well Sir, he's a mighty fine creature for sure. I very much hope we are able to return the compliment of a worthy gift to you some day."
"Charles Lamb?"
I nodded.
"It's marvellous to meet you at last. Everyone has spoken so highly of your work... and of your character."
"Why thank you... likewise is true."

Active and curious, the puppy was the centre of attention. "He's the people's dog," Albert said.

"Does he have a name?" asked Emma.

"We named him Malachi," Albert replied. "But I guess you have the freedom to choose another, should you so wish."

"Could you repeat the name?" Emma asked.

"Ma – la – ki," he said, stressing the pronunciation.

"I believe it means the messenger," I suggested.

"It does so," replied Albert.

"I find it a fine and befitting name for him. I say we keep it," said the Captain.

We all exchanged eye contact, and settled things with a nod.

Lady Plumer and I smiled at each other; recalling my earlier encounter with a fully grown Samoyed of the same name.

"Come Malachi... have you a message for us?" I asked in all innocence.

The puppy licked my hand.

13 December 1822

Today is a Friday; a most unwelcome date. Superstitious, I largely kept to my room to play at cards with Sarah Battle; in my mind, she still plays a fair hand. Around us, life at Blakesware had been re-invigorated. From my window, I witnessed many of the expanded household venture with the puppy into the Manor's wilderness garden. Lively, animated and bristling with energy, it was impossible not to grow fond of Malachi.

Feelings were blossoming elsewhere too. It was abundantly clear that the boy, Emerson, was attracted to Emma. I had overheard him tell her that in America he assisted his brother in a school for young ladies at his mother's house. With an enquiring mind, he was a confident man and lover of nature - I warmed to him. Although somewhat gaunt and with a very lean upright figure, I suspect he will do well in life. He's a youth of promise. Let me recount his words, "To Britain I come, a young son of America, to the land of my ancestors, this glorious land of memory and legends, and Shakespeare."

The boy Anderson surprised me greatly. He told us how he loved the art of banter and had set up a group of like minded 'banterers' in his native land. His nature was quite feminine. He didn't shy from revealing his wooden dolls, with which, apparently, he used to enact his tales of Shakespeare, 'All the world's a stage and all the men and women merely players,[36]' he told us in defence of his behaviour.

15 December 1822

Amid the growing anticipation of the Salon, I am haunted. I am confused. Gaia, I made a list to help focus my mind. Maybe you can inspire me to find the answers:

❤   I must return to Adam. I cannot forget his tiny fingers wrapped around mine. Sweet child – he must be over six months old now. I am no closer to understanding who he is or where he came from. Where is the child's father – he who stood in the porch at Keeper's Cottage – he who Fanny once told me claimed, "If I ever met him, then God help me?"

❤   Mr Phipps still has the handkerchief – not my handkerchief. Why was the hanky in the infant's basket? Does it indicate the identity of the father of the child?

❤   What of the rose? Does it still bloom, everlasting? Tom Watson claimed he saw Richard carrying the rose, saying, "The rose is dying!" Has it died?

These enigmas – what are they? So, Gaia I took a walk along the Nimley Bourne stream – amid the cold and an icy wind - and I discovered…

Climate Change – the ticking bomb 💣

♥ *Humans are using the world's resources so fast that the planet cannot replace them quickly enough. Many of the Earth's species of animals had lost nearly one-third of their population in the last 30 years.*

♥ *Do the maths? If nothing changes, by the time a new born child today reaches adulthood the world will be entering a disaster so huge it is unthinkable.*

♥ *Global warming was set to tip many countries into crisis. Mass migration, terrorism, civil war, disease, want and starvation - this was the future.*

Such strange ramblings, but I wonder, could there be something deeper unfolding? I looked to you, Gaia, for inspiration and you delivered; you found a way to reach me as you thought fit.

What to make of such a list? Mathematics – I leave that to the likes of Malthus. Global warming – strange words indeed and what, pray, are terrorism and want? Take a look at the hearts – the three drawn hearts. Has someone been reading my journal? Am I spied upon? If so, let me tell you reader – I have no shame. Let the world know I'm writing it – I dare thee, for what value art if produced for its own sake. Be my champions - join me.

18 December 1822
(Evening)

My eyes surely have deceived me. As I put the words to paper, I can hardly believe it. What to do? Let me explain Gaia, truthfully.

For several years now publicans and traders in Ware have hosted a pre-Christmas fete. What better opportunity for our guests to enjoy some Hertfordshire customs - a night of music, magic and carnival? I had to shield them from temptation – peepshows, waxworks, and readers of fate! Yet, if I'm honest, I hoped to find Mlle Lenormand amongst them. What if I should meet her, that famed reader of cards – what of my fortune?

The night was cold and a full moon – yes my friend – a full moon. Pray, let me shield my eyes from it. I took courage, for Bill Richmond came too. I kept him in view, should fate choose to be cruel. Well, destiny led us to a magician, a masked man with the stage name, 'The Emperor'. I recall now I had seen a glimpse of this man before – at Wareside, when the White Wolf unbalanced the kegs – remember Gaia. I digress. Let me continue - such wizardry the man performed with cards and dice. But what of this volunteer?

"And what's your name, my child?" asked the magician.

"Sarah."

"Are you cold Sarah?"

"Yes, but that's okay."

"Sarah, do you believe in magic?"

"Oh yes... it's because of the Captain. He likes to play tricks on people."

The audience cheered, me amongst them.

"The Captain you say. So where is this hearty fellow then?"

"There. He's the soldier... just there." Sarah pointed at Richard Lewin, in all his finery.

"Three cheers for our hero the magnificent Captain. Hip-hip..."

"Hooray!" cried the crowd. But what was this child to Richard?

The Emperor marched before his audience declaring,

"Allow me to give you an education! Dice have a history as rich and old as man and were very popular with the Greeks and Romans. They say, too, that departed spirits in the underworld play at dice.

Oh, and these dice I have in my hand are no ordinary dice. No, they were found in mysterious Royston Cave, when it was excavated. Some say the Knights Templar took them from the Holy Land."

Oh, Reverend North was going to tell me something about the cave – I digress.

The magician stood beside the girl.

"They talk to me and me to they! So cast the dice and I will control their will. Blindfold me?" The girl did as he asked.

"Tacta alea est," he commanded. "The die is cast and I am seeing double."

The dice danced across the cobbled streets.

"Snakes Eyes!" he cried, much to Sarah's delight. She looked straight at me and smiled. Such a dear sweet child!

"Can you see into the future?" I heard the girl ask, as the magician led her away.

"Time Is, Time Was, Time's Passed," he replied.

Those words again. Oh the conundrum! I shuffled closer, making my way through the crowds. The throng meant I witnessed only parts of their conversation. I heard,

"It's a survey about what happens in the future." It was a man's voice. "I only need three questions - that's all."

The girl replied, "Okay then, three questions. Oh, that's easy my favourites are:

- ❤ Have you ever helped the poor?
- ❤ Do you have a favourite flower?
- ❤ Have you ever searched for buried treasure?

That's it. Those are my questions."

They were enchanting questions. A survey for the future, how fascinating! Now there was an idea. Although, I hadn't much time to ponder it further because of the puppy. The dog was suddenly beneath my feet, tugging at my laces.

"What is it with Samoyed's and boots... these are staying on," I insisted, before gathering up the mischievous puppy.

"Oh Malachi! What are we to do with you?" I asked. He'd obviously fled from the Captain's side.

19 December 1822
(Very early morning)

Another clandestine entry under moonlight! So, what was the girl Sarah to Captain Richard Lewin? We all saw it, but he casually dismissed the evidence. "I won't play these frivolous games," he insisted. "You all know full well I have no connection with the child, or any other child, so let that be the end of the matter." He clearly hopes the encounter will quickly be forgotten. I just wish Lucy were with me to witness it. Still, I have Sarah's questions. What to do with them?

20 December 1822

Gaia, I've had some remarkable and deep discussions with the eloquent Ralph Emerson. He is a kindred spirit and so bright for one so young. They taught him the art of conversation at Harvard. He is here against his elders' knowledge, in the hope of a meeting with the Duke. He described himself as a young scholar who finds it happiness enough to live with people who can give an insight to the world; to share anecdotes, thoughts and ideas with each other - to play 'Bo-Peep' with celebrated scribes. He already finds writers superior to their books. He will make a natural teacher. Proficient in Latin, he is winning Emma's heart, of this I am sure. He is content to impress and has good humour and wit too – together I heard them quoting Latin at the puppy and rewarding him with treats, "Qualis artifex pereo![37]"

As for young Hans Christian Anderson, he claims to have already succeeded in publishing his first story – about a ghost at a grave. He's caught the imagination of King Frederick VI of Denmark who has paid for the scholar's education. Hans really is a most amusing fellow – with a dashing magical waistcoat and a pair of squeaky boots which, he claimed, talk to him. He is most welcome.

21 December 1822
(Morning)

Ralph has served to wet my appetite. I am enthused beyond words at the imminent arrival of so many like minds and friends. A mythological gathering of extraordinary proportion awaits! Each harbours a message - all have come to participate. All have an interest in verse and art, and a sense of adventure. Hail, sound representatives of humanity. Welcome one and all. I am always longing to be with men more excellent than myself. For we gain nothing by being by ourselves as such - we merely encourage one another in mediocrity. I am under no illusions. The voice of a few, the Blakesware Set, will hardly shape the world, but I see it as my duty to scribe. Faithful Gaia I hope not to disappoint.

21 December 1822
(Afternoon)

Oh how majestic. Today, on the winter solstice, an unnerving foreboding date, we have welcomed the majority of our guests. The Captain and Lady Plumer have done themselves proud with their hospitality. Some I know well, others I met for the first time. I can hardly keep from smiling. The splendid twelve Caesar busts in the Marble Hall have met their equals. Greetings, wonderful artists – William Turner and Richard Westall; saluté, Thomas Malthus and John Rickman – men of numbers; but the best I save to last – dearest Samuel Coleridge, the magnificent William Wordsworth and the beautiful gothic Mary Shelley. No sign yet of William Blake, nor word of the Duke – but Blakesware's foundations shake with glee. Bring the Doubting Thomases to the door – those who said it would never happen. Let them eat humble pie.

Although bitterly cold, the weather had been kind to the travellers. Many chose to warm themselves beside the fire that spat, seethed and crackled in the Great Hall. I watched the smoke from the fire escape like a ghost, drifting up and out through the funnel. I thought of Percy Shelley's recently departed soul and beseeched him to join us, if it were possible. Somehow, Mary sensed my wish – we first met when she was a young girl, for I knew her father William Godwin. Now slender, but sadly mournful, she stood beside me. Her long dark hair glistened as we looked into the flames, she that creator of our modern Prometheus[38].

"Charles Lamb, when times were kinder to us, Percy often spoke admirably of you, so when Samuel told me of this venture I thought and I pondered, vainly. I know what terrifies me will terrify others. Like Percy, I understand we ought not over-reach, which is why I came."

"Mary Shelley, make no apology. You are more than any man's equal. None here doubt you." I took her fragile hand and, with her permission, kissed it. "Besides, you were kind enough to quote me in your masterpiece, so who am I to quarrel?"

"Ah, the Old Familiar Faces! Well Charles, these last few months I've seen the face of tragedy often enough. I seek some light relief – for new hope at this festive time. What joy I feel in my heart in such jocund company. Inspirational faces to flash upon my inward eye in times of solitude[39]," she knew she had William's ear. He smiled at her.

"If it's joy you seek then look here," suggested Wordsworth, for many of the guests were being entertained by Malachi - Thorvalden's gift to us.

"How enchanting. He's so adorable," said Mary. She knelt before him. "Look at the magic in his eyes. Comfort for a restless soul. What is he?"

"A Samoyed - herder, hunter, guardian and creator," said Albert Thorvaldsen.

"Worthy of a monument of his own," she replied.

A local hero, Richard Westall[40], was especially taken to him, "Worthy of that painter of dogs, George Stubbs, I'm sure," he suggested. The lively puppy looked at the artist and barked; he obviously had much to say for himself. Oh for a translator.

"Vox populi," contributed Emma, to everyone's surprise.

"It means, he's the people's voice," said Emerson. "Emma and I have been teaching him Latin." The comments triggered much laughter and more barking.

"Where in America are you from?" asked William Turner.

"Why, I'm from Boston, New England," he said proudly.

"Patriot, before you return, you should visit my gallery in London," offered Turner.

"Why thank you sir, I'd like that very much."

"I'm from America too," said a timid voice. It was young David.

"You're a long way from home, for such a young fellow."

"I'm with my Grand-pa – we've been to Jersey." Although not blest by nature with looks and obviously rustic, he was strangely confident. Mary's surviving son, Percy Florence Shelley, befriended him. The boy whispered something in David's ear and the two of them set about chasing Malachi, which made us all laugh.

21 December 1822
(Evening)

Our esteemed guests began to settle with their belongings into their rooms. I have seldom known Blakesware so alive and bustling. It's very reassuring to know that Bill Richmond and Tom Watson are on duty to deter any potential intruders – word must be spreading of the arrival of so many famed people of our time. We need to keep the evil out and the good within. I mentioned this to dear Samuel once we were alone in the majesty of the Marble Hall. The two of us paced the room, our footsteps and voices echoed into the night.

In the eerie candlelight the Caesar busts appeared almost human. Samuel and I studied each in turn. We observed that many of them resembled the faces at the Salon.

"Goodness, this one reminds me of Wordsworth, and this is the double of Turner," he claimed. I had to agree.

Samuel sat before the grand piano and toyed with the ivory keys. He played the opening bars to Ludwig Beethoven's famous fifth symphony. This giant amongst dwarfs[41] was enduring a crisis of confidence. His health may have benefited from a spell in Italy, but his quill had run dry.

"My friend, I fear my vigour and poetic powers have escaped me," he said. "To be replaced with a dark obsession[42]. The torment of my thirst, I am the Ancient Mariner[43] with an albatross round my neck." I knew Samuel craved attention but his melancholy surprised me.

"Dear Samuel, have courage. Don't doubt - your reputation is intact. Smile, be happy. The deep magic is unfolding. Come with me," I suggested, leading him to the Justice Chair.

"Where are you taking me?" he asked.

"To some place inspirational."

I invited him to sit on the cold hard Justice Chair. He understood its reputation and did as I proposed. "I may never sit in this chair again," he said. Tenderly, he stroked the grain, then reached down to feel the carvings at the chair's base. Samuel closed his eyes and sat in silence for several minutes, before whispering, "Water, water everywhere, nor a drop to drink." These were lines from his epic poem. He opened his eyes as a changed and fortified man, recollecting the magnificence of his creations. I took my opportunity to show him the list I'd found.

319

Climate Change – the ticking bomb 💣

♥ _Humans are using the world's resources so fast that the planet cannot replace them quickly enough. Many of the Earth's species of animals had lost nearly one-third of their population in the last 30 years._

♥ _Do the maths? If nothing changes, by the time a new born child today reaches adulthood the world will be entering a disaster so huge it is unthinkable._

♥ _Global warming was set to tip many countries into crisis. Mass migration, terrorism, civil war, disease, want and starvation - this was the future._

Together we shared these new horizons. "What does it mean?" I asked him.

"A curious mixture – a rouse to provoke our imagination. We should show it to the others," he proposed. But how? My credibility was at stake. Most know my history and I remain under Captain Lewin's watchful eye. Samuel as good as read my mind. He rose from his temporary throne as an emperor of wishful thinking. "Kubla Khan," he whispered, "Rejoice in the beauty of creation - savour the joy of Nature's majestic pleasure dome decree[44]. Let us unleash the deep magic. In that knowledge, I shake off my apathy." His theatrics drew the attention of someone stood in the shadows. It was Lucy. My faith in Samuel restored, I longed to introduce her but she, the unannounced and uninvited, put her whimsical finger to her lips to plea for silence and solitude.

Samuel's voice drew me back to him,

"Do you know if William Blake will join us? Has he confirmed? It's just when I visited him at Fountain Court, I thought him a genius. He would grace our Salon. A man ridiculed for claiming to have seen a tree filled with angels... we need him Charles. I know the world is divided in its opinion, but this strong opponent of slavery and advocate of sexual equality, is our true friend and compatriot."

"Sadly Samuel... it would seem not. Though we have not had a word of confirmation or decline," I replied.

"Maybe the presence of the Duke has kept him at bay – for his association with remarks against the King and praise for Napoleon linger," whispered Samuel. "And our good friend William, thinks him insane."

"It is a pity. Is there no justice?"

Samuel was still seated in the grand chair.

"I sense, dear Charles, that the mystical fellow that is William Blake will one day be celebrated as one of the greatest British artists."

I tend to agree.

"I shall scribe the words of the Blakesware Set with him in mind."

21 December 1822
(Approaching midnight)

Tomorrow, Captain Lewin and Lady Katharine Plumer are to wed. Envy, I beg thee, don't cloud my weary eyes.

22 December 1822

How distasteful is the complacency and satisfaction in the faces of newly-weds. There's little more I want to say, other than Reverend North conducted the service at St John's Church. He, this man of the cloth, reminded me that he would like to attend the Salon, claiming he had something spectacular to offer. Who am I to deny the will of God?

Gaia, I must put right an omission. I've said very little about the tree and squirrels that Albert Thorvaldsen brought with him. Allow me to use his words to educate you. Imagine Albert sat upon the Justice Chair with the collective guests mingling about him. The supposed mystical tree – he named as Yggdrasil - stood only about 12 feet tall in a huge pot. Frankly, it looked fragile and nothing akin to the powerful guardian of humanity Nordic legend would suggest. To begin with it was far from gigantic. It was also a most unusual name. It meant 'Odin's Steed,' and describes his self sacrifice, although the pessimistic sometimes call it, 'Terrible Horse.' Albert quoted Odin's sacrifice at us,

> "I – that is Odin[45] - hung on that windy tree for nine nights wounded by my own spear. I hung to that tree and no one knows where it is rooted. None gave me food. None gave me drink. Into the abyss I stared until I spied the runes. I seized them up, and howling, fell."

We studied the innocuous tree. Mary Shelley stood closest to it. She ran her fingers through the needles of one of its branches. "Brave Odin," she stated, entering into the spirit of things; this was a woman after my own heart.

"Brave indeed, but the real magic of the tree before you is that it comes from the Russian Arctic Tundra. There reside the Samoyed tribe – they who care for the Samoyed dog. It's a World Tree to represent the folklore of Siberia."

In impeccable timing, the puppy ran in to the hall. It slid ungraciously on the marble floor and yapped excitedly. He regained his footing and ran towards Albert to paw his breeches. Ceremoniously, Albert lifted him on to his lap and continued his tale, "In the mythology of the Samoyeds, the World Tree connects realities together – the underworld, this world and the upper world."

Malachi seemed to nod in approval – a wise puppy was he.

"But, here is the rub - in Samoyed mythology the tree is the symbol of Mother Earth, for the Samoyed tribe has a belief system which stresses respect for animals, the land and its resources. At these times, when we have begun to abuse our world – to drain its sap and bleed it dry – I believe we can look to the Samoyed people, their tree and their wisdom to inspire and guide us."

The puppy licked Albert's face.

"One more word – the Samoyed tree is famed for showing how the past and the future coil around the present."

"I believe the tree was created for a glorious future," suggested Hans. Oh sacred tree, I honour thee!

24 December 1822
(Noon)

Twas Mary's idea to adorn Yggdrasil for the Christmas period. We left the tree in the cool Justice Hall and laced it with apples, berries and nuts, sweets, bells and tiny dolls that resembled fairies. We carefully placed candles on a few of the branches and planned to light them when darkness fell. The children adored the tree, though the more conservative amongst us were not amused - the likes of Rickman and Malthus. Regardless, I have a feeling the practice could grow common and widespread. We shall see. I do wish Lucy was here to witness it – why do we exclude her so? Did she not once tell me, "I am everywhere you turn Charles. You'll find me in the wind, the rain and the sun. I am in the breath of every living thing?" Yes, those were her words. Dear Lucy, I Forget-you-not.

On a cold and frosty morning, some of us took a walk in the grounds of Blakesware. We explored the wilderness and the rose garden and admired the late John Plumer's lion head statue. Although overshadowed by his dying lion monument of Lucerne[46], when Albert saw it, he greatly approved. He favoured its proud expression, realism and detail. "Time Is, Time Was, Time's Passed," he said as he, and others, circled the beast. As we did so, Samuel taught us his ode for a poet,

> "Weave a circle round him thrice,
> And close your eyes in Holy dread.
> For he on honey dew hath fed
> And drunk the milk of paradise."

Nourished by his words, Albert asked,
"Tell me Charles, do you know why your uncle had such a fascination with time?"
"No, all I know of John is that he was a man of business. Deputy Lieutenant of the County, Colonel of the County Militia and Justice of the Quorum."
"Quite a title," he responded. "You must regard him highly, as a man of much influence."
At these words, I felt an icy gaze from a presence at the window of the room that overlooked the lion statue. I dared not turn to look.
"Perhaps, yet if he had his way I would probably be far from a man of Art, Love and Nature... of that much I am certain."
"Why then would he have inscribed, 'verbatim ac literatim' on the base of the plinth?"
"Word for word, letter for letter," translated Emma Isola.
"Don't you find that mysterious, a rouse Charles?"
"I suppose... now you say it," I replied.
I mused. So, word for word, letter for letter, we have:

- 💙 A set of questions from a strange young girl,

- 💙 A ticking bomb called climate change, and

- 💙 A riddle about time.

Enough material to get the Blakesware Set in motion.

24 December 1822
(Afternoon)

My quill is creaking under the strain. I have crept to my room several times since the guests arrived to scribe what I can, when I can. Forgive me, Gaia, if my words appear disjointed. I feel constantly under surveillance. I have to look over my shoulder, watch my every word. I cannot relax. In case my actions are discovered, let it be known, I have no shame or regret. That is except for my behaviour at the wedding of Richard and Katharine. Here I seek to repay these loyal hosts. I forget that without them I would linger in the 'work-a-day' world Lady Katharine regularly warns me about. Contrite and sincere, I offered apologises for my silence and mood on their wedding day.

I was surprised to learn they had no quarrel with me, finding my behaviour on the day entirely as they had expected. Love is truly blind! Besides, Emma and Ralph had a plan; a surprise to deny the Lewin's any chance of lamenting my actions. Bless these visitors. Imagine the grand piano; a temporary stage and performers. Picture Emma and the controversial Beggar's Opera[47], composed by John Gay. Hark, I, the beggar, introduced the play,
"Life is a jest and all things show it, I thought it once but now I know it."[48]
Hark, Emma's nightingale voice:

♫ The turtle thus with plaintive crying, her lover dying,
The turtle thus with plaintive crying, laments her dove.
Down she drops quite spent with sighing
Pair'd in death as pair'd in love. ♫

The turtle doves were the newly weds, Richard and Katharine! Once Emma finished her brief solo, the audience took up with, "Two turtle doves and a partridge in a pear tree." Oh, how we laughed, the Twelve Days of Christmas had begun.

Albert Thorvaldsen had yet another surprise for us, in the form of a poem recently composed by an Austrian priest called Joseph Mohr. With the candles on the world tree aglow, Albert played the grand piano, whilst Emma sang. The poem was *Silent Night*. It was a beautiful lament about sleep in heavenly peace. The creative mind of William Wordsworth toyed with the opening lines and sang, "Silent flight, owl of white," which amused me. His words reminded me of my recent spontaneous ride to Keeper's Cottage to seek Lucy, when the silent white owl flew over me, as though a ghost in the night. I shall do all I can to involve Lucy in tomorrow's joyful celebrations.

Hans Christian Anderson was besotted by the tree. He staged a puppet show for young Percy and David to tell a story of a little match girl, concluding with the words, "The light of the Christmas tree stretched higher and higher like stars in Heaven." He has the making of a renowned author and poet, I wager.

25 December 1822
Christmas Day

How can I account for such a day as this? Oh Gaia, the responsibility overwhelms me. Distracted, I can hardly think, let alone scribe. The excitement fuels my adrenalin. Focus, concentration and flair – these qualities I need. Oh quill, don't fail me now. Where shall I begin?

Yesterday eve, we took a vote on whether to conduct our Salon on his Saviour's day for fear of being distracted or disrespectful. None of us crave to live forever in shame. Yet, on this day we wanted to do something memorable – to make our choices and leave an impression. This was not about religion but about symbolism: all champions need a great stage on which to perform. What better opportunity to send our gift of hope to humanity in the face of darkness – those creeping Satanic Mills - words perhaps immortalised by one W.Blake Esq.

Although many of us were much older, greyer and wiser than I had imagined we had a wonderful mix of people – the reserved and the charismatic; the stoic[49] and the emotional; the witty and the dry. Whatever our background, age or experience, we had one thing in common – we were witnesses to life – all contemplating where the dawn of the age of the machine would take us. We vowed to speak with one voice, for one world, to find one solution. Hear us now.

Although many argue that he had more gladness in his youth, it was only right that the Ambassador of the Romantic's, our poet laureate in waiting, should have the honour of opening the Salon. I'm referring to William Wordsworth of course. Our leader stood in the limelight beneath the *Haymakers*, in the full glare of Lucy Ebbs' watchful eye. Yes, the *Haymakers* by George Stubbs. Now, I owe you an apology Gaia. How remiss of me. Wrapped in my own preoccupations around Lucy and our guests, I neglected to tell you that the newly-weds decided to display the *Haymakers* in the Great Hall.

Allow me to explain. You may recall that Captain Richard Lewin resembles the man at the top of the hay cart. Well, he fancied that our visitors should get to see the likeness for themselves. Frankly, I wonder of the wisdom of giving Stubbs pride of place at the Salon, whilst masterpieces by J.M.W.Turner and R.Westall are hidden from view in the Gallery. I digress.

William Wordsworth clasped his hands behind him, cleared his throat and began,
"Oh this splendour. Welcome one and all, welcome to our Salon – to

the Blakesware Set! Such honour befalls me, the glory of this hour on our saviour's day!" We were due to begin at noon, but it was five minutes to twelve. Another digression! Let me continue. William Wordsworth verbatim, enjoy,

"How wonderful it is to be graced in such exalted company. Do you feel the spirit, so profound? Let us recognise ever and anon the miracle of nature in our hearts."

William paused, and brought his hands forward, as if in prayer. The expectation! The silent awe, as we congregated in a horseshoe about him.

"But first on this day of kings, let us not forget our absent friend, our Skylark sadly taken prematurely by the cruel sea. Let us make a covenant to Percy Bysshe Shelley, one of our finest lyrical poets - a vow to embrace his sense of freedom, beauty, truth and love."

I looked upon Mary, stoical and proud, yet tearful; her bemused surviving son beside her. William continued,

"May his spirit be with us - the Triumph of his Life![50]"

Mary nodded in appreciation.

Being tardy is better than not at all, though had we a messenger to alert us we'd have timed the opening better. I guess it's only human nature – to anticipate something unwelcome yet carry on regardless, perhaps hoping it might not happen anyway. Sorry Gaia – I must be more concise. An emotional Bill Richmond had the courage to interrupt William,

"Sir, if I may, we have more visitors."

Three men stepped forward. The first was the elderly Reverend North, unsteady as ever on his feet, the second was the remarkable appearance of the humanitarian William Wilberforce, and the third – yes Gaia it was Field Marshall Arthur Wellesley, 1st Duke of Wellington. Alas, no sign, though of William Blake.

"Make way for the Duke," insisted Captain Lewin.

Malachi was a dog for ceremony. The feisty puppy ran straight to the boots of the 'Saviour of the Nations.' and yapped enthusiastically.

"He's a lively one, got plenty to say for himself. Still, nothing great was ever achieved without enthusiasm," said the Duke, kneeling to stroke the puppy's head. Malachi licked his hand - that mighty fist which had clung to the reigns of Copenhagen on the fields of battle, now succumbed to an embrace from the animal kingdom.

The wise late-comers were followed into the Manor by their wives and families. Richard Lewin requested extra places at the table for the festive feast!

"Just cold meat and bread for me," quipped the Duke. Wilberforce nodded at the irony of the Duke's words. As for Reverend North he was rejuvenated, for the Holy man had a revelation of his own to share.

The Duke encouraged William to continue, waving him on, "Come William, make haste. Don't tarry so. And please don't mind my presence, be merry. It's Christmas Day!" he ordered.

"Sir, if I may, we were just honouring Percy Shelley."

"Good, good," he nodded.

To be candid, it felt peculiar to have this senior man of the military amongst us. We knew he feared the anarchy of the French Revolution may spread to Britain. He also had a growing fondness for mechanical gadgets.

"Halt! Who goes there? Friend or foe?" I imagined saying, before sight of the gallows whisked me away from such foolish thinking.

"For Percy, you say," chirped Wilberforce. "Then before we continue, may I have a moment to pass this eternal rose to Mary."

Wordsworth accented, of course. I later discovered it to be the rose from the table I thumped in anger when I visited the Ware workhouse. Reverend North knew Mary was attending and thought it honourable that she should take ownership of it. A tearful Mary much appreciated the gesture. The young Anderson captured the moment perfectly when he later told Mary, "Just living isn't enough - one must have sunshine, freedom and a little flower." I digress. "To a Skylark!" began William.

> "Hail to thee, blithe spirit!
> Bird thou never wert-
> That from Heaven or near it
> Pourest thy full heart
> In profuse strains of unpremeditated art…"

Ending,

> "The world should listen… as I am listening now."

The party were true to the Duke's word. Conversation, laughter, food and wine flowed freely. Let me remind you Gaia of those at the table – the Duke; the Captain; the Reverend; romantic writers, poets and painters; philosophers and politicians; mathematicians; a sculptor; scholars and their loved ones.

Captain Lewin was quick to honour his new wife. I raised a toast of good health to them. As Captain Lewin was one for a wager; he announced,
"Friends, my friends. How heartened my beloved Katharine and I are to find our home so blest this day. Some have travelled across continents to join us and brought greatly cherished gifts too. Our thanks in return seem trifle in comparison, so allow me to surprise you. You see, I had a wager with the Duke. Yes, I wager, it's true. A gentleman's agreement shall we say. If our swathe Marshall joined us today I vowed to reward him with a turn of 'Yankee Doodle' in honour of the Union, whilst the Duke promised to play the fife. Yes my friends – to acknowledge our American companions I shall put a feather in my cap and call it macaroni."

330

Oh the frivolity. The pair got up from their seats. The Captain began to stomp to the beat of the ditty, with the feather in his cap, whilst the Duke blew his whistle. What's more, Ralph Emerson tapped on a small drum. What could we do but participate? To do otherwise would have been disingenuous and rude to our New World guests. Picture it Gaia: song and dance – happy days!

♫ Yankee Doodle went to town,
A-riding on a pony.
Stuck a feather in his hat
And called it macaroni.

Yankee Doodle, keep it up,
Yankee Doodle dandy.
Mind the music and the step,
And with the girls be handy. ♫

Now, Gaia, my spirit is willing, but my body weak. I can scribe little more on this day. Fear not, I shall honour thee.

During the course of the next few days I shall record all that unfolded and add them to our journal: word for word, letter for letter. There will be three inserts.

I shall call the first, *The Magic of the Stones*.

Book 1: The Magic of the Stones

You will remember, Gaia that 'Yankee Doodle' was sung by a few good men. Well, as the Captain passed his feather to the Duke as a keepsake, Reverend North coughed pretentiously and loudly to bring us back to order.

"Please, lest we not forget to whom the day belongs," he announced, as people fell silent.

"Peace on Earth! Remember some have made great sacrifice to be here today... Lord forgive me. Still I sympathise with the mission. So, people of the Blakesware Set I am compelled to surprise you... 12 surprises to be exact." He shuffled with a bundle in his large stubby hands. Wrapped in silk were a collection of small stones that resembled pearls.

"I have searched into my soul. Now please... silence if I may. I need to choose my words carefully. This isn't a sermon, there is no set script. It's not a call to arms or a judgement... just a curiosity to ponder and inspire us in our mission. Am I understood?" He looked about the table at puzzled faces.

"Many years I have waited to tell this tale. Only Thomas Watson here... that's him next to the pugilist..."

"Pugilist? Bill Richmond!" remarked Wilberforce.

"Aye Sir."

The human rights ambassador realised the former boxer was standing beneath the *Haymakers* painting.

"A horrid ugly word... call him a Haymaker[51], that I suggest would be a kinder term for a tower of a man such as he."

"Thank you Sir, God bless you, hero of my people."

Reverend North continued, "Next to the Haymaker, his father can bear witness to the tale."

Tom Watson nodded.

"Confession is good for the soul. These are no ordinary stones! Where once Roisia's Cross stood in the town that assumed her name, a cave was discovered by chance by workmen. A milestone was found in the ground which, when lifted, revealed a vertical, well-like shaft about two feet wide and sixteen deep. Some eighty years ago, when I was but a boy, I was volunteered to make the first descent into the cave. I injured my leg when I fell the last few feet, which is why I have this constant physical reminder of my act. When I emerged from the darkness, I told those that dared to ask that, 'the cave contained no treasure, at least not that I could tell. Just earth and some strange carvings - with eyes that beseeched me to repent.' Forgive me - they knew not that I found these within a jar of clay."

"Twelve stones?" confirmed Tom Watson.

"Always warm... never cold to the touch. All the same size. Hypnotic! Hold them to the light and they sparkle inside. I'd say I've even seen them move on their own. If you hold them in the palm of your hand... well just try and see for yourself."

We fell into a stunned silence, which I broke.
"Why are you telling us this after all this time and on this day to all these people?"

"Charles Lamb, do you never cease to question?"

He continued, "I'm an old man... Heaven awaits me. I lay my reputation before thee. He teaches; have faith. How would the good Lord judge me if I neglected my duty. We must all do our duty." He looked into the eyes of the Duke.

"Please, do continue," the Field Marshall invited.

"They are not pearl or diamond, gold or alabaster."

"Alabaster?" Mary Shelley asked.

"The purest marble." He toyed with them like a child. "They won't break or chip, can withstand the mightiest blows or the hottest furnace. They seem weightless. They puzzle me.

I have always believed I found them for a reason. Maybe that reason was to share them today in the hope of an answer to the question, 'What do these stones mean?' "

"You were the first person into the Royston Cave?" asked Professor Malthus, his interest heightened, as he was employed locally - Hertford Heath, in fact. "Why did you not share this with me?" he asked, exhibiting embarrassment over his hare lip.

"The Lord moves in strange ways," replied Reverend G. North. He got to his feet and began to offer each of the Blakesware Set a stone. "I am just the gate keeper. Trust me... hold out your right hand."

He progressed around the table placing a single stone into each outstretched palm. It reminded me of a Communion. Was I dreaming? I, of dubious mind, saw these things with my own eyes. Strange events indeed.

"Reverend North are you challenging our faith?" asked 'Population' Malthus.

"Not at all, I'm sure. The stones were my destiny... they shaped my future. I share them now so they may shape yours too," he replied.

"What, is this not a blatant sacrilegious act? Are you not now condemned?" asked Thomas Malthus, once more.

"I tell you that out of these stones God can raise up children[52]," replied Reverend North, as he dropped the stone into his palm. He added, "I tell you, if they keep quiet the stones will cry out[53]."

We fell silent. Did the stones speak? I held mine. I believe Reverend North was right to invite us to speculate on the stones potential to inspire. None of us had any answers – just questions. Time would be his judge.

"They are like stars in the night sky! We should visit this cave," suggested Mary, holding her stone against the flicker of candlelight.

I shall call the second book – *A Delicate Investigation*. I warn thee – the arguments were many and profound. I shall scribe as best as I can. Reader of Gaia, if you are of faint heart, read it not, for Book 2 is dark and foreboding. Book 3 is full of hope, read that alone if you will. The tale will still unfold. If you are stoical and of strong heart and mind then plough on – follow the narrow furrow with me my friend. Join them as they seek out the Golden Ticket![54] Listen to your ancestors – react to their words. I implore you.

Book 2: A Delicate Investigation

Where were we, oh yes, the Stones!

"So are you inspired?" asked Reverend North. "A few good men and women... one and all... each may hold our future in your learned hands."

"Extraordinary Reverend North, spoken like a true politician," said Wilberforce.

"I've no interest in popularity Sir, just the greater good."

"Laudable, my friend, most laudable," said Malthus.

"Votes, votes, votes," whispered the Duke, clearly musing on the prospect of becoming Prime Minister shortly. "So, what's on the other side of the hill? The machines, is there really anything to concern us. What say thee?"

Feather in one hand, enchanted stone in the other; the leader of nations played the role of Devil's Advocate[55]. He succeeded in stirring our guests into action. For me, his words were akin to a pistol let off at the ear; not a feather to tickle the intellect.

Motivated by her own haunting experiences, the courageous Mary Shelley responded first, "Now that the war with France is at an end, presumably you have time to read? Are you conscious of the real meaning of my tragedy, 'Frankenstein, or Modern Prometheus'? A deliberate ploy by Percy and I to show the

---

potential destructive effects of the mechanical age - a thing created by man that escapes his control and ultimately turns and destroys him."

"A magnificent work of fiction Mary," replied the Duke. "But we have mastered fire, invented the wheel and it turns apace. That which unfolds now will be the natural outcome of all that went before. I, for one, am not afraid."

"Still, we should beware as we pursue science, for we may discover something unwelcome and destructive," she replied.

"Try looking into the fire, Sir. Hear its crackle, is it trying to warn us?" invited Westall, pointing towards the blazing hearth. "Watch the smoke, how it rises and taunts. Have not our northern winters already worsened by the coal smoke lit by blast furnaces? For me, the 'Year without a summer'[56] was no surprise. I fear it an ill omen that our use of coal and iron will return to haunt us. What invisible spectres have we set free? The smoke of the industrial revolution could destroy much more than it will ever create!"

"You paint a solemn picture. What would Admiral Nelson say? You claim these new industries might destroy; well I would have it Richard that we succeeded in the Napoleonic Wars not by chance, but because of the wealth created by the mechanical age and the fighting qualities of our men. Yet now you argue against it!"

Old Nosey was on top form, until William Wilberforce spoke. "Sir, if I may, we are living through the greatest change in our way of life since we began to farm the land. The Reverend spoke of sacrifice - well the British people never suffered such a deadly blow. We have swept aside a primitive but pleasant and socially stable world, replacing it with an inhuman system, where people are regimented by the time-table of the machines. Children, who were once put to family work early, are now herded like sheep into the factories and mines. Human bodies in a factory culture are soulless, behaving like machines in the mills and looms they work in. Our land is suffering too. Great areas of country lost and blackened by Satanic Mills, brass founding and potteries. Dear Duke, I fear it is just the beginning. The iron horse[57] and the iron road will spread like a plague on our delicate Earth, our one Earth... our home. What next, an iron bird? We will be sucked into a vortex to drown in the mire of our own making."

Perfectly put, I would suggest. The Duke was deep in thought; a great actor as well as a genius in war! Samuel, dear Samuel, spoke in rhyme,
"A bold pleasantry, their country's pride,
When once destroyed, forever we cried!"
It only brought the Duke time, that most precious commodity.
"What of the progress of nations, prolonged life-expectancy, and a broader human experience?" he asked.
"The industrial revolution has left us both stimulated and penalised – we have a more brutal individualism and a cult of money – 'brass' they called it. Yet that man is the richest whose pleasures are the cheapest. All this while the engine runs and the people must work... men, women and children are yoked together with iron and steam. The animal machine – of flesh and blood - is chained to the iron machine, which knows no suffering or weariness. What price exploitation?" said Wilberforce.
"All this sorrow, the good Lord will see us prosper. Fortune favours the brave," feigned the Duke.
"Jest not. Listen the mighty Being is awake," said Wordsworth.

His words greatly amused the puppy. He barked excitedly at the king of poets, dancing in circles around his feet. "Ah, you like poetry do you?" he asked, before reciting:

"Great God! I'd rather be
A Pagan[58] suckled in a creed outworn;
So might I, standing on this pleasant lea,
Have glimpses that would make me less forlorn;
Have sight of Proteus[59] rising from the sea
Or hear old Triton[60] bellow his wreathed horn."

"Appeal to my intellect my friend, not my heart," asked the Duke.
Emerson responded,
"Sir, what if our world is enchanted? What if there's a world-wide-web that links everything together. Invisible strands of Earth energy. What if we upset the balance, break the communication by stripping everything down, digging everything up, replacing green with grey, burning, pillaging our Earth? These are the times that try men's souls. Where will it end?"
Richard Westall added, "Perhaps the ice I painted in my mind's eye might melt – vanish before our eyes. What if 'Nelson and the Bear' be a portent of doom?"

The Duke shook his head wildly.
"Such pessimism. Fairy tales – one and all. Next you'll tell me, 'The sky is falling in.' If we dither others will prosper at our expense, our Empire will falter. Why should we be the ones to make the sacrifices without clear evidence that we suffer from our actions? Our caution and restraint will be our demise!" claimed Wellington.
"Sir, if I may, I suggest to you life itself is the most wonderful of fairy tales," spoke Hans bravely.
The Duke merely raised his eyebrows in disdain, so I played my trump card.

"Sir, you ask why? Let me show you," I said. "Recently, I was out walking by the Nimley Bourne stream…" Hey, Gaia you know the detail. To surmise, I showed them the list I found – the one that read:

Climate Change – the ticking bomb 💣

💜 *Humans are using the world's resources so fast that the planet cannot replace them quickly enough. Many of the Earth's species of animals had lost nearly one-third of their population in the last 30 years.*

💜 *Do the maths? If nothing changes, by the time a new born child today reaches adulthood the world will be entering a disaster so huge it is unthinkable.*

💜 *Global warming was set to tip many countries into crisis. Mass migration, terrorism, civil war, disease, want and starvation - this was the future.*

It certainly provoked a response.

"Are you suggesting this list is a vision of the future?" asked Professor Malthus.

My credibility was at stake.

Samuel tried to help but dug me a deeper hole, "Maybe the proposition is that the list is from the future?"

The Duke was immediately dismissive, "Nonsense! I don't like it - with all this talk of civil war, is this a clandestine message from the Radicals in support of the French?" he asked.

I shrugged my shoulders. The Duke continued,

"Is this a fantasy land? Give me facts, I implore you! Malthus, Rickman, you are men of facts and logic – what say you?"

Malthus decried, "If it was from the future, it would vindicate my 'Principles of Population' and my predictions of catastrophe... these may be the consequences of the struggle for existence, the lack of food for an unchecked expanding population."

The Duke suspected foul play, "Remind me of the numbers," he asked.

"Our Crowded World! Oh millions Sir, if not billions. How many people can the world effectively support?" mumbled Malthus.

"Billions of people... no, the sword, disease, famine, will keep our numbers in balance," said J.R.[61] or John Rickman, as more commonly known.

"Not if this note is anything to go by. Maybe the machines provided the means for humans to flourish and devour all the resources, leaving nothing for the animals. Maybe the machines warmed up the world," I suggested.

"I'm sorry but are we taking this list as Gospel? Ah, the machines! Besides, I still need an answer. How many people does it take to fill up the world?" asked the Duke.

"Now that Sir is the key question," responded John Rickman. "It's one reason why we do the British Census.[62]" Rickman sat back with a smug expression and folded his arms, "It shows from 1750 - 1801 the population has risen from 6 to 9 million, with people in the factories in their thousands."

"Frankly, I'm not convinced by any of this!" replied the Duke.

Our famed leader played cynic and sceptic – but Captain Lewin later assured me he did so for all our benefits.

"Maybe electricity was the culprit," suggested Mary.

"Try reading Candide... 'All is for the best in the best of all possible worlds,'[63]" the Duke proposed, with an ironic grin.

"With all respect Sir, the work is pure satire! The mass of men lead lives of quiet desperation and are regular witnesses to tragedy," claimed Emerson. He then offered a solution on how the list may have reached us.

"This list, what if time was littered with gaps, like a web, and sometimes things slip through at the right place, at the right time, such as at dawn or dusk at the equinox or solstice? I, for one, would not discount such a possibility."

"I have seen fish fall from the sky like rain," said Bill Richmond, from nowhere, adding,

"Our world is more mysterious than we know."

"Entirely so. My Uncle the late, great, John Plumer built a lion's head statue in the grounds of the Manor – many of you have seen it. Around its base is engraved a riddle, 'Time Is, Time Was, Time's Passed' and the Latin 'Verbatim ac literatim' - word for word, letter for letter."

"Implying?" asked Wellington.

"Ah, Lord Byron's, Don Juan," said Samuel. "Like Friar Bacon's Brazen Head, I've spoken. Are none familiar with the legend?"

Samuel explained, "In the 13th Century a wise English Franciscan Monk made a head of brass with the power to speak. The monk was linked to stories of magic and alchemy. He expected the Brazen Head to become an Oracle[64], truthfully answering questions about the future. However, one night whilst the monk slept, the head spoke to his assistant. It spoke three times. First it said 'Time Is,' then after a long pause it said 'Time Was' and finally, after another interlude, it said 'Time's Passed'. After this, the head fell to the floor and broke into thousands of pieces, never to speak again. When he awoke, the Friar was distraught to learn his assistant had failed to wake him. The assistant was certain he had remembered every word... letter by letter."

"Was it a human head?" asked Albert Thorvaldsen.

"No one knows," replied Samuel. "That's just part of the mystery. But what do the words mean – who can tell?"

"More to the point, why did John Plumer erect the statue in the garden with the words carved about it?" I looked at Lady Lewin as I spoke. What secrets did she keep?

"If there's truth in the legend, then maybe it was a message... a warning... an anagram?" proposed Emma.

Old Nosey presented an image of leather and iron. He brushed the talk of riddles aside. He had a rare instinct for timing the decisive stroke, "Enough of this fancy talk, myth, riddles, unfounded portents of gloom. Heavens, what is it with poets and artists – this is now, this is fact. I accept we should investigate, gather the evidence, and I am happy to lead that... but I know one thing, the people of Britain must be governed by persons who are not afraid. We shall not have a commotion. We shall have order and law." He thumped the Christmas table determinedly.

Dare anyone challenge him? Step forward Mary Shelley, she had the final word,

"I see a Lost Man[65] standing alone and forlorn... in the shadows of humanity... stood on the Arctic ice lamenting our actions. He is the victim of our unchecked creation. I see the ice crumbling around him, shattered and breaking up. This man is you and me. He is our Frankenstein, our future unless we modify our ways we will make the Earth our enemy and it will strike us down."

The last, I shall call, *Hope Springs Eternal*. Now Gaia, Mary was so prophetic. Her talk of the 'Lost Man' reminded me of my horrid nightmare, when the animals fled in terror from the bird of fire and a wall of water. Alas, I was not bold enough to tell it. Still Gaia, I feel the Blakesware Set has flourished – champions one and all for our cause – Art, Love and Nature. Read on...

Book 3: Hope Springs Eternal

The Duke mellowed. He began by saying he had seldom seen such passion for a cause and appreciated the candid nature of the discussion. He invited Reverend G. North to comment on all he had observed, "Preacher, speak!"

"Sir is it not curious how millions the globe over, of all colours and creed, put so much faith in religion, yet when presented with evidence and facts by men of science and reason it is dissected, picked apart. I ask the question, what would any God say on the 'State of the Nations'? Would he not say,

'Humankind, think of your footsteps, about what you do. My Earth is my precious gift to you. Savour its fruits yes, but do not indulge beyond reason. Respect all nature for you, humanity, hold the key in your hands. Act today for all our tomorrows – Rush, Save My World.'

So, I say let us do as he would wish."

The Duke showed little expression as he asked, "What do we propose we do, within reason?" The question was directed at all of us.

"Life is a jest and all things show it, I thought it once but now I know it," I said, gripping my stone so tightly in my hand that it felt part of me and me a part of it. I continued,

"There are those who care what we do with our future, such people are thee. We strive today to become an idea. Let me provide an example, a girl I met at the Ware festival before Christmas. On stage, I heard her volunteer three questions to a magician:

- ♥ Have you ever helped the poor?
- ♥ Do you have a favourite flower?
- ♥ Have you ever searched for buried treasure?

That's it. Those were her questions."

My stone grew warmer still, absorbing my tension.

"Charles... we are all terribly bemused... clarity please. How exactly does this help?" asked the Duke.

"Sir if I may, she suggested the questions should form part of a survey for the future, one being prepared by her father. It set me thinking. I wondered whether we should contribute some questions." I stumbled on my words, appreciating how foolish the idea appeared at first sight. I saw the frowns and raised eyebrows.

"Do you mean like the census?" asked John Rickman.

I gripped my stone tighter still - it burned and trembled in my palm.

"Possibly, I don't know. Look, I know it's strange, but I feel we must do this. It's beyond rational explanation! I feel this is our duty, our destiny – transcendentalists[66] and romantics. If, as the Duke says, the wheels of industry turn inexorably, we, who are bound, need to convey a message of hope to future generations. Not through prose, essay or poetry, but something spectacular. If the world of the future struggles so as we fear it may... let us give them inspiration to find the solution!

Many of us here are giants amongst dwarfs. Alas, fame is temporary, yet some questions are eternal. I say let the people of the future hear our voice, so they may find the means to give theirs. Let us present them with a list of questions to stir their imagination and encourage them to look afresh at Mother Nature. Creative questions such as, 'Have you ever searched for buried treasure?' Perhaps we will find a way to keep these questions hidden for centuries, to let fate reveal them when the time is right to an unsuspecting world. This, my friends, would be pure genius, Art in its widest sense - what say thee?"

Silence – what had I done?

"An extraordinary affair!" The Duke was again in a tenacious mood.

"Eureka!" said Malthus.

"A secret inheritance," suggested Captain Lewin.

"Art, let us not underestimate the power of the imagination to influence and provide a vision," commented Westall.

"We see the world not as it is, but as we are!" so spoke Thorvaldsen.

"We desperately need to restore the love and empathy for nature lost as the affair with the city takes root, so I for one endorse Charles' idea. It is a wild and delicious venture," were Wordsworth's words.

"Our voices heard from beyond the grave," said Mary.

"To reveal our enchanted living Earth," spoke Emerson.

"Inventive splendour... with all the making of a fairy tale," said Hans Christian Anderson.

"I, too, am in. Life, universe, consciousness... all these things are beyond comprehension," commented William Turner.

"We will astonish them all!" proclaimed John Rickman.

"Haymaker, what say you, can we achieve the impossible?" asked Wilberforce.

"Deliver the coup de grace," pronounced Richmond, with his fist raised, "I say now is the time for action! Set free Mother Nature!"

"Hail to 'The Haymakers Survey!' " we cried.

"Most splendid, to give our people in their hour of need the insight to know when to retreat, and to dare to do it," championed Wellington. I had seized the day. All others consented, wishing to be part of the magic. Oh joy, oh triumph. Let the games commence. I for one have a head full of questions – where to begin? Yet, the question I most wanted to ask was, "Is she the one?"

Oh Gaia, although we have gained so much on this day – I so wish Lucy had been able to join us. I told Samuel that she was weary with fever so had to rest, but I would introduce him to her soon enough. I read the suspicion in his eyes. Am I alone in this world - me, myself and I?

Certainly, I was not prepared for William Wordsworth's finale; a reading of his poem – Lucy.[67] It took me by surprise. My cheeks glowed. I felt all eyes upon me. I quietly trembled, hearing only the early verses,

> "Strange fits of passion I have known;
> And I will dare to tell,
> But in the lover's ear alone,
> What once to me befell.
>
> When she I loved look'd every day
> Fresh as a rose in June,
> I to her cottage bent my way,
> Beneath an evening moon.
>
> Upon the moon I fix'd my eye,
> All over the wide lea;
> With quickening pace my horse drew nigh
> Those paths so dear to me.
>
> And now we reached the orchard-plot;
> And, as we climbed the hill,
> The sinking moon to Lucy's cot
> Came near and nearer still.

In one of those sweet dreams I slept,
Kind Nature's greatest boon!
And all the while my eyes kept
On the descending moon.

My horse moved on; hoof after hoof
He raised, and never stopp'd;
When down behind the cottage roof,
At once, the bright moon dropp'd.

What fond and wayward thoughts will slide
Into a lover's head!
"Oh mercy!" to myself I cried,
'If Lucy should be dead.'"

Oh to bed, to sleep and dream, but what of the questions? Why, here are my notes of the one hundred questions and who chose them.

The Haymakers Survey
Our Secret Inheritance

Prepared this day, 25 December 1822 by the Blakesware Set as an unexpected historic inheritance for the generation threatened by such ills as climate change, global warming and mass animal extinctions. It is our genuine and sincere hope that our questions will inspire you in your hour of need to find the creative solutions for your almighty struggle. May our enchanted Earth behold the caring voice of its people!

Blakesware Set: Full Members

Field Marshall Arthur Wellesley (1st Duke of Wellington)
Captain Richard Lewin KB (Host)
Reverend G North (Preacher)
Charles Lamb (Romantic Poet and Essayist)
William Wordsworth (Romantic poet)
Samuel Coleridge (Romantic poet)
Mary Wollstonecraft Shelley (Writer and widow of Percy Shelley)
William Wilberforce (Pioneering Politician)
Richard Westall (Artist)
William Turner (Artist)
Albert Thorvaldsen (Nordic Sculptor)
Thomas Malthus (Professor in Political Economy and Anglican Parson)
John Rickman (English Statistician)

Associate members

Lady Katharine Plumer (Hostess nee Lewin)
Ralph Waldo Emerson (son of Reverend Emerson)
Hans Christian Anderson (Scholar and budding writer)
Emma Isola (Latin Scholar)
Bill Richmond (Pugilist and Haymaker)
Thomas Watson (Tradesman)
Mrs Elizabeth Field (Beloved Housekeeper)
Friends and family of full members, including David Thoreau and Percy Shelley (the younger)

<u>Our Absent Friends</u>

Late Percy Bysshe Shelley (Romantic Poet)
Late George Stubbs (Artist)
William Blake (Poet and Artist)
Lord Byron (Romantic Poet)
John Constable (Artist)
Sarah - the mysterious confident young girl (our inspiration)
Lucy Ebbs

<u>With special thanks</u>

Malachi (mischievous Samoyed puppy)
Yggdrasil (the World Tree)
The Sacred Stones (from Royston Cave)

26 December 1822
(Early morn)

Oh restless slumber – insomnia[68]. I really must say a little about how we decided the questions. Twas Captain Richard Lewin's idea – for us to sit at random upon the imperial Justice Chair, with its runic carvings, and offer our instinctive questions - which may explain the eclectic mix. We even let the dog have its say, of which more to tell.

One hundred questions – now that took some doing. Twas the Duke's idea to coincide with the 100 days of the Waterloo Campaign and the final conflict in the Napoleonic Wars. A huge number of questions, granted. However, the Duke claimed, "Numbers do not guarantee to win a battle but they help." Still, a few of us had reservations about the scale – we resolved it thus. Participants need only answer those questions that mattered most to them. I found this most agreeable.

It all took place after a spontaneous tour of the Gallery, where we wondered at the works of art. Gaia, my disappointment was beyond words – not one soul commented on my painting of Lucy. No, for the Set were obsessed with mere masterpieces, 'Nelson and the Bear', and 'Hannibal Crossing the Alps'. Sleep engulfs me, rest scribe, rest.

The Haymakers Survey
The Questions

Q1. Do you believe your life has a purpose? (Charles Lamb)
Q2. Are you an art lover? (William Turner)
Q3. Do you have a good imagination? (Mary Shelley)
Q4. Have you ever wanted to stop the clock? (Reverend G North)
Q5. Do you believe in fate? (Duke of Wellington)
Q6. Do you believe in fairy tales? (Hans Christian Anderson)
Q7. Have you ever dreamed of being a champion? (Bill Richmond)
Q8. Do you crave a better life? (Samuel Coleridge)
Q9. Do you feel in control of your life? (Charles Lamb)
Q10. Have you ever seen a ghost? (Emma Isola)
Q11. Do you believe in justice? (William Wilberforce)
Q12. Is our Earth enchanted? (Ralph Emerson)
Q13. Have you ever been mistaken for someone else? (Captain Lewin)
Q14. Do you believe your stars? (Ralph Emerson)
Q15. Do you sometimes fear the worst? (Professor Malthus)
Q16. Have you ever had a psychic experience? (Mary Shelley)
Q17. Can you speak another language? (Emma Isola)
Q18. Do you let your heart rule your head? (Samuel Coleridge)
Q19. Do you love hedgehogs? (Elizabeth Field)
Q20. Have your eyes ever deceived you? (Charles Lamb)
Q21. Have you ever hugged a tree? (Albert Thorvaldsen)
Q22. Do you love our Earth? (The Complete Set)
Q23. Do you believe all the laws of physics? (John Rickman)

Q24. Do you get enough time to yourself? (Duke of Wellington)

Q25. Do you believe in fairies? (Mary Shelley)

Q26. Do you take poetry seriously? (William Wordsworth)

Q27. Do you like gardening? (Mrs Elizabeth Field)

Q28. Have you ever lived in poverty? (William Wilberforce)

Q29. Could you live without machines? (Captain Lewin)

Q30. Did you ever watch the rain on your window? (Mary Shelley)

Q31. Are you a charitable neighbour? (William Wilberforce)

Q32. Are you afraid of the dark? (William Turner)

Q33. Do you believe in life after death? (Reverend G. North)

Q34. Have you ever restored something? (Albert Thorvaldsen)

Q35. Do you trust your instincts? (Albert Thorvaldsen)

Q36. Should a good life cost the Earth? (William Wordsworth)

Q37. Do you know how to have fun? (Richard Westall)

Q38. Have you built a house of cards? (Charles Lamb)

Q39. Do you believe in magic? (Albert Thorvaldsen)

Q40. Can you play a musical instrument? (Captain Lewin)

Q41. Do you like surprises? (Duke of Wellington)

Q42. Do you enjoy drawing? (William Turner)

Q43. Do you believe in happy endings? (Hans Christian Anderson)

Q44. Is there anything worse than a fly buzzing around your room at night when you're trying to sleep? (Richard Westall)

Q45. Are you good at marbles? (Tom Watson)

Q46. Do you value a good education? (Lady Katharine Plumer-Lewin)

Q47. Do you know your history? (Bill Richmond)

Q48. Have you ever played Solitaire? (Charles Lamb)

Q49. Do you ever think about the old days? (William Turner)

Q50. Do you miss someone you love? (Mary Shelley)

Q51. Have you ever taken part in a protest? (William Wilberforce)

Q51a. How many people does it take to fill up the Earth? (Rickman/Malthus)

Q52. Do you believe in miracles? (Reverend G. North)

Q53. Do you like to keep warm? (Richard Westall)

Q54. Do you enjoy a bit of a mystery? (Reverend G. North)

Q55. Do you believe in truth? (William Wilberforce)

Q56. Do you believe rules are there to be broken? (John Rickman)

Q57. Have you ever spied on anyone? (Tom Watson)

Q58. Do things happen for a reason? (William Wilberforce)

Q59. Do you like surprises? (Charles Lamb)

Q60. Have you ever experienced déjà vu? (William Wordsworth)

Q61. Have you ever worn fancy dress? (Captain Lewin)

Q62. Have you ever helped the poor? (Sarah - The Mysterious Girl)

Q62a. Is life logical? (Reverend G. North)

Q63. Do you like the way you look? (Professor Malthus)

Q64. Do you know whether or not you are sometimes indecisive? (Lady Plumer-Lewin)

Q65. Have you ever wished you could fly? (Duke of Wellington)

Q66. Do you have a favourite flower? (Sarah - The Mysterious Girl)

Q67. Have you ever decorated a tree? (Albert Thorvaldsen)

Q68. Does the Earth have a spirit? (Ralph Emerson)

Q69. Do you ever procrastinate? (Emma Isola)

Q70. Do you like to look at the stars? (Samuel Coleridge)

Q71. Is there something missing in your life? (Professor Malthus)

Q72. Are you a good time keeper? (Lady Plumer-Lewin)

Q73. Do you like nursery rhymes? (David Henry Thoreau)

Q74. Do you like puzzles? (Charles Lamb)

Q75. Have you ever put on a show? (Bill Richmond)

Q76. Are you going to take action now to save our world? (The Complete Set)

Q77. Do you get bored easily? (Duke of Wellington)

Q78. Do you want to be part of the picture? (Malachi)

Q79. Have you ever looked into the shadows? (Richard Westall)

Q80. Have you ever searched for buried treasure? (Sarah – The Mysterious Girl)

Q80a. Do you keep a diary? (Mary Shelley)

26 December 1822

Gaia, I awoke this morning with mixed feelings. The Blakesware Set had exemplified itself for sure, compiling our list of questions – 'The Haymakers Survey'. I had also been enriched by the company of so many spirited, creative and inspirational people. However, as I alluded in my notes yesterday, my key question was, "Will she be mine?" I refer to Lucy of course. Would I ever receive an answer? So, whilst others prepared to participate in, or watch, the traditional Boxing Day hunt, I schemed on a meet of my own; to seek out my beloved.

Gaia, I know some may object to the moral of riding to hounds, so I shall not dwell long on the detail, but the animated aesthetics of a hunt in flight cannot be denied. My Uncle, the late great John Plumer, Deputy Lieutenant of the County, Colonel of the County Militia and Justice of the Quorum, rode every year until his death and was a member of the Hunt Club. He was most familiar with the easy-going Master of 'The Hertfordshire' hunt, Mr Sampson Hanbury of Poles. Uncle had an extraordinary knowledge of breeding, selecting and breaking hounds, but he also understood the need to preserve the noble fox.

We watched the riders, many in their pinks, gather in the light drizzle in the court yard at Blakesware. Amongst those preparing to depart was the Duke of Wellington, an avid and regular foxhunter, going so far as to introduce it to France recently. The horses circled each other erratically before the off, uncertain of their route. Malachi, the puppy, yapped furiously at his larger cousins, tugging at his leash. Emma did well to restrain him. Indeed, if not for her swift intervention, I fear the puppy would have come to a premature end at the hooves of a zealous horse, eager to depart. It kicked out, just missing the head of our beloved friend. I fear the hound may develop an aversion to the horse. Let us see! I digress, as ever.

I followed the pack with Mary Shelley riding alongside. A vegetarian – I apologised sincerely for my meaty name - she respected the tradition of the hunt but heartedly disapproved of the practice. She chose to accompany me, regardless, to witness directly any distress to the pursued animals. This was Mary Shelley; a remarkable and pioneering woman - unafraid, challenging and open to new ideas and interpretations. William Wilberforce chose to remain at the Manor, arguing that hunting was cruel and placed unnecessary suffering on the fox. I believe he wants to establish a society against the cruelty of animals. Is there no end to this man's magic – the Wilberforce Way? What a magnificent specimen of humanity, he who shows what can be achieved against all odds. Wordsworth too remained behind. He stood in doleful silence as he surveyed the scene, mumbling, "Another horse, and another."

Keeping clear of the pack, I led Mary towards Keeper's Cottage. This was my motive. Our pace slowed to a trot.
"Charles, you lead me astray," she suggested teasingly.
"I know the way of the land, the pattern of the copses and the direction of the wind. We can expect the pack to head this way soon. You have my word."
We could hear the call of the hunting horn.
"You are *the* spirit of this place Charles," she said.
"Accepted, though I doubt the Nimley Bourne compares in any way with Lake Geneva[69]," I replied.
"True Charles, though I should like to holiday here one day too. I feel it has the roots of a novel in it – you ought to scribe again Charles, really you should. Do try, I sense you have further tales in you," she said, as the cottage came into view.
"Do you keep a journal Mary?" I asked.
"Why Charles, of course," she replied, "Do you?"
The light drizzle had eased. We were side by side. I looked into her eyes – our collective sorrow united.

"My Little Journal of my Foolish Passions," I replied cautiously.

"And what is your passion Charles?" she asked, with Keeper's almost upon us.

"Art, in all its forms, nature and love; on these things all hangs."

"Laudable, romantic Charles – small wonder that Samuel and William admire you so."

I looked ahead for sight of Lucy, with Wordsworth's recital of his poem of her name, fresh in my mind.

I spied a rider ahead, at peace on his thoroughbred.

"Oh mercy!" I cried, thinking, "If Lucy should be dead."

"Charles is something wrong?" asked Mary.

The rider was in conversation with a young woman – a spirited individual.

"Lucy," I replied.

"Ah, if Lucy should be dead," said Mary, as though she read my mind. She recalled the next verse:

> "She dwelt among the untrodden ways
> Beside the springs of a Dove,
> A maid whom there were none to praise
> And very few to love."

Lucy was half hidden from my eye by the rider. We knew him well – it was the Duke, estranged from the pack. Captured in the misty rain, he looked almost ghost like.

"Do you see him too?" I asked.

"I do," she replied. Those two little words again.

Our arrival disturbed the great man. He tugged on Copenhagen's reigns, twisting the horse's head our way before galloping towards us. He left Lucy in his wake. Improbable as it sounds, before departing, I believe I saw him adorn her neck with gold.

"Be discreet in all things, and so render it unnecessary to be mysterious about any… I lost the scent!" said the Duke, as he reached us, lifting his head at the sound of the horn.

"When Mother Nature calls, I must answer," he announced, promptly fleeing in the direction of the horn; with mud kicked up from Copenhagen's hooves flying about us. Mary and I were perplexed by his cryptic words and actions. We had seen another side of the Duke.

"Lost the scent, he's lost leave of his senses!" remarked Mary, laughing.

As the Duke sped away, Lucy chose to ignore our presence. She ran swiftly back to the cottage, with, it seemed, one hand firmly clasped around the object hanging from her neck. Perhaps Mary's presence unsettled her, I wasn't certain. Whatever the reason, I felt Lucy's icy blast.

28 December 1822

Many of our distinguished guests have departed from Blakesware, leaving in their tremulous wake a cryptic message of hope for future generations. Of the esteemed arrivals, only a famous five[70] remained, Mary Shelley, Samuel Coleridge, Ralph Emerson, Albert Thorvaldsen and the puppy, Malachi. William Turner and Richard Westall had taken their inspirational paintings with them, leaving shades of grey on the wall to frame where they'd once hung. Our memory of their presence alone remained – perhaps the characters in Stubbs' Haymakers wept! Who can tell? Whatever, Bill Richmond's presence alongside Tom Watson had kept them safe! With Malachi in mind, Richard Westall's final words to us were worthy of recount.

"If you do one thing in your life, let it be this...
take good care of the polar bear."

Seeking respite from the task of scribing the Christmas Day events, I returned once more to my favourite dwelling – The Cottage of the Keeper. At last, Lucy was able to greet me. Let it be written, this unfolding story appears more myth than truth. A gallant Duke had presented my young maiden with a heart of gold - a repository and embodiment of romantic love to thy beloved! Gold, that eternal shining gift of Heaven that can outwit time. Bewilderment!
"What mystery unfolds?" I asked. "A pendant such as this, from a man such as he? Be it a token of love?"
"The Duke is much more than a man of war Charles, he knows my common predicament! It's an act of faith, on which I cannot speak."

She looked over the undulating landscape to the rear of the cottage – it was her wilderness, her rarely trodden way. A chill wind swept back her hair, but she was oblivious to it. A white dove sprang from cover and took to the skies. Lucy clasped the locket in her palm. Her eyes scanned the horizon, from east to west. Half of the sky was dark with rain clouds, whilst we had clear sky overhead. A double rainbow spread across the land, but wait – yes it was that rarest of sights, a third appeared, faint and fleeting, but I saw it – a beauty and a phenomenon previously unknown to my eyes. No philosophy shall clip this Angel's wing.[71]
"Is this a kind of magic?" I asked, because emerging from beneath the centre of the rainbow's arc was the Samoyed, Malachi. Not the puppy, but the adult dog - the White Wolf of Wareside! He bounded towards us, as if in a celebratory mood. Lucy received him warmly, "Malachi, look, I, a mere commoner with few who cherish me, am the Guardian of the Heart." She showed him the locket.
"Lucy – I don't pretend to understand any of this. Like the Blakesware Set, I've a head full of questions." Oh, I had so much I wanted to tell her about the Set.
She seemed oblivious to me, choosing instead to gaze serenely ahead at the rainbows. So I put the question to the dog,

"What's so special about Lucy's locket?"

He barked. Oh for a translator.

"The Duke wore it every day under his shirt for good fortune during the one hundred day campaign."

"Well, it obviously worked a charm. Where did he get it?"

"He says, from Caroline of Brunswick, our injured Queen."

"She of 'The Delicate Investigation!' Is this the truth? So it belonged to the people's queen. But why give it to you?"

"The Duke was adamant... I am not to speak of it again."

"But why pass it to you."

One word resonated in my head – succession!

We stood hand in hand.

"Do you know what's inside?"

"Imagination," she replied.

"Imagination?"

"Creation," she added.

"Creation?"

"And affection."

I looked at the rainbows, "Art, Love and Nature."

I warned thee of the surrealism. The beauty of these things is that they are free, eternal, span generations and culture, and they bind us together, weak and strong, rich and poor.

"Can you open it?" I asked.

"Only in our mind's eye! Try, close your eyes, picture the locket, open it and see the three hearts - feel all the love you have ever given or received, wonder at the miracle of creation and the beauty of the animal kingdom."

Most wonderful.

"The contents are valuable enough, but the source of the locket is the real magic," she added.

"Please Lucy, speak plainly."

"All will unfold in time," she replied.

"In time?"

"Time Is, Time Was, Time's Passed."

Malachi barked. I speculated on his meaning, "Vox Pop!"

Alone in my room Gaia, curiosity grabs me – what if I had taken Malachi the younger with me to the 'Cottage of the Keeper of the Three Hearts' – what then? Could adult and young have met?

30 December 1822

Unable to speak to the Duke about the validity of Lucy's tale, I had to take her at her word. I was hugely curious about what she had said about Queen Caroline, our tragic royal. It might explain the spies and the over-protective, dreary Fanny Ebbs. Still, the mystery of life. Just ask Mary Shelley – a woman who grows in my affection, particularly at this hour for only six years ago to the day, Mary and Percy were wed. Oh cruel sea!

Together, she and I stood after dusk on the terrace overlooking the wilderness garden. On a misty night, only one star broke through to shine in the sky overhead. Confidently dismissing the myth that the star can cause madness, we secretly dedicated the bluish white light of Sirius[72] in the constellation Canis Major to the late Percy Shelley. His light shall not fade!

"You know Charles; I travelled amongst men to lands beyond the sea. Yet my travels taught me much more of home than I knew. All that occurred this past year seems but a melancholy dream at times. No more shall I quit these shores – this jewel of a place. For once I returned, I love her more and more, this Sceptred Isle.[73] To look upon these green fields as though they might be the last."

1 January 1823
New Years Day
Early morn'

New Year's Day is everyman's birthday, this I believe. Greetings all New Year babies. Welcome Gaia to our collective new dawn. What wishes have thee for the coming year – a golden age? What, I wonder, has fate in store for me? A whole 52 weeks! How akin to a year is a deck of cards, sacred symbols of the ancients:

- ♥ 52 cards for 52 weeks.
- ♥ 13 cards in each suit for 13 lunar cycles.
- ♥ Four suits for four seasons.
- ♥ Red and black for night and day.
- ♥ The value of the pack, plus one for fun, gives 365 days.

Triviality? Let me see. I shuffled mine when I awoke and turned the first card low. Oh fate be kind, the 'Ace of Spades'[74] – the trump card. I shuffled again Gaia - the 'Seven of Hearts' – much improved, personal happiness, creative inspiration and romance – these things await me. I chose this destiny over power – oh weavers of fate, hear my plea!

1 January 1823
New Years Day
Evening

Gaia, something incredible occurred today. The Lewin's, Bill Richmond and I gathered, with the famous five, by the World Tree in the Marble Hall to hear Thorvaldsen reveal his wish to plant the tree. Oh, how remiss of me, Hans Christian Anderson, of course, was with us too – but he doesn't count as famous, at least not yet. "On this day, when the year is reborn and the days begin to lengthen, I say let us set the spirit of the Earth free. Let us release it upon all living things in our fragile world. People get ready. I proclaim, let us do this new thing."

I looked up at the *Haymakers* painting as he spoke – at the man at the heart of the picture, next to Lucy. He who was only a shadow, loomed large in my mind – oh, there's more to this world than meets the eye. I know there's more – I feel it so. There's something beyond the material world – an eternal beauty. I wondered then could planting this tree really save our world as Thorvaldsen suggested? Come, 'Friends of the Earth', let us awaken a new age of enlightenment for all humanity – I think of it as a 'green peace'!

"Are you ready to join the 'I Count' campaign? Raise your hands – let me see them," asked Albert.

It was pure theatre!

"Let us find our tree a home beside a stream amongst the wind, the rain and the sun. Some place far from the meddling hand of progress."

"I know such a place," I suggested. "It's a rich and fertile ground. A place where folklore has it that the pulse of life of the Earth runs beneath the soil."

Where other than Keeper's Cottage? Home to a bounty of snowdrops in January, snowdrops for hope!

So, we undressed the evergreen, stripping it of its artificial load and transferring it back into the great outdoors. However, I was not along in being anxious about this, for Twelfth Night was a few days away yet. Fortune, do not forsake us!

"Oh fear not Charles, it's just a foolish superstition, nothing ill will arise from it I assure you," said Ralph Emerson with enthusiasm. "Besides, what better opportunity is there to plant a symbolic tree of peace and hope – a tree to unite us all as Champions of Mother Nature?"

We lay the tree onto a cart and drew it swiftly towards Keeper's, securing it with rope. In some ways, as we toyed with the tree, we mimicked small and fragile Lilliputians from *Gulliver's Travels*. Fortunately, the weather was most kind to our mini-parade – a remarkably mild day for mid-winter – allowing the good Captain Lewin the opportunity to don his military finery for the ceremony.

The Captain led us on foot, playing the fife bestowed to him by the Duke. Malachi walked beside him for much of the way, wagging his tail excitedly. Bill, Samuel, Albert and I did our best to ensure the tree remained secure. The two boys, David Thoreau and Percy Shelley sat together at the helm with Hans. All three jumped down now and again to race ahead and wait for us to catch up. Mary Shelley and Emma Isola sat at the rear to keep the cart in balance. Wedged between the women were the two caged grey squirrels – for them it was a journey of emancipation. For Mary, it was one of reflection - she travelled most of the way in silence. I speculated she was pondering the year ahead without Percy. I vowed to urge her to stay at Blakesware a little longer.

Our decision to plant the tree at Keeper's had been spontaneous. The wilderness garden at Blakesware would have been the obvious choice, but Albert was adamant; to prosper and work its magic, the tree had to be close to a stream, not that many of us *actually* believed that the tree was empowered! Still, life without carnival is empty, so we played along. I wondered how Fanny and Lucy might greet us! When we arrived, I'd knocked loudly on the front door and called for them to join us, but the door did not open.

The procession drew up beside the cottage and sent a flock of birds skyward. For a fleeting moment, all was quiet. Until the Captain played his favourite ditty again 'Yankee Doodle'. He marched towards the clusters of snowdrops beginning to appear at the rear of the cottage. Albert examined the location, weighing up points on the horizon for the rising and setting of the sun at the equinoxes and solstices.

"Ah, a well, magnificent!" I heard him cry, as we cut loose Yggdrasil. Albert entertained us with more detail on the Nordic myth,

"The Well of Wyrd, by the side of which live the three Wyrd sisters, makers of destiny. The Wyrd sisters will nurture the tree.

Under the light of the moon, the Wyrd sisters will sprinkle the branches so it shall neither wither nor die. Its roots will grow mighty into the realms beneath us, whilst the branches soar to the heavens."

Improbable, but utterly agreeable! To a logical mind, a World Tree must surely grow naturally in a sacred place and reach real maturity in height, girth and age before it can lay claim to such a crown; Thorvaldsen would have none of it.

"Charles Lamb, you of all people - where is your faith? Has the power of imagination deserted you?"

We dug deep into the soil at a spot which Albert decreed as sacred.

"What makes the land sacred?" I asked.

"The soil... the stones... the air... the wind... I feel it. I know it. This is the place! Here she will grow in sun and shower, amid the loveliest flower Earth has ever sown[75]."

"I believe you are reciting Wordsworth!"

"Why yes - the poem 'Lucy'. William wished it. I promised to honour him in this way if we chose to plant the tree."

So, with our own labour in the heart of Hertfordshire, we planted our very own Axis Mundi[76] – around which we turn and turn.

"But Albert really, what's so magic about this tree – it looks just like any other?" asked young David Thoreau.

"Credulity is the man's weakness but the child's strength," I suggested, "We must make him believe."

What was Albert Thorvaldsen, cultured world famous sculpture to do? God gave him a gift and it was his duty to use it. Albert climbed on to the shoulders of Bill Richmond and used Captain Lewin's tomahawk to shape the top branches, claiming confidently that the pruning would do nothing to diminish its mystic powers. As he worked, some of us gathered up the fallen branches as keep sakes. Not to be outdone, Malachi snapped one up. He scampered around the tree excitedly. Percy and David shrieked in excitement as they tried to rescue the stick from Malachi's jaws.

Once the commotion and sculpturing was through, we stood back to admire Albert's creation. The tree had undergone a transformation. Yggdrasil's crown had been re-born in the shape of a horse's head – befitting Gaia, as the literal translation of Yggdrasil means, Odin's Steed! He even shaped the tree with a fore leg, raised as if to break into gallop, with the coronet[77] pointing to where he was told the sun set at the summer solstice.

I looked up at Keeper's and wondered whether Fanny or Lucy might show themselves. The window to Lucy's bedroom was the closest to us. I saw a faded face at the window, like a spectre. Would one of them join us? Lucy, I hoped would feel the overwhelming power we were about to kindle.

Bristling with enthusiasm, Albert announced,
"Behold, I have reshaped Yggdrasil into Odin's Steed."
Let me be candid Gaia, to me the great man's work appeared rather sinister, ghoulish, goblin-like even. I quickly imagined an infamous reputation might grow, but Thorvaldsen was optimistic.
"Have we ourselves belittled nature?" Mary whispered in my ear, with her shawl wrapped ever tightly for warmth.
"I think not Mary, besides its good to love the unknown," I replied.
Ralph Emerson was more upbeat,
"Let us hope we may reshape man too, in a new image with ideals and values beyond personal gain and the individual. Let us hope that in planting this World Tree we help bring forth - now or in some future time - the dawning of the Age of Aquarius."[78]
I agreed, "Yes, let hope forever grace this tree, Yggdrasil."
"Let us raise all good cheer... waes hael," cried Captain Lewin. "Good health!"

We replicated his gesture, lifting invisible goblets in its honour. Oh Gaia, the drama, as Captain Richard Lewin KB concluded the ceremony with an oath,

"On this new day we commend our services to you, Tree of the World - symbol of life. Do you find us pure of heart and untarnished by ambition or revenge? Are we worthy champions of nature? Do you honour us… simple Haymakers with the greatest challenge of all, as Mother Earth's Keepers?"

How unrealistic of us to expect a reaction. Malachi broke the silence – yapping and running off in the direction of the Nimley Bourne, the crazy young thing!

Oh, how remiss of me – the squirrels – Mary and Emma had set them free at the base of the tree. With a swish of a bushy tail, they vanished up into the branches. "It's all part of the legend," explained Thorvaldsen.

The more I observed the tree, the more I was in awe of it. You know, Gaia, its strange how when we sow a seed in our mind – an idea or a vision - we may be sceptical at first, doubting, but after a while we may wonder – what if it were true? Suppose we really had planted a magical World Tree? Could Yggdrasil help us – the Blakesware Set – to achieve our aim? Could we use it to harbour the 100 Questions – 'The Haymakers Survey' – for use by future generations? Did not Albert Thorvaldsen imply that it can influence time and space? Maybe that's why my great Uncle, the esteemed John Plumer, introduced me to the Brazen Head riddle. It's all falling into place.

Awash with such thoughts, I let the others return to Blakesware ahead of me, yet the puppy was reluctant to leave – so he stayed. Hunger, thirst and cold had defeated them, but my needs went beyond the elementary. Why did Lucy hide herself away? I called to her again,

"Lucy, it is I Charles, do come down, I implore you, see what we have done."

I waited for her face to appear at her bedroom window.

"Please Lucy – come see our tree – amongst the bed of snowdrops," I cried.

Nothing stirred, so I serenaded her with our favourite tune,

> ♫ And the lady fair of the knight so true,
> Aye remembered his hapless lot:
> And she cherished the flower of brilliant hue,
> And braided her hair with the blossoms blue.
> And she called it 'Forget-me-not.' ♫

The door to the cottage opened:

> ♫ Oh enchanted thee,
> Sweet Lucy my fawn,
> To skip and dance across the lawn,
> And wave your ribbon with glee. ♫

"Charles, you do tempt me so," she said.

"The tree Lucy, what say you of the tree?" I asked.

"Sh! Charles do you hear it, the voice of creation? Can you hear its heartbeat?" she replied.

Malachi yapped excitedly to greet her.

"Oh look at you, so creamy white, adorable and young."

Gaia, have you ever noticed how sparingly pure white is found on Mother Nature's canvas.

- ♥ Fleeting things, like snowdrops, dandelions and snow.

- ♥ Creatures or things to inspire the imagination, such as unicorns, Samoyeds, white rabbits and alabaster marbles.

- ♥ Elusive creatures, including barn owls and polar bears!

Yet the colour white in nature is just an illusion. The magic and mystery of pure white is it reflects back all visible light – so the creatures stand out. Breakdown the spectrum of light and you have all the colours of the rainbow – the magic is in the diversity, savour it. I digress once more.

"Didn't you see us Lucy? The members of the Blakesware Set! Twas Albert's idea to plant the World Tree. He shaped it with his own hands into a horse's head... oh Lucy, you have missed out on so much. I wish you could have joined us. There were so many wonderful people... even William Wordsworth, I know how much you admire him! And Mary Shelley, dark and mysterious, prone to melancholy, she is inspiring and so talented. Oh Lucy... the questions, all the questions... and Reverend North's stones, you must get to see them you must. Lucy, enigmatic you!"
"Charles please. I so cherish the artists of this world, with their tender patience, leading us by such visions of truth, beauty and goodness. And the tree, the tree! I proclaim this... that the world is alive and has a soul! It's in me, in you, in all living things, in every stone, stick and grain of sand. Each has a voice waiting to be heard... listen, do you hear it? The sound of the World Tree is deafening! It's the sound of the deep magic."

I agreed. This world is more than an object for logical scientific study, void of the understanding and experience of nature found in poets like Wordsworth. The 'red glow of sunset' should be as much a part of nature as the electric waves by which men of science would explain the phenomenon.

Lucy's mood grew playful. "Come Charles," she said, taking my hand to lead me about the tree. "Dance with me!" She skipped around the tree singing, "Ring a ring o' roses... we all fall down."
"Am I right to assume you like the tree Lucy?" I asked, when we returned to our feet.
"But of course Charles, I just adore it. Come, let us embrace it!"

"Embrace it?"

"Why yes. Let's share our love. Come, if we hug her for long enough, she'll hug us back!"

Oblivious of the needles on the evergreen, Lucy hugged Yggdrasil with such passion that I felt only admiration and awe. What's more – she chose to tie her blue ribbon onto one of the branches as a mark of quality.

"There," she said, "First prize, for the majestic mystical tree. May she grow mighty and wise and bestow all her kindness and shelter upon the globe."

Oh sweet Demeter[79], bring humankind the fruits of the harvest, continue to permeate the imagination of painters and writers alike.

5 January 1823

Gaia, you'll remember my commitment to scribe all that happened at the Blakesware Set - well I've honoured my word. I have scribed all that I recall. Now I need to lay down my quill and rest. I long to get on with the business of living, and return only infrequently to you. This I make my resolution for the year, to surrender the largely solitary pursuit. Even young Sarah cannot tempt me with her cards. It feels good to be free.

Gaia – before I bid thee farewell I ought to tell you that Yggdrasil has grown several feet in just a few days! Lucy is adamant of this. She has also seen an owl take roost within its branches and, that most rarest and mystical of sights, a white stag deer, come to nestle at its base. In the heart of winter, what magic have we unleashed?

6 January 1823

I break my promise already. The rain falls incessantly, lashed by the wind against my window, as though wandering spirits had been set free. Is someone watching over me?

7 January 1823

Gaia, how swiftly I renege on my promise, but I must record events of last night. In a dream he came to me. I expect it was my own doing. I fear I invited him into my mind through my obsession with that painting – the *Haymakers*. I have paid the price for my indulgence. Do you recall the times I have woken in my room believing a presence was with me? Remember when I'd stood beside the lion's plinth in the wilderness garden at Blakesware and imagined I saw a figure at my window? Well – the artist revealed himself, a big-boned broad featured man. The glowing apparition beckoned me to rise from my bed,

"Who's there?" I asked.

"It is I, George Stubbs, a country boy at heart[80]," was the reply.

"Stubbs – the man who painted the *Haymakers*?"

"And the *Reapers*!"

"The Reapers… am I… have I died?"

"No Charles… come, rise. I must show you something you have never seen before."

"But you're…"

"Fear not death Charles. Come," he requested.

He led me by candlelight through the cold, eerie corridors of Blakesware and down the staircase to the Great Hall, where his picture hung above the fire. He invited me to stand before it.

"Charles Lamb, tell me what you see?" he asked.

"Mr Stubbs, Sir if I may, before we proceed. We would very much have liked for you to have been part of the Blakesware Set this Christmas. Your presence was deeply missed."

"I know Charles; I have been observing you for some time now. I am reassured to know I was missed, for I died a lonely man – known as a mere painter of racehorses! But I'm not here for vanity's sake. No, I came tonight because he sent me."

"Who sent you?"

"I was asked to show the power of art to persuade us of truth. Let me enlighten you Charles. He commissioned it... this vision of nature, human and animal. One of aristocrats, peasants and creatures equal under the sky. He wanted to bring an infusion of the aesthetic and the scientific!"

He stood close to me... I felt the chill of his breath. I rubbed my arms for warmth.

"And Charles, twas such a pity that William Blake was unable to join the Set for he inspired me. He saw them Charles, walking amongst the figures. He told me so as I painted."

"What did he see?" I asked, but the response was a cryptic one.

"Look Charles, what does the work reveal and what does it hide? Study the images, compare and contrast them, do. Uncover the secret and help to guide our souls."

"I cannot see – I need more light," I insisted. How could I possibly do this by candlelight alone? So I said,

"I don't understand – do you mean the man in the shadows?"

"Ah, the man in the shadows! Well Charles, you must recall Mary's question – she asked it of Malachi – What is your question?"

"She did so, I remember it most clearly. She said he wanted to be part of the picture."

I did my best to study the painting but it was no use.

"Bring your light closer," I urged.

Alas, his light faded.

> "Wonder though thy senses look,
> Behold now, throw down thy book,"

I heard him say, poetic and softly spoken in a voice that faded with the light. The darkness closed in and I slept.

It was Mary Shelley who found me, slumped in the armchair close to the hearth in the Great Hall. I had walked in my sleep. Oh the horror!

8 January 1823

Gaia, I gave a simple explanation to the curious residents of Blakesware Manor. I claimed I had trouble sleeping, so had ventured into the night to bring solace to my restless mind and fallen asleep whilst musing. Yet, I suspect Mary Shelley knew the truth. She noticed my increased obsession with the painting. Prompted by George Stubbs' impressions I observed afresh. What does it reveal? What does it hide? I saw,

💜 The solidity and triangular form of the figures.

💜 To Lucy's left, what might be perceived as a Wheel of Fortune or a Spinning Jenny?

💜 The horse's head - which may have served as a model for the Goblin Tree, as I now fondly dub our tree!

That was it – I was through with looking – seeking the truth that Stubbs suggested. I had studied the sky and the clouds, the shape of the tree, the clothing and gestures of the figures and looked into the remaining shadows. Nothing more!

"I can't see it," I said aloud. Mary understood me.

"Oh, the *Haymakers* painting... do you believe there's something more to it than meets the eye? Is that why you couldn't sleep last night?" she asked.

"Maybe... it's just by now I should have fathomed what it is I'm supposed to do![81]"

Malachi dashed into the Great Hall. Maybe, he was the one to save me? I gathered him up, so he could look at the picture at eye level.

"Is this the picture you want to be part of?" I asked.

The puppy licked my face. Mary laughed, but from the corner of my eye I swear Gaia that I saw Lucy – that beauty with the cool blue pastoral drapery - reach her right hand forward from the canvas,

371

as if to beckon the dog to join her in a partnership of human and animal. Oh the fear of insanity haunts me! So I set down the dog.

Gaia, I must confess, Mary Shelley's qualities go far beyond her literal skills. She's a wonderful listener and passed no judgement on my deeds. Walking in the wilderness garden, I spoke candidly about the visitor to my room – one George Stubbs.

"Charles, come now. Remember, I of all people have some insight into the mysteries of life. Where do you think I found the inspiration to write Frankenstein? It didn't just come from within, but from without too. No, I'm certain there's much more to life on Earth than we can see... maybe that's what George was trying to say."

"So you don't think me insane?" I asked.

"No Charles Lamb... we're all prone to moments of insecurity. I think you are a brave, honest and most likeable man."

"I am!"

"Charles, I know you saw him... because I saw him too! Let me explain, I'm an insomniac Charles. It's been worse since Percy died. Sometimes I take from my bed from frustration to scrawl at my travellers desk, but this was different. I rose with a purpose. You both passed me on the stairs. I watched you walk with the spectre. I followed you both. I saw every movement, heard every word. Verbatim ac literatim, 'Fear not Death Charles, come...' he said."

I was astonished.

"Heavens, weren't you afraid? Oh Mary, why didn't you wake me?" I asked, as I leant against the great lion plinth.

"Because he came to us in kindness... with a message to reveal something we have yet to see."

"How can you be sure?"

"Because I was expecting him," she replied.

"You were? How?"

"This may sound strange Charles... I saw it in the rain."

"The rain?"

"I see patterns in the rain in the dark. The night before last I saw him... the visitor who came to bring a message of hope."

"That's why you asked the question – Do you ever look at the rain on your window?" I replied.

"So Charles, I believe he wanted to help with our questions. I feel he wants us to look beyond the painting. To me it's not about comparing the images with each other, but with something else. This is my instinct."

"Mary Shelley, you really are a remarkable woman."

"Do you remember his last words?

'Wonder though thy senses look,
Behold now, throw down thy book.' "

I had a vague recollection.

"I think therein lies the truth," she suggested.

9 January 1823

Gaia, when I began to keep this journal I had not anticipated any revelations. All I proposed was to give a picture of how life was changing due to the age of the machines. Yet a simple tale of simple folk has become a story of enchantment – of magical stones, hidden messages in paintings, wandering spirits and playing cards, a World Tree that now resembles a Goblin, an everlasting rose, a dog both young and mature at the same time, a riddle about time, an enigmatic Duke, an enthralling golden locket, 100 Questions of Hope, prophetic visions and a cryptic list from the future.

Yet this is the real world – I scribe not one falsehood. How it must seem a place of fantasy, brimming with symbolism and metaphor beyond all expectation. Will people believe me if I share it with them? How curious is this Earth we inhabit? What magic flows through its veins?

Gaia, how strange is the period of reflection when things return to normal after such eventful days. I have mused and despite the still and cold of winter, I believe this is the start of an adventure. So, I returned to you today with this new sense of optimism. I have shied away from your company for too long – simply to keep the madness at bay! They say time takes care of everything. Well, what of my dreams? Did I ever really share them with you? Contented with little, yet wishing for more. Let me be clear, I do not champion wealth or land, gold or jewels, status or power - these things mean little to me.

I stake my claim for happiness – it will come from the lips of my Lucy. Pray, one day I shall hear her say, "I love you Charles. I have always loved you from the moment I first saw you." I live in hope, Gaia, that she will be mine. For these lonely, cold, drawn out nights of winter chill the bone. I feel my aching heart beating as if to say, "Charles, fulfil your longing. Go to her." Peculiar then, that I was reminded, Gaia, of the last words to me from my Late Uncle the great John Plumer, "Charles, my dear boy – remember, only you can make it happen. I'm counting on you Charles, we all are – you must not disappoint." Did he have my love for Lucy in mind?

7 February 1823
(Morning)

A magnificent deep white snow has settled about the Uplands. Sadly, Albert Thorvaldsen, Hans Christian Anderson, Ralph Emerson and my dear friend Samuel Coleridge departed in January, long before the cold spell arrived. I have tried many times to muster the will to scribe about their departure, but it pains me so. All I will say is this. Fearing an arduous journey ahead of him Hans said, "My friends I foresee it, a day a thousand years from now when the ship of the air will come, crowded with passengers, and this will be much faster than cruising by sea." I suspect there's a truth in that, for I have seen it in my dreams – a bird of fire.

There is one blessing, the inclement weather has prevented Mary Shelley and her son from leaving, or so she says, for I believe she has warmed to the Manor. Like me, she simply adored the sight of the heavy freshly fallen snow. The whole Uplands had changed into a fairy tale world. I wish Hans and Albert had remained behind to witness it. Hans could have recounted his Snow Queen tales, and Albert could have borne witness to the majesty of Yggdrasil in deep snow – yes Gaia, for he claimed that the real magic of the tree is only witnessed at that time. Come now Albert, how you tempt me to visit the cottage to see for myself.

This morning, Captain Lewin and Emma Isola joined us with the young Malachi – my how he has grown already – to venture into the glistening, radiant landscape. The snow was swept high in drifts, new and frozen, deep and silent. Most things were half buried, like monuments scattered in a strange new world. It was Malachi's first real snow since coming to England. He stared out, at first suspiciously, then tentatively, and finally he ran and jumped in, as though greeting an old friend. Emma cried to him in Latin, "Veni, vidi, vici.[82]"

Thoroughly wrapped to keep out the cold, young Percy borrowed my sled. It was Captain Lewin's suggestion – to tie a leash between the dog and the snow cart. Malachi was remarkably powerful for his size and drew Percy along at some speed for a short while. Oh, how we laughed. We made balls of snow too and chased each other around the wilderness garden, as best we could before the cold set into our bones.

7 February 1823
(Afternoon)

Gaia, temptation got the better of me – having feasted on Mrs Field's broth, I surreptitiously set out into the snow again, taking young Malachi with me. Under a bright clear sky, I tramped slowly through the heavy snow towards Keeper's Cottage, with my scarf covering my mouth and nose to keep out the cold and warm my breath. By the time we'd reached Yggdrasil I was quite frozen. What I found when we arrived astounded me.

♥   The World Tree, Yggdrasil had surely doubled in size since we planted it on New Year's Day. The snow on its branches sparkled like little diamonds and the two grey squirrels we had set free were at its peak, watching me as I drew closer. A ribbon still hung upon it, but one of regal purple[83], not blue. Had Lucy's ribbon changed colour due to the snow?

♥   Near the foot of the tree were three perfectly spaced snow heart shapes, each about three feet across. They would have formed an equilateral[84] triangle, were I to join them. Curiously, none of the hearts showed any signs of footprints about them. What hands had created them?

♥   Beyond these, I saw them – with my own eyes Gaia. I swear it so until they take me to my grave. I counted 12 in total. The shape of angels in the snow! Each was about the size of a small person, each with a set of wings, each with a gown. The snow about the angels was undisturbed too. I immediately recalled Samuel's words about Blake's claim to have seen angels in a tree, which made me pause and wonder!

Entranced by these things, I hardly noticed the fresh flurries of snow. Lucy changed all that. She crept up on me and whispered in my ear like the wind,

"The entire ocean is affected by a pebble[85]."

I span around to find her lightly dressed despite the cold. She held a long stick, like a crook, to help maintain her balance. I suspect it was the same staff she'd used to perform her strange spell near Nimley Bourne – the incantation cast to protect against fear and dread.

"I'll put a wager on that," I replied.

"Charles, you came. I anticipated you would. Just look at the snow. Isn't it simply beautiful?" She held out her palm. A huge flake fell into her hand, with fern like crystals[86], branches and side branches. "Wonderful isn't it how no two snowflakes are alike," she suggested. I agreed and watched astonished as the fragile flake in her hand refused to thaw. The young Malachi stretched up to greet her.

"Hello, my little polar bear – enjoying the snow are we? Make the most of it my friend, for it'll disappear before you can say Jack Frost[87]."

Lucy gently blew the flake from her palm and watched it settle with its thousands of unique companions on the ground.

"Albert said Yggdrasil blossomed in the snow, but this is beyond my wildest imagination," I said, gesturing towards the shapes in the snow.

"I know… its so exciting isn't it. Anything can happen in life. It's just a question of will power… of faith."

There she goes, talking in riddles again.

"Faith – a belief in something for which we have no evidence," she added.

At the rear of Keeper's Cottage was an area of sunken land which during times of prolonged or heavy rain turned into a temporary pond, several feet deep. At times like these a thin sheet of ice often covered the surface. Today, a layer of snow hid the fragile ice sheet. Some animals are perfectly adapted to life on the ice; others are hardly able to stand, let alone make it home, Malachi included. As he ran ahead of us, he glanced back, as if to announce his arrival as a performer on ice. However, unlike the famed polar bear, this little fellow was most unsteady on the ice. He slipped and yelped on the frozen surface. As fractures appeared on the ice beneath him, I saw the spectre of fear in the animal's almond shaped eyes.

"Malachi!" I cried, trumping through the snow. "How deep is it?" I called to Lucy, as the inevitable happened.

The ice broke into chunks. Our baby bear clung on for survival as the meltdown began. The harder he fought to free himself, the more the ice shattered about him. As the helpless creature slipped through the ice and disappeared beneath the surface, I was thrown into panic. I was his life-line, the bear's only hope of survival. I had to set aside my own comfort and act quickly and selflessly to save him. No sacrifice, no victory.

Oh Gaia, how irresponsible I had been to allow this to happen. The 'little bear' was obviously at risk, but I ignored the signs. Thankfully, Lucy was beside me, with her long slender staff.

"Charles, make haste, go." she said, imperiously passing me her staff. The image of 'Nelson and the Bear' flashed in my mind, though I was no admiral and held no musket. Behold, Richard Westall, if you could see me now, I give you a picture to paint of man seeking to save. Capture me, reaching out a helping hand. Capture me with my arms around the bear, using all my strength to haul him from the freezing water. Capture me, rejoicing as the creature lives!

7 February 1823
(Late evening)

Malachi showed tremendous resilience and powers of recovery. There were no ill signs, so I chose to keep the ordeal a secret.

8 February 1823
(Early morning)

Gaia, he came to me again in the night – the spectre of George Stubbs. In my dreams I imagine. It was probably the Stilton – Mary warned me, but I neglected her advice.
"Charles, today you did a most noble deed. You were an example to all mankind," he told me, as I sat up in bed with a start. The light of the full moon was upon him.
"Oh, be gone blithe wandering spirit – haunt me not," I replied. I buried my head under my bed covers to will him away.
"Charles – be patient. I bring good favour… behold… my reproduction of the *Haymakers* has begun." My curiosity stirred, I slowly peered out from under the bedding.

Tucked discreetly in the corner of my room, I saw a canvas upon an easel, with the artist, brush in hand painting in the moonlight.
"Pray… my eyes see too much," I declared. "What are you doing?"
"Putting a simple wrong to right, my friend! Malachi was right. He merits a place in the picture. You proved that today. Let it be so." Sheer lunacy! I threw the covers over my head once more and decried my fortune.

8 February 1823
(Dawn)

Oh, what foolish passions besot me! The canvas stands in the corner of my room – an alternative *Haymakers* was emerging before me, even as I sleep. The brushes and oils stand idle, but my imagination rampages through them. Is there no end to the mirages?

8 February 1823
(Night)

The artist returned again – for a second night – oh weary eyes, sleep. Oh weary ears, hear not one sound.

At his third and final appearance - George claimed it so;
"Thank God it is all over," he announced. So, he'd been conversing with Lord North! I digress.
I dragged myself from my bed.
"Think of it as a birthday gift Charles - by way of a thank you."
"A gift, from whom?" I replied, making to shake his hand. Oh spirits – how thy tease thee. My hand passed directly through his. Oh cold shudders. Oh, creeping flesh! Oh, vanishing soul! No time for an explanation – I was just able to see Malachi sat beside Lucy Ebbs, where he rightly belongs. Malachi was in the picture!

10 February 1823

A rapid thaw greeted this day of my birth. I'd like to grow very old, as slowly as possible. Alas, I fear we grow grey in our spirit long before we grow grey in our hair. For certain, ghostly painters frequenting my room will turn me grey overnight – let me check my appearance Gaia. All is well!

What to do with the painting? There she is as plain as day – a replica of the *Haymakers* in every detail, except for Malachi's presence.

"The brushes have gone – the paint is dry –
what to do but wonder why?"

Who to tell? Come forth Mary Shelley! Be my witness Emma Isola. Be entertained, Bill Richmond - knighted as Haymaker by William Wilberforce. Shall I invite them to come before the painting? The image is part of me and me of it. The *Haymakers* speaks to me – I listen. I feel as though part of my soul is wrapped up within it. I shall ponder it the day through!

Gaia, I feel it would be vain and remiss of me to dwell much on the gifts bestowed to me this day, for I want to make plain this 'Little Journal of My Foolish Passions' is, in truth, a message of hope for mankind. I am just one man amongst millions. What is my life as a mere mortal compared with all our futures? The greatest gift is life itself, and all the life about me – these are my presents. Nature - it's the one thing for which there is no substitute. I pity those isolated from the joys of nature – for it's free to rich and poor alike!

I should reveal a third and unexpected gift – a letter from Samuel Coleridge! He left it with Mary Shelley for her to pass to me on his departure. It read so:

Dear Charles,

You have said often enough how nothing brings you greater pleasure than to do a good deed by stealth and have it discovered by chance. Well Charles, I surprise thee – birthday greetings! Be assured, it gives me great pleasure – to think of you now, receiving my greetings. In the highest degree Charles! Call me mystic if you will, but I can picture your face now, glowing, nodding, eyes wide open! O' smile, O' smile, I'll sing the while.

Enough of this banter. I must convey how I enjoyed the perfect ease and delight whilst at Blakesware. Hearty congratulations must go to the hosts. Oh Charles what a majestic Set we compiled. The beauty and neatness of 'The Haymakers Survey' – to honour Gaia, our living planet. What to do with the questions? How might we persuade them – the doubters? It overwhelms me as I sit down alone I must content myself with the memories. Happy days! I trust, Charles that we helped to soften the anguish of your spirit.

I trust you find Mary Shelley good company? She is a fine, creative woman. Percy would have admired her fortitude. She is candid too. Charles she shared this truth with me. A spectre haunts Blakesware Manor – she and Emma have seen him pace the corridors at night. A benevolent spirit. I am perplexed and have no opinion, but Mary swears it so. Sweet Emma, so bright and eager to learn. I feel she has developed a love for Emerson – Cupid's bow has captured her heart. Mind her Charles, she needs a paternal figure!

Charles I grant you health, hope and a steady mind. I leave from Highgate, once the weather permits, to visit Victor Hugo in France. I hope you can join us soon. It would do you mightily well to leave the shores of England for a while – to touch new lands. God bless and protect you, friend!

Yours,

Samuel

PS: Did you ever hear word from William Blake? If not, I feel it my duty to share our scheme with him. Confer, Charles, if you will!

14 February 1823
(Morning)

Gaia, on this day when lovers openly express their feelings for each other, I woke with a start to the tune of a playful, 'knock, knock, knock[88]' on my bedroom door. I scampered from my bed to open up - only to find the corridor was deserted, void of life. Behold, a Saint Valentine's Day note had been slipped under my door. I unfolded the paper, perfumed like the rose.

<u>*Valentin – Prvi Spomladin*[89]</u>

I have heard you declare that hearts are your favourite suit!

I declare they be mine too.
Lest not our love stay unrequited!

14 February 1823
(Evening)

Gaia, I face a crisis of confidence at the unwitting hands of Ralph Emerson. Allow me to explain! I happened to frequent the Library in search of inspiration to respond to Lucy's gesture. I believe I told you the Library is a further extension of the mind, with a rich collection of books and artefacts, most collected by my late Uncle John. At first glance, a most serious room with two huge stacks of reading material either side of a majestic desk, at which I scrawled my Essays, and now housed Emma's study materials.

I scrabbled through the dusty shelves, switching through the pages of poets and authors from home and abroad. Masterly works many of them, yet tired, well-read and predictable! Where might I find the words to surmise all that Lucy is to me? My Celia! Disappointed at my own lack of creativity, I sat at John's desk and drummed the surface with my fingers, playing the tune to the rhyme, ♪ Solider, soldier won't you marry me with your musket, fife and drum. ♪

Emma's books on Latin – the language of love – were arranged neatly on the desk, as if to confirm her as a disciplined and committed scholar. Amongst them was a work of much recent conversation and praise, 'Ivanhoe' by Sir Walter Scott. I picked the book up to find Emma had marked her place with a letter from Ralph Emerson. In dreary silence, I chose to read the private correspondence. Sin can carry a heavy and immediate price. I rehearse some of his words…

My Darling Emma,

Forgive my impatience Turtle Dove, for my heart runs wild. I am sighing since we parted, yes... we agreed, give all to love... obey your heart! I confess, when I came to the land of my fathers I did not expect to find love. By the rarest of luck I found you my sweet, graced with beauty, elegance and intellect...

Forgive me any indiscretion. I just longed to renew our engagement. We must make the most of the opportunities life presents. Do not go where the path may lead, go instead where there is no path and leave a trail. Join me Emma.... once my tour is done and your studies at Dulwich are through. Better that than yearning letters from America. A land where the imagination can prosper, where all modern women find fulfilment...

Emma, you know how I dislike scandal, it goes against my better nature. Be wary of the lingering tragedy. For dear Charles wears a mask of gaiety over his sorrows. You know how it pains to see someone so cared for in such deep trouble. Emma, do not try to console him for he will tell you that he is already comforted. He believes his condition so natural that he would be surprised to hear you speak ill of him. Let us not betray his loneliness, however genuine we may be. Take care not to smile too broadly at him, an expression of distress and concern that will be clear to his eyes. Be charitable and discreet, should he mention his Lucy again. None have seen her ,Emma. She is but a metaphor - The Earth Spirit! We know it. She is nothing but the wind, the rain and the sun. Lucy, the girl in rock and plain. Poor Charles, he is in a minority of one ...

Yours for...

Master Ralph Waldo Emerson

Oh Gaia, 'The Earth Spirit!' Do they imagine me crazy? The revelation grieves me. Now I see too late the error of my ways – to keep this journal against the kind counsel of Captain Lewin. I steadfastly ignored his warnings. Now, at this news, have I the strength or will power to continue? Am I a deluded, hallucinating man? I am in love with something in my own head. "O' mercy," to myself I cried. If Lucy should be... I cannot scribe. To Keeper's...

15 February 1823

Gaia – my senses have abandoned me! Lucy - fate binds me to thee for ever and a day. I saw her today in the wilderness, beside Uncle John's Lion. She, the sprite as they would have me wonder – as natural as can be. I ask, who's seen her beside me? Fanny, Bill Richmond, Captain Lewin, Mary Shelley, the Duke himself? What converses between them once I'm gone? To preserve my mind, I lay down my quill. I give it up for Lent.

28 February 1823

Solitaire – I have returned to thee these last few weeks, to ease my troubled soul. The cards do not judge me. Yet whenever I play, the Three of Hearts appears as a constant reminder of the solstice last June when Lucy told me of the mischief fairies can conjure. Am I destined to live my life in some kind of fantasy world of the kind young Hans Christian Anderson aspires to create? Is my legacy to be remembered as a figure of ridicule in history, rather than the heroic champion of Art, Love and Nature!

I have failed to observe my vow. How can I, as troubled as I am, find the determination to rise out of my crisis of confidence and champion the causes of the Blakesware Set? Where is my courage and fortitude that Bill Richmond helped to instil? As I look back over my journal Gaia, I see question after question. It concerns me deeply. Why do I always pose them and seek answers? How can I be guided? Perhaps I should pass the survey's questions into safer hands. Wait... I'll pull them together here.

5 March 1823

Gaia, my incompetence is beyond comprehension. The final 20 questions posed by the Set have gone astray! Cursed, irresponsible, fragile me! Occupied with my own self doubt I have done a terrible thing. Oh, the consequences of neglect reach far. I have searched my room thoroughly, thumbed through every book in the Library and tactfully and cryptically asked my companions if they had, by chance, discovered anything of interest of mine. All to no avail. What would Uncle John Plumer make of me now? So much for his instructions to Katharine!

Alas, I now carry so many secrets – the loss of 20 questions, knowledge of the content of Ralph's letter to Emma, Yggdrasil in the snow, the spirit of G. Stubbs, the alternative *Haymakers* painting and you, Gaia, my journal. To whom may I turn? To Mary Shelley – as confidant!

23 March 1823

They call today Passion Sunday in Lent! Well, there's little evidence of saintliness, for further robberies have occurred at the market town of Ware. Rumour has it that a gang of highwaymen, dressed in all concealing smocks and with soot-blackened faces pick out their victims – they who leave the market fair with the fullest pockets. A life has been taken. I fear these dark arts will cause folk to desert the market in their droves.

As for Mary Shelley, it seems her late Percy's father denies her financial aid. She shared with me correspondence in which he insists he will only provide for Percy the younger if Mary relinquishes custody of him. Oh the irony, as we await the Maundy Ceremony.

27 March 1823

I fear, Gaia, that the ugly spectre of the industrialised world is out of control. Cotton mills, mines and factories are spreading like a rampant plague across our land – devouring all before it. Is this Mary Shelley's Frankenstein unleashed? Our mountains of green are fading to grey – a world of bland monochrome, shy of colour. How magnificent is nature in reply. Evidence of renewal and rebirth is everywhere at this wonderful period in the calendar. I take comfort in this and in humanitarian acts like the Maundy Ceremony.

Let me be clear. Fanny Ebbs was nominated by Reverend North as a beneficiary of the ancient annual ceremony – held today at Keeper's. So, I set aside my pride to return to the scene of my dreams and my apparent delusions. Mary Shelley, Captain and Lady Lewin (nee Plumer), Emma Isola and Bill Richmond joined me at the cottage to await the presentation by the Duke of Wellington, on the King's behalf. The Captain brought Malachi too. When I saw him at Keeper's again I remembered the incident of the Polar Bear on Ice. I'm convinced Malachi recalled it too, for as we gathered in the bridleway to the fore of the cottage, he regularly looked at the gully where he nearly lost his life.

The Duke arrived riding Copenhagen with a gallery of soldiers in escort. His unexpected appearance, on behalf of King George, sparked great excitement, drawing the workers of Noblin Green farm away from their chores. The reluctant beneficiary of the peculiar ceremony, Fanny Ebbs, pleaded she was far from unfortunate or poor. Abashed at her sudden fame, she sought comfort by leaning against one of the pillars that held up the front porch; it seemed to bring her strength and courage. Gaia, I'm beginning to sense a magic about Keepers Cottage that spreads beyond what the eye can see!

The Duke dismounted and beckoned Fanny into the early spring sunshine.

"Mrs Ebbs … Fanny… please… do step down."

"You've all be'n waiting… come to greet me… oh!"

"Why, yes… it's noon on Maundy Thursday, as we agreed," announced Captain Lewin, as he emerged from the throng.

"Ah Richard… quite… of course… I hadn't forgotten. My memory is as strong as ever. It'll live beyond my grave," she replied. The Captain took Fanny by the arm and led her graciously towards the onlookers.

"Come, it'll be perfect. Just think of it as a reward for your determination … he is most pleased," I heard.

Richard led Fanny towards the Duke. At the Field Marshall's side stood the Yeoman of the Guard, carrying the alms. He passed the Duke a small leather spring purse. The Ceremony had begun.

"A new commandment, give I unto you," said the Duke, ahead of presenting Fanny with three silver coins – specially minted. Dominations of one, two and three pence, carrying the obverse GEORGIUS IIII D G BRITANNIAR REX F D! The Duke and the Ebbs' clearly had a special relationship. I have seen him present Lucy with a locket, now he has bestowed Fanny with silver coins, at the King's favour! This, after everything that Lady Katharine had implied about the Ebbs' status.

Oh enough. Where was my Lucy? This day being known as Kiss Thursday, with the promise to, 'love one another'. Might I honour it! The presentation underway, I saw her - my Lucy - wandering under Yggdrasil's shadow. Was I alone in noticing how mighty the tree had grown; its presence now marked on the Uplands landscape? I avoided any temptation to go to her. I sensed she understood. She waved discreetly. Malachi, however, was unfettered. He ran to her side, preferring her company to the tedium of a formal ceremony. Oh Happy Dog!

On our return to Blakesware, Mary Shelley made a telling observation. As we walked with Malachi in the wake of the others, she casually remarked,

"Charles, tell me. The young woman befriended by the Duke at the Boxing Day hunt... why should she choose to stand alone... in the shadow of Yggdrasil? Ought she not to have joined us?"

I stopped in my tracks.

"What did you say?"

"The young woman at Keeper's! You must have seen her, playing with Malachi under the tree!"

"So you saw her too?" I asked.

"Why of course Charles. Why act so perplexed?"

I grabbed her arm.

"Mary... thank you... I am of sane mind! Lucy is real... thank you Mary, thank you truly."

We dropped off the pace. I told Mary everything about Ralph's letter and the perception many in the Blakesware Set appeared to have of me.

"I see. How unfortunate... a cruel twist of fate, but please Charles, be reassured."

"They believe her to be the Earth Spirit!" I said.

"The Earth spirit... most curious! Charles, think do, has anyone else besides you, I... and the Duke seen her?" she asked.

"Why Fanny Ebbs..."

"And Captain Lewin, Emma and Lady Plumer?"

Unclear, I shook my head.

"Charles, let's reason this out. Either they mislead you... or they can't see her, or... or she chooses by whom and when to be seen."

"No... I doubt they mislead. I believe in them... in their integrity. It must be something more, but what you and they suggest, its pure fantasy."

Malachi danced about us as we spoke.

"Well, let us hypothesise… and assume she is the Earth Spirit."

"But she is flesh and blood and my bel'… no, I won't have it."

Mary was determined.

"Let us suppose all the same. Put your feelings aside, for it is a magical proposition."

"If you must…" I replied.

"How wondrous… to imagine that Mother Nature would choose to show herself in this way… as an Earth Spirit personified. Let's be clear Charles, if she were such a deity would she…"

"If Lucy was such a deity…" I interjected.

"If Lucy is such a deity, she would behave as such… enigmatic, unpredictable and beautiful, yet harvesting the potential for wanton cruelty and devastation. She'd be capable of sending a bolt of lightening, as much as able to paint the horizon with a rainbow. Does this sound like the woman you know and care for?"

"Lucy is complicated, this I know. There is something about her, but it cannot be this."

"Well Charles, with a little imagination… it's easy. She can be the Earth Spirit should you wish it."

"She could. I picture it."

"Then let it be."

I nodded.

"Whatever the truth Mary, at least my mind is less troubled. Thank you!"

"Don't thank me Charles, thank my father. He was the one who encouraged me to keep an open mind to all things, especially where Nature's concerned, which reminds me, I've something I need to share with you… something equally curious."

Gaia, Mary's revelation would wait until the morrow. For I rejoice - I woke this morning with one disturbing notion of my place in this world and retired this good night with another. I am, again, of sound and open mind and opinion!

31 March 1823

Mary Shelley came to my bedroom to share her curious revelation. In doing so, she witnessed, first hand, the alternative version of the *Haymakers*.

"There's more mystery and suspense unfolding in Hertfordshire than I ever imagined possible," she said, once I'd explained how the ghost of George Stubbs had seemingly re-painted the image, so as to secure Malachi's place in history.

"Let me get this right... his spirit came to your room every night for three nights... to paint this? Well Charles... there is clearly more magic in the *Haymakers* than anyone might have imagined possible, for let me share my revelation."

In the full gaze of the painting, Mary Shelley unfolded a letter. It was written in the hand of one William Blake Esquire and addressed to Lady Shelley. The startling sections read:

My Lady,

I write to you in good favour and hope I find you well. Samuel has shared news of the magical endeavours of the Blakesware Set - such visionary wisdom. I find it most wonderful to know that George's painting inspired you all. How befitting. If George were with us still, I wonder, would he have been so bold as to tell you of my role in the work? Mary, let it be known that I have seen angelic figures walking amongst haymakers as they worked in the fields. In my minds eye, I see them too within the canvas that is George Stubbs' Haymakers. Let if be said, art can be illuminating, puzzling and powerful! Art is part of the Tree of Life! And, a fool sees not the tree that a wise man sees.

Mary, if I had my time again, I'd do my utmost to be part of the picture… to offer some questions for the survey. I wish it were so! How I rue my ill-health. Alas, it prevented me from attending!

In some vain hope, I say, there is an intricate web of symbol and meaning that connects word and image. May that be my contribution to 'The Haymakers Survey.' Let some future host assign pictures to the questions.

> *O Earth O Earth return,*
> *Arise from out the dewy grass!*

W. Blake Esq

"So, William Blake once watched haymakers at work, and believed he saw angels walking among them?" I asked.

"So it would seem."

"I think George alluded to this. In fact, I'm certain of it."

"That's most mystical," she said, as she folded the letter away.

She asked if anyone else had seen the alternative version.

"No, not to my knowledge… apart from Malachi. I brought him to my room the day after it was completed. He just adored it. You ought to have seen his face. I'd love to have been able to read his mind."

"Well, if Emma persists in practising her Latin on him, who knows where it might lead."

"Mary… I sense there's something most unusual about Malachi too. I think he belongs to Lucy, for she says, 'He is here to convey a message'. Although she also says, 'He goes as fate decrees', but this doesn't explain how he was mature before he was a puppy. Ask about... and people will say, the White Wolf of Wareside was the same dog as he, yet the White Wolf was here last autumn. I saw him with my own eyes. He startled me... stole my handkerchief."

"The same dog?"

"Yes... the very same dog, but one with a disc about its neck. It had the name, Malachi, and a set of numbers."

"Maybe the numbers were a clue to help get the message across? Can you remember the numbers?"

"Yes... well a few of them... 01920."

"1920? Sounds like counting! Ready or not, here I come," suggested Mary.

"Or a date in the future."

"How unlikely. A dog from the future... from 1920!"

"Malachi... our messenger from the future," I speculated.

1 April 1823

Here cometh April again and as far as I can see the world hath more fools in it than ever, myself included. I still have no trace of the missing questions. What a travesty! In their absence, I try to recall those on the list... I think some were:

- ♥ Can a dog speak Latin? (Ralph Emerson)
- ♥ Will a man ever walk on the moon? (William Turner)
- ♥ Do you believe in a European Union? (Duke of Wellington)

Oh foolish me – I can't be certain of this.

I bring good news Gaia! Inspired by Reverend North's tales of Royston Cave, Captain Richard Lewin has made arrangements for us to visit. Our party consists of the Captain, Reverend North, Bill Richmond, Mary, Emma, Malachi and I. We depart for Royston today at 11.00 sharp on the twice weekly coach service. We are booked into the Bull's Inn at the heart of the town. I shall leave you behind at Blakesware, Gaia – and keep separate notes of the visit.

3 April 1823
(Evening)

As we headed north up Ermine Street, an old roman road from Londinium to York, the weather was most unkind. Hail swept across the exposed landscape, perhaps to test our character. It unsettled the horses and thumped the roof of our fly, as if to warn us to turn back. Our journey delayed, we arrived weary and with insatiable appetite. Let us hope the elements fair us better tomorrow and we are not disappointed.

4 April 1823

I awoke in relative luxury and full of optimism. My room was comfortable and I was untroubled by rumours shared the night before that it was haunted. I looked out over stables the like of which I'd not seen before, capable of keeping up to 100 horses if required. I judge this unsettled Malachi as he yapped incessantly from dawn, despite the Captain's best efforts to restrain him. Still, twas a bright clear morn, so we were set well for the day.

Our guide, William Stukeley Senior, met us in the lobby. A most handsome man, if not quite the dandy, his father was a draftsman and scholar of sacred history and an antiquary. He had inherited a passion for stone circles - Stonehenge and Avebury - and, unlike his father, imagined there was an invisible mystical thread that linked these and places like Royston Cave together.

A master at recreating the past, he possessed the kind of voice and expression that was irresistible to the ear. We listened intensely as he gave us a most thorough account of our location. As I recall, Royston is where Ermine Street crosses the Icknield Way, two of the oldest roads in Britain. He told us the Way was 2,000 years old and probably named after the Iceni tribe of Ancient Britain, as they used the route for trade. The Royston Cave is directly under the point where these ancient roads cross. Above ground, a cross was erected at the crossroads by Lady Roisia de Vere.

Probably once known as Roisia's Town, Royston is a very early settlement. As we made our way towards its famous cave, I felt as though I was walking with history. We heard so much about the cave from Reverend North. It had developed a sense of mystery in my mind. I hoped not to be disappointed, yet experience had taught me not to crave too much.

Our procession, led by Captain Lewin and his dog, passed the Roy Stone, which was said to have first marked the crossroads. An impressive obelisk, like the Diamond Stone at Avebury - so say locals – known to turn full circle at midnight. Whilst here, Emma said that Roy Stone could also mean Stone of the King, as Roi in French means king! Good point, but as confusion reigned, our host replied,
"I prefer to think of it as a Diamond to mark the centre point of the world. Based on celestial observation, we are at true north-south and east-west. We are at an Axis-Mundi!" I think Albert Thorvaldsen said something similar when we planted Yggdrasil, but I digress.

Enthused by Stukeley's words, we reached the entrance to the cave. Reverend North paused at the very place where many years prior he had descended into the darkness; an inconspicuous site, now almost hidden from view. The preacher turned to me and smiled.

"Come walk with me… just one more mile!" he said metaphorically, adding, "To think I climbed through that hole… the first person to enter the cave for hundreds of years…"

"Through here… six shillings each to enter… but to you, my friends, it's free," announced Stukeley. He led us to a tame looking door, which was the gateway to the small dome shaped cave. Yet, one of us was denied entry: "The dog… tie him here," insisted Stukeley. "For the Royston Cave's too sacred for an animal."

At first, Captain Lewin hesitated, before reluctantly complying with Stukeley's advice; he tied Malachi to a tethering post. We left the dog, protesting and struggling to break free and join us in the cave.

It was only right that Reverend North should be the first to follow our guide into the passage dug by Tom Watson and his workers, albeit with some difficulty negotiating the steps into the cavern. As we descended, George North warned us of his feelings when he first entered the cave more than half a century ago. He'd felt breathless, touched by something unseen; an experience that provided the stimulus for his faith. All these years on, his shortness of breath now was due to his declining years. With each step, he mechanically prodded his walking-stick, as if to punch out a coded rhythm to the ancient inhabitants of the cave – to awaken them from their graves. I imagined his message to be, "Though a tree may grow high, the fallen leaves return to the ground."

Up to 1,000 years old, the Royston Cave is unique in Britain – if not the world for its numerous medieval carvings, mainly Pagan in origin. I marvelled at the mysticism, so did Mary Shelley. As she reached the final step, the original stone that once covered the entrance, she swooned. I kept her from falling.

"In manus tuas Domine," I believe she said.

"Mary! Are you hurt?" I asked.

"No Charles… just lost my footing on the last step," she replied.

"Forgive me. It's the rain… I ought to have said. The moisture creeps into that stone," explained Stukeley. "It's irrational I know. The cave keeps a constant temperature… except for that one step. It replicates conditions outside, as though it's still guarding the entrance to the cave."

"Guarding?" I said, "To keep us out… or to keep something within." Reverend North changed the mood,

"To think, where we stand now was just a pile of rubble when I dropped down into the cave."

"A fall of about 26 feet?" said Stukeley, pointing to the skylight.

"A fair drop for a young boy…. I still bear the scars to this day… physical and emotional. The experience is so deeply etched into my memory… like the carvings on the wall themselves."

"You didn't uncover any buried treasure then?"

A slight smile came to the Reverend's face, "Ah, well I can say I've had plenty of time to ponder the meaning and purpose of the cave."

"It's remarkable to think this place was out of reach of human kind for so long," said our Haymaker, Bill Richmond.

Stukeley hung his perforated lantern on a swivelling hook. Before it settled, its light swung like a pendulum, casting grotesque shadows that danced about the cave. As the carvings flickered in the unnatural light, I wondered about the invisible people from days gone by whose feet had traversed the floor of the cave, whose hands had carved the figures into the stone. What would they make of us?

Gaia, I have added copies of William Stukeley's illustrations, here:

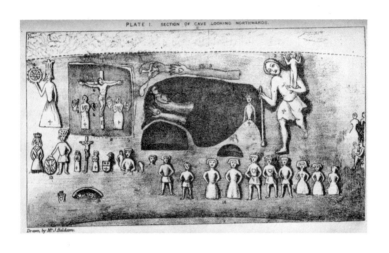

PLATE I.   SECTION OF CAVE LOOKING NORTHWARDS.

Drawn by Mr J. Baldam.

PLATE II.   SECTION OF CAVE LOOKING SOUTH-WEST.

Drawn by Mr J. Baldam.

398

My first impression was of a powerful sense of divination, which developed into a feeling of tranquillity. William Stukeley's hypnotic voice told us about the carvings, directing us to images of crucifixion and effigies of saints - St Catherine, St Christopher and St Lawrence. A figure with a drawn sword was said to be St George, pointing out the 12 apostles. He showed us Richard Lion-heart and an uncrowned queen. There were Pagan symbols too. Although in apparent chaotic disarray, we learnt the carvings may in truth be placed to represent the constellations.

"So what was its purpose?" Captain Lewin asked, on our behalf.

With the help of our guide, we speculated on the possibilities for the 'Origines Roystoniae!'

♥ A chapel of devotion used by the Knights Templar, as the cave's shape was said to be modelled on the Church of the Holy Sepulchre in Jerusalem.

♥ A cool store, because the Templar held a weekly market at Royston in 1200.

♥ A grave used in ritual... there were some bones recovered during excavation – who's and where did they go?

♥ The tomb of a martyr or hero, Boudicca or King Arthur, perhaps!

♥ A secret hideaway or refuge for our early ancestors!

♥ A symbolic gateway to an underworld!

♥ A cell, created by Lady Roisia!

♥ A sanctuary or hermitage – oh my, imagine being trapped down here alone for days, weeks on end.

♥ A medieval art gallery.[90]

To me, Royston Cave was a circular Wonder Wall – a place of salvation and hope. A wall of the Art of God! I speculate – could it be a cure for body, mind and soul? In some ways the carvings were a skull at our banquet to remind us of our mortality. It evoked feelings in me - what hath thou not done? Not naturally disposed to a deity, I pondered – Has God been kind to me?

"I just wish my Uncle, John Plumer, had been here to see this… he a member of the oldest, ancient family in the county."

"Plumer you say… ah yes, he was a regular visitor. My father knew him well," claimed Stukeley. So much for Katharine's implication that he was just a man of science and business!

We had come in the hope of making some perfect discovery. Then it struck me – like Robinson Crusoe lamenting in his cave on his Island of Despair - the impression of my dream resurfaced. What wild things dreams are? That strong vision of the burning forest, fleeing animals and a great flood came alive here in this cave, just because I happened to touch one of the three hands with a heart etched into the palm. The strange carvings revealed their inner secret to me. A radical opinion, which I kept to myself! The cave told a story beyond the religious and the revered. Beyond my dream, I saw similarities in the images and in the curious events unfolding in my life… and in the work of the Blakesware Set, captured in 'The Haymakers Survey.'

Let me see – with a little imagination the carvings could have a secondary coded meaning!

♥ The long Staff at the centre of the carvings could represent Yggdrasil.

♥ The animal near to Yggdrasil could arguably be a dog or a polar bear, not a horse! Could it be Malachi?

♥   The spoked wheel could be the Spinning Jenny – a warning to use the machine wisely.

♥   The woman holding the supposed iron grid could represent Mother Nature, holding aloft a list – the questions from 'The Haymakers Survey'!

♥   The sun shapes – could symbolise the world heating up because of all the smoke and fires from the dark Satanic Mills.

♥   King David drowning … if the Earth warmed up the Arctic would melt and all would be drowned! Hear him say, "I am come into the deep waters."

Reverend North knelt upon some raised stonework ahead of the main wall, and removed a red purse from under his cloak. The very purse used at the Maundy Ceremony. He dipped his large hand inside and withdrew one of the famed stones. Trembling, he held it before the carved figures, and urged, "What do these stones mean?"[91] He spoke with the intense conviction of a hungry man – a man who had harboured this curiosity for most of his life. He had returned in the hope of a resolution; to secure an answer to settle his mind or confirm his faith. An irrational act – could the cave respond?

His words had hardly ceased to echo about the chamber, when the excited clamour of a dog scampering down the stone stairs replaced it. Malachi was free! The loudness of his bark in such a confined space was overwhelming – enough to wake the dead, assuming they still slept. Surprised at the verocity of the sound, Reverend North mishandled his purse, scattering the contents about the floor of the cave. I watched bemused as North's twelve stones fell like hail, then began to roll, wither wander, about the cavern. "Heaven's above! Restrain him… silence him!" insisted Stukeley, shaking his hands in fury, adding, "Banish him this instant."

I confess it was really most amusing! The sight of exalted company, grappling forlornly to capture the stones. All the while, Captain Lewin KB tried to calm the excited dog. Young Percy laughed uncontrollably, in a little, "Hee, hee, hee!" Hysteria, for try as they might, neither the dog nor the stones could be tamed. Then Gaia it happened – exactly as I describe. A miracle emerged from the chaos! The stones clustered at the centre of the cave and began to swirl at speed in a dynamic spiral – a helical twist. The stones gave out a luminous glow as they span. Clockwise, then anti-clockwise. How long did they spin? It was hard to tell. The stones were hypnotic, seeming to suspend time and space. It was a moment when the ideal and the practical collided. A fushion of time and space.

Stukeley broke our collective silence. "What are those things?"
"I have brought them home… in search of meaning… of truth," was all Reverend North could muster.
"It reminds me of a whirlpool," claimed Mary.
The Reverend's eyes widened. "As water washes away stones and torrents wash away the soul, so you destroy man's hope[92]," he said prophetically, as the stones finally settled at the cave's core. Mary Shelley was the first to gather up a stone.
"De profundis clamavi[93]," she declared. As she held it, I could immediately tell from her stance that she was a witness to something beyond our five senses.
"Did you see what I saw?" she asked, as we left the cave, but more of her testimony later – better I think to be sequential – to tell you as I was told. I digress!
"What force is this to defy the laws of gravity… and in my cave?" announced Stukeley, before he made Malachi the focus of his wrath.
"And that beast… out damn you. Out I say."
Captain Lewin's tolerence finally elapsed,
"Sir, if I may. First, what claim of ownership do you suppose on this national treasure? Second, Malachi is, frankly, no beast. And third,

yes third…. that was a force for sure – the *Force of Nature* – a warning to mankind to mend our ways." Richard had spoken with authority. "Incredulous nonsense! No matter… no matter," replied Stukeley, his hands raised in defence. "The Duke commended you to me… and I respect and trust him. Continue… do as you wilt! But I have just one question. What do you propose to do with the stones?" he asked, as the last stone was safely gathered in.

"Why, return them to where they belong… I am done with the responsibility… it is too much!" claimed Reverend North.

"But you can't just leave them here… they'll disappear, as sure as night follows day." I said, convinced others would undoubtedly find them again.

"Not if we put them out of sight and out of reach … in the nooks high up," he suggested.

It seems that the cave once had two levels, probably divided by a wooden structure supported by beams that slotted into square holes carved into the dome – 12 holes. One for each stone!

"Dare I suggest Reverend that the sacred stones were left so they might be found… by you?" proposed Mary. "Besides would it not be a betrayal just to hide them away… can't you see what they can do? They inspire us to look beyond the world of reason and facts and into the world of creativity… the kingdom of the imagination."

"Sacred! Did I say they were sacred?" fumed Reverend North. As a repost, he produced a copy of the Bible from an inside pocket of his cloak.

"Now… please do as I say. It is my duty, my calling. The Lord wills it! But first I need each of you to swear an oath of secrecy on the good book," he announced, tenderly dusting the surface.

We were perplexed by the Reverend's behaviour. What did he fear?

"George patience please… we need a moment or two to think this through a little," said the Captain.

"Do you not have ears? Can you not see? What kind of injustice would it be to hide the stones away? Why deny the world a little magic?" I asked.

The Reverend approached me, book in hand.

"It is my duty. Swear to secrecy Charles, I implore you before it is too late. We must act now."

He was sweating profusely. Perhaps he anticipated what was to follow.

"With respect Reverend, why are you so afraid?" I replied. Stukeley had an inkling, "Does this have anything to do with the boy?" he asked. "The one left here last May. The boy you took in at the workhouse at the Duke's request?" This was an unexpected turn of events.

"The boy! He... he is well cared for... that is sufficient for now." The Reverend was troubled. He put his hands together and looked to the heavens for guidance. Stukeley delivered it.

"And the Duke was here too! Just before the heavy snowfall – to see the cave for himself. He came with a couple of Scandinavian fellows... Anderson, yes that was it.... and the famous sculptor.... he was just in awe of the carvings. He mentioned something to do with a lion that weeps. Curious people... must be the lack of sunshine during winter! Look, they even carved their initials into the rock. "

I can confirm Gaia, the initials AT and AW were carved into the wall.

"This is all very well... but what to do with the stones?" asked a persistent Reverend North.

"Frankly... I think your spirituality has got the better of you. What you propose is highly irrational to me." The Captain surveyed those of us in the chamber. "As Charles has said, in the course of time, people will search the chamber afresh ... it's a natural curiosity. If we seek to preserve them, we need to find another, more secure, place," he added.

"But they belong here. It's what I believe. I've always sensed it wrong of me to take them... I sinned."

Unexpectedly, the cave had now become a confession box too – perhaps that was its real purpose – a place of repentance and reflection.

"Ah… so we come to it. This is about your sin, nothing more," said the Captain. Mary Shelley tried to reassure him, "Dear Reverend, allow me to speak plainly. Positions of authority bring with them great responsibility… you have carried a heavy load for many years. God would surely judge you an honourable and worthy man… whether you keep or replace the stones, you have more than done your duty."

The Reverend mellowed, "Maybe… maybe that's so." Our expressions indicated our support. He felt vindicated, pardoned.

For me, the open forum about the stones and the boy that had been found in the cave, were a distraction. I wanted time alone to admire the beauty of the carvings and to do so in silence. I requested it. My wish was granted. I traced my fingers around the full circumference of the cave, feeling the contours of many of the carvings. In common with the Captain, I was convinced we were viewing a story-board. A message was encrypted here and the stones were part of it. I wondered if Mary's vision – for that is what she experienced – might provide some answers.

She revealed everything once we had vacated the chamber. In the part of the cave which most assumed was once a grave, she had seen a despondent ageing figure of a man hunched over a wooden chest. He was diligently placing items into the chest – a feather, some dice. The dog, Malachi, sat calmly beside him. On the wall to their rear was a copy of the *Haymakers* by George Stubbs! The distinguished gentleman – for that was how she perceived him - looked up at her and drew the shape of a heart in the air with his hands. There was nothing more. What did her vision imply?

Gaia, I scribed so furiously last night to try to capture everything that my wick ran out! Today, I shall by necessity be brief – oh weary quill. Although the cave revealed more than its carvings, our visit had, in truth, raised further questions.

♥ Where did the stones come from before they first entered the cave? Were they made or did they form naturally? I shall remain alert in the hope of discovering their source.

♥ Did Reverend North choose to leave the stones in the cave? We believe we persuaded him against the idea. Besides, a man of his fragility could never place them so high alone, and none of us were willing to assist him.

♥ Why did the Duke, Albert and Hans visit the cave ahead of us and without telling us their plans?

♥ Why didn't Uncle John Plumer disclose to me his deep interest in the cave?

♥ Lastly – that child again! Who is he? Why is he so significant? And, what is he to the Duke?

1 May 1823
(Morning)

I can hardly believe that a year has passed since I began the journal. Unable to resist, I've reviewed the content and believe there's much truth in the saying, 'A book reads better that which is our own.' I've witnessed much during the past year. In this life, let me count my blessings. I've had the most joyous company - mixed with the most sacred minds of the modern world, who came together to produce a list of hope for future generations; I have been greatly inspired by brilliant art; I have seen nature in its many guises and beauty; I have experienced things my senses can hardly behold. Yet my love still eludes me. Tell me Gaia, how on this day – of song and dance – might I fulfil this need?

My heart skipped back to last May, to the vision of the rose cloud in the zenith over Philosopher's Point. A time when I sung Lucy a ditty Capt Lewin taught me,

> ♪ And the lady fair of the knight so true,
> Aye remembered his hapless lot:
> And she cherished the flower of brilliant hue,
> And braided her hair with the blossoms blue.
> And she called it 'Forget-me-not.' ♪

1 May 1823
(Afternoon)

Had my Lady Fair escaped me? Amid the colour and spectacle of the Wareside Maypole celebrations, I set off alone to Keeper's once more in search of the enigmatic and mysterious Lucy, and the promise of eternal love.

I found her walking bare feet by the banks of the Nimley Bourne stream with Malachi beside her. As I approached, I noticed she'd braided her hair with the blossom's blue that grew in abundance by the water's edge. Flowers in her hair; most becoming!
"Lucy, there you are. I hoped I might find you here... heavens, Lucy Ebbs, where are your shoes? Did you forget them?" I called, as I descended into the basin.
"I love the touch and feel of the Earth... and take every opportunity to satisfy this need." She held out her hand, "Walk with me Charles.. Don't let your modern culture separate you from who you really are. Come, feel the Earth breathe. Every step I take brings a sense of belonging, of being."
"You really are most peculiar... I'll keep my boots on, if I may,"

I replied, recalling my hapless lot - the time I went bare feet with the dog about.

"But I wish for you to experience an eternal truth," she claimed.

"You take care not to slip or hurt yourself," I urged, as Malachi ran to and fro in the flowing waters, sending up a spray.

"Carefree... wherever you may be," she said. "As it was when you were a child."

She strolled into the centre of the stream to let the fresh cold water rush by her ankles. She was abandoned, free! A passive, yet powerful act! Envious, I cried, "I'll do it! I'll join in."

Hand-in-hand with Lucy, I did none other than stand. As the water flowed, it played around the tops of my feet and swirled around my ankles and toes. I was gifted with a delicious and sensual pleasure that invigorated and lifted my spirit. The rivulet danced its merry way about us. A beauty born from murmuring sound passed upon her face. Oh Lucy, my great teacher – she told how all other creatures in the world walk barefoot, yet we clothe our feet. When we take our first giant steps, our feet are bare. I fear we have lost something deep and precious that our ancestors cherished. We're out of step with Nature – our footprints heavy, laboured and lost.

"Oh poet, behold for soon enough tomorrow will take us away from this happy dell, to leave but a shallow memory of this moment," she whispered.

"Speak it not... silence is better," I replied.

"Charles I promised... I have an eternal truth to share," she said, untying the blue ribbon from her hair.

"Lucy... tell do. For nothing can surprise me now... after these recent days I know all things are possible. My mind is an open book."

She let the ribbon dangle freely from her fingertips. "I know of the Blakesware Set... the magic of the stones... and of the carvings at Royston Cave," she told me as the stream ran beneath our feet, with Malachi darting freely amid the waters.

"Oh! Who told you?"

"No matter..."

She turned to face me, taking my other hand. She let the ribbon fall gently into the stream. Caught in an eddy, it formed a heart shape.

"Charles, I love you!"

She had said so at long last, but my enthusiasm was quickly tempered.

"As I love all living things on this Earth, for I am its keeper!"

"Keeper?"

"I am the keeper of our common inheritance."

I watched the blue ribbon slip away down stream.

Gaia, Lucy asked me to promise not to tell another soul about the nature of the inheritance. Oh the dilemma. All I will say is that it concerns the locket. She opened it. Gaia, I have seen the inheritance for myself. The phenomena of the magic circle astounded me! Should the chance arise, I shall share the truth with you.

"Now you know how miraculous life is... on this living planet that circles the sun, accompanied by the moon and the stars."

"I do, I know."

She led me from the stream. Malachi followed, the blue ribbon dangling between his teeth.

"But why me?" I asked.

"Time's Passed!" she replied.

"Riddles... you always talk in riddles!"

On a day like this with scent and colour abound, Lucy's mood changed like the wind.

"Charles... I shared the truth with you as I'm afraid for the future. I am in grave danger. There are so many demands on me. I've only so much to offer," she said, clinging to the locket. She broke into verse:

> "They hang the man and flog the woman,
> That steals a goose from off the common.

But leave the greater criminal loose,
That steals the common from the goose."

"I think I understand," I replied.

"Charles, let me speak plainly. Our achingly beautiful world is set to change far beyond what we see today. It's why Malachi came to my aid as my defender. My work here is almost through. I need you to be strong for me Charles. Promise me, you'll stay strong."

Despite her hair being adorned with the Forget-me-not flowers, she looked pale, insipid even - so, I promised.

"Just one more thing Lucy," I asked. "We couldn't understand why the Duke gave you the locket?"

"We? Do you mean Mary Shelley?"

"I do."

Those three little letters again.

"Surely Charles the question for you and Mary is, why I chose to allow the Duke to have it?"

"Are you saying you own it? It's engraved with your initials."

"Charles, you're not listening... I am the Keeper. That is my role."

"I have the stones too," she whispered.

"The stones!"

We were well on our way back to the cottage.

"Reverend North returned them to me. In the wrong hands they have the capacity for evil, as well as for good."

I was astounded.

"Are they safe?"

"Quite safe!"

We reached the shadow of Yggdrasil, the World Tree.

"It grows as mighty as any oak," she said.

"It's also kept the shape carved by Thorvaldsen's creative hand!"

As in most things I encounter now – reality was stranger than fiction. For me the Goblin Tree would forever be synonymous with the curious carvings in the snow – the angels. Gone, perhaps for ever, but never forgotten.

3 May 1823

Gaia – I do question Lucy's confidence in her capacity to keep the locket and the stones safe! Now that the kinder weather had returned, it had brought villains with it; the highwaymen had emerged from hibernation. Yet Lucy persists with wearing the locket so openly – as if to invite the thief to her door. I warned Lucy of this before I departed. She replied,
"Beauty was made to be conceived and cherished by the senses, not hidden away for all eternity."

17 May 1823

A long journey must begin with a first step. Well, Lady Plumer's step when she heard the news was a backward one, before she sank into her favoured chair to catch her breath.   In her shaking hands, she held the King's telegram.
"No. He mustn't go. I deny it. Surely he can speak to the Duke. We've only been married these few months. I cannot bear the prospect of being alone again… a mournful Lady in Waiting for him to return. To lie awake at night helpless, pondering his fate," she said, between sips of water passed to her by Mrs Field.

Gaia, allow me to clarify. Richard has been commissioned to serve as ambassador for our land. Another venture in the New England awaits him. As the Captain stressed, it was ironic that the post arrived to coincide with the anniversary of Nelson's knighthood, 26 years ago. He judged it a sign,
"Katharine, duty is the great business of a military man. All private considerations must be set aside, however painful."

"Duty, speak not of it. What of duty to me, your wife... and to your child?"

I heard it, for sure. You see my Aunt Katharine was much younger than my late Uncle John. Some say she married for money, not love. Maybe, but none would doubt her loyalty to him.

"But Katharine, please don't fret so. I shall return; there will be no battle, no bloodshed."

"Then go, if you must to where glory waits thee, but while fame awaits, oh my captain, I urge do remember me," she replied, melodramatically.

"I go, but my heart remains... I shall write frequently of my travels."

"But when you are gone far away... out of sight and mind... you will forget me."

"I'll forget you not! Hey, let me grow a new moustache to remind me of you every hour of every day. Fashion and protocol move aside, I shall keep it until my return. My love won't die. You have my word."

25 May 1823

Captain Lewin has departed Blakesware, leaving in his wake a tearful wife, bemused dog and sad friend. I shall miss Captain Richard Lewin KB greatly. He left on horseback, side by side in the saddle with Bill Richmond.

"Live the sunshine, swim the sea and drink the wild-air," he advised, picking up on something Emerson had said during his stay. "Here," he added, throwing me his fife. "Learn to play Charles, entertain me when I return." I caught it single handed. He smiled broadly and gave me a hearty wave, as I tooted a comical tune. He stroked his dashing new moustache. "King George commands – I obey... for the King's shilling!" Richard cried, before he spurred his horse into action.

Malachi was most distraught at Richard's departure. I have seldom seen such a commotion – he really does dislike horses! Whimpering, then growling and tugging at his lead. Richard was unable to pacify him, poor hound – such sadness in his eyes.
"Don't worry little bear, you've not seen the last of me yet, I promise."

How the dog howled once the Captain left – I fear Gaia he was more troubled at Richard's farewell than Lady Lewin. Would he ever recover from the loss?

In his haste, it seems the Captain neglected to take his favoured military jacket with him. I was most surprised to find it hung in my bedroom next to the alternative version of the *Haymakers*! A note was pinned to the lapel. It read:

> *"Charles....*
> *I am certain the Captain would*
> *have wanted you to have this...*
> *Ben!"*

Most ominous and strange. Who, I wondered, was Ben?

Oh – there is something else. It's about the fife. Something that the Captain said to me – I look at it now he has gone. I wonder at my wisdom. Why did I not have the courage of my convictions – to put a stop to Captain Lewin's venture? Still – it's just words that's all, whatever the soothsayer, Mlle Lenormand might have advised him. I shall not scribe it. I shall bury it in my mind and speak no more of it.

Mary Shelley's qualities are unbounded. I find myself drawn to her. I know she is committed to leaving the Manor soon, and frankly the prospect troubles me. I fear my circle of friends grows smaller by the day. Emma was the latest to leave. She departed yesterday for Dulwich to resume her schooling. At this rate, Blakesware will soon fall into silent slumber – a refuge for wailing spirits and fading memories.

Gaia, Mary is such a wonderful confidant. I find I can talk with her freely. Our tragedy is our common bond, such that she takes thee at thy word. I had no qualms about sharing with her a copy of the note left for me. I produced it as we meandered at leisure through the fragrant and colourful rose garden.

"Do you know, Mary; I feel Uncle John Plumer ought to have commissioned a maze in the grounds of Blakesware, as my life is full of twists and turns leading to inexplicable events. They follow my every move, like a shadow. I know not whether I imagine it… Do I imagine this Mary?"

I passed her the note. She read it aloud.

"Charles… I am certain the Captain would have wanted you to have this… Ben! Who's Ben?" she asked.

"Precisely! I found it in my room, pinned to the Captain's scarlet military jacket."

"The Captain's jacket you say! Does he possess another?" she asked, as we walked towards the Blakesware pond. Did I ever mention the pond? It's beyond the wilderness garden. In truth, its size makes it more of a small lake. Whatever, the waters were still today and offered a perfect reflection of the heavens.

She repeated the question, "Does he possess another?"

I eventually answered,

"Not so far as I'm aware."

"I'm certain he was wearing a fine scarlet jacket when he left. I remember it most clearly Charles. I've a strong visual memory for such things."

"We digress… the note Mary, what can it mean?"

She shrugged her shoulders.

"Maybe it's a rouse Charles. A joke played on you by the Captain?"

However, her jovial mood changed when she studied the writing. "I know one thing Charles… I wager the same hand scribed this note as scribed the list which informed the Blakesware Set."

"Is that so?" I took the note back from her. She really has beautiful hands – so sleek. Our fingers touched. I sensed an energy betwixt us; let me call it electricity! I studied the hand-writing. It did indeed look familiar.

"Do you know… you may well be correct? Perhaps we ought to seek out this Benjamin fellow. He sounds quite the dandy!"

We sat beside the pond; a most peaceful and tranquil scene.

"Here… let me see the note again," she asked. I obliged. "What do you propose to do with it, for I want to share something with you?"

"I've no particular plans… beyond being sure in my mind that the writing is the same."

So, she began to fold the paper – Origami I believe the art was known as. Soon enough, she claimed to have made a small boat. I thought it resembled a hat, but no matter.

"When he was a boy Percy developed an endearing habit for making and sailing paper-boats. He and I often sought out a local pond or such. Somehow enlightened, I'd watch as he made his craft and set the boat afloat. It really was most appealing," she said, kneeling by the water's edge to set her own creation to sea, so to speak.

"Percy always claimed it was the inspiration for Samuel's *Ancient Mariner*… and Samuel has never denied it."

Fate decreed that the word – Captain – was at the peak of the sail.
"Mary, are you sure you want to do this?" I asked.
"Charles… I find it comforting. It helps me to remember… but also to let go, move on. A wanderer… here I seek a home."

Mary's eyes frosted over as we watched the boat drift towards the middle of the pond. Brave Mary Shelley!
"I had a passion of my own as a child too." I said, collecting a flat oval stone from the bank. "I loved to skip stones across the water. I once made a stone skip ten times… my record on this pond's eight! Here give it a try, it's such fun," I said. "The stone has to be a good shape and size, and needs to hit the water at the right angle and speed… watch me!" I boasted.

Oh my, Gaia. The stone slipped from my hand as I threw it and skipped three times in the direction of Mary's paper boat, hitting it directly. The stone must have nestled within the boat, as it sunk from view. In its wake, it left ripples that spread out across the pond. I couldn't apologise enough, but Mary insisted that Percy would surely have been amused.
"Maybe he had a hand in it… who knows. Some say that when you lose a loved one they have a window to your world, until they feel the time's right to move on," she suggested.

I saw no reason to dispute that.

6 June 1823

A glorious summer, this is not. Stormy weather has swept in from the Atlantic bringing floods, unseasonable low temperatures, hail and strong winds. It began a few days ago and looks to have set in. Little wonder we British have a preoccupation with the weather. However, the silver lining to the dark cloud is that Mary Shelley's long stay at Blakesware continues. She seemingly has little desire to leave; especially as young Percy has regular tuition. Samuel's loss is our gain!

Lady Plumer – apologies – Lady Lewin has been fraught with worry as the Captain has already set sail from Plymouth to Newfoundland when the depression hit. We all understand her fear, but the ship – the Mountstone I believe - was most sturdy. I do so regret telling her how my stone had sunk Mary's boat. I know she dwells on it so – assuming it an ill omen. The dreadful weather is simply feeding her fears. Where is the sun?

10 June 1823

The gloom continues unabated, perhaps because there's still no news of Captain Lewin! Where has the summer gone? There's a strange feeling around the Manor as we wait to learn of Captain Lewin's safety. It's most unsettling! I can hardly scribe nor sleep. The restless nights have returned. Welcome Solitaire, old friend.

11 June 1823

Gaia, I met Fanny Ebbs today. She came directly to the Manor! She has heard a rumour that the Mountstone has sunk! It cannot be – an iceberg they claim. Her source, she would not say.
"Tell me it isn't so Charles, please. I urged him to stay, but he wouldn't listen." She sobbed incoherently, "The foolish man, gone and be'n… 'wittingly…bury… at sea… killed."
I felt a shiver of fear crawl over me. The Captain lost at sea – not so?

Fanny stood in the courtyard, dressed in grey with her shawl wet through. The very courtyard in which we'd recently bid the Captain farewell. I could almost hear the whistle of 'Yankee Doodle' echo about the courtyard.
"Come in out of the rain," I urged.
"I just had to come… to see if you knew. I could wait no longer," she said, as I helped remove her shawl. She continued,
"Oh, think of it! He did so much for us, just as John Plumer had asked. He was true to his word, such a cruel and tragic end for a man such as he."

417

"Uncle John Plumer?" I asked.

"I hoped otherwise, but it's just as he said it would be," she said with a face that crinkled with sorrow.

Fanny sobbed openly as I led her to the servant's quarters, where Mrs Field came to our aid. As she wiped the tears from Fanny's eyes, she said, "We'd best keep this from Lady Katharine for now… it's probably nothing more than a nasty rumour, you'll see."

I was silent; my voice strangled by dread, so Fanny spoke,

"Well… I say go see Reverend North. He'll say… he knows the truth about everything!" she claimed.

"But he might be mistaken… Charles, tell her so," said Elizabeth, but my voice was strangled with fear.

Fanny wailed, "Oh poor Captain Lewin… what did he do to deserve this? He promised he'd return… he did. Pray if I see his face… once more, I shall be overjoyed… we've lost so much, all of us… the poor lady in waiting." Her words were broken. I hoped she was deluded.

12 June 1823

Gaia, as the mid-summer approaches I long to tell of hope and joy, of new beginnings. Who wishes to read of melancholy and loss? It pains me so – this was not my aim. I stare truth head on and say, 'No – the Captain survives, he lives I will it so'. Make it happen!

13 June 1823

Gaia, I have an idea – I have witnessed the magic of the stones and the miraculous power of Lucy's locket, maybe they can shape the Captain's fate? Would that be possible? There is magic in the air – I feel it. The circles in the field and the Goblin Tree at Keeper's that grows furiously; and the dog, Malachi, maybe he can guide us? Am I losing my mind? Is this what desperation can do to a man – lead him to clutch forlornly at straws? So, I confided in Mary Shelley.

Where better to do so than the Justice Chair? Malachi was with us as Mary sat upon the Justice Chair. It seemed the only place to ponder the Captain's fate. Malachi joined us. Gaia, the poor hound. He seems lost without the Captain. He pines so for our soldier. Mary stroked the dog saying,

"Charles, there are many things we don't understand… so many questions in need of answers. The truth is, we don't know if the Captain's alive or dead, if he's lost at sea… we may never know. Some say they have pulled survivors from the wreck."

"I have heard, so has Lady Katharine. The suspense is hard to endure… it's intolerable."

"It is; which is why I wanted to share something with you." About her she had a small silk purse, from which she revealed a tiny musical automaton.

"I call it the fairy ship." She took a key and wound it. The golden ship was close to rocks and guided by a light house. It moved on a sea of silk. The music played – I believe it was Piano Sonata No 16 by Mozart.

"See the pitch and toss of the ship… is it not like life? Are we not at the whim of the elements? Can we not be guided by the light?"

"It's beautiful, so revealing and delightful."

"Samuel gave it me after Percy died - to honour the *Ancient Mariner*." She cupped the ship in her hands. The motion and sound had a curious calming effect on Malachi.

"I feel we must leave well alone Charles… the stones, the locket… my instinct is that these things are not for meddling with. I believe they show us the way, bring a deeper meaning to life. They guide us and reveal there is more to this world than we can see. Take comfort from that Charles. Be at peace with the Captain's fate… what will be, will be."

"A soldier's real enemy is the fear of death. It was one of the Captain's favourite sayings," I said.

"Guard yourself in your spirit and do not break faith," claimed Mary. Malachi barked, as if in agreement. It was a time for courage and resolve.

15 June 1823

Gaia, we have confirmation in writing that the Mountstone struck an iceberg in the Atlantic Ocean. Captain Richard Lewin was not amongst the surviving crew. Lady Lewin was inconsolable. The wicked misfortune. Richard… the cruel sea has made a hero of you! Oh God! It's all over!

I weep.

18 June 1823

Emma Isola has rejoined us from Dulwich. She has delayed a planned trip to Brighton to take in the sea air!

20 June 1823

Malachi is deeply sullen. The Samoyed, famed for its smile, has glazed eyes as though in mourning. Perhaps Lucy can come to his aid.

21 June 1823

Lady Plumer has commissioned a small memorial for the Captain at St John's Church in Widford. The Reverend North will conduct the service. Many dignitaries will be invited. I'm sorry if this sounds so formal.

Contrast today with last mid-summer's day, when Lucy and I met at dawn to search for fairies. Oh for some escapism – for reality is too sad. So I walked with Malachi, Mary and young Percy to the banks of the Nimley Bourne. It was mid-afternoon. Sprinkles of sunlight spread through the trees, flickering like diamonds on the water of a stream flowing freely from all the recent rain.

"This is where Lucy revealed the meaning of the locket to me," I said, as we stood on the banks of the stream. "We were side by side, as you and I are now. We were hand in hand."

"Like this," asked Mary, taking my hand.

It felt like betrayal.

"Yes… like this. Lucy opened it… and I witnessed the miracle of its inner beauty for myself."

"What did you see Charles?"

As I prepared my answer, Malachi - seemingly bouyant once more - ran along the stream into a tangle of branches that overhung it, darting through twists and turns of wood. We did our best to follow him, only to become distracted by a swirl on the water.

"Look there… do you see it?" I asked.

"I do," replied Mary.

"Its magic!" cried Percy.

At the very place where Lucy revealed the locket's wonder to me a small whirlpool appeared. In water that would barely reach my knees, it circled rapidly with hardly a sound. We watched a newly fallen leaf spin in its vortex; around and around. It was hypnotic. I thought of the Captain and his demise, yet it was a beautiful moment - as though he spoke to us from some place else. It was a fleeting reminder of the stones that span at Royston Cave. We counted the revolutions – up to 21 to celebrate the solstice, before it vanished right before our eyes. The folly! Where was Malachi? I called for him to return. It was the first of many fruitless cries. Betwixt our calls, Mary asked,

"The locket Charles... what did you see? Do tell!"

"I wish I could… but I promised."

"Why Charles, what harm could it do? Tell do!"

I shook my head.

We called for the dog again. No response.

"Do you believe in fairies?" I asked.

"Why Charles, don't lead me astray," she urged.

"I believe in fairies," said young Percy. "Mother does too. We saw them in Switzerland," he claimed. "They live in the mountains by the lakes."

"Percy, you mustn't say such things. You know the rules. They'll be cross with you!"

"Well, you shouldn't hold his hand then should you. Father would be cross with you!"

As we released our grip, I told Mary about last solstice's mischief making with the Three of Hearts and my straw hat. I had brought both items with me as mementos.

"The trick is not to let them catch you sleeping… because that's when they play games on you," I told young Percy, showing him the card.

"It says – *Thank You Ben*," he replied. "Do we know him?"

"Yes Percy, I believe I do… in some strange way," I told him.

"Charles Lamb, you have a vivid imagination," said Mary.

"Sometimes a bit too vivid, I'd say!"

Gaia, we were most distracted by the whirlpool and our hunt for the tiny people with wings that we plain neglected to keep track of Malachi. The dog had vanished from sight. We thought little of it at first. As we waited by the Bourne for his safe return, Mary and I conjoured up a little poem called, 'Shadows'. I shall rehearse it later. Let it be our gift – a thank you for the spirit of creation - and in honour of Captain Richard Lewin KB. Now, where had that Samoyed gone?

Twas the strangest thing. I swear Gaia that no sooner had we completed the poem did we catch a glimpse of Captain Lewin at the peak of the Nimley Bourne gully. It was his silhouette – we were certain. I saw Malachi run to him, our calls ignored. The Captain left with the animal. Does he live still or am I deluded by my sorrow?

21 June 1823
(Midsummer night)

Malachi has vanished. We fear he may be lost. We will search anew tomorrow. Until then, our poem reads,

Shadows

See the magic in the shadows
Standing next to Nature true,
Tiny seeds of hope o' sowing
Tiny wings of Aqua Blue.
Ah, be ours the task to stop it
Ours the task this Earth to keep.
With imagination blot it,
Woe decry industrial creep.
Woe decry that Icy Tear
"Forget-me-not," the Time is Near.

See the stones, pure o' glowing
Circles in a darkened cave.
Tiny seeds of hope are growing
Tiny hands for us to save.
Ah, be this our task to find it
So the Artist shall not weep.
With imagination stop it,
Woe decry complacency.
Woe decry that Icy Tear
"Forget-me-not," the Time Is Here.

On our return to the Manor, scribing the ode came easily to me. I had perfected it to memory. The ink from my quill flowed like sweet wine. Twas an attempt to capture much that we had experienced and stood to lose at the advent of the age of the machines. It warns us not to disregard Mother Nature – forget her not, for the Blakesware Set shall weep.

24 June 1823
(Morning)

Malachi is still absent – whilst others fret, I feel he is keeping guard over Lucy. I shall seek her out.

24 June 1823
(Evening)

Tales of further villainy! Our Mrs Elizabeth Field heard the news direct from Mr Phipps; remember him Gaia - the bulbous Governor of the Ware workhouse. Elizabeth was returning from one of the four annual fairs at Hertford. Goods, trade and bargains were to be had. Alas, not everyone returned safely. The latest victim was a wealthy farmer, from Bennington, called Kent. It seems Kent put up a fight before he was murdered for his wares. The farmer's mangled body was thrown back into his cart and the horses left to bring him home. They have dubbed the head of the pillagers the 'Murderous Pie Man of Ware' as the evidence mounts that he disguised himself as a local trader.

25 June 1823

I found Lucy beside Yggdrasil in silent sympathy. The grace that moulds the maiden's form, subdued at the Captain's fate.
"Lucy, I'm over here," I cried, as I approached, for she seemed not to see me.
"Charles... you finally came. I assumed you had forsaken me, distracted soul."
"Distracted... sadly yes... you look pale, are you troubled... or unwell?"

"These are testing times… the Captain was a good man. I was sorry to learn of his fate."

Lucy eyed Yggdrasil from top to bottom. "It reaches ever skyward and ever to the depths… linking life with death. And look, see how the arm points towards the cave," she said, implying a connection.

"Do you mean the Royston Cave?"

"I do."

Those words again.

"It's strange to think we planted it merely as a gesture to encourage a new dawn."

"Take heart Charles, the deed was most worthy."

"I was hoping Malachi would be with you, is he?" I asked.

"No Charles… he's some place else now."

"Really, oh! Do you know where?" I said, as I shuffled my feet in the dirt.

"Where his spirit takes him!" She raised her hand to stroke my face and said, "You're unshaven. Your hair is wild. Mary deserves better of you!"

"We miss him. I was hoping he was here with you… protecting you… and…" The Earth stirred at the base of Yggdrasil. I continued, "The locket… there's so much at stake! Why did you say that about Mary?"

"You care for her, don't you?" she asked.

"Not in the way, I care for you. If you die, I die."

She put an index finger to her lips to urge silence. Yet I had further questions.

"Lucy, when Fanny came to the Manor she was distraught… she said the Captain did everything Uncle John had asked of him, but it wasn't enough. What did she mean by that?"

"Charles you have a head full of questions…"

"An enquiring mind needs to know."

"Come walk with me," she took my hand and led me towards the Nimley Bourne. She explained how, "It began when I was younger at the bequest of the Duke, Reverend North and Uncle John, they entrusted my care to Fanny Ebbs. They bestowed on her a duty to care for me... for us to live in partnership! I, a mere commoner, have no place in a grand estate so John believed Keeper's was the right place for me to be at this time – a sanctuary from which to prepare to share my story."

"And the Captain?"

"As I matured, your Uncle commissioned the Captain. His duty was to protect and serve me. I shall forever be indebted to him for convening the Blakesware Set and to you Charles for 'The Haymakers Survey'. They both surpassed my wildest dreams. Alas, now he is lost, I am under greater threat."

Entranced by her words, we had walked beyond the stream and on towards Philosopher's Point. We reached the peak and looked out across the Uplands. It prompted me to say,

"If you fear your future so, then why not leave this place... to begin anew... I shall come with you. Let me be your protector," I asked.

"Charles... you forget, I am the Keeper... and I prefer it here... in the wide open spaces, with the wind in my hair and bird chorus in my ear. Besides whether I stay or go depends upon the actions of others."

"Why then do you say your time here is nearly done? I am bewildered."

"It is the way of things... I too am entangled in the web of life. Here look again into my eyes Charles."

I did so and saw the colours of the sea and the sky. I was entranced, hypnotised even. Unable to turn my gaze, I saw a lone white bird fly inside her pupil – from one eye to the next. I saw our Earth spinning on its axis with the moon trapped in its orbit. I felt like that moon – tied inexorably to Lucy. Was this real or my imagination?

"Charles Lamb... you may never find all the answers you seek, but some day your name will ring across the globe in celebration. The man who gave back what was so nearly lost."

Lucy ebbs and flows. I cannot fathom her capricious ways.

The arrangements for the Memorial Service at St John's Church are firmly in place. We shall remember Captain Lewin at noon on 7 July. Our congregation will encircle a plot set aside for a large Celtic cross erected in the Captain's honour. We shall be able to see the Manor from the Captain's symbolic resting place.

Many members of the original Set: the Duke, William Wilberforce and Bill Richmond, William Wordsworth and my good friend Samuel Coleridge - all have committed their time. We shall welcome them back to the Manor. Rumours fly that the King himself will frequent Widford. Let us see.

6 July 1823

On the eve of the service we have a letter from Albert Thorvaldsen, with a few words too from Hans Christian Anderson. I share an extract with you,

"Our condolences given for the sad loss of the much revered Captain. We are led to ask, how many steeples would have to be stacked one on top of another to reach from the bottom to the top of the sea? Lest not forget the ocean floor is our 'Ice Prince's' domain now. May his spirit be eased by mermaids! Hans wishes it so. In the Captain's honour, he promises to one day write a tale of how a mermaid saves a prince from a shipwreck. May that thought lighten your hearts at this mournful time!

Do please keep the puppy in good health... I have a Samoyed of my own too. We have called her Foxy, for she is somewhat daring. Perhaps one day the two shall meet in the shadow of Yggdrasil... how grows she? Mighty fine we anticipate. I speak the truth Charles when I say the Earth spirit abides... a living, feeling, breathing organism. I sense it now more than ever."

7 July 1823
(Morn)

Anything awful makes me laugh – I misbehaved once at a funeral, but not today. For Captain Richard Lewin KB has gone before that unknown and silent shore. I wish there were such things as mermaids. Oh stay! Oh stay! I try to accept it as so – but, I still have a seed of uncertainty in my mind. I recall the dog, Malachi and how I feel I saw him run to the Captain on mid-summer's day. Life is indeed a mystery, for I'm sure I saw the Captain ahead of his return to the Manor and again after his departure. As Lucy says, 'We shall never have all the answers'.

7 July 1823

Gaia, is there no end to the mystique? The service went as well as we could have hoped; although His Majesty did not attend, which was a trifle unfortunate. I judge it a good thing on the whole for the day was not about King George. It was about Captain Richard Lewin KB. It was comforting to have so many kind and knowing faces about us, especially Samuel Coleridge, though I fear he may persuade Mary Shelley to finally return to Highgate with him. I digress.

Gaia, rather than dwell heavily on the ceremony – though it would be remiss of me not to comment on the stoical performance of Lady Katharine – I should like to tell of the curiosity – the mystique. It happened thus. It may take a while to scribe – word for word. I shall try nonetheless. I shall write as an insert... I call it, *A Ball of Blue in a Sea of Black.*

A Ball of Blue in a Sea of Black

Several days ago, I persuaded Lady Plumer that I should play the Captain a lament on his fife. That I should do so alone – after the other mourners had gone. I had promised it so to the Captain. I know not why, but he had said to me before he left – yes I recall it now,

"Charles should I ever succumb to the deep, you must honour me thus. You must play me a solo farewell on this fife. Do so at my graveside. Mlle Lenormand insisted upon it. She knew not why my brother… for so you are in my heart… but you must know and act upon it."

So I did.

I nestled in the shade at the base of the stone monument and played a simple tune – a slow tempo of 'Yankee Doodle'. No hand clapping or foot stomping today. Just solemn remembrance – and a lingering flicker of hope. I hung my head for a second or two to reflect on the Captain's rich and varied life.

"Charles, I know that tune. It's about Lucy and her lost locket. She can't find it anywhere," claimed a voice that startled me.

"Who says?" I asked, confident I'd heard her somewhere before.

"I do… I know the whole song," she claimed.

I located the voice to some bushes close to the monument.

"Well… may I correct you young miss. I was playing 'Yankee Doodle'. The Captain was most fond of it." I took quiet steps towards the voice. I was within arms reach when a head poked through the foliage.

"Malachi!" I gasped in surprise.

"He's staying with us now," said the girl, whose features remained hidden.

"Is the Captain with you?" I dared to ask.

"No! Grown-ups are so stupid sometimes," I heard her say.

"Come out where I can see you?" I asked.

"Lucy said I could come here, but only if I kept hidden and quiet. Those were the rules."

"Well you've already broken one rule… so what harm will it do to break another?" I asked.

The girl giggled. I'm sure it was the girl who'd offered the three questions to the magician at the Ware festival; the inspiration for 'The Haymakers Survey'. Trouble was I'd forgotten her name.

"Okay… promise not to tell," she requested, before I heard her tell the dog, "It'll be okay. There's no way they'll know, and you'll look after me won't you."

This troubled me.

"Do your parents know you're here?" I asked.

Silence.

"A young girl like you ought to be more careful. You shouldn't talk to strangers."

"But you're not a stranger. We know so much about you already… and Malachi will look after me… and I have my mobile (I think that's the name she used for the machine) so can call them if I need to."

It felt extremely unnatural holding a conversation with some bushes.

"You should go home… young lady."

"I want to but I can't. I have to wait."

"How do you mean?"

"Lucy needs to help me… I can't get back on my own."

I sat crossed legged on the floor in front of the bushes.

"Lucy who?" I asked, as Malachi emerged fully from the bushes to greet me then survey the monument.

"You're a silly man Charles. Lucy Ebbs who else? Mali, come

back here," she asked.

"He doesn't do as he's told, does he?"

"No," she said abruptly. "Sometimes he makes me really cross."

"So… have you returned him to us?" I asked.

"Mali… oh no Charles. I can't do that. He has to stay with us now. Lucy says so."

"So why are you here?" I asked.

"I'm waiting for Lucy to come get me… to take me home."

"How long have you been waiting?"

"Since the start," she replied.

"Are you going to stay in there, until Lucy comes to get you?" I asked.

"I don't know."

"Are you the girl from the show… the one who asked the questions?"

"What questions? Mali, come here. Daddy will be so cross."

"Shall I fetch him for you?"

"You can try."

"What's you favourite flower?" I asked.

"Hey… that was one of my questions," she replied.

"I know… that's why I said it. Look, this is really remiss of me, but I've forgotten your name."

"It doesn't matter," she said.

"That's a strange name," I replied, as Malachi returned.

She giggled again.

"Do you know you're going to write this in your journal?" she asked.

"You know about my journal?" I said, suddenly feeling most vulnerable.

I got to my feet and began to pace around.

"Please don't walk in circles," she asked. So I stopped.

"How do you know about… about my journal?"

"Oh that's because we..." she stopped.

"We! Who's we?" I asked.

"Oh this is going wrong. Let me call Mum," I heard her say. Gaia, the strangest noises you could ever imagine came from within the bushes. Curious sounds, like a bird or a bell.

"I can't get a signal... oh no my battery's low. Oh come on..." I heard.

We shared a few minutes of silence, whilst I tried to decide what to do.

"Is Lucy coming for you? You're sure about that?"

"She promised me."

"I'll just wait here till she returns then."

More silence, until the sound of weeping.

"Please don't be upset," I asked. "Shall I go find your mother for you?"

"Oh this is ridiculous," she announced, suddenly crawling from her hiding place.

"Hello... I'm Sarah Whittenbury, aged 13."

She raised her hands to stop me from talking.

"It's so wonderful to meet you Charles Lamb. We're all so very proud of you... but please don't put this in your journal. I know you will, but I'm not supposed to be here."

She was a bright young thing, adorned in clothing of a kind I'd not seen before. She came and sat beside me to wipe her tears.

"Hello Sarah. I'd offer you a handkerchief but mine... well, let's say I lost it."

"I know. We're sorry about that... and the stitching."

I was most perplexed. She spoke quickly and emotionally.

"Charles... this must sound crazy. I must tell you. It's why Lucy invited me. There are some really important things you need to know. My Daddy... Ben. He wrote the list and left you the notes – the ones you found. I need to tell you that we did what the

Blakesware Set wanted, but it's not enough. The people aren't listening... well some of them are, but most of them aren't. It's really getting very worrying now – floods, droughts, melting ice. We don't know what to do. It makes me sad. That's why I came - to try to warn you."

She paused to tip some food into her palm. The objects - she called them 'Dry Roasted Peanuts' - came from within a strange bag of crinkled blue. She offered the fruit to me.

"Its okay - they're fine - unless you have an allergy to nuts! Do you have an allergy to nuts Charles?"

"I absolutely have no idea."

I took a nut from her palm and rolled it between my fingers as she spoke and nibbled on her food.

"Lucy doesn't know it, but you mustn't be late Charles. Have you still got the Three of Hearts? Don't lose that card. That's it I've told you, now I can go."

These were strange words indeed.

"Lucy! Lucy, where are you? LUCY I want to go home now!" she called, once she got to her feet again, jumping up and down as she cried in the hope of encouraging a response.

"Sarah wait... please don't go. I'm confused. Look I'll even eat this nut for you... watch me."

"Oh Charlie, 'yes Gaia she called me Charlie' you're always confused. Look, it's very simple. All you need to do is make sure you're not late, that's all."

"Not late for what?" I asked.

"We thought... I thought... that if you knew, not to be late then maybe everything would somehow be alright again."

"What would be alright again?"

"You do ask so many questions Charles... you're worse than my parents." She folded her arms and looked at me sternly.

"I'm sorry. It's just you're talking in riddles. Everyone talks to me in riddles. I can't make any sense of it."

"The thing that needs to be alright again, is the global warming. The climate change is melting the ice in the Arctic. The polar bears are losing their home. They're going to die out. I don't want them to die."

She finished her small basket of peanuts. I still held mine.

"You mean the polar bears, like the one in Nelson's painting?"

"Yes. Many animals are dying Charles. The weather has turned really strange. It's a crazy world too – six billion people and so many with little respect for nature. They're cutting down forests, flying in planes, driving their cars and leaving on all the lights. I wish I could stop them – make everyone slow down. They're just too busy or don't believe it. Dad says people live like ostriches with their head in the sand. Don't they care? Can't they see the Earth must come first," she said.

"What language is this, Latin?" I asked.

"No! I can't speak Latin silly. No one speaks Latin anymore, except in movies about Goblins. And Malachi... he talks Latin too, at least Dad makes out."

"What language is it then, for your words - I do not understand."

"Ah... of course. I'm not a very good Time Lord am I?"

"Time Lord."

"Yes Charles... you must not tell a soul. You promise."

I nodded. She came over and whispered into my ear,

"I'm from the future, the year 2008."

It was my turn to laugh.

"Look, here's a picture of a plane," she told me.

Gaia, may the Lord forgive me should my senses deceive me! The young Sarah had a machine with moving pictures so real I cannot describe. Pictures of the future! I saw a large metal bird soar in the sky leaving a trail of small clouds behind it. I saw a cart that moved without a horse. What witchcraft was this? I dared to touch the shiny purple thing with the dancing pictures she called her mobile.

"Everyone has them in the future," she told me.

"I have seen the metal bird… in my dreams. I have seen a ball of fire."

"I know. Don't be afraid, Charles… I just wanted to show you, so you knew."

"I see."

"Look I secretly took a photo of the Duke, here."

She passed me the hand machine. It was true. I saw Mary Shelley too, with me stood beside her.

"Why does it say, 'Emergency Only'?" I asked, but she replied, "Quick… we've not got much time. I'm nearly out of charge."

She held the device in front of us and came up close to me.

"Okay… I just want you to show your nut to the mobile then say…' Hi people of the future… I'm Charles Lamb from the 19th Century and this here's Sarah Whittenbury. Come on… in memory of Captain Lewin and for the sake of the polar bears... take action to help stop climate chaos today. Join in... do 'The Haymakers Survey'. Rush save our Earth!' " So I did.

Gaia, I fully accept how unlikely my experience was. Perhaps the emotion of the day deluded me! I hold my breath and count to three. Scribe on. Lucy did come for Sarah. She led her and Malachi back to Earth Day 2008. No questions asked from me. Such courage from a young child in the hope of salvation for the polar bear and all the other creatures she says are at risk. What kind of a world has she returned to? A charitable one, able to comprehend the future and make the sacrifices needed to keep the Earth from further harm? Have they Sarah's courage and vision?

Alas, this child of the future left something behind. Her purple device called a mobile. A machine that carried an image that I will keep in my mind and heart forever! Her screensaver - that was what Sarah called it. "It's a picture of the Earth, our home, taken from space. Isn't it a miracle! There's nothing more beautiful or precious." I stared in bewilderment at the blue planet in a sea of black. The machine bleeped at me time and again – its mysteries trapped inside, waiting to be released. Until it fell silent and the Earth vanished, gone from my sight, forever. Fear not Sarah, I shall keep it safe. I shall keep it hidden. I shall keep it - and the peanut - with my journal.

15 July 1823

Gaia – it has taken me this long to find the opportunity to scribe in full my recollection of events on 7 July. I feel I have captured Sarah's every word. I know she asked me not to write about her visit, but she's such a brave girl, an example to us all! An ambassador for the world! There's just something in particular that puzzles me – what did Sarah mean when she told me not to be late? Be late for what, when? Maybe time will tell. I shall be on my guard – punctual always. As for the Three of Hearts – I have it still.

28 July 1823

We have correspondence from William Turner. I must tell you Gaia. He has been truly inspired by his encounter with Albert Thorvaldsen and his Lion! He has promised to take a trip to Switzerland to Lake Lucerne, where he proposes to paint a *Blue Mount Rigi!* We shall see. "I shall dedicate my watercolour to the Captain," he vowed. "I shall paint a small boat in one corner in memory of the man and of the paper boat that you and Mary set sail in his honour." I wait with impatience.

436

30 July 1823

An enthusiastic Mary Shelley told me her essay, Giovanni Villani, appeared in the periodical publication, *Liberal*. In it she has alluded to my papers of Elia. She described the work, when collected together, as ranking among the most beautiful and highly valued specimens of the kind of writing spoken of in the text. In turn, I told her that Frankenstein was the most extraordinary realisation of the idea of being out of nature which had ever been affected.

1 August 1823

Gaia, you may recall my painting of Lucy Ebbs. It hangs quite lonesome in the Gallery at Blakesware. To be truthful, I have neglected its presence of late. I rarely venture into the Gallery, not since its glory was lost. Imagine my surprise to find the colours faded. My memory fails me. I am sure I painted in oil, yet the picture now resembled a watercolour. I could hardly make out Lucy's features. She is just a ghost of her former self. Her spirit seems to be evaporating before my eyes. Most curious!

2 August 1823

Gaia, how can I possibly allow Mary Shelley to leave Blakesware Manor? She has gained a special place in my heart. I could hardly bear the sight of her belongings stored in a trunk ready for the journey to Highgate. I certainly couldn't allow her to leave without sharing the secret of Sarah's visit with her. It would be a travesty of justice. So, I invited Mary to my room.

"Charles, how long will it take?" she asked, seemingly eager to continue her preparations.

"Mary please… not long. It's something you must see. It's of the utmost interest," I replied.

An intriguing look crossed her face.

"Charles, I know you despair at me for leaving, but…"

Yes, its true Gaia, when I was lonely, Mary was there to comfort me. I feared her departure. I stumbled on my words.

"Oh… well… look we're wasting time," I said, kneeling before the chest in which I kept the journal, Ben's list, the Captain's fife, my playing cards, the purple mobile and my nut.

"You're quite a curator in the making Charles Lamb… still, it's bound to be of interest to someone someday," she said.

"Here's hoping! Here, it's from the future… the year 2008. It belongs to a girl called Sarah," I explained.

"Charles Lamb, that's nearly 200 years from now. Have you lost leave of your senses?" she asked, taking hold of the machine.

"She called it a mobile phone. Here I've written everything down… it took me a few days, but I'm very confident it's a good account of events."

I held my notes – *The Ball of Blue in a Sea of Black* – in my hand whilst Mary examined the object.

"What does it do?" she asked.

"It's a gallery… it has pictures, moving pictures… and it makes music too."

"Show me?"

"I fear it is sleeping or damaged. I cannot repair it."

"Is it dead?" she asked.

"Who can say?"

Mary asked more questions. "Look at all the numbers. Is it a counting machine? What are these symbols? A star, a fence, a cross! Look at the large circle at the centre with arrows pointing north, south, east and west. And this, is this an eye? Can this thing see?"

"It's the eye that draws the pictures… the ones that move."

"This machine… such invention! Do the letters and signs mean something? Is it a clue to why we are here, like the carvings at Royston Cave?" she asked.

"Here read this… it explains everything," I said, finally handing the notes over.

I paced the room as Mary read them twice, then asked,

"Charles Lamb, what does this mean… don't be late? And the card – the Three of Hearts?"

"I live in a world of riddles Mary… all she said was, 'It's simple, just make sure you're not late,' nothing more."

"We are tomorrow's past. It's a magical world Charles – a fantastic world I favour. One more agreeable than my writing! Charles Lamb your life helps concentrate my mind. You of independent mind and spirit! You are a torrent of light in a dark world. Shall I stay?"

3 August 1823

Gaia – Mary Shelley stays! Her inquisitive mind keeps her here – and perhaps her purse, for she is in a precarious financial position. She claims too that the rural air promotes her writing – having produced a deeply moving poem - *The Choice* - she is now very involved in a historical romance, *Valperga!* Our distinguished mourners left without her, all but Emma and Bill Richmond. The mourners had questioned her decision, claiming she should do well to rehabilitate back into society. If it helps, let them deceive the populace by encouraging them to believe she resides at the Godwin's residence. Let her rehabilitate with me. We make for fine company.

Mary and I discussed sharing the news of Sarah's visit with the others before they left, but we decided against it. We reached an understanding as we meandered in the wilderness garden.

"Charles, I believe fate has brought us together for this purpose… to make sense of all that unfolds before us. I feel it from within. Do you feel it too Charles? Our tragic lives have merely shaped us as people able to respond to the challenge. My dear Charles, I suggest we keep these events to ourselves and endeavour to find a way to return the machine to Sarah. If we share the discovery with the others, who knows where it might lead! Scepticism, curiosity, jealousy... they are all bound to want to be involved. And, the journal Charles, do they know you scribe so? How your quill must quiver from all your labour."

"They know nothing of it, other than they entrusted me with the 100 questions... and, sadly, I have failed them miserably." I revealed.

"In what way Charles?"

"Twenty questions have vanished... from the chest. Try as I might, I cannot find them. I kept them all together... but they have disappeared."

"Taken? Are you sure no-one else is aware of your journal?"

We approached the lion-head statue.

"No, nobody... other than you."

I studied the statue once again.

"Why did your uncle have this statue built here?" Mary asked.

"I don't know, but given everything, it's no small coincidence that it speaks of time and being verbatim... word for word."

"I think your Uncle anticipated the whole thing. I believe he knew this would happen. He prepared you."

"It might explain why he left me the journal to write in!"

"He did?"

"Yes. And the chest in which I store it."

"Lady Katharine regularly says she wanted me to aspire and achieve as he would wish. Maybe I misunderstood him. Maybe Uncle John has given me the tools to find the answers," I suggested.

"How old were you when he died Charles?"

I said I wasn't sure. I could only recall that he went when I was just a child.

"Where is he buried?"

I said, I didn't know. I hadn't thought to ask.

"Don't you think that's strange?"

I had no answer, so just shrugged my shoulders as we paced the statue.

440

"Weave a circle round him thrice,
And close your eyes in Holy dread.
For he on honey dew hath fed
And drunk the milk of paradise."

Mary had rehearsed the words. "Don't you remember, Samuel said this when we circled the statue before Christmas?"
"Sarah told me not to walk in circles."
Mary stood still and speculated.
"What did the picture of the Earth from space look like?" she asked suddenly. "I would love to see it – just the once."
I took the communicating device out of my pocket and pressed the small buttons at random.
"I saw her do this… to bring it to life." The machine sprang into action!
"It makes music," cried Mary excitedly.
"Maybe the sun awakens it… like a reptile… maybe it draws energy from the rays."
The machine showed me a 'key' sign and invited me to enter a magic code - A 'SIM PIN'.
"Try the year… enter the year!" urged Mary.
I pressed the numbers… 1… 8… 2… 3.
The picture of the ball of blue in a sea of black appeared.
"Quickly, rush... this is what it looks like."
Mary took hold of the mobile.
"Charles, it's the most beautiful and precious thing you could ever wish to see."

It was just a glimpse. Sadly, the machine fell silent and empty.
"Hold it up to the sun. Maybe it needs global warming to make it work… Sarah mentioned that."
We held it directly skywards… until the surface grew hot to the touch. It made no difference. The globally warmed Earth had died.
"I have seen it Charles with my own eyes. A gift from God! A magic,

special thing… our living Earth as few other people have seen her. Maybe it'll come back Charles. Maybe the machine needs time to rest."

"All I know is Sarah told me not to be late… rather she warned me. Whatever it is, we need to do we need to act fast, otherwise it'll be too late."

"And the Three of Hearts… what does that mean?"

"For me, it means… love… nature and art." I claimed. "But, as a card, it could be taken to mean we are gambling with our future."

"Oh this is wonderfully exciting Charles. Have you any idea what this means? It means a child from 200 years in the future has come to us… to you. A human has turned back time. She has found a way. But how? Maybe this is a time machine! Why not enter 2…0…0…8, should it awaken?"

"It may be so, but why would Sarah need Lucy to get her back home?"

"Let's go seek Lucy … the Earth Spirit… she knows the truth," asked Mary.

I calmed her.

"Wait. It's not that simple… I see it in her eyes – all our future's are at risk. She's fading away. I fear that Lucy is dying." I had finally said how I felt. I hoped it otherwise.

"Just like my rose… the eternal rose that William presented to me. It wilts. The petals have begun to drop."

"The rose that came with the child Adam?"

"Adam! Who's Adam… apart from the biblical Adam, of course?"

"Oh. It's very confusing. You've not seen him have you? He must be a good year old by now. The orphan's cared for at the Ware workhouse. The Phipps' say they found him at Keeper's Cottage last May. The rose was in the basket. Oh my! Fanny Ebbs was obsessed with the child. She had a visitor about this time last year – a sorrowful gentleman who offered her money in return for the child. She believes he may be the father. She believes he will come again to reclaim his child."

"Charles, all these experiences are very perplexing, mysterious and, dare I say, disturbing… where's the morality?"

I had no reply to offer.

18 August 1823

Gaia – apologies for the absence of scribing these last two weeks. I fear I use my brain all too much. A fever has struck me low. It is deeply frustrating, especially as there is so much to uncover. This is no time for ailments. Forgive my weaknesses. Mary has left the wilting rose beside me and kept my chest hidden from view. The rose lifts my spirits.

The alternative *Haymakers* remains on display - it hangs in the Great Hall. You see, Captain Lewin's Will decreed that William Turner should house Stubbs' painting at his new gallery. So, William had it taken away – the picture leaving with our departing friends. I could just sense Stubbs' presence in the Hall as the painting was taken down. Farewell to an old friend. I had the replica put up in its place. Nobody asked how I obtained it - I guess they assumed I'd simply commissioned the work - nor did they object to the sight of Malachi, sat beside Lucy. It was judged an endearing reminder of his presence at Blakesware! Oh, the house feels lonely and abandoned without him. Still, he's in good hands now. Treat him kindly Whittenbury's, until the day he should return once more. When I think of it now, my passive acceptance that Malachi was with them surprised me. How strangely I behave under such circumstances. I digress, as ever. No, this is not why I return to my journal.

In the height of my fever, I had a most disturbing dream, or should I say, nightmare.

I was on a beach of golden sand, lain flat by a retracting sea. It stretched ahead of me like a blank canvas, with one exception. Tiny human footprints spread erratically across the sand. I followed them. I carried the Captain's fife and piped out the tune, 'Yankee Doodle'! To my left, I spied the sea gradually encroaching on the sand. Wave by wave it began to cover the tiny footprints. I ran - sometimes on the sand, occasionally in the shallow sea. Ahead of me, the waves teased with something at the shoreline. It was a handkerchief. I picked it up. I pondered the meaning of its presence. I hesitated, trying to convince myself of reality. I stood motionless as the sea level rose about me.

Only when I looked back to the beach, did I act. I let the handkerchief float in the sea and returned towards shore, driven by an urge to pursue the remaining footprints. Those left led me to a basket, tumbling as the waves reached it – an infant's crib. I rescued the basket from the sea. I raised my head to find the sea coming in more swiftly than before. A wind picked up. The waves grew stronger. I saw a young child struggle to keep his footing ahead of me. Now waist high in the water, I waded through the sea. I threw the crib to one side to ease my way. The surf splashed about me. I cried to Adam. The rising sea levels threatened to drown him. I reached out a hand. His eyes made contact with mine. "I'll save you Adam," I cried, before the waves took him. I was too late. The last I saw was his silhouette beneath the waves. Adam was just a shadow.

I awoke to find Mary Shelley and Elizabeth Field hear me cry, "Water, water everywhere, nor a drop to drink," - a line from Samuel's lament.

25 August 1823

During my fever, Mary wrote to Horace Smith – who once took part in a writing competition with her late husband. Horace is one of those few men with a flair for the arts who knows how to make money and is generous with it. Horace is a man of action. Mary says he once told Percy that, "Thinking is such an idle waste of thought," which amused me a good deal! In her letter, she told Horace they are staging Frankenstein at the Lyceum, London and vilified the monster in such a manner as it caused the ladies to faint away and a hubbub to ensue. However, they diminished the horrors in the sequel and it is having a run. She proposes to see the show on 29 August. Should I be well enough, I shall go with her.

29 August 1823

Mary Shelley was strangely impressed by the stage adaptation of her story. She told me, "Lo and behold, I find myself famous! Frankenstein had prodigious success as a drama and is about to be repeated for the 23rd night at the English Royal Opera House." She was most pleased with the set and the acting performances. "He lives!" she cried in triumphant jest. I could not help but compare with irony how the launch of the play coincided with the creeping curse of industrialization – the true monster unleashed on mankind. The crucial difference between Mary's work of fiction and this narrative; if you think you know how it will end, think again!

30 August 1823

Today is Mary Shelley's birthday. Her mood is most capricious – a head and heart awash with memories of her lost loves – Percy, Clara and Will. She reveres her husband's memory and seeks to continue still to rebuild his reputation. That is her public face, at least. Clearly emotional on this day, Mary said,
"Charles, its funny how one of my most abiding memories is when Percy and I eloped to France. Father forbade me to see him, so Percy threatened to take his own life. Elopement was a bit of a habit with him. To think it was nearly 10 years ago... yet it feels like yesterday.

To think my father and I did not speak for over three years. Oh the relationship was far from idyllic... free love has its price Charles."
I asked Mary how it felt to elope. She said simply, "Life is for the living Charles. Don't let it pass you by."
In some ways, Mary reminds me of Lucy – remember her Gaia? She, my first love! At summer's end, I shall seek her out.

30 August 1823
(Night)

A hot sultry night – and the sight of Mary shedding tears in memory of her lost love disturbed me. Rest, slumber haunts me. Determined not to succumb to a night pacing my room I scribed... Beauty's Tear! I think of it as a sister to Shadows.

1 September 1823

Gaia, Lucy needs a miracle! I rode this morning to Keeper's Cottage to see her. I found her bedridden - fragile, subdued and pale.
"Fanny, how have you allowed her to suffer so? Has she not seen a doctor?" I asked. Fanny was most displeased that I doubted her.
"Charles Lamb, I'm innocent I tell you. I could have changed my behaviour, maybe. Yet I have raised and loved this child as my own as the Captain asked. Of course she has seen a doctor, but it's not medicine she requires. There is no ready cure... not now."
"You are mistaken, oh Lucy. How has it come to this? Had I known your condition I'd have come sooner. I've been so preoccupied with my little world that I neglected you."

Fanny stood, arms folded within the frame of the bedroom door. "The Captain's her only hope... she told me so herself. Alas, Charles she barely has a voice now. Not that anyone listened before. Why should they listen now? Why should they listen in the future?"

"Well the Captain's dead… he can't help us now."

Fanny shook her head. "I shall wear my grey… I suggest you talk to the Lady," she said with an unexpected sternness.

So, I sat beside Lucy's bed and took her hand. She had a fever. She tilted her head towards me.

"Sarah is such a sweet brave child. She got her message through!"

"Oh Lucy - to speak kindly of others when you ail so! What becomes of you?

"Even you dear Charles, you hear but don't listen. My time in this place is nearly at an end."

"Come Lucy – the fever deludes you. I had it too. Look at me now. Why I'm as fresh as a daisy in spring. I could run all the way to Philosopher's Point and back before you could say Haymaker."

"Ah, the *Haymakers*."

"Oh, my foolish passions," I replied. "They have led me astray, when you are all that matters to me."

"Charles please…when a door closes a window opens… I need you to have something, for safe keeping."

She unfolded her right hand to release her blue ribbon. She whispered,

"Take it Charles… it is my gift to the Haymakers… as a *Thank You* for all they strive to do in Nature's name."

She fell silent.

Fanny Ebbs still stood in the doorway.

"I'll best let some air in," she said, before shifting to the window that overlooked the Goblin Tree.

"That tree… it's a ghastly thing. It's blocking out all the light. Someone should cut it down," she suggested.

"No… it must stay, please. The tree must stay," urged Lucy.

"Come now. Don't weary yourself so. As you wish it, so shall it be. At my time of life, after all that I have seen and done, I just wish to make you happy. It's my purpose in life, now that I am alone.

Now sleep Lucy, sleep. You need all the strength you can muster."
Fanny beckoned me from the bedside.

"It's for the best Charles. We have to let nature take her course."

I left with the ribbon firmly in my grasp and a determination to give it the credence it so deserved. A Star Question to add to 'The Haymakers Survey' sprang to my mind.

5 September 1823

These last few days, I have been a frequent visitor to Keeper's Cottage. Lucy remains weak and listless. The more time I spend at her side, the more I feel as she does. Sometimes it seems I think her thoughts. It's as though I can read her mind. How could that be? As I held her hand, I saw what she saw. Strange visions indeed:

♥   She and I dancing bare feet about the lion plinth statue to her words, "Oh so close your circles lace, that I may never leave this place."

♥   One by one, Lucy placing the sacred stones inside a jar to store within the hollow of a tree bordering the cottage.

♥   The boy Adam held aloft by a man wet through, such that the rain dripped from the tip of his nose. The figures reminded me of one carved at Royston Cave.

♥   Under a setting sun, a horseman riding at pace along the bridleway that leads to the cottage.

♥   Two white dice tumbling into the Nimley Bourne stream, settling into the water at Malachi's paws.

♥   The uncrowned Queen Caroline - I am sure it was her - walking in a light covering of snow, head bowed and clutching the remains of a bloody rose.

♥   A list of questions caught on the wind, the paper leaf fluttering towards tall chimneys, the like of which I'd never seen before. Chimney's that sent dark smoke to the heavens.

Had I seen glimpses of the future? Visions of things before they happened?

7 September 1823

During my latest visit to the cottage, I found the courage to ask Fanny Ebbs,

"Do you know who Lucy's real mother is?"

"Why do you ask Charles? Some questions have no answers."

"Are you hiding something from me?" I asked.

"No Charles… my instinct today is to protect and I made a promise to the Captain. I keep my promises."

"But Richard's no longer here…"

"You didn't speak to the Lady! The choice is yours, yours alone. Remember Charles, Katharine knows…"

"What does Katharine know?"

"The truth Charles… though whether she wishes to share everything with you, who can say!"

"I assumed you and Katharine were worlds apart."

"Oh Charles never assume… it can lead to all kind of chaos."

In an everyday world, this was a strange conversation. In my world, it was nothing out of the ordinary.

10 September 1823

Gaia – I heeded Mrs Ebbs' advice. I had always been in awe of Aunt Katharine, inhibited even by her presence. She was not always very approachable, especially in the confines of her own home. In conversation in the Great Hall, I assumed Lady Katharine Plumer-Lewin would talk and I would listen. It was often so. Yet I found my Aunt was in a curious mood, she had mellowed. Perhaps the

449

unexpected premature loss of the Captain had affected her more than I imagined. I began by thanking her for all her kindness to me, before I gradually probed for the 'truth', as Fanny Ebbs described it. "I knew this day would come," she said. "Uncle John taught you well. He would be most proud Charles... you've given everything. You've made a very good impression."

"The more I learn of John, the more I see I misunderstood him. The more I see my purpose unfolding."

"The measure of choosing well is whether a man likes and finds good in what he has chosen," she advised, pouring herself a glass of port.

"Please, Charles... sit, do. The truth is long overdue."

I sat at the table where the Blakesware Set had convened. I could picture their faces in my mind; the smiles, the banter, the mission. It seemed a different world. Katharine sat opposite me.

"Charles, when you were young, Uncle John had a frightening apocalyptic experience. He witnessed a harsh grey world regimented by the timetable of the machines. A world where the lush green to bless us was laid bare and turned to dust. A world where desert spread far beyond the equator and the ocean rose to flood many lands."

It was hard to believe these words came from the lips of Lady Plumer.

"What do you mean an experience?" I asked.

"A lion like creature led him, as if in a day-dream, to the vision."

"Why wait until now to tell me this?"

She ignored my question.

"It changed John beyond all recognition. Nobody would believe him, not even Reverend North. Not one word. So John had a statue built in the grounds of the Manor...with the engraving... word for word."

"Who built it?"

"Albert Thorvaldsen. It was the inspiration for his Lion of Lucerne."

I sat open mouthed.

"It's why Albert brought the puppy… as a gift in memory of the late Uncle John Plumer."

Surely my ears deceived me.

"What else do you know?"

"I was wrong. The spirit of the revolution isn't dead Charles. It has just begun and you are at the heart of everything. It's just as John foretold. Your mission was to begin to unravel the mysteries of life. To grasp an understanding of the wonderful force of nature and give our world a picture of the real magic that is our enchanted Earth. You are succeeding Charles, beyond our wildest expectations, and you have recorded every word, verbatim, in your journal. You have gathered the evidence to help convince and persuade a doubting, sceptical world."

"The journal, you know of my journal. I assumed you forbade it!"

"Come now Charles… my instructions… my words to you were…"

I interrupted.

"I know it full well. I am astounded that you too know of Gaia. Allow me a moment."

"Think of the bigger picture Charles. Think of how far we have come. We will be judged not by what we do, but by the actions of people living hundreds of years from now. When our bones have turned to dust our names will be immortal. We are so close Charles. So close. Your hunger for the truth has made the difference. We can still save the Ball of Blue in the Sea of Black."

"You know of the planet blue…"

"I do."

Those words again, in most unexpected circumstances.

"Did Mary tell you?" I began to pace the Great Hall.

She refused to answer.

She poured herself another drink and gulped it down. I could see she was shaking.

"Something happened… Charles… to rekindle my interest. I had lost all faith until 7 July. Ever since, I had to find out what you knew. Forgive me."

"What happened?"

"You shouldn't have a funeral without a body. Captain Richard Lewin walks. I have seen him with my own eyes. I shall wait for him Charles. He will return. I know it."

Gaia – Lady Lewin wept.

13 September 1823

When your whole life is turned upside down by those you know and trust, it's difficult to begin afresh. I've spent many long hours going through everything in my mind to try and make sense of it all. I've had many games of Solitaire – often playing with an unhealthy obsession into the small hours.

"I must win… I must, just one more game will do it!"

Perhaps it took my mind of things, who knows. For certain, I was oblivious to the impact my reclusive behaviour was having on those about me. Its just the sense of being used that hurts the most – I feel akin to Mary's Frankenstein's monster; part of some cruel experiment to see if I had what it takes to succeed in the mission laid down by the Plumer's, as were.

I feel betrayed! Oh, no doubt the mission is a laudable one and I pray it succeeds, but the knowledge that many others know my fate incenses me. I'm no toy for the amusement of others. Step forward Captain Richard Lewin wherever you may be. Dead or alive, show me your true colours – I dare you.

14 September 1823

Oh Captain Lewin – my brotherly spirit. Forgive me. Do you live still? Hope is a dangerous thing. I wonder – does his double haunt us? I have seen him before, remember.

15 September 1823

The worst of all of this is the prospect of Lady Plumer's hands turning the pages of my journal in secret. Reading every word - the infringement of my privacy! I am offended. The pages with corners turned over – my favourites. They seem untouched – but who can say. I feel as though my soul has been exposed to the world. How could they?

16 September 1823

Lady Plumer may well have revealed the truth – but mysteries remain!

- ♥ What happened to Uncle John Plumer?

- ♥ Why was I chosen to do his work?

- ♥ Is Lucy genuinely the Earth Spirit or Mother Nature as we suppose, and who are her parents?

The time for games is over Charles Lamb. I shall lock my cards away for all eternity. The ground is prepared in my mind.

17 September 1823

How selfish of me to hide myself away in solitary confinement these last few days! Dwelling in self-pity at a time when Lucy Ebbs is so weak. Have we not all suffered enough? Besides, with the passage of time, I mellow. I begin to see the brilliance of Uncle John's scheme. I begin to feel pride that he chose me to conduct his mission; a mere artist, poet and romantic - a man who lives in the omnipresent shadow of tragedy. I begin to remember everything that is at stake. This is not about me. It is about the future of the *Planet Blue in a Sea of Black*. How could I have been so selfish? Uncle John Plumer's mission is a work of art; a kind of magic. I am the star witness to our enchanted Earth and have captured every word for a baying public. I shall be strong for Sarah. The people and animals of her time need me. This needs to be about much more than 'The Haymakers Survey'. If only I could find a way to ensure people from the year 2008 are able to see this journal.

In my hour of need, I turned to Sarah's machine. It has a curious possession over me. It will be my inspiration and provide me with the courage to succeed in my mission. As if to vindicate my new found resolve and shun the sceptics, I took Sarah's peanut and crushed it. The granules reminded me of sand. In truth, I was but one human amongst many; akin to a grain of sand on a beach. We all are. Yet each of us have a responsibility to our planet Earth - we all must do our duty. Humbled, the enormity of the challenge ahead was clear - but Uncle John Plumer had sculptured me. I raised my fist to the heavens and cried, "Now is the Time for Action!"

I shall bury my passions, once and for all. I know just the place to hide my journal from the world, to be recovered when the time is right. I shall lay down my quill, for I wish not to write of Lucy's demise. If I do not put ink to paper, perhaps the inevitable can be prevented – in some other time, some other way. Maybe Sarah's people will find the key to save her. It is my undying wish. Let them have faith. Vanity, I accept but what value art if produced for its own sake? Let the world know, I am writing it!

Charles Lamb's Journal Ends Here

Part Three

Nature

Does spring hide its joy when buds and blossoms grow?

So, that was Charles Lamb's journal. What an extraordinary account of how 'The Haymakers Survey' came into being. We're astounded that so many famous and influential people had a hand in the creation of our 'Secret Inheritence'. We are in awe and privileged to be able to share the contents with the world and wish to applaud Charles Lamb for succeeding in his aim of revealing the curious, yet wonderful, events of nearly 200 years ago to today's world.

It's almost beyond belief that Mother Nature chose to take the form of a human - Lucy Ebbs - and that persona should be captured by George Stubbs in the *Haymakers.* How marvellous to speculate that Mother Nature did so in an attempt to show the people of the world the miraculous, but tenuous, splendour of planet Earth.

What of Malachi? How delightful that he should have such a prominent role in helping to deliver the message of the Blakeware Set. Coupled with the Goblin Tree - that 'fearsome' icon - they have helped provide the focus of all the activity. We pause to draw breath.

However, what puzzled and - if we're honest - disappointed us, is that the journal ended abruptly, with several unresolved issues. Oh, much is implied because of Lucy's poor health and we can make a good guess that the ghostly horseman was Charles Lamb in a desperate dash to help Lucy in some way. We just wish Charles had continued to scribe. We very much wanted to know how everything concluded! Yet, once when we dwelt on this, we realised that this may be a never ending story!

Could it be that whether Lucy died or recovered depends on our actions today across the globe? It's down to us all - you, your neighbours, the person reading the news or delivering your mail, even those people who flew to the moon. We've reached a tipping-point in history that will forever define the human race.

What's especially interesting is that a few of the things described in Charles' journal had yet to happen, such as Sarah somehow travelling back in time to use her mobile phone to show Charles the picture of the Earth from space, *The Ball of Blue in a Sea of Black*.

Sarah was very excited that her questions were captured by the Blakesware Set, and really enthusiastic about the incident with the mobile phone. Curiously, we had already arranged for Sarah to receive a phone identical to that described in Charles' journal. Only trouble is, if Charles is to be believed, she will soon find a way to meet him and show him the planet blue from space!

What, too, of Charles' claim that the Blakesware Set posed 100 questions for 'The Haymakers Survey', yet he only told us about 83? Where are the remaining 17 - 20 questions, depending on your logic? We sense there is something more; we're on the look out.

For Jonas – the news about Adam was deeply emotional. We were very unsure how to react to what's said about him and suggested to Jonas we could edit these sections out. He would have none of it; his view was that the boy Adam was a metaphor to show that our behaviour today has put at risk all tomorrow's children. Only a look into the past can provide the inspiration to take the necessary and sustained climate action needed worldwide. We respected his decision.

For Julia - the source of the *Shadows* poem was a revelation. To think, the work passed to her by her Grandmother had been penned by Charles himself, collaborating with Mary Shelley. Magical!

We know, for sure, we've witnessed a rare and precious vision which suggests there is a force greater than our own at work. We feel a sense of awe, humility and hope. Everyday, we remind ourselves how lucky we are to be on this beautiful planet.

All the more so, for one of our New Year resolutions for 2007 was to monitor world events – to keep watch from a 'Haymakers Survey' perspective. We decided to call this *Whittenbury's Watch*. In doing so, we were mindful of the things Charles Lamb cared about the most – Art, Love and Nature! We pledged to remember this as we looked for signs to vindicate the unique and mystical power of 'The Haymakers Survey' - as we were advised to do by whoever, or whatever, left the messages marked ✉.

At first, we monitored the obvious things, but gradually we began to realise that something unexpected and beautiful was taking place. As the days, weeks and months went by - we grew astonished at what we found. We flagged these as *Watch Wonders*.

The Watch is all truth - our take on world events from New Year's Day until 7 July 2007, *Live Earth* concert day. We feel events started to turn really interesting from about the spring, onwards. Forgive us if, at times, our findings appear in note form; its just we hadn't planned to include them.

Before we present the Whittenbury Watch, we ought to say that Bill Darvill's reaction to it was predictably cynical and negative. He dismissed it as a folly and a fraud, claiming we simply adapted our tale to fit with world events. Nothing could be further from the truth and we have the early drafts to prove it. Bill also argued that *The Watch* will soon become dated. In his words, "Nobody cares about yesterday's news - what matters is today. Yesterday is history!" Well, Bill Darvill we have news for you. Julia's instinct is that the evidence in Whittenbury's Watch will prove an enduring record for future generations; hosting evidence that will bring about a fundamental shift in the way that humanity relates to Nature and our place in the Universe.

The watch continues on our website. We urge you to read every word. It's history in the making,' that every child may joy to hear'.

Whittenbury's Watch

Early January 2007

We began by watching a global warming week, featured on British television. If the experts are right, we face the end of Europe as we know it - an end to skiing in the Alps, no more sunbathing in the Mediterranean, and the loss of vineyards and olive groves. *Question 36: Should a good life cost the Earth?*

In Britain, the average night temperature in the second week in January has been 12.6°C compared to the norm of just 1.5°C - the hottest average January temperature for 350 years! This is hotter than the average for July. In the USA, people sunbathed in New York as temperatures reached over 20°C. Separate figures also revealed that last year was the warmest on record in the USA. *Q53: Do you like to keep warm?*

10 January 2007

A newly discovered Comet shines brighter than Venus in a fiery night sky. In the past, bright comets inspired panic and hysteria and were generally thought of as bad omens. They've been viewed with awe and feared throughout human history. *Q70: Do you like to look at the stars?*

17 January 2007

A climate change map drawn up by scientists predicts the severity of change by 2100 on a chunk of the Amazon rainforest, with rises of up to 11°C. Swathes of the tropics show the most changes. *Q34: Have you ever restored something?*

The Doomsday clock has been moved on two minutes – it's now at five to midnight – the point of self-destruction! Initially set up to warn of the threat of nuclear apocalypse, the clock is now almost equally influenced by the danger of climate change. *Q4: Have you ever wanted to stop the clock?*

18 January 2007

Northern Europe was hit by 100 mph winds. In the UK, ten people died and there was massive travel disruption. It was described as a tropical cyclone! Strong winds and heavy rain have been around for several weeks now. Countless trees have been lost. Many predict that extreme weather will become the norm. *Q30: Did you ever watch the rain on your window?*

1 February 2007

The lights on the Eiffel Tower in Paris were dimmed for five minutes to help raise awareness on global warming. The tower's made of iron – which, of course, is so symbolic of the industrial revolution. *Q32: Are you afraid of the dark?*

Britain is the world's third highest importer of illegally felled timber, according to a report by the World Wide Fund for Nature. *Q21: Have you ever hugged a tree?*

3 February 2007

The Inter-Governmental Panel on Climate Change Report is in the news. Not for us to go into the detail – it's splashed all over the media. Extra, extra... read all about it! Humans fuelling the hellish vision of life on a hotter planet! *Q76: Are you going to take action to save our world?*

6 February 2007

The Thames Barrier closed three times in the past week, amid fears climate change is affecting sea levels. The barrier was built in 1984 at cost of £1b. *Q9:Do you feel in control of your life?*

9 February 2007

The Global Crop Diversity Trust has set up an International Seed Vault in the Norwegian Arctic. It will store seeds from all the main food crops across the world. The seeds will be kept in foil wrappers in boxes at -18°C. The vault could survive a 61 metre rise in sea-level and is insulated against rising temperatures. *Q15: Do you sometimes fear the worst?*

15 February 2007

A survey shows more than two in three drivers in London are refusing to use their cars less, even though they know they may be ruining the environment; they want significantly better public transport first. *Q8: Do you crave a better life?*

1 March 2007

William Turner's the *Blue Rigi* has been saved by the nation thanks to a phenomenal response from the public to a fund raising appeal and Artfund.org. Mary Shelley would be delighted. The magic of the Blakesware Set lives on! *Q2: Are you an art lover?*

4 March 2007

Most of the UK has been treated to a wonderful spectacle – a blood moon. A total eclipse of the moon, caused by the Earth's shadow, turned it to a coppery red. In ancient times, a blood moon was viewed with dread as an omen of disaster; that, coupled with the comet – okay! *Q79: Have you ever looked into the shadows?*

16 March 2007

Confirmation that the winter in the Northern Hemisphere was the warmest since records began more than 125 years ago. *Q53: Do you like to keep warm?*

The Arctic sea ice has reduced by 38,000 square miles every year for the last quarter of a century. Computers predict sea ice could have disappeared by 2040. That's just 33 years away. *Q46: Do you value a good education?*

A survey by the Royal Society for the Protection of Birds suggests fewer songbirds visited British gardens this winter. The evidence is that birds are adapting their behaviour to fit the changing conditions. *Q65: Have you ever wished you could fly?*

The ultimate green machine – a car which runs entirely on compressed air – is apparently on the horizon! For us, it can't come quickly enough. There are over 600 million cars in the world today; that would be some traffic jam, if lined up end to end! Numbers are predicted to rise to over 1 billion by 2030. 35 million new cars are produced every year. That's an unimaginable amount of road building, raw materials, petrol consumption and CO_2 emissions. *Q55: Do you believe in truth?*

A study by the University of Wisconsin-Madison in the USA warns of new 'fatal' climates in many parts of the globe by 2100. The greatest changes will be in the Amazonian and Indonesian Forests. *Q21: Have you ever hugged a tree?*

It's only one year to go before Terminal 5 opens at Heathrow Airport. It costs £4.3bn to build. About 40,000 people will go through the terminal each day. *Q35: Do you trust your instincts?*

Scientists for the International Fund for Animal Welfare reveal that global warming is causing the deaths of thousands of harp seal pups – they fear a catastrophe because the ice conditions are amongst the worst on record. *Q18: Do you let your heart rule your head?*

The tiny Indian island of Ghoramara is gradually disappearing into the ocean because of global warming. Farming has contributed to its demise as it has ruined the ecology, leaving the soil to be swept away! *Q34: Have you ever restored something?*

2 April 2007

The Energy Saving Trust have launched a Green Barometer which shows there is a huge gap in Britain between people who care about green issues and those prepared to reduce their energy use. Only 4% of Briton's have made major changes to their lifestyles, despite the large majority accepting that climate change is already having an impact on Britain. Sadly, 40% have done nothing at all. *Q1: Does your life have a purpose?*

A record 2.5 million Britons are flying abroad for Easter to, 'chase better weather.' Ironically, it will be warmer and sunnier in Britain than in the Mediterranean. Q36: *Should a good life cost the Earth?*

3 April 2007

Has the tide turned? 'Love' has been voted Britain's favourite word – Charles would be so pleased! However, neither Nature nor Art are in the top ten. Other favourite words include, 'smile… happy… chocolate… family… sunshine… holiday.' There's also a really odd one called, 'antidisestablishmentarianism.' Does this mean - *Q22: Do you believe rules are there to be broken?*

The amount of on-line information about environmental issues is huge. There's just so much activity – much more than is ever reported in the media. Congratulations to all those working tirelessly for the cause – what Earth Champions!. We're sure Gaia appreciates you! If we have a sick patient, they need tender loving care just as much as medicine. *Q22: Do you love our Earth?*

4 April 2007

Purrfect: the RSPCA is celebrating the Animal Welfare Act. The landmark legislation is about to come into force and means a brighter future for neglected animals. William Wilberforce would raise a glass of cheer. *Q31: Are you a charitable neighbour?*

6 April 2007

The second IPCC report confirmed the impact climate change is likely to have on the world. Billions of people face shortages of food and water, and an increased risk of flooding. The poorest people in the world are likely to be the worst hit. *Q28: Have you ever lived in poverty?*

In the Vancouver Aquarium, a pair of otters has been videoed floating and holding hands. Apparently, otters do this in the wild to help them stay afloat in choppy waters. You can see the video on our YouTube collection. *Q12: Is our Earth enchanted?*

12 April 2007

In Taiwan, a Nile crocodile has bitten a Vet's arm clean off! It took seven hours for surgeons to sew it back on. *Q52: Do you believe in miracles?*

15 April 2007

The first crop circle of the 2007 season in Britain has appeared in a field of oil-seed rape in Wiltshire, at a place called Oliver's Castle. It was aligned precisely east to west in a high hill-top field. Its 333 feet in diameter and in the design of a megalithic sundial with eight overlapping circles. In the late afternoon, several nearby trees cast their shadows upon it to give the impression of a 'gnomon' - which is an object, such as a sundial, used as an indicator. *Q12: Is our Earth enchanted?*

16 April 2007

Whilst the UK basks in near record April temperatures, there is speculation that mobile phones are helping to wipe out millions of bees. The phone signals are thought to upset the bees navigation systems - it seems they don't return to their hives if nearby phones are left on. The phenomenon is called Colony Collapse Disorder. It's bad news for pollination of flowers and honey production. We've a video about that too. *Q8: Do you crave a better life?*

18 April 2007

Predicted high levels of heat, storms and smog, mean this could be the worst summer ever for hay-fever and asthma sufferers. Assuming, of course, nature follows a predictable, logical path, and summer temperatures match or exceed those seen in Britain in 2006. Yet, from what we know of Lucy, somehow we feel nature has a surprise or two up her sleeve for this year. *Q41: Do you like surprises?*

Global warming will cause the Himalayan glaciers to melt, leading to mass migration and possible wars over resources, such as agricultural land and fresh water. *Q31: Are you a charitable neighbour?*

Food in Britain could be in short supply by 2030. Climate change will put pressure on supplies and staple foods will be harder to get. *Q69: Do you put off until tomorrow what you could do today?*

On the side of a London bus, Jonas saw the slogan, 'Yes, I was born to shop!' He then read a news article stating British people face a £1 trillion debt mountain!. *Q36: Should a good life cost the Earth?*

Over 200,000 people have registered for the UK leg of the 'Live Earth' concert at Wembley on 7 July. *Q75: Have you ever put on a show?*

The journal, Nature, has published a study by Cardiff University on the discovery of a fossil of the world's oldest known tree, with its roots and leaves still intact! It's a Wattieza tree and 385 million years old! It's a spectacular find, recording a significant moment in history. Monsters of their time, the Wattieza tree covered large areas of land. They lived at a time when carbon dioxide levels were much higher than today. The rise of the trees removed the carbon dioxide from the atmosphere, and caused the temperature to fall, bringing conditions very similar to those we see today. *Q21: Have you ever hugged a tree?*

The British Museum has hinted the Elgin Marbles could be lent to Athens. Lord Elgin brought them to Britain during Charles Lamb's lifetime and he referred to them in his journal. Is the trend that began in Charles' life about to be reversed? *Q45: Are you good at marbles?*

Spring is now the new summer, claims the Woodlands Trust. Results from its spring survey showed Hawthorn bushes are flowering early and swifts returned prematurely. These are traditional signs of summer and three weeks ahead of normal. *Q72: Are you a good time keeper?*

20 April 2007

Britons are migrating to Australia in their droves – 71,000 in 2005 - yet the country is faced with its worst drought in 1,000 years, with record heat-waves, droughts and wildfires. Since the 1950s, temperatures in Australia have risen faster than the global average. There is a serious threat to food crops, as farmers are set to be denied water for irrigation to ensure enough water for people to drink. *Q36: Should a good life cost the Earth?*

April in Britain is also set to be the driest on record. Runners in the London Marathon are preparing for the hottest day in the event's history. *Q62a: Is life logical?*

In the 1986 football World Cup, Maradona scored a magnificent goal against England. In 11 seconds, he ran half the length of the field, beating many defenders before scoring. 21 years on and another Argentina star, Messi, scored an almost identical goal - this time for Barcelona. It also took him 11 seconds to score. *Q60: Have you ever experienced déjà vu?*

A ghost yacht has been found off the Australian coast, near the Great Barrier Reef. When bemused rescuers boarded the catamaran they found the sail was ripped, but the boat was otherwise undamaged. Yet, cutlery was set for a meal, laptop screens flickered inside the cabin and mobile phones and sunglasses were placed on tables in front of empty chairs. The three crew members had simply vanished. *Q54: Do you enjoy a bit of a mystery?*

22 April 2007

It's International Earth Day, and they're running the London marathon in record heat. There's also a race to be won, called the Climate Change Challenge. Now then, 6 billion people are lined up. On your marks, set – go! *Q51a: How many people does it take to fill up the Earth?*

23 April 2007

William Wilberforce would despair that the RSPCA had to rescue 44% more pets this year, than last. The figure included nearly 3,000 cats. Almost 150,000 domestic, wild and farm animals were taken in by the charity, because of sickness and injury. The number of pets and domestic animals recorded hurt in road incidents reached nearly 10,000. The figure excludes the countless number of wild creatures who die on the roads. *Q31: Are you a charitable neighbour?*

Millions more Londoner's face life under a flight path, when Britain's airspace is redrawn to accommodate a million extra flights a year by 2015. The expansion of dozens of airports is planned –

doubling passenger numbers by 2030 to 470 million a year. *Q44: Is there anything worse than a fly buzzing around your room at night when you're trying to sleep?*

Each year, around 500 billion plastic bags are distributed worldwide. That's nearly 100 bags per year for every man, woman and child alive today. A new eco-movement has declared them as Public Enemy No 1. Tied end to end, the 4 billion plastic bags that end up as rubbish in Britain each year, would encircle the Earth 64 times. The bags can end up in all kinds of places, often caught by the wind and blown into trees! *Q67: Have you ever decorated a tree?*

24 April 2007

'Kryptonite' has been discovered in a mine! In fiction, it's supposed to drain Superman's energy. Well, as Ben fancies himself a superhero, should he fear it? It's not green and it doesn't glow, but it reacts to ultra-violet light by turning a pinkish-orange. *Q7: Have you ever dreamed of being a champion?*

A fossilized rainforest has been discovered in a coal mine! Revealed in the journal, *Geology*, it covers 40 square miles and is a natural Sistine Chapel of incredible well-preserved images of sprawling tree trunks and fallen leaves. Such sweet irony! Is this Mother Nature demonstrating against deforestation in a bid to persuade us to change our ways? *Q2: Are you an art lover?*

Villagers in Africa have replanted a whole forest to coax back dwindling flocks of flamingos. They say, "It was wrong to cut down the trees. We burnt them all when we started farming." The farming caused erosion and left Lake Nakuru virtually uninhabitable for its famous birds. It will take decades to reverse fully the harm done. *Q46: Do you value a good education?*

25 April 2007

A super Earth-like planet has been found in a galaxy far away. They've called it Gliese 581c. It's three times the diameter of Earth and has a system of three known planets. It orbits in the 'Goldilocks zone' around a star where the conditions are just right for life. On the treasure map of the universe, we could mark it with an X. Could it provide an alternative home for us? Only trouble is, it would take five billion years to get there! *Q80: Have you ever searched for buried treasure?*

A loggerhead turtle has broken a marine world record – holding its breath under water for 10 hours and 14 minutes. It's the longest dive ever recorded for a marine vertebrate, smashing previous records! *Q75: Have you ever put on a show?*

Doctors have used amazing 3D X-ray technology to help in an operation to remove a metal chair leg from a teenager's head, after it was speared 4ins into his eye following a brawl! It was an intricate three hour operation. *Q39: Do you believe in magic?*

Alan Ball MBE, the youngest of England's World Cup winners, has died of a heart-attack, aged 61. He regularly wore the number 7 shirt! *Q7: Have you ever dreamed of being a champion?*

26 April 2007

British Physicist, Stephen Hawkins, has taken a zero gravity flight in a specially modified plane. He was able to float free, unrestricted by his paralysed muscles and his wheelchair. His next goal is to go into space. He believes the human race doesn't have a future unless it goes into space, because a catastrophe is just a matter of time. He quoted Global Warming as an example. *Q23: Do you believe all the laws of physics?*

More party tricks from nature - a coastal area of Kent, the Garden of England, was hit by an Earthquake measuring 4.3 on the Richter scale. In the minutes before the quake struck, 'Dave the Dolphin', known to local fishermen, regularly leapt from the sea as if to try to warn them that something was about to happen. *Q17: Can you speak another language ?*

29 April 2007

In Bangor, North Wales, two teenage girls were issued with a fixed-penalty notice when they were caught by a police officer drawing hearts and rainbows in chalk on a pavement. The father of the girls plans to appeal because rain washed the drawings away. *Q2: Are you an art lover?*

30 April 2007

The celebrity-obsessed artist, Andy Warhol, is now regarded by many as the most important international artist of the 20th Century. His painting, *The Green Car Crash*, is set to become the most valuable Warhol picture ever to go to auction. It shows a mundane suburban street with an overturned car in flames and a catapulted body of the driver. Did you know an anagram of Andy Warhol is, 'An Hay World!' *Q2: Are you an art lover?*

The latest observations indicate that Arctic summers could be ice-free by the middle of the 21st Century – that's just 40 years from now. The studies suggest the IPCC's latest climate change analysis underestimated the rate of loss. *Q76: Are you going to take action now to save our world?*

1 May 2007

On this day in 1822, Charles Lamb began his journal. Nearly 200 years later and another Charles, this one a Prince, issued a 'Mayday' climate alert to businesses to curb greenhouse gas emissions. The Prince said, "This is an emergency we face. The crisis is far too urgent and discussion simply isn't enough." We need a low carbon-economy. *Q76 : Is now the time for action to save our world?*

2 May 2007

Remember the earth tremor on the coast of Dover? Well, a commercial airline pilot and his passengers reported bright yellow lights shaped like flat discs in the sky near Guernsey. The light show may have been a warning of the quake to come. There have been previous examples of light shows elsewhere in the world ahead of quakes, in blues and reds. One theory is that the lights are due to moving plates that produce an intense electrical field which ionizes the air and reveals a light show. *Q12: Is our Earth enchanted?*

The pace of life is speeding up. An experiment in 32 world cities has shown average walking speeds have gone up by 10% since 1994. Psychologists believe the findings reflect the way technology, such as the internet and mobile phones has made people more impatient, leading us to cram more into a day. The biggest rise in foot power has been in 'Tiger' nations, like China and Singapore, with people walking between 20 – 30% faster. *Q24: Do you get enough time to yourself?*

Sir David Attenborough has leapt to the defence of the moth. He will launch the first phase of a 'Moths Count Campaign' to help stop an alarming decline in numbers, which have halved due to pesticides and 'too tidy' gardens. Moths perform an important role in pollinating flowers and are an important food source for other animals. We will lose familiar birds unless we protect them. *Q48: Have you ever played Solitaire?*

In New Zealand, a brave tiny Jack Russell gave his life to save five children from two snarling pit bulls. The pet stopped the pit bulls from attacking the children, but his injuries were too horrific for him to survive. The pit bulls had carried out previous attacks and officials plan to put them down. *Q50: Do you miss someone you love?*

In Brazil, home of more animal species than any other, poaching and trafficking in wild animals, such as monkeys and parrots is reaching critical proportions. Police confiscated more than 50,000 captured animals in one part of Brazil's rainforest. *Q34: Have you ever restored something?*

On a bank holiday weekend designed to celebrate the re-birth of nature, an estimated 750,000 people will use Heathrow Airport over the next four days. Motorists can also expect the worst bank holiday congestion Britain has ever seen. The RAC expects motorists will drive 1.8 billion more miles over the weekend than during the same bank holiday in 2006. *Q60: Have you ever experienced déjà vu?*

5 May 2007

The quest for eternal youth has led to long queues at a pharmacy chain to buy a long-awaited anti-ageing 'miracle' cream. The reputation of the cream received a boost when it featured on a documentary. The company has been working round the clock to produce enough of the cream to meet demand. *Q63: Do you like the way you look?*

8 May 2007

The most powerful supernova ever recorded has been observed by NASA scientists. The supernova star, SN 2006gy, was originally discovered in September 2006, which was when Ben took on the role of Earth Champion! It has shone an incredible five times brighter than any supernova seen in the past. It has been described as a truly monstrous explosion – the king of all supernovas. This is an incredible signal to us from Nature: they are coming thick and fast now. There's something deep and mysterious unfolding. *Q70: Do you like to look at the stars? A Watch Wonder!*

The ancient tomb of King Herod has been 'found' in a place south of Jerusalem. Herod was infamous for his 'Massacre of the Innocents'. If confirmed it will rank as a major archaeological discovery. *Q80: Have you ever searched for buried treasure?*

May 2007 will see a record number of airline flights taken worldwide, with figures boosted by a huge increase in budget carrier operations. A total of 2.51 million flights are timetabled, which is 5% higher than the same time last year. An aviation spokesperson was quoted as saying, "This healthy growth bodes very well for the future." *Q17: Can you speak another language?*

10 May 2007

Artists have created two grass walls on the National Theatre, London. They're expected to last six weeks and aim to remind people in the city of the countryside. The grass will turn yellow - the colour of hay - symbolizing the artists' concerns about climate change. One of the artists said, "Climate change is an epic drama unfolding before our eyes. Yet you still see people who have their head in the ever-warming sand." *Q75: Have you ever put on a show?*

A new internet tool will create the soundtrack to regions from around the globe, as users zoom in using Google Earth. It will be possible to hear the crack of melting glaziers! The recordings cover several decades, so virtual visitors will be able to experience the impact of human activity on the environment. *Q57: Have you ever spied on anyone?*

Scientists have discovered a distant planet that glows like a hot coal. It has a surface blacker than charcoal and gets as hot as 3,700 degrees Centigrade! To reach that temperature the planet has to absorb all the light that reaches it then re-radiate it as energy! *Q74: Do you like puzzles?*

A statue of Bobby Moore OBE, England's 1966 World Cup-winning captain, has been unveiled at the new Wembley Stadium. The acclaimed hero was regarded as the perfect gentleman - a role model in public life. He died in 1993, aged just 51. *Q7: Have you ever dreamed of being a champion? Watch Wonder!*

13 May 2007

A design for the Chelsea Flower show with a honey bee theme has been withdrawn for health and safety reasons. The garden was due to have four hives with some 300,000 insects. *Q27: Do you like gardening?*

15 May 2007

Latin, the root of all romance, is making a comeback! A study by the Cambridge Classics Project discovered that over 450 state secondary schools in Britain now teach Latin, including inner city schools in Tower Hamlets and Kilburn. The Iris Project, which runs a campaign for the study of classics in state schools, says it is a valuable way to help improve literacy skills. Latin also helps develop the English of those with English as a second language! Id quod circumiret, circumveniat - What goes around comes around. *Q17 : Can you speak another language?*

The Taj Mahal, India's famed white marble monument to love, is being turned an unromantic yellow by pollution! A therapeutic mud pack has been proposed to restore it! *Q45: Are you good at marbles?*

Trafalgar Square - home to Nelson's Column - is to be turned into a 'village green' when it is covered in grass for the first time next week. The square, a focal point for many protests and celebrations over the years, will be transformed with more than 2,000 square feet of turf! *Q51: Have you ever taken part in a protest?*

Researchers at Stanford University have offered an explanation for Claude Monet's distinctive style. The explanation for his blurred, discoloured images is simple – the artist had cataracts. They recreated Monet's famous Japanese Bridge, showing, for the first time, how he would have seen it. *Q20: Have your eyes ever deceived you?*

Astronomers have identified what appears to be a ghostly ring in the sky, which is made up of dark matter. Dark matter does not reflect or emit detectable light, yet it accounts for most of the mass in the universe. *Q79: Have you ever looked into the shadows?*

16 May 2007

Fifty students from the University of Japan have set a world record by cramming the most nationalities into one sauna at the same time. That's 50 people from different parts of the world crammed together in one hot house, securing their place in history. *Q63: Do you like the way you look?*

An international study has shown that flies have 'free will.' When they buzz about your head, they know exactly what they are doing and where they are going. The study was of fruit flies and found their actions appear to be spontaneous rather than random activity in the brain. *Q44: Is there anything worse than a fly buzzing around your room at night when you're trying to sleep?*

A life jacket worn by a survivor from the Titanic fetched £60,000 at auction. It showed the market for Titanic memorabilia was as buoyant as ever, as we approach the 100th anniversary of its sinking in 2012. *Q5: Do you believe in fate?*

18 May 2007

Satirical TV series *Spitting Image* is due to return to the small screen with a new 21st Century look. 3D computer animated graphics will be used to lampoon its victims. Celebrities will be top targets for the show. *Q13: Have you ever been mistaken for someone else?*

The discovery of a Roman skeleton, buried beneath Trafalgar Square 1,600 years ago, is forcing archaeologists to rewrite the history of London. The find proves the Romans stayed in London longer than people previously thought. Whilst in China archaeologists studying ancient rock carvings say they have evidence that modern Chinese script is thousands of years older than previously thought. *Q47: Do you know your history?*

An 11 year-old male gorilla called Bokito escaped from his enclosure at a Netherlands Zoo. He climbed a high wall and swam across a moat, before he was eventually tranquilised by zoo staff. Despite his venutre, nobody was seriously injured by Bokito. We believe zoo's have an invaluable role in conservation, so perhaps the gorilla was making a statement about poaching. *Q51: Have you ever taken part in a protest?*

19 May 2007

A record haul of half a million silver and gold coins from a 17th century ship wreck have been found of the coast of Cornwall. The gold coins are dazzling mint-state specimens. The discovery is estimated to be worth $500m. The site of the wreck is also of huge historical importance. *Q80: Have you ever searched for buried treasure?*

21 May 2007

The historic 19th Century *Cutty Sark* may have been the victim of an arson attack. Stored on dry-dock at Greenwich, the 138 year old sea clipper is an iconic landmark on the route of the London Marathon.

♥ For us, the curiosity is that the ship rests at the home of the Prime Meridian – the zero line of longitude. The Meridian is the symbolic home of 'time' - an imaginary line that runs from the North Pole to the South Pole.

♥ The ship was built for speed and achieved a record-breaking wind powered voyage from Australia to England in 67 days. Odd that, as Australia is enduring its worst drought in 1,000 years!

♥ Should this be an unfortunate accident then we wonder – is Mother Nature trying to warn us of calamities to come?

Fortunately, the Cutty Sark Trust is hopeful that the ship is salvageable, as much of it was off-site at the time of the blaze undergoing restoration. So, all is not yet lost! *Q58: Do things happen for a reason? Watch Wonder!*

22 May 2007

Scientists say that face creams containing vitamin A really do fight wrinkles! Beauty products with Retinol had a significant rejuvenating effect on a group of volunteers. The study comes weeks after a documentary endorsed a product produced by a leading pharmacist. *Q39: Do you believe in magic?*

Britain's first miniature 'spy drone helicopter' has taken to the skies. Designed for the military, it's a three feet wide battery operated remote-controlled craft, fitted with CCTV cameras. *Q57: Have you ever spied on anyone?*

The surprises from Nature just keep coming – a 'virgin birth' that has baffled scientists. Researchers have confirmed that a hammerhead shark, born at a zoo where there were no male sharks, has identical DNA to its mother. There were three potential mothers in the same tank. All had been in capacity for at least three years. This means the shark did not mate before being captured and store the sperm for fertilization. *Q23: Do you believe all the laws of physics?*

A British climber has become the first person to make a mobile phone call from the top of Mount Everest. The caller sent a text – "One small text for a man, one giant leap for mobile kind!" All this was possible as China installed an antenna just 12 miles from the peak and the caller had special batteries tied to his body to keep them at a high enough temperature to power the phone. Take a look at our image for *Q42: Do you like drawing?*

A forensic examination on the remains of the Cutty Sark, has failed to establish how the fire started. The police say tests have proved inconclusive. We ask again, is Mother Nature trying to warn us of calamities to come? *Q68: Does the Earth have a spirit?*

The TV series 'This is Your Life' is to be re-launched. It involves a 'Little Red Book' where famous people are caught unawares and have their life story revisited with a live audience, meeting friends and families from their past. *Q59: Do you like surprise?*

24 May 2007

Another escaped primate! This time an orangutan escaped from its cage in a zoo in Taiwan. The most curious thing was the orangutan went in to a rage against a motorcycle. He knocked it over and pushed it down a hill! Was this a protest by Mother Nature against our continued over-use of fossil fuels? *Q68: Does the Earth have a spirit? Watch Wonder!*

Nelson went green in London today! For a few sweet days, Britain's famous Admiral will enjoy a rural square, rather than the usual grey paving slabs! *Q58: Do things happen for a reason?*

Anti-wrinkle cream sales have trebled, following the frenzy caused by experts saying that vitamin A creams really do beat wrinkles! *Q63: Do you like the way you look?*

Fashion experts claim that electric blue is the 'must have' colour for spring and summer 2007! Blue is not only beautiful, but works for most skin tones. So, Lucy clearly has an eye for fashion. *Q63: Do you like the way you look?*

The latest incarnation of HRH Prince Charles at Madame Tussauds is the most eco-friendly waxwork in the history of the museum. The self-declared greenest member of the Royal Family can take pride in knowing the figure is 'carbon-neutral' being made from a recycled 1989 version of the Prince. *Q13: Have you ever been mistaken for someone else?*

25 May 2007

More magic from nature! Barbow, a barnacle goose took just five hours to fly from Scotland to Norway, the natural home of Yggdrasil. The bird knocked three hours of the previous record. A satellite-tracking device clocked an average speed of 80mph, all the more remarkable as there wasn't a strong tailwind. The team measuring the bird's progress were amazed at the speed at which he was able to make the crossing. *Q65: Have you ever wished you could fly?*

Humans are performing magic too! A woman has given birth less than two minutes after her waters broke. She could hold the world record for the fastest ever delivery. *Q51a How many people does it take to fill up the Earth?*

Meanwhile, a man has claimed a new record by succeeding at staying awake for 11 days as part of human sleep research. *Q44: Is there anything worse than a fly buzzing around your room at night when you're trying to sleep?*

28 May 2007

So much for global warming – more like global wetting! It's the second bank holiday in May and both have been complete washouts! The weather is so unpredictable! Still, Julia's had plenty of opportunity to practice her art! *Q30: Did you ever watch the rain on your window?*

The world's oldest camera has been bought at auction. The daguerreotype camera, made no later than 1839 fetched about £400k. The first photograph of Abraham Lincoln was believed to have been taken using a daguerreotype, in the 1840s. *Q78: Do you want to be part of the picture?*

30 May 2007

Researchers from Aberdeen and Loughborough universities predict that British society faces a return to Dickensian inequality. The authors claim that many young couples and families have levels of debt that leave them as no more than bonded labourers. Little time is left for family life, with little disposable income with which to enjoy it. *Q62: Have you ever helped the poor?*

Michael Jackson memorabilia was under auction in Las Vegas. The sale of more than 1,000 items included a scarlet military-style Jackson stage jacket. Despite what Charles' journal says, Ben still has his jacket. *Q61: Have you ever worn fancy dress?*

In the TV Big Brother House at Elstree in Hertfordshire, the opening twelve housemates included a pair of identical twins. As if to celebrate, a spiral shaped crop circle consisting of 57 circles has appeared near Avebury in Wiltshire, England. *Q57: Have you ever spied on anyone?*

31 May 2007

In Devon, a group of orphaned baby hedgehogs have been rescued by a farmer from a freezing barn. The five tiny and blind mammals were less than a week old and close to death. They are being cared for by an animal rescue centre and could soon be fit enough to be released into the wild. We've named them Ben, Julia, Sarah, Jonas and Caleb! *Q19: Do you love hedgehogs?*

London's biggest casino has opened for business, on the site of a former ballroom in Leicester Square. An unlucky punter lost £10,000 on a single spin of a roulette wheel! The business man gambled the ball on red but came up black! *Q4: Have you ever wanted to stop the clock?*

1 June 2007

It was 40 years ago today, that Sgt Pepper taught the Lonely Hearts Club band to play! The ground-breaking album from the 'Summer of Love' inspired us to think of Billie Shears. The album included 'Lucy in the Sky with Diamonds!' It seems, a Surbiton housewife. called Lucy, was at a school with John Lennon's son, Julian. One day, Julian took home a drawing of her surrounded by stars. She imagined Julian telling his famous father, "That's Lucy at School," and John Lennon, asking, "What's in the sky - diamonds?" *Q40: Can you play a musical instrument? Watch Wonder!*

At a *Beyond Belief* exhibition at the White Cube Gallery in London, a platinum cast skull by Damien Hurst will go on sale for £50m. The skull, 'A celebration against death' is studied with 8,601 diamonds. *Q33: Do you believe in life after death?*

Saturn's glowing blue rings have been captured in stunning detail by an orbiting spacecraft. Scientists say it is also the first image of the clouds covering Saturn's surface, 746 million miles from Earth. *Q70: Do you like to look at the stars?*

More than 1,600 guitar players took part in a rendition of a Deep Purple song, 'Smoke on the Water'. It beat the record set in 1994 for the most people playing the same song at the same time. The tune is often one of the first songs players learn. It was released in 1972 on the album, 'Machine Head'! *Q40: Can you play a musical instrument?*

Desperate news about tigers! There are now believed to be only 5,000 left in the wild. The animal is on a catastrophic path towards extinction because humans are encroaching on their habitat and killing them for traditional medicine. Their territory has shrunk to just 7% of its historic area, with most of the land lost within the last 10 years. *Q48: Have you ever played Solitaire!*

5 June 2007

It's the United Nations' World Environment Day. To celebrate, a globe shaped crop circle has appeared in Wiltshire. The creation shows a planet in half light and half dark – resembling an equinox, when our adventure began. *Q12: Is the Earth enchanted? Watch Wonder!*

Sarah marked Environment Day by toying with the heavily criticised 2012 London Olympics logo, which cost £400,000. She cut out the pieces and rearranged them into the shape of our messenger, Malachi. We took a photo and placed it on our website. *Q74: Do you like puzzles?*

New Zealand's famous Kiwi bird, is facing extinction from climate change, deforestation and habitat changes. Does this help explain why a type of heron not seen in London for nearly 150 years has taken up residence in Abbey Wood? The bird has attracted hundreds of camera twitching birdwatchers. *Q65: Have you ever wished you could fly?*

The heat continues with London's property market. A record price of £3m has been achieved for a one-bedroom flat in Eaton Square - the most expensive one-bedroom flat in London ever. So, to buy or not to buy? *Q64: Do you know whether or not you are sometimes indecisive?*

6 June 2007

Department of Health data shows that more than 8 million Britons are problem drinkers – that's one in six of the adult population! *Various questions may apply.*

The oldest man in Britain was 111 today. The number 111 is sometimes known as Nelson, after Admiral Nelson who allegedly only had, 'one eye, one arm and one ball' at the end of his life. The number is considered an ill-omen in cricket and is the emergency telephone number in New Zealand – try telling the Kiwi! *Q5: Do you believe in fate?*

7 June 2007

Nature's producing more miracles! In a previously barren field in Holyford Wood in Devon, a sea of foxgloves has appeared after lying dormant for more than 100 years. Experts believe they were simply waiting for the right conditions to germinate! *Q12: Is our Earth enchanted?*

A study of elephants in Namibia and Kenya in Africa has discovered they have a secret sense - they pick up noise through their feet. The mammals 'talk' to each other, by picking up sound waves along the ground. Their pressure sensitive feet are also thought to be used by herds to warn each other of danger. The chief researcher said, "People are amazed." *Q17: Can you speak another language?*

We're celebrating 30 years of bottle banking! Since the first empty jar was dropped into a bottle bank, more than 23 billion jars and bottles have been recycled in over 50,000 banks across Britain. Mr

England, the man behind the idea to recycle glass said, "At first everyone thought of me as a crank, but there were pressures which made it all make sense – depletion of resources, the energy question and the landfill issue." Oh, isn't glass made from sand? *Q34: Have you ever restored something?*

8 June 2007

In Canada, a team of surgeons operating on a man were shocked to discover the patient had dark green blood! It's claimed the colour was due to large doses of migraine medication. *Q58: Do things happen for a reason? Watch Wonder!*

In the USA, a teenager found a diamond on a path – just minutes after praying she would discover one. She found the 3 carat stone whilst leaving the Crater of Diamonds State Park. *Q5: Do you believe in fate?*

A United Nations report has found Britons toil longer every week than any nation in the developed world. Around 7 million people, put in more than 48 hours per week. It puts Britain far ahead of the rest of Europe! *Q24: Do you get enough time to yourself?*

In the last two decades, Europe's rapid economic growth has 'seriously degraded' the quality of the continent's seas. The main causes have been pollution caused by shipping, coastline development, over-fertilization and fishing. *Q36: Should a good life cost the Earth?*

A 33 year old Hertfordshire man has discovered the most distant black hole ever – 13 billion light years from Earth. According to scientists, the discovery may shed light on the evolution of the universe. *Q79: Have you ever looked into the shadows?*

10 June 2007

A world record has been achieved for Napoleon memorabilia. A gold-encrusted sword which belonged to the emperor sold at auction in France for some £3m. The sword was used in battle 200 years ago. It has an intricately decorated blade and a distinctive gentle curve. The inspiration for the unusual design was said to be Napoleon's Egyptian campaign. Aside from being a weapon of war, the sword is regarded as a work of art and a piece of history. *Q47: Do you know your history?*

11 June 2007

In 2006, Britons spent nearly £6billion on health and beauty products. A study into the spending revealed that many people splash out on health care, skin and hair products because of their anxiety and desire to look like their favourite celebrities. *Q63: Do you like the way you look?*

A 70 ton seed made from 300 million year-old silver-grey granite has arrived at the Eden Project in Cornwall. The seed weighs as much as ten elephants, with a pattern as intricate as the head of a sunflower. It's one of the biggest sculptures ever made from a single piece of rock. The oval seed measures 4 metres high and 3 metres at its widest point - so it's somewhat larger and heavier than the Royston Stones. It will form the centrepiece of the Core Education Centre, helping the Project's mission of regeneration – to reconnect people with their natural environments locally and nationally. Q58: *Do things happen for a reason?*

12 June 2007

A survey has shown that, on average, people who commute to work in London spend the equivalent of a full working day travelling each week! Add that to the amount of time people spend at work – 7 million putting in 48 hour weeks and that doesn't leave much time for the things Charles Lamb valued most – Art, Love and Nature! *Q24: Do you get enough time to yourself?*

A controversial artist has made sculptures from animal road kill he has collected. The art is designed to shock! The father of three has attached a hefty £35,000 price-tag on the work to provoke a reaction, rather than secure a sale. His work includes the skins of squirrels, deer and badgers killed on the roads. He said, "We live in such a pre-packaged world with environmentally damaging processes and it's important to identify that." *Q2: Are you an art lover?*

13 June 2007

Given our experiences leading up to the discovery of Charles Lamb's journal, the significance of the enigma of President Bush's disappearing watch is intriguing. Video footage shows that whilst greeting crowds in Albania, his watch appeared to vanish from his wrist. The watch has a Mickey Mouse design and was inscribed with the date Mr Bush became president. The White House claims he put the watch into his pocket, but the footage is inconclusive - at no time does it show him removing the watch! We believe this is an act of nature to reinforce our message, 'Now is the Time for Action' on climate change. *Q4:Have you ever wanted to stop the clock? Watch Wonder*!

21 June 2007

Up to 20,000 people were at Stonehenge or Avebury to welcome the sun as dawn broke on the summer solstice. In London, the day saw a symbolic 'light's out' to encourage people to conserve energy. Famous landmarks such as the Houses of Parliament, The London Eye and Piccadilly Circus switched-off at 9.00pm and came back on at 10.00pm. Some 3 million people took part. *Q51: Have you ever taken part in a protest?*

A squirrel has gone 'nuts' in Germany, attacking three people. The bushy-tailed baddie found its way into the house of an elderly woman and she ran into the street with the squirrel clinging to her hand. *Q51: Have you ever taken part in a protest?*

22 June 2007

We watched a television documentary about an Arctic expedition. The scientists kept a Samoyed named Alcatraz at their camp. The footage included several close encounters between the dog and some hungry polar bears. *Q78: Do you want to be part of the picture?*

Britain has experienced almost constant rain during May and June. Global warming sceptics are rubbing their hands triumphantly, saying, 'We told you so!' *Q30: Did you ever watch the rain on your window?*

A crop circle has appeared in a field in Wiltshire which has a flower formation that resembles the wild native 'Forget-me-not.' As the flower was dear to Lucy and Charles, are we to assume this is a clear reminder to us all not to forget our precious natural world? *Q66: Do you have a favourite flower? Watch Wonder!*

25 June 2007

Areas of northern Britain have received the heaviest rain ever recorded in a single day! Sheffield, Britain's 'City of Steel' has experienced very severe flooding, with loss of life and damage to property. *Q58: Do things happen for a reason?*

Pilots are so exhausted that the industry is 'skating on thin ice' when it comes to passenger safety. An aviation expert claims the number of pilots he treats for chronic fatigue has doubled in the last five years - 81% of pilots say they have been affected by fatigue! *Q24 : Do you get enough time to yourself?*

27 June 2007

As northern Britain deals with the aftermath of the flash floods, south-eastern Europe is experiencing extreme temperatures. In Greece, June is set to be the hottest on record with all public offices closing at midday to allow people to keep out of the sun. Temperatures in Romania are set to reach there highest level in 90 years, and Turkey and Bulgaria are sweltering too. The advice is to keep in the shade. *Q79: Have you ever looked into the shadows?*

On a brighter note, scientists at the University of Edinburgh are converting ordinary peanuts into precious gem stones, using pressures up to a million times greater than the normal atmosphere. Bill Darvill will be going nuts! *Q62a: Is life logical? Watch Wonder!*

A United Nations report, 'The State of World Population 2007' found the number of people living in cities in Africa and Asia increases by about 1 million each week. This wave of growth in urban living is unprecedented. By 2008, more than half the world's population will live in cities, most of them in the developing countries. *Q51a: How many people does it take to fill up the Earth?*

Another remarkable archaeological find – this time in Egypt! A tomb has been discovered to rival that of Tutankhamun. *Q80: Have you ever searched for buried treasure?*

28 June 2007

Fire chiefs are mounting the 'biggest rescue effort in peacetime Britain' in response to the floods. 3,500 people have been rescued and there have been more than 600 casualties. Crews are exhausted and at the point of collapse. Further heavy rain is forecast for the weekend. *Q30: Did you ever watch the rain on your window?*

29 June 2007

Sales of honey are soaring as Britons are preferring sweet spreads. It now has 26% of the market share, up 16% in the last two years. *Q8: Do you crave a better life?*

A report published in *Science* reveals only 17% of land on Earth remains free of direct human influence, and practically nothing remains completely untouched. It states, 'We are domesticating nature and as we attempt to bend it to our will, we damage not only the planet, but ourselves. 50% of the world's surface has been directly converted to pasture or crops, with more than 50% of the world's forests lost in the process.' *Q36: Should a good life cost the Earth?*

30 June 2007

Flooding in parts of the USA has been as bad as in Britain. Is the melting ice having an impact on precipitation rates? *Q35: Do you trust your instincts?*

1 July 2007

Forecasters say our summer will last for just one day this year – 15 July! So, we have a 'Year without a summer!' Strange that, as the Blakesware Set discussed the 'Year without a summer,' which occurred in 1816. It was the year that inspired Mary Shelley to write her novel Frankenstein. *Q60: Have you ever experienced déjà vu? Watch Wonder!*

A tiger in the Indonesian jungle has survived against all odds, after having its front foot ripped off by a poacher's trap. To keep alive, the tiger is thought to have chewed its own leg off or pulled its leg away, leaving the foot behind. He would normally have been expected to die through blood loss, infection or an inability to feed. But despite having only three legs, the big cat has amazed observers by managing to catch enough prey to stay healthy. *Q12: Is our Earth enchanted? Watch Wonder!*

2 July 2007

If we ever needed reassurance that our famous ancestors had a hand in 'The Haymakers Survey' - we have it now. That majestic seabird, the Albatross, has found its way on to British shores for the first time. The RSPB said the discovery of an endangered Yellow-Nosed Albatross was 'incredibly exciting' for it is believed the bird – which has a two metre wingspan – flew thousands of miles off course before landing near Brean in Somerset. That's just three miles short of the birthplace of the poet Samuel Taylor Coleridge, author of the famous 'Rime of the Ancient Mariner' which features the arrival of an Albatross as a sign of hope to a ship stranded in Arctic sea ice.

As we know, Samuel was a close friend of Charles Lamb. Charles' journal shows that the pair discussed the poem when the Blakesware Set came together. Given the problems with the Arctic sea ice melting, it's worth looking again at some of the lines from the poem:

"The ice was here, the ice was there, the ice was all around.
It cracked and growled and roared and howled, like noises in a swound...
At length did cross an Albatross, through the fog it came."

How poignant and strange is this? Are you a believer yet? *Q12: Is our Earth enchanted? Watch Wonder!*

3 July 2007

Huge hail stones, the size of 50 pence pieces, have fallen in the streets of South London, turning July into a winter wonderland. Hail, of course, is basically frozen rain-water or ice. We wonder - how many have fallen as ice-tears? We wonder is Mother Nature crying? *Q75: Have you ever put on a show?*

Odd that these things should happen in the build up to the 'Live Earth' concert on 7 July, to promote action to reduce carbon emissions. When the date was first set, the organisers must have anticipated a heat-wave - not the wet, chilly, blustery conditions we've experienced in Britain recently. So, it comes as no surprise that many people are sceptical about 'Green-Spin' believing the case is being overstated, or that people are exploiting the situation to make money. *Q78: Do you want to be part of the picture?*

Caleb's view is that people want unequivocal evidence that humans are responsible for climate change, and proof that the consequences may be as bad as scientists fear. Well – neither of these things can ever be totally proven, so it comes down to a matter of faith. Our view, is that 'The Haymakers Survey' and all that has unfolded since, tells us that Nature means business! We continue to disrespect her at our peril. *Q69: Do you ever put off until tomorrow what you could do today?*

A study has shown that two out of three British managers will not be using all their 2007 annual leave entitlement, compared with two in five in 2003. Many blame heavy workloads. *Q24: Do you get enough time to yourself?*

4 July 2007

Global warming has caused Mount Everest to shrink by 50 metres since 1953! Peter Hilary, son of Sir Edmund Hilary who reached the summit in that year, said, "In 1953, the base camp sat at 5,320 metres, today it is 5,280 metres." See our online survey image for *Q42: Do you enjoy drawing?*

493

Sarah thought it a good idea to look more closely at the crop circles that have appeared in Britain during June. We were truly amazed. We found:

♥ On 14 June, a reversed *S* eclipse formation at the Westbury White Horse. Does this suggest a Survey prepared in the past?

♥ On 12 June, a formation of a bird in flight. Does this represent the Albatross that came within touching distance of the home of Samuel Coleridge?

♥ On 28 June, a 3D chess board effect design. Could this represent a Scrabble board, used to decipher the deeper meaning of, 'The Haymakers Survey'?

♥ On 29 June, a formation said to be a worm-hole design that allows for time-travel!

What's really curious is that during the last 3 years, the Whittenbury's have been to all the key archaeological sites in the south of England – Stonehenge, Silbury Hill, Dragon Hill, Royston Cave, Avebury and the West Kennett Long Barrow. Did they unwittingly open a secret door of understanding? *Q12: Is our Earth enchanted? Watch Wonders!*

However, our excitement has faded as a major oil company has announced plans to seek oil in the Arctic Ocean. Many fear it could spark a scramble by other fuel giants. We see this as a huge insult to our beloved polar bear! *Q11: Do you believe in justice?*

As if in response, a grizzly bear in Pennsylvania, USA scaled an electricity pylon 100 metres high. The pylon was beside a highway. Was this an act of defiance on behalf of his polar brothers in the Arctic - a symbolic message to the world from the animal kingdom? After all, the bear was amid two examples of the greatest forms of creators of carbon emissions! *Q51: Have you ever taken part in a protest? Watch Wonder!*

7 July 2007

The 'Live Earth' concert is underway. Performances are taking place in seven continents across the globe – that's 150 countries with an estimated 1/3rd of the world's population predicted to watch. The most striking thing has been the cynicism and complacency about the events – with the media focusing on the lifestyles of many of the performers, and the energy used by people in getting to the event and in staging the concerts. Well, some of the most startling things we heard were:

"The lights are on, but no-one's home."

"We're re-writing the atlas and the dictionary."

"It's very easy to be cynical."

"We're fair-weather environmentalists!"

"Will our Earth ever be this good again?"

"It's not what happens today, but tomorrow and the day after."

"We're calling SOS!"

"This is a wake-up call – an avalanche of awareness that we are running out of time."

"We're at a tipping point."

"This is the last chance to show we care about the planet."

"At times like these, we learn to live again."

"We are humans - we have faith, hope and vision."

"You must be the change you wish to see in the world."

"If one leaf on a tree changes colour, the tree is different."

"There's no need to stop living, just start living in a different way."

"We asked... you answered."

Still, as the musician's play, in the USA record heat in the west is turning hay crop to dust. In the words of a Montana farmer, "It just gets crisp and falls apart!"

Is that why Madonna sang,

> "Hey you... open your heart... Poets and prophets will envy what you do."

Is that why the BBC TV coverage ended with the question:

Who will speak for Planet Earth?

Answer:

'The Haymakers Survey'

Q12: Is our Earth enchanted?

Star Question: What happened to the Blue Ribbon?

We've agonised over how best to conclude our experience. Given the magnitude of everything we discovered, we had to ask the questions: 'Why here? Why now?' For the final time, we sought inspiration from the *Haymakers*. Ben recalled how George Stubbs had told Charles to 'Behold look, throw down thy book'. So, we looked at things from a new perspective.

♥ The figures in the *Haymakers* were no longer representative of 21st Century Britain. The country now had one of the most cosmopolitan and diverse populations in the world. Britain was a global village in every sense. For sure, the messages within 'The Haymakers Survey' applied to each and every person, regardless of colour or creed.

We found many other reasons why the Earth Spirit chose Britain as the place to unveil the mysterious wonder of 'The Haymakers Survey' to the world:

♥ Britain has a rich cultural heritage, with an abundance of famous artists, poets and writers, such as Shakespeare, Dickens and Bronte - and the members of the Blakesware Set.

♥ Britain is steeped in myth and folklore – King Arthur, Merlin and dragons, and ancient monuments, like Stonehenge. It's a place where magic abounds; just ask Harry Potter!

♥ Britain is the home of Time and the Greenwich Prime Meridian, at zero longitude.

♥ Britain gave the world popular music, including the Beatles.

♥ Britain's a country with genuine champions of the Natural World – Peter Scott, founder of the World Wide Fund for Nature, and current day ambassadors, such as Sir David Attenborough.

♥ As the birth place of the industrial revolution, Britain arguably has a moral responsibility to show leadership to the world on the consequences that have arisen from the spread of William Blake's infamous, 'dark Satanic Mills.'

♥ In the past, the British people have shown tremendous courage and strength in the face of adversity and extremism. It remains a country of influence in the world; so at a time of climate chaos, where better to launch a renaissance of Art, Love and Nature?

As for us, working on behalf of the Blakesware Set, we've shared with you everything we've discovered thus far. At this point, we can do no more. We suspect we've not given people quite the conclusion they might have imagined – we've just put our interpretation on recent events. Arguably, this doesn't really count as an ending in the conventional sense; it's all largely inconclusive.

But, hey… this is 'The Haymakers Survey'. It's not about logic, science or hard facts. It's about Art, Love and Nature. For 2007, a 'year without a summer,' we feel it was our purpose to share the truth with you through this tale, our website and our video selection.

Yet, for us, the most astonishing thing was that at the final proof stage for typesetting this tale, the following note appeared. It left us pondering a potential explanation for the Brazen Head enigma:

Time Is: 2007
Time Was: 1822
Time's Passed (for Action) 2100

Is this how you want the story to end?

Hey you! I've left enough notes from the future to give those humans with the chance to change things a better understanding of the message and what they need to do.

I'm not sure what more I can add to convince you. I'm going to put my copy of 'The Haymakers Survey' back in its secret place, with my Interludes inserted. Most of the many thousands of copies of the book in circulation were destroyed long ago. With them went the results of the survey, and the hopes and dreams of humanity.

In 2100, the authorities were determined that people shouldn't know the truth – what you've never had you never miss – that's the philosophy of Dr. Darvill.

Only a few of the thousand or so people still alive today know that England used to be a green and pleasant land – not the shrunken, dry and barren place it is today; that Britain once had a 'year without a summer'; that there were rainforests or that we had a frozen Arctic with polar bears; that we once had a population of 6.66 billion people, and three babies were born every second.

As I look at the last remaining copy of Stubbs' Haymakers upon the wall of our sanctuary in Royston Cave, a single tear runs down my cheek. Have we failed? Let me open the locket and take out the key to the treasure chest, so I can put everything safely away in the hope that someone will one day find it and discover the truth.

Inside everything must go; each served a purpose. Oh, the truth is, I'm the one who likes making lists.

♥ *Acorn* - Preserved, fossil like, as a reminder of the mighty Oak that once flourished in Britain.

♥ *Art* – A few drawings, honouring the wonder of imagination.

♥ *Dice* – Representing numbers - people and animals and the odds against a living planet.

♥ *Feather* – A symbol of independence and the spirit of revolution.

♥ *Handkerchief* – To show sorrow and sadness at the loss of so much beauty.

♥ *Locket* – Oh sweet thing, representing the tenuous gift of life on this planet.

♥ *Peanut* - To appease the cynics and sceptics.

♥ *Penny* – The global currency, that made the world go around!

♥ *Postcards* – From Tate Britain and the National Maritime Museum of 'Hannibal Crossing the Alps' and 'Nelson and the Bear'.

♥ *Ribbon* – Oh this fragile Earth - let me wrap it with a ribbon, for it's a gift so precious.

♥ *Sacred Stones* – Symbolic of the imagination and creativity needed to preserve the endangered Earth.

♥ *Watch* – A reminder that time is of the essence.

Then, some applause for the things that cannot go into the chest:

♥ *Goblin Tree* – A reminder that nature is evergreen and can recover from the darkest of days.

♥ *Owl – Delivering a message of hope, belief and faith.*

♥ *Rose – Sweet symbol of love and beauty.*

♥ *Squirrel – A reminder that the time for talking is over.*

As I sit on the Philosopher's Chair, with a strand of hay dangling from between my teeth, I accept my tricks may have flattered to deceive. I take off my top-hat.

Oh, I nearly forgot, the Three of Hearts, bless them. ♥ ♥ ♥ *Yes, there is the playing card, which is about gambling with our future. 'Thank you, Ben,' for all you did to champion the cause. The card goes into the treasure chest too. But, the clear truth is our future lies in the palm of our hands. It is so, here engraved three times on the wall of Royston Cave, as a blatant warning – STOP!*

Still, the world keeps on turning, has been for millions of years, and will hopefully continue to do so for millions more. Malachi , my everlasting symbolic polar bear. An iconic voice of nature, an irresistible and amazing animal! It seems I sent you for nothing my friend, but wait, what's that you say,

🐻 *Key - Rush Save My Earth.* 🐻

Now that's what I call magic.

Signed,

THE EMPEROR
1 May 2100

Caleb's Notes

1. Runic - A form of alphabet used in the 1st Century. In Norse mythology, the invention of runes is attributed to the god, Odin. Early runes were used as magical signs of divination.

2. *Luddites* - A social movement in the early 1800s of English textile workers led by General Ned Ludd. They destroyed textile factories, in response to changes produced by the Industrial Revolution. There was a mass trial at York in 1813, leading to death penalties and deportation.

3. *Hesiod* - His writings serve as a major source of knowledge on Greek mythology and ancient time-keeping.

4. Mlle Lenormand - A famous Parisian fortune teller using her own system of cards. Each of the cards contained rhymes and artwork. Her readings used three spreads of three cards – for past, present and future.

5. *Sixteen-String Jack* - The nickname of John Rann, so called because of his audacious robberies and courtesy to his victims, and his habit of attaching eight strings to each knee of his silk breeches. He was hanged in 1774.

6. *Peterloo massacre* - Occured in 1819 and was the result of a cavalry charge into a crowd of protestors in St. Peter's Field, Manchester, England. About 80,000 people were protesting for reform of the Corn Laws.

7. *Robin Goodfellow* - A fairy from William Shakespeare's 'A Midsummer Night's Dream.'

8. Oberon, Titania - More fairies from, 'A Midsummer Night's Dream'.

9. Château de Malmaison - In 1799, Empress Josephine established a magnificent rose garden at Malmaison, gathering specimens from all over the world.

10. *Romantic Movement* - In America followed that in England 20 years or so before hand. Creative individuals, such as William Wordsworth, used art, poetry and literature to express nature and love.

11. Three Thumbs – We all know that I have three thumbs, but I know nothing about any of this. Is this a work of fiction?

12. Tithes - The right to receive tithes was granted to English Churches by King Ethelwulf in 855. They were given legal force in 1285. Adam Smith criticised the practice, in the Wealth of Nations 1776, arguing that a fixed rent would encourage peasants to farm more efficiently. The system ended with the Tithe Commutation Act 1836.

13. *Pugilist* - In the 19th century a satirical definition for a pugilist was someone ringed-in and on the ropes who never gives in until they are out! It's also another way of describing a Haymaker!

14. *Nelson and the Bear* - Housed in the National Maritime Museum, Greenwich, the painting from 1806 shows Nelson standing on one part of the ice with the bear, just separated by a fissure. The bear has one paw raised and bares his fangs, as if in self-defence, whilst Nelson attacks the bear with the butt-end of his musket until the ship fires to scare off the bear. It's unlikely that a more iconic vision of man and polar bear will be repeated, given the current plight of the beautiful hunter of the North.

15. *Triviality* - I find this issue about who owns the handkerchief extremely trivial and distracting. Whilst we're on the subject, Reader you ought to know of the debate we've had on whether there should be an apostrophe in 'The Haymakers Survey' eg 'The Haymaker's Survey' or 'The Haymakers' Survey.' We wager it may have crossed your mind too. Well, there's more than one Haymaker and the survey's named after the *Haymakers* painting, and it looks much better without. Forget the small print, what matters to us is the bigger picture!

16. *Teach us, Sprite or Bird, what sweet thoughts are thine*! - An extract from 'Ode to a Skylark' by Percy Shelley. A poem written by William Wordsworth in 1827 had a very similar title, 'To a Skylark.'

17. *It will not be long, love, till our wedding day* - From, 'She moved through the Fair.' It is a traditional Irish folk song, though some claim it stems from medieval times.

18. *Vein of love* - Traditionally the fourth finger of the left hand. It's where the vein is said to link directly to the heart. I, of course, have four fingers and two thumbs on my left hand, which confuses things a bit.

19. *Radicals* - In the early 1800s the Radicals sought political change aimed at abandoning Government policies of repression, such as the right to demonstrate.

20. *George Washington* - The first President of the United States of America – fondly known as the 'Father of the Country'.

21 *England expects that every man will do his duty* - A signal sent by Admiral Horatio Nelson from his flagship HMS Victory as the Battle of Trafalgar was about to commence.

22. *National Gallery* - In April 1824, the House of Commons agreed to pay £57,000 for 38 pictures to form the core of a national collection. Initially, the paintings were housed in a private house in Pall Mall, London.

23. *Emma Isola* - The history books show she was adopted by Charles Lamb.

24. *Flat Earth Society* - We have the eccentric English inventor, Samuel Rowbotham to thank for the Society through a theory known as Zetetic Astronomy!

25. *Spinning Jenny* - A multi-spool wheel invented in 1764 for use in the cotton industry. It dramatically reduced the amount of work needed to produce yarn.

26. *The sky is falling in.* - In January 2007, an economist employed by the car industry infamously used these words as an attempt to belittle the facts about climate change. The phrase comes from the fable, 'Chicken Licken'. It's commonly used to indicate a hysterical or mistaken belief that disaster is imminent.

27. *Woe is me* - A phrase that appears in the Christian Bible a few times and Shakespeare's Hamlet, "Oh woe is me to see what I have seen. See what I see."

28. *Christ's Hospital* - Charles and Samuel attended the school together.

29. *Salon* - A gathering of stimulating people of quality to increase their knowledge or taste.

30. *George Stubbs* - I fear Charles must be mistaken, George died in 1806!

31. *Ex silentio* - Translates to, "In the absence of contrary evidence."

32. *Colebrooke* - Now Mr Lamb, it may be coincidence but you too lived at Colebrooke Cottage.

33. *I circle our world…*, - Taken from a Charm from the Lacnunga spell book.

34. *Carpe Diem* - Translates to "Seize the Day."

35. *Copenhagen* - The name of the Duke of Wellington's horse and Albert Thorvaldsen's home town.

36. *All the world's a stage…* - From Shakespeare's 'As You Like It,' Act II.

37. *Qualis artifex pereo* - Translates to "What an artist dies in me," the last words famously spoken by the controversial Roman Emperor, Nero Caesar.

38. *Modern Prometheus* - Mary Shelley's gothic 1816 novel was titled, 'Frankenstein; or modern Prometheus.'

39. "*In times of solitude…*" - Mary was toying with words from Wordsworth's famous Daffodils poem, about a wandering lonely cloud.

40. *Richard Westall* - The artist was born in Hertford.

41. *Giant amongst dwarfs* - Samuel Coleridge was fondly described in this way.

42. *Dark obsession* - For long periods in his life Samuel Coleridge was addicted to opium.

43. *The Ancient Mariner* - Samuel's most famous poem. Odd that he should liken himself to the mariner whose actions cost the lives of the rest of his crew!

44. *Pleasure dome decree…*- This plays on some lines from the poem, 'Kubla Khan'.

45. *Odin* - The chief god in Norse mythology. He was complex; the God of war and wisdom. He was also attested as the God of magic and poetry.

46. *Lion of Lucerne* - The American writer Mark Twain described the monument as the saddest and most moving piece of rock in the world.

47. *Beggars Opera* - A satirical comedy of corruption and immorality. The characters include Lucy Lockit, the jailer's daughter at Newgate prison.

48. *Life is a jest…* - John Gay's epitaph.

49.*Stoicism* - In Greece over 2,000 years ago, Stoics saw the universe as fundamentally rational. They believed that wisdom and happiness can be found by reserving our emotions. In other words, we should learn to accept events with a stern and tranquil mind.

50. *Triumph of Life* - The title of Percy's unfinished poem at the time of his death.

51. *Haymaker* - The Duke was right; a Haymaker also means someone who can deliver a powerful blow!

52. *I tell you that out of these stones God can raise up children* - Adapted from the Christian New Testament, Luke 3-8.

53. *If they keep quiet the stones will cry out* - Adapted from Christian New Testament, Luke 19:40.

54. *Golden Ticket* - A prize in Roald Dahl's, 'Charlie and the Chocolate Factory'. What prize awaits the winners of the Earth Championships?

55. *Devil's Advocate* - A person who takes a position for the sake of argument. Their job may include taking a sceptical view of a person's character or pick holes in the evidence, and to argue that claims of miracles are fraudulent.

56. *Year without a summer* - In 1816 temperatures in the Northern hemisphere plummeted, causing widespread crop failure.

57. *Iron horse* - By 1825 the Stockton and Darlington railway would be operational.

58. *Pagan* - Emanates from the Latin term 'Paganus,' meaning rural, rustic or of the country.

59. *Proteus* - An early sea god known as the 'Old Man of the Sea'.

60. *Triton* - A Greek God, the messenger of the sea. Triton is also the largest of Neptune's moons.

61. *J.R. Ewing* - The main villain and character in a 1980's TV series, Dallas. J.R. was a wealthy, greedy and amoral oil baron.

62. *British Census* - The First Census was taken in 1801 and recorded a British population of 10.9million.

63. *In the best of all worlds* - In Voltaire's satire published in 1759, Candide remains true to the belief that "Everything happens for the best, in the best of all worlds," despite ridiculous examples of injustice, suffering and despair.

64. *Oracle* - Ah yes – wasn't there an Oracle in the film, 'The Matrix' which involved a hidden system of governance.

65. *Lost Man* - In 1824, Mary Shelley began to write 'The Lost Man'. Her darkest and gloomiest novel, which told of a disastrous future.

66. *Transcendentalists* - Emerged in New England. Its pioneers included Ralph Emerson and Henry David Thoreau. They believed in an ideal spirit state that transcends the physical and scientific world and is realised through intuition.

67. *Lucy* – A collection of enigmatic poems by William Wordsworth, written in 1802.

68. *Insomnia*. Famous insomniacs have included Vincent Van Gogh, Napoleon Bonaparte, Charles Dickens and the inventor of the light bulb, Thomas Edison.

69. *Lake Geneva* - Where Mary Shelley began to write Frankenstein.

70. *The Famous Five* - Four fictional children detectives and their dog. Created by Enid Blyton, every time they met up they solved a mystery. The characters are outlined with very few words and there is very limited description of scenes. This is designed to encourage the reader to use their imagination!

71. *The Angel's Wing* - In 1820, John Keats in his poem *Lamia,* lamented the effect of Isaac Newton's deconstruction of the rainbow.

72. *Sirius* - The best time to view Sirius in the Northern Hemisphere is on 1 January when it reaches the meridian at midnight. As the big star from Canis Major the Big Dog constellation, it's often known as the Dog Star. Sirius is one of the nearest stars to the Earth – only 8.9 light years away! The spacecraft Voyager 2 launched in 1977 to survey Saturn and Jupiter is due to pass relatively close to it in 250,000 years time!

73. *A sceptre* - An ornamental staff held by a ruling monarch. 'This Sceptred Isle' is the title of a BBC Radio series about kingship and taken from a quotation from Shakespeare's, 'Richard I'.

74. *The Ace of Spades* - I asked Julia about this, "Why Caleb, the 'Ace of Spades' is sometimes known as the death card. It also promises worldly power, but at a price as challenges lie ahead. Obstacles must be overcome with the power of positive thinking and faith."

75. *The loveliest flower ever sown* - Another line from the lyrical 'Lucy' poem.

76. *Axis Mundi* - In many religions or myth the Axis Mundi is the centre of the world, a sacred place connecting Heaven and Earth.

77. *Coronet* - On horse anatomy, the coronet is the band around the top of the hoof from which the hoof wall grows. A coronet is also a small crown worn by nobles, princes and princesses – maybe this is what Charles had in mind!

78. *Age of Aquarius* - In Astrological terms this won't occur until 2600. In popular expression, the Age of Aquarius refers to the heyday of the hippie of the 1960's and 1970's and of New Age phenomenon.

79. *Demeter* - The Earth goddess in Greek myth.

80. *Country boy at heart* - In support of the Tate's *Haymakers'* appeal campaign, a London newspaper ran an Essay competition on the paintings. A boy, Daniel Bennett of North London, came closest to identifying Stubbs' intentions with remarkable honesty and innocence. Part of what he said was, "When I look out of my window I see boring cars and I hear horrible pop music...In my head I am a town boy because this is what I know... But when I look at this painting, I am sure that in my heart I am a country boy. I think George Stubbs was a country boy at heart... He liked painting trees and fields and animals and the people on the farms and fields. There is a feeling of joy and happiness."

81. *What is it I'm supposed to do?* - This reminds me of the song 'Wonderwall' by Oasis, a group famous for saying, "This is history!"

82. *Veni, vidi, vici* - Translates to, "I came, I saw, I conquered." It's an example of a Snowclone, a formula based cliché. A modern example is, 'Green is the new Black.'

83. *Purple* - Often used to symbolise magic and mystery. Being the combination of red and blue, the warmest and coolest colours, purple is believed to be the ideal colour and one most favoured by artists.

84. *Equilateral* - A triangle whose sides are of equal length. A broad example is the region known as the Bermuda Triangle, where the known laws of Physics are said to be violated or altered. Another famous triangle is Pascal's used in algebra and probability.

85. *An entire ocean is affected by a pebble* - A quote by Blaise Pascal, a French philosopher and mathematician from the 17th century, famous for his probability theory, which changed the way we regard risk and predict the future.

86. *Crystals* - Fernlike Stellar Dendrites are the largest snow crystals, often falling to Earth with diameters of 5cm or more. They are single crystals of ice.

87. *Jack Frost* - An elfish creature who personifies crisp, cold winter weather. He is also a fictional superhero from 1941 in Marvel Comics. He is a man covered in ice and able to project ice. Well – those polar bears could do with him right now!

88. *Knock, knock, knock* - A ritual of Cartomancy – a form of fortune telling using playing cards.

89. *Valentin, prvi spomladin* - Translates to "Valentine – first Saint of Spring."

90. *A medieval art gallery* - In the South of France, there are two fabulous examples of prehistoric cave paintings, in Lascaux and Chauvet. The paintings were from over 30,000 years ago! A common theme is large wild animals, bears, lions, bison and mammoths. The original cave in Lascaux is closed to the public to protect it. Maybe that's why they originally sealed up Royston Cave too!

91. *What do these stones mean?* - Christian New Testament - Joshua 4.21

92. *As water washes away stones and torrents wash away the sun, so you destroy man's hope* - Christian Bible, Job 14-19.

93. *De Profundis Clamavi* - Translates to "Out of the depths I cry." The Christian Bible, Psalms 130 "Out of the depths have I cried unto thee."